THE
PATIENT'S
DAUGHTER

BOOKS BY JENNA KERNAN

THE ROTH FAMILY LIES

The Nurse

AGENT NADINE FINCH

A Killer's Daughter

The Hunted Girls

The Adoption

The Ex-Wives

THE PATIENT'S DAUGHTER

JENNA KERNAN

bookouture

Published by Bookouture in 2024

An imprint of Storyfire Ltd.
Carmelite House
50 Victoria Embankment
London EC4Y 0DZ

www.bookouture.com

ISBN: 978-1-83525-169-0
ebook ISBN: 978-1-83525-168-3

For Jim, always

PROLOGUE

TAMPA, FLORIDA

August 2023

She told me to go. Threatened me even! And I was scared. I can't deny that. My hands were shaking, and I backed down immediately.

Why do I always do that?

I relive the conversation as I pack my suitcases in the dead of night. My hands still tremble as if I'm some old woman instead of one in her prime.

With each item carefully folded, the conversation morphs into other ways it could have gone. I could have refused. Insulted her or ordered her out of my room. Instead, I am rolling my underwear into neat little bundles. Preparing to leave, just as she ordered.

As I pack, my initial shock evolves to fury. How dare she make such demands and issue such threats? As if she'd follow through with it. It's ridiculous. This is my home, too.

My father says the only way to stop a bully is to stand up for yourself. Make them move on to someone weaker.

Why am I always the weaker one? How do they know?

I can't believe this is happening again. I'm an adult for goodness' sakes. I've been bullied before. By my mother and, later, by the kids at school. That's why they finally tried a private school, just to get me away from those nasty girls. Girls can be so mean. Women too, apparently.

Why am I a target again?

Now, as I carefully fold and place my shirts into the open case, my breathing comes in angry draws of air through flared nostrils.

And what would she do, really, if I refuse to go?

Maybe I should settle this for myself. That thought has me pausing as if frozen in some tractor beam. Indecision immobilizes me. Should I put all my things back in the drawer or keep packing?

Honestly, I don't want to go through this again. It's not just being intimidated, it's knowing I'm a coward and somehow that it's obvious to everyone.

I know how to fight, in theory, at least. My father showed me how to throw a punch and where to kick a boy. Where do you kick a girl?

I remember those lessons. And if I have to, I'll use them.

Yes. That's what I'll do. I'll march down the hall and tell her...

My feet don't move. I do not charge into battle. I just shake like a stray kitten lost on a highway, crying for its mother.

The mewing sound in my throat humiliates me. Am I crying?

Yes. Because I know that I can't handle myself. And everyone else knows.

So, I am going for help. Again. Like always. To my dad, or a teacher, or that middle school counselor, trying to overlook the eye roll as I appear yet again in her office.

But this time I am going to the police and telling them to

come here and arrest that terrible woman. I could press charges. Stand up before a judge and tell them what she said.

It's illegal to threaten to hurt someone. My finger taps my upper lip as I deliberate this course. It would be my word against hers. Would they believe me or just be angry that I am wasting everyone's time?

It's impossible. I'll never do it. But I'm sick to death of being bossed. At work, at school, at home.

I lash out at a safe inanimate object, take the larger suitcase, and upend it on the bed, spilling all the neatly folded and rolled garments. Then I throw the suitcase on the floor.

Spinning, I march to the dresser to recover my phone. Maybe I will just call 911 and say I don't feel safe. That much is true. I'm still shaking, the combination of fear and fury rocking my entire body.

The device is in my hand and the screen awake when I hear something behind me. Whirling, I spot her in the door.

She glances at the bed and the mess I've made. Then she takes in the picture of me, mouth open, phone clutched and glowing in my hand.

She glides forward and I know from the set of her jaw and the scowl lowering her brow that she is livid.

My back is already pressed against the bureau. I can't back up any farther, so I lift my chin in an attempt at defiance. She will ask what I am doing, and I'll order her out. No, I'll tell her I am calling the police and that she is the one who is leaving.

But I say nothing. I feel sweaty all over. Damp and quaking with a cold, shivery panic.

These kinds of fights always begin with yelling and name-calling. I know this spot, have found myself here so many times. It won't matter if I back down. The conflict will escalate to a shove or slap. Perhaps the argument will alert the others and they'll come to help.

But she doesn't say anything. She just keeps coming.

I don't know what makes me look down, but when I do, I see it there, gripped in her hand.

A knife.

A long, shining silver blade. I recognize it as the narrow kind my dad used to fillet a fish.

Only I am the fish.

She is right before me.

"No," I say. And there it is. My first time standing up for myself.

She rams the point into my diaphragm. It hurts. I gasp as the knife angles up and into my heart. The pain steals my breath. Shock. The slicing blade lancing deep. I feel my heart shudder, cramp, and then stop.

My heart isn't beating.

I stare up into her cold eyes. My killer grips my shirt, pressing the blade to the hilt, holding me upright as my knees give way.

Tears stream from my eyes and the cellphone drops to the ground at my feet.

ONE

TAMPA, FLORIDA

Mid-July

Did she feel guilty about this? Yes, a little.

Taylor Roth Parker kept her eye on the hostess stand of the expensive restaurant she'd chosen to make her announcement. Her husband, Seth, had agreed to forfeit one of his practicum hours to meet her.

She perched on an upholstered bench in the waiting area, one hand resting on the new satin sheath-dress that covered her enormous baby bump, and forced herself not to fidget. The effort to remain outwardly calm made her armpits sticky and she feared she'd stain the finicky fabric. Taylor had selected this addition to her maternity wardrobe, special for this occasion, because none of her rows of designer garments fit her now and this steel blue accentuated her eyes. Carrying twins made her look as if she were past her due date when she was still four long weeks away.

Before getting pregnant and right up until month five, she had been an avid runner, something she'd started while out west

s she had once spent shopping. Now she waddled
e in November.

gust 17th could not come soon enough.

One of the twins kicked. She placed a hand over the little
boxer.

"I know. I'm excited, too. Wait until we tell Daddy."

She jiggled one swollen ankle with impatience and then
leaned in her seat to see past the couple arriving at the hostess
station, and to give herself an unobstructed view of the
entrance.

With the hurried step of a man who had somewhere more
important to be, her husband strode through the glass doors,
bringing an unpleasant blast of heat. He paused, blinking as his
eyes adjusted from the brilliance of a summer morning to the
cool, dim interior of the posh restaurant. He wore his scrubs,
unfortunately. Though she had to admit that he did wear them
well.

Not yet in his residency, he was currently finishing a series
of short rotations in a variety of units. Seth combed his long
fingers through his thick black hair, which stood up in an artful,
messy pile on the top of his head and revealed a distinct
widow's peak at his broad forehead. In profile now, his
perpetual dark stubble emphasized his strong, square jaw. With
a pale complexion and rugged masculinity that came from his
ancestors in Eastern Europe, he was, as always, a striking man.
Even without spotting his unusual eye color, you noticed him.
His height ensured that, but the combination of his unique eyes
and his muscular build made her tease that he should give up
his medical training and try out for the role of Superman in the
next movie. It didn't seem fair that he'd won the cosmic lottery
for looks, brains, and those haunting eyes that were a grayish
blue but had a distinctive splash of amber in each.

Seth was sweet, loving, and usually a pushover. And since

she was an only child, used to getting her way, well, that worked out.

It had taken some convincing, but he'd accepted help from her father to apply for and pay for medical school. She wasn't thrilled that he'd picked medicine, but it was his dream, and he wasn't interested in psychiatry, like her dad, thank the Lord.

Now he just needed a little more persuading. They'd discussed this purchase, but she hadn't swayed him. So, she'd gone ahead anyway.

At the hostess station, Seth leaned in to speak to the pretty blond in the short, tight black dress. To his credit, he didn't even drop his eyes at the bounty of female flesh visible above her neckline.

He lifted his gaze to sweep the waiting area and spotted Taylor. His face lit up and she felt that familiar drop in her stomach. That smile and his eager expression—they were just everything. Their eyes met. Her breath caught, and his lopsided grin warmed her all over.

She lifted a hand and gave a little wave. He stepped before her as she rocked forward, preparing to stand. He assisted her to her feet and then pulled her into his arms for a kiss on the mouth, making her skin flush and one of the twins kick.

"I only have an hour," he said.

The hostess held the menus, waiting for Seth to nod before she guided them to a table with a white tablecloth and fresh blue pompom-like blossoming hydrangea and a sprig of tiny pink flowers in a green ceramic vase.

Taylor felt a little nervous and wasn't sure why. He'd let her have her way before, on everything from their wedding venue to the honeymoon destination.

At their table, her husband helped her settle. Once she had her napkin on what was left of her lap, he bent to kiss her on the mouth, then took his seat beside her, still gripping her hand.

He leaned forward and kissed her knuckles just below the cluster of diamonds her mother had picked for the engagement ring and matching bands, both top and bottom. The two surrounding rings really did keep the larger stone in the engagement ring from spinning. She didn't like the setting or the ostentatious size of the diamond, but when your mother offered to pay for a large gemstone, you said yes. At least that was what her father had advised. She'd lost count of the times she'd spun the diamond to hide the stone, afraid the darn thing would get her mugged or killed.

Taylor wasn't small but felt that way beside Seth. Unlike his jet-black hair, her light brown hair had honey highlights, thanks to her stylist. The cut was long, and her thick hair fell straight without much fussing. She wondered if the babies would inherit her pale blue or his blue-gray eyes? As long as they weren't the cold gray of her mother's, she'd be happy.

"You look beautiful," Seth said.

"I look like a barn wearing satin."

"I like barns."

She chuckled, knowing he was serious. He really did love barns, animals, the outdoors.

His smile broadened as he met her gaze, and she noticed the circles under his eyes and the bluish smudges on either side of his narrow nose. He was losing weight again. Working too hard to remember to eat.

"Not much longer now." He grinned.

"How goes the practicum?"

"Well. There is so much to learn! My hospital supervisor is a bit of a jerk, bedside manner of an ice statue, but he knows his..." He cocked his head and lifted his dark brows. "That was a polite question. Right?"

She chuckled and squeezed his hand. "Yes. I want you to do well, Dr. Parker, of course."

"Of course. But not so interested that you need to hear about the care and treatment of diabetic skin lesions?"

"Definitely not." She drew back her hand, fiddling with the wedding bands, using her thumb to roll them in circles, as she did when nervous.

He winked, and his big blue eyes sent off a flutter that caused the twins to kick again.

"Oufh! They're getting so strong. If they were girls I'd say they were ready for the Bolshoi."

Seth chuckled.

The server arrived, smartly dressed and well spoken. He explained the specials as he confirmed that tap water was fine, then continued his spiel as he filled their water glasses from a carafe.

Seth didn't ask the prices. She'd explained early in their relationship that you picked a restaurant you could afford and then didn't ask. The specials were either fresh and the chef's recommendation or, in a few cases, overpriced and made with food they needed to move.

Seth ordered a steak, medium, and a double side of vegetables without butter or sauce, as per usual.

She ordered a Caesar salad with grilled salmon, hoping it wouldn't upset her stomach which now seemed to be the size of a golf ball.

"So, what's the occasion? Not your birthday. Not *my* birthday. And I don't finish my classes until the end of the month."

"How do you know it's a special occasion? Can't I just want to share a romantic meal with my husband?"

"You're up to something. I know it. Phone calls with your father and mysterious outings."

She grinned and he lifted his brows expectantly.

"It's true," she admitted. "You're on to us."

He pressed his lips together and nodded in satisfaction. "Knew it."

"So, what's your best guess?"

"I think you bought a bigger car for the twins."

"Close." She lifted the mortgage agreement from her designer bag. "We bought a house!"

The warm smile dropped away, and Seth's eyes rounded.

TWO

Seth blinked as if Taylor had begun speaking in a foreign language. She waited, holding her brittle smile as she watched for joy to flood his features.

Instead, his skin went ashen. He drew his hands from the table as he sank back in his seat.

"What?"

"I said, I bought us a house. Our first home!" She bounced in her seat, the excitement momentarily making her forget the extra weight that kept her from drawing up to the table. She held her smile but it now felt forced.

"Where?"

"Here in Tampa!"

"How?" He breathed through parted lips. Panted, really. "Your father?"

"Well, yes. I signed the loan agreement, but he handled the downpayment. And he'll cover the mortgage payments until you get your practice established."

He stiffened. "My practice? I haven't even started my residency."

Taylor gave a dismissive wave. "But you will."

"What if I fail or I want to specialize?" The fears poured out, one upon the other. His hand pressed flat to his forehead as stress tugged at his features.

"Don't be silly. You're brilliant and you certainly can specialize."

"Taylor, we agreed to wait."

"I did." She stretched out the words. "But that was before..." She motioned to her stomach. "This."

"But what if I want to establish my practice in New York or Chicago?"

"Well, then we'll sell and relocate because even if you want to move to Anchorage, Alaska, I'll follow you."

"But you bought a *house,*" he said, exasperated, his voice loud enough to turn heads at nearby tables.

"Because you're doing your residency here. Specializing, leaving the area, establishing a practice, that's all years away. And I need a house for these babies yesterday." She leaned forward, extending a hand across the linen cloth.

He didn't take it. Instead, he covered his face in his hands.

"Oh, Taylor." This was not a groan of happiness. She needed to turn this around.

Was he afraid they couldn't afford it? She'd just explained he needn't worry.

A glance around showed they'd attracted the interest of a couple dining to their right. Taylor arched her brow, and both looked away. The public setting had been intentional. Her mother always said a fancy restaurant lowered the chance of anyone raising their voice.

"We said we were waiting until after my residency."

Now she found herself losing her enthusiasm and her footing. He so rarely took issue with her decisions. But he had asked her to wait, and, at the time, renting seemed like an acceptable compromise.

"You try walking from the carports to the elevator carrying groceries and this." She rested a hand on her huge stomach.

"I told you I'd do the carrying."

"Yes, but you are never home! I need to be in a house *before* I give birth."

"Nesting. A woman's need to find a safe place—"

She cut him off with a scowl and uplifted, open hand. "Don't quote from your textbooks. These babies need a nursery, *now*."

"They don't. Babies need to be clean and dry and fed."

She pressed her lips tight to keep from saying something mean.

"Those babies will fit in a dresser drawer until they're several months old. By then I'll have started my residency and we can talk about this."

"Talk about it? It's done. We own this house."

His head dropped and his chest rose and fell as silence stretched and her irritation grew.

Now she folded her arms. He wasn't shouting, but she'd never seen him look so sad. Or perhaps it was worried?

Defeated? That made no sense. This would make his life easier. Both of their lives easier.

Finally, he lifted his chin and met her gaze.

"I turned down Tampa."

"What?" She sat forward, staring.

"I said, I turned down Tampa. I took the residency in Orlando. It's a bigger hospital with a better pediatric program."

The shock had her gasping. "Orlando? No. It's Tampa." She shook her head. He wasn't making any sense.

"No, it's Orlando. I already signed the paperwork."

Now *she* was exasperated. "When were you going to tell me this?"

"Today, actually. You'd tell me about the minivan and I'd tell you I got accepted in Orlando."

"But you got into Tampa."

He broke eye contact. "Yes. But really, your dad got me in. Called some people in administration. And I wanted to do it on my own."

He gave her that look, the one that was both pleading and apology. The one that begged her to recognize that he needed to stand on his own two feet.

She respected that. Hadn't she gone west for exactly the same reason?

Taylor wanted to be angry but also understood why he was reluctant to tell her and disappoint her father. Especially after all the help he had been.

But Orlando! That was over two hours away.

"Seth, what are we going to do?"

His reply was a huffing sigh. Then he scratched his chin. "I really thought you two were picking out a car."

"I can't move a house, Seth."

"I'm sorry, Taylor. I should have told you sooner, I know it. But I was worried that I'd offend your dad. And since he got sick, you feel you need to be close by. When I mentioned a residency up north..."

He didn't need to finish. She'd shut him down with no discussion.

Why did she do that?

"I just kept putting off telling you. I wasn't sure how you'd feel about Orlando."

"How I'd feel? You're going to be two hours away and working eighteen-hour shifts. And I'm delivering twins in four weeks. How do you think I feel?"

"I was hoping we could rent a small place near the hospital."

"We own a *house*!"

Taylor groaned.

It wasn't his fault.

But her announcement wasn't going at all as she'd intended. Though her concern that he would not be exuberant about this was the very reason why they now sat in this pretentious interior with all these well-dressed people, being served by young, hungry-eyed wait staff.

Meanwhile, she was the one raising her voice. Taylor reined in her upset, sipped her water, and tried not to cry.

Across the table, the muscles in Seth's jaw bulged as he locked his teeth. He got himself under control first, of course.

"We could rent the house out and get something near the hospital."

Her heart ached to think of someone else moving into their home. "HOA rules say long-term rentals only. We'd have to rent for a minimum of a year."

"That could work."

The sense of loss flooded through her, and she clasped her hands, as if that could help her hold on.

"Oh, but Seth, I had my heart set. It's such a perfect home."

He rolled his lips inward as if to keep from objecting again. Finally, he asked, "Just what did we buy?"

Taylor again offered the listing details, setting them on the table between them.

"When?"

"Closing already happened. Moving truck tomorrow." She should have told him earlier. Definitely. But then he might have talked her out of it, and they'd have backed out and lost this house. Her ideal home.

And despite what he'd told her, she still wanted it. They could make this work. Couldn't they?

"Wait until you see the inside. You'll love it."

Taylor fiddled with the charm on her gold chain, zipping it back and forth.

Guilt niggled.

"Don't you want out of that small, dingy apartment and into a home of our own?"

"Yes. I would. But I was hoping to have you and the boys close by."

"I know. This is terrible, Seth. I'm so sorry."

"Don't be. I have the spot I want. We have the home you want. Right?"

When they rented their first place, it had seemed charming. But the second-floor terrace apartment would not do when there were strollers involved.

He scanned the papers before him.

"Thirty-six thousand square feet? Three bedrooms." He flipped to the last page. "One point three mill?" He lifted his gaze and gave a slow shake of his head. "Oh, Taylor. This is a lot."

"But we'll be able to afford it. When you're at a hospital and with my income."

"I have no income until my residency, and I won't make this kind of money for decades."

"We can do it."

"What about your decision to take a longer maternity leave? With a house like this, you've eliminated that option. You have to go back."

She didn't. Her father had assured her. And there was no shortage of job postings for engineers on the Gulf Coast.

He cast his gaze at the photos of the grand property she'd selected, and his expression turned wistful. She felt a glimmer of hope.

"It's nice. Right?"

"Beautiful."

"Three bedrooms, a screened pool, two-car garage, and an unfinished attic bonus room. The primary bedroom overlooks the pool. And it borders a reserve. It's a beautiful neighborhood. Stunning."

"Taylor, this is—"

She interrupted his objection. "I can't even make it up the stairs to our floor anymore."

"Then use the elevator."

"Which is often broken. After I deliver, I'll be carrying two babies. Do you want me to fall down the stairs carrying our children?"

"Of course not, but..." His words fell off and he stared glumly at the real estate listing.

"It's not in Orlando. I know that. But what else is your objection?" she asked.

"I want to provide for my wife."

She clasped his hand. "Oh, sweetheart, that's so nice."

"And it's emasculating, even, having him buy you the things I should provide."

Taylor pressed her hands to her enormous belly. "This should serve as proof of prowess. And why not spend some of what will be mine now when we can enjoy it? When we need it?"

"It feels wrong."

"I'm an engineer. I make a good salary. I don't need his money."

"Then why do we keep taking it?"

Her parents had paid for their wedding and Seth's education, leased their cars, and bought her this honking-big engagement ring. But she'd turned down the country club membership, the more expensive cars, and the vacations, hadn't she?

He met her gaze with an earnest open expression that melted her heart.

"At least include me in the discussion."

"Yes. You're right. And you, as well."

"Point taken."

"I wanted to surprise you is all." And she was a tiny bit

afraid he'd draw a line in the sand, and she needed a house before she brought these babies into the world.

He rose and carefully set his linen napkin on his seat.

"I've got to get back to the hospital."

She opened her mouth to protest and then thought it best to give him some time to process everything she'd told him. He'd come around to see this as the incredible gift it really was. He always came around.

And whatever problems with his residency in Orlando, they'd work them out. They always did.

The waiter arrived, eyes on her departing lunch companion.

"Wrap his to go please."

THREE

Taylor's surprise had fallen flat like a souffle in an earthquake. Worse than she could have imagined.

Once Seth had left the restaurant, she'd lost her appetite. Taylor paid and waited until they boxed both meals before heading out.

The first low rumble of thunder vibrated through her chest. She hoped the valet would bring her car before the skies opened.

She made it to the apartment in a driving rain, wishing she was already in their new home. Instead, she parked in her assigned spot, out in the open parking area, and was drenched before reaching the front door of their second-floor apartment.

This, she thought, was pointless, even more determined to move out of this place and into their first real home.

It was going to be so great. Seth would see once they moved. It was going to be epic.

Once she stowed their meals in the fridge, she changed into dry clothes, grabbed the oversized golf umbrella, and hurried back to the office where she and Milena Smigelski went over the progress reports on the I-75 Interchange improvements at Big Bend Road.

Milena was the newest hire, tall, with fair skin, and straight, short, blond hair, given texture with the application of some gravity-defying product. She was inexperienced but had some good insights and Taylor took careful notes. A staff meeting about the I-75 ramp reconfiguration from SR 574 to I-4 and her inbox ate up the remains of the afternoon.

By the time Seth returned to their apartment that evening, Taylor felt dizzy and faint. She should have eaten without him, but she kept expecting him to return any minute.

Seth got her a glass of orange juice and the fructose seemed to help boost her flagging blood sugar. It was fortified with calcium because her lactose intolerance made it difficult for her to enjoy dairy products. She ate half her salad, feeling a little like a lioness tearing the salmon to pieces with her teeth as Seth offered a wilted napkin. Once the protein landed, she felt remarkably better.

Seth collected his meal from the microwave and sat across from her at the round table that just fit in the space provided in their eat-in kitchen. There was no dining room. The carpets were a dull, dirty beige and she hated the entire place.

"Feeling better?" he asked.

"Yes." She gave him a weak smile. Her stomach now felt too full, though she had eaten only half the salad. "How's your steak?" she asked.

He tried a slice. "Good. Want to split it?"

"You need to eat that," she said, but her gaze was on the pink, juicy section remaining on his plate.

He chortled and sliced away a large hunk, adding it to her salad.

"Eat up," he said.

And she did, ravenous for more protein.

When she finally had done all she could with the salad, he

took over, finishing what she could not and carrying the plates to the sink.

She sipped her water as he washed the dishes and tossed the takeout containers.

"Mind if I do a little more studying?" he asked.

She didn't. Seth went to work at their little dinette and Taylor headed to the bedroom to open and tape the boxes she'd ordered. She began packing in the bedroom and Seth was so preoccupied with his laptop and textbooks, he did not even notice.

He was often so worn out when he dragged himself home, he just had nothing left in the tank.

She finished packing the bathroom, except for their travel bag and one suitcase. At ten, she shuffled out to kiss him goodnight.

At his elbow, beside the open laptop and medical textbook, was the real estate listing.

"You still mad?" she asked.

"I'll get over it. It looks like a beautiful place."

"Still going to opt for Orlando?" she asked, hoping he'd changed his mind.

"Yes. I'm sorry and I know it will make things more difficult for you. But, yes."

"Okay."

"Are *you* mad?" he asked, repeating her question.

"No. It's what you want, so go for it. This residency is going to be very hard, so you need to be in the place that you think is best."

He gripped her hand. "Thank you."

Taylor gave him a warm smile, filled with tenderness and gratitude. Then she leaned down and kissed him on the mouth. They lingered there, tongues blending as her body quickened. His arms went around her and he drew her into his lap.

It would be all right. They'd work everything out together,

just like always. Seth would love the new place and when their boys were playing in that backyard, it would be the perfect home.

If they needed to sell it after his residency, she'd be happy to put it on the market and move wherever he liked.

Goodness, their boys would be nearly four by then.

They headed to bed early to cuddle and dream. This was their last night in this little upstairs apartment and Taylor could not wait to see that moving van arrive in the morning.

As per usual, she didn't sleep well. The need to visit the bathroom and the impossibility of sleeping in any position than on her back ensured that. So she was up before Seth on Friday as he appeared in the kitchen, bleary eyed and smiling.

"There's my girl. How did you sleep?"

She kissed him. "The usual."

"I'm sorry."

"That's all right. It won't be long now."

An hour later, she waved him away.

Taylor attacked the kitchen, taping boxes and wrapping fragile things. She had the kitchen, living room, and bathroom packed before the movers arrived. Then she stashed most of the clothing in their bureau into her matching luggage set. The movers would pack the closet and the bureau would go only as far as the curb along with much of their old furniture. And good riddance.

One good thing about a small place, packing was a snap.

The squeal of truck brakes broke into her thoughts.

She glanced at the time displayed on the clock in the wonky stove beyond the four electric burners. Seth had cleaned the stove last night, along with the surfaces and bathrooms, hoping to get their deposit back. He'd even patched the holes from the nails she'd used to hang some artwork, using toothpaste and tissue paper instead of Spackle.

"Resourceful," she added to his list of attributes.

Taylor headed out to the second-story overlook. Below, the moving truck parked before the entrance.

She waved. "Right on time."

The movers were very quick, which was great because she intended to be back at the office after lunch.

She directed them to clear most of the furniture to the curb for the city trash collection on Monday. The rest was loaded and delivered to the new place. Once there, Taylor had time to unpack only a few of the meager boxes, realizing just how big this new house really was.

With only a few of the kitchen gear boxes unloaded, she reluctantly abandoned the job to head to the office.

Seth called while she was en route to work.

"Did the truck show up on time?"

"Yes. It was there. I unpacked two boxes of kitchen things. The rest is piled in the garage, living room, and upstairs."

"What about our bed?"

"I kept it. That way we'll have a place to sleep until the furniture delivery."

"Great. See you at home."

"The new home."

He laughed. "I remember. See you soon."

* * *

Taylor arrived at their new home under threatening skies and the first drops of rain with takeout Mexican. Taco Friday, she thought, as she turned into the flagstone drive.

The three-story home included a turret on the second floor, a wide porch, hurricane-resistant windows, a composite slate roof, and an unfinished attic that offered all sorts of possibilities later on.

The gray exterior with white trim had a classic feel but modern construction. Taylor nearly danced from the two-car garage, up the three steps to the laundry room, delighted to finally have covered parking out of the sun and the rain. There, she paused to admire the large front loader washer and dryer, the shelving for detergent and the rack to hang clothing to dry. There was even a small utility sink. No more hauling their clothing to the building's laundry or scrounging for quarters for the machines.

Continuing to her bright new kitchen, she set the takeout bag on the gray veined granite surface of the generous island beneath the three blown glass pendant lights. Beyond, the stainless-steel hood sat suspended over a five-burner gas stove.

Soon, she promised herself, she'd be trying out gourmet recipes and whipping up breakfast on the center griddle.

The doorbell alert announced Seth's arrival at the front door and she hurried to let him in. He stepped into the foyer with a bottle of champagne, shaking off the rain that she'd just missed. Droplets spattered the solid Brazilian cherry flooring beside the grand entrance that featured clear stained glass, flanked by matching sidelights.

"Why didn't you park in the garage?"

"No remote."

"I'm sorry. There's a control box outside. I'll get you the code and a remote."

He leaned to drop a kiss on her lips, and she hugged him tight. He was home. *They* were home. And her toes were curling in joy.

When he drew away, she said, "Welcome home, Dr. Parker."

"Thank you." He glanced around. "Wow. There's an echo."

"Because we don't have any furniture." She turned to take in the view from the foyer.

From here, she could see both the dining room to the left with a picture window that offered a view of the drive and front yard, and the living room to the right with the three glass sliders which gave a great panorama of the pool and yard beyond. The open floorplan included a wide-open entrance to the kitchen adjoining the living room where she pictured turquoise stools and accent pieces. Perhaps a cookie jar or teapot to match. And beyond, out of sight, was the family room where she imagined her twins playing happily for years to come.

"High ceilings," he said.

"And crown molding. We have a chandelier in the dining room and this one." She pointed up to the large fixture overhead. "Though I'm not a fan of the wrought iron. What do you think?"

He shrugged. "I like it."

She eyed the champagne. "You know I can't drink."

"It's non-alcoholic sparkling cider."

"Oh great!" She clapped her hands, delighted. He pulled her in for another kiss, spinning her in a circle in the entry under the twelve-foot ceilings and leaving her breathless. When they finally stopped, she was dizzy and giggling and so very happy.

"Tour the upstairs first?" she asked.

His smile was generous. "Sure. Show me everything."

He set the bottle in the kitchen, taking time to admire the custom oak cabinets and appliances, running his hand over the cool stone counters.

"What an upgrade," he said.

She giggled and then headed to the stairs beyond the foyer. At the top, they paused.

"So, this is the walk-over. Allows for a higher ceiling in the foyer and gives a partial view of both the dining room and living room."

"Perfect spot for the boys to spy on us," he said.

She loved that he imagined them old enough to peek through the railings.

"Or wait for Santa."

They shared a smile, and he looped an arm over her shoulders and tugged her close as they admired the view.

She pointed to the left. "At that end are the two guest bedrooms each with walk-in closets. To the right and left of the hall are the two bathrooms."

"Posh. Think they'll be in one room for a while?"

"Yes. That's the plan. I'm not sure which for the nursery, yet." She pointed in the opposite direction. "That way, in the turret, is the primary bedroom and primary bath with double sinks and a huge closet."

"What are the other two doors?"

"Linen closet and stairs to the third floor and the unfinished attic. Where do you want to start?"

"Top to bottom."

They set off, arm in arm, but she let him go up to the attic alone. It was stuffy because it lacked insulation and the floor was splintery plywood. Plus, the stairs were narrow, dark, and a little creepy. Nothing that some paint and proper illumination wouldn't remedy. Maybe a skylight?

When he returned, he was still smiling. "Big," he said. "What are you planning up there?"

"Could be a home office, exercise room, man cave, or playroom for the boys."

"Like your boathouse?" he asked.

The mention of her childhood escape room sent a jolt of panic scissoring into her chest. She tamped down the unease. Taylor was not going to spoil this day with thoughts of her childhood.

Should she tell Seth the truth about her old sanctuary?

FOUR

Taylor had told her husband about that room above the boathouse, framing the space as a playroom. But it was more than that. It was a haven from her mother before she discovered Taylor's refuge. Then no place was safe.

Back then Taylor had been good at hiding. She had to be.

She recalled curling into a tiny ball and lying motionless behind the piles of old seat cushions and floats, hardly breathing as her mother stormed past her secret place shouting her name. Taylor shook off the dark memories.

After touring him from room to room and heading back downstairs to explore the pool, with its two-story screened cage, they paused in the sunshine, staring out at the wildlife reserve behind their house.

"Looks like a jungle," he said.

"It is."

"Any ponds?"

She knew why he asked and shook her head. "No. So no gators."

"That's good."

"Did I smell food back there in our ginormous kitchen?"

"Yes. I picked something up."

They headed in and shared their first meal at the granite island, Taylor seated on a stepladder and Seth standing because she had left their old kitchen dinette on the curb for Monday garbage pickup.

"It's a beautiful home, Taylor. I love it."

If you switched off the lights, Taylor was certain she would have been glowing with pleasure and pride.

"Thank you. I'm glad you like it."

"I love it." He kissed her again and she knew it would be all right.

After dinner they unpacked the bathroom, admiring all the fixtures and details. Seth seemed happy as he hung his small wardrobe in his side of the huge walk-in closet.

She left the suitcases because they had no bureau until the new bedroom suite arrived, hopefully next week. So, they headed to the kitchen to tackle those boxes. She sat as Seth unpacked. It had been a busy day.

Her phone rang.

Seth retrieved her mobile from her purse, glancing at the screen on the third ring.

"Your mother," he said, offering the device.

She growled her annoyance and silenced the call. Her mother's mental illness had gotten worse, to the point where her father had hired a personal nurse.

"Not going to answer it?"

Since returning from out west, Taylor had avoided her mother when possible. Their relationship had always been diffi-cult, exhausting, and nearly as troubled as her mother was herself.

"It's probably a pocket dial." She placed the phone on the granite. She hoped so. Her mother almost never called her but when she did it was to complain that Taylor was neglecting her or to criticize Taylor's dad.

"Complicated. Right?" he said, repeating how she'd explained her relationship with her mother.

She nodded. "Extremely."

He glanced at the phone. "She's leaving a voice message."

Outwardly, she appeared calm, but inside her body was twitching and shuddering as if she'd trod on a live wire. This was potentially catastrophic, but if her mother had taught her anything it was how to mask her emotions.

Taylor retrieved two glasses and Seth opened the cider. Her phone rang again. This time it was her father. Now a jolt of panic fired in her belly. Having her mother call was unusual enough and a voicemail completely uncharacteristic. Having her dad call immediately afterwards sent a cold shaft of fear through her.

Visions of her father's last emergency surgery popped into her mind as apprehension lodged in her throat like an oversized pill.

She took the call.

"Hi Daddy," she said, trying for an upbeat tone.

The voice that replied was not her father's.

"It's your mother. Interesting that you pick up his calls on the first ring, while mine are relegated to voicemail."

"I was in the bathroom," she lied.

"Hmm."

"What's up?" asked Taylor, one hand clutching her forehead and the other holding the phone with all the enthusiasm of gripping a live grenade.

"Now don't panic. An ambulance just took your father to the hospital."

Taylor's body went rigid as she gripped the phone. "What? What happened?"

"He showed me his latest little purchase. And I put my foot down. Told him we weren't buying you a house. We argued.

And he had some kind of event. They're taking him in for I don't know what all."

"Who is?"

"The paramedics." Her mother's voice was devoid of emotion. She might have been discussing an annoying plumbing problem instead of her husband's life.

"Is it his heart again?"

"I don't know. He has chest pains."

"What hospital?"

"Winter Haven. I'd hurry." Her mother disconnected the call.

Taylor sobbed and then Seth was there, gathering her up and cradling her in his strong arms.

She stammered and choked but told him what was happening. Seth guided her to the stool. Taylor folded onto the seat, still shaking. And then he was there again, holding open her raincoat, with her purse slung over one arm.

"I sent Rubin a text. Told him about your dad."

"Why?"

"In case I get called in, hoped he'd sit with you. But he's still on the road."

Taylor slipped into the coat, with his assistance as her fingers were sweaty and clumsy.

She was muttering to herself as she accepted her purse. "This is bad. This is so bad."

The thought of losing her dad terrified her. And just like that, a moment later the selfish little voice reminded her that their deal with him, for him to pay the mortgage, had been verbal only.

What a thing to think of when her father was ill. She chided herself. But still, it was a threat to her family and her dreams depended on her father.

How had she let this happen again?

FIVE

Seth drove to the hospital in torrential rains. Roadways were flooded and the windshield wipers could not move the water fast enough.

They were both soaked when they reached the ER at eleven in the evening and were directed to admissions. Her dad was in surgery.

This was Seth's hospital. So, he left her sitting with her mother and went to find the kind of answers that took families hours, sometimes days to obtain.

Her conversation with her mother was strained. Taylor asked how her new personal nurse was working out and Sabrina spent much of the next half hour complaining on a myriad of topics, ending with Taylor herself.

When they were joined in the waiting room by a man around her father's age, her mother quieted. Taylor drew a breath in relief, until she found the man staring at her with a disturbing intensity. He was big with a body that reminded her of a rancher or farmer because his muscles were wiry and his skin deeply lined and tanned. He wore jeans and a long-sleeved cotton shirt and glasses with transition lenses that made it hard to see the color of his eyes. But she could see he was staring at her.

Hadn't he ever seen a pregnant woman before? Finally, Taylor got tired of his rude ogling.

"Did you need something?" she asked, her tone sharp with annoyance.

"You know if it's a boy or girl?"

"Boys," she said. "Twins, actually."

His widening smile creeped her out. "That's fine. Congratulations."

"Are you waiting for someone?" Taylor asked.

"Yes, I sure am. My grandson. Think I'll take a walk. Might be a while."

His accent told her he was not from Florida. Somewhere out west, perhaps. After he left, her mother said, "The man has the manners of a pig. Did you see how he was staring?"

Taylor watched the guy disappear down the corridor.

"I hadn't noticed."

When Seth finally returned, he cast them a reassuring smile.

"He'll be in surgery for at least another ninety minutes. Can I get you something from the vending machine?"

Taylor accepted a water and a granola bar. Her mother ate nothing. The surgeon arrived two hours later, still in his scrubs. Seth stood to speak to him then returned to Taylor and her mom.

"They gave him a catheter to check his heart. He's got two stents and is in recovery. He'll be fine."

Taylor dropped back to her seat and exhaled, releasing the tension in her shoulders.

"That's good news," said her mother, in a monotone voice that relayed nothing.

Taylor repressed a shiver.

Seth dropped a kiss on Taylor's forehead then squatted

beside her as she started to cry, the pent up worry now flooded by relief.

"We can see him once they have him in his room. He'll be groggy. Kind of out of it."

Taylor's tears came faster. Her mother rose.

"They're keeping him?" she asked.

Seth stood to face his mother-in-law. "Yes. At least overnight."

Sabrina lifted her purse from the chair. "It's already tomorrow. I'm going home."

She didn't wait for objections or goodbyes, and just sailed out of the waiting area.

Taylor looked from her mother's retreating back to Seth, whose mouth parted as confusion drew twin lines between his brows.

She used both arm rests to push to her feet and stepped into Seth's arms for a hug.

"Thank you," she murmured into his chest, her tears soaking the front of his T-shirt.

Seth rubbed her back in large circles and hushed her.

"He'll be all right."

"What are stents?"

He explained and she grew more worried. But he reassured her. "Routine," he said. "He'll feel better. Caught it early."

Taylor's tears slowed and she realized she was sitting again with Seth crouching before her, one hand on each knee.

Her father would recover. And he'd be there to see her twins born, attend their first birthday, and maybe buy them their first bike. But this episode underscored the things she took for granted, like her father always being there.

Seth's phone chimed with a text. He glanced at the screen.

"Want to go see him?"

* * *

Taylor and Seth stayed long enough for her to be certain her father was all right, then headed home.

Upstairs, Taylor found the bedding and Seth made the bed which now looked very small in the huge space. She barely roused when his alarm buzzed and he was up for a quick shower, before heading back to the hospital. She'd meant to get up with him, but fell immediately back to a sound sleep.

This was not the way she'd pictured them spending their first night in their new home.

Seth's text woke her at seven with an update. Her father would be coming home today.

Taylor dozed after Seth's message. When she woke to daylight, she sent a text to her dad to call her when he got home, then waited all morning for his reply.

The call came at noon.

"Daddy?"

"Yes, pumpkin. It's me."

"How do you feel?"

"You know, it's amazing, but I feel so much better. More oomph, like I'm running on high octane."

Her father loved cars. Sports cars especially.

"And everything is working. I'm not short of breath and my energy level is through the roof."

She wasn't sure that was good. "Is that the medication?"

"Blood thinners and cholesterol meds? No way. It's the improved blood flow. Should have done this years ago. It's amazing."

Relief warmed her. She smiled. "I'm so glad."

"I'm home until Monday. Then checking in with my cardiologist. If that goes well, I'm cleared to return to work."

Should she tell him Seth had turned down the residency he'd arranged in Tampa?

No, she decided. Not today. That could wait.

"Do you want me to come with you?"

"No, it's just routine. I'll be fine."

"Okay. Let me know if you change your mind."

"I will," he said. Even his voice was stronger.

"Daddy. Mom said you two had a fight."

There was a long pause.

"I'd characterize it as a disagreement."

"About the house?" she asked.

"She told you?"

"Yes, I mean she told me you weren't buying us a house." Taylor gnawed on her lower lip as she waited for his denial.

There was no reply.

Taylor's worry leaked into her voice, making her words take on a pleading note. "Daddy? What did she mean?"

"She's a no on covering the mortgage payments going forward."

"Did you change her mind?"

Nothing.

"Daddy? You still there?" The concern grew, tightening in her chest and blossoming to panic.

"Listen, honey, I tried. And I tried again this morning. But she's just not coming around."

Now she was the one adding a stretch of silence to the call. Was she an idiot for trusting her dad? It wasn't the first time he'd chosen her mother's side. Possibilities jabbed at her, making her twitch.

Finally, she spoke. "What does that mean?"

"I'm so sorry, pumpkin."

Taylor felt the guillotine blade fall, cleaving her dreams of owning this house.

"Daddy? Can you help?"

"She said if I do, she's leaving me. My hands are tied."

"But you promised to cover the mortgage."

"I did. And it breaks my heart, but I can't keep that promise."

And then the tears welled up, bursting forth with a cry that might have seemed like anguish, but the emotion pouring from her was not heartache or grief but something more painful. She'd signed the papers with the understanding he'd keep his promise. But his name was not on the dotted line beside hers. Was she naïve to have trusted her father?

No. He'd never let her down like this before. The recent problems in her parents' marriage must be more serious than she realized.

"She put her foot down. She said she's not funding the lifestyle of a daughter who can't remember her own mother's birthday."

She'd remembered. But stupidly had not called or sent flowers.

"What about the house?"

"It's yours. You signed the papers."

"Because you said you'd help!"

"I can't. You'll have to handle it or, if not, you could sell it again."

She wasn't doing that.

"Will you tell me if she changes her mind?"

"She won't, Taylor. I've seen her like this before. She's stopping payment on your cars, too."

Taylor felt sick. "Really?"

"Yeah. You two are going to have to do without us for the foreseeable future. Reclaim your independence and all that."

What a lovely notion. But it would have been better to hear this advice before she signed the mortgage agreement. Oh, God! What was her interest rate? She didn't even know.

"Daddy? Will you please call me after you see the cardiologist?"

"Yes, pumpkin. Thank you for everything. You rest up. Okay? Love you, Taylor."

"Yes. I love you, too. Bye-bye."

Taylor ended the call and sank to the stepstool, her only seat in the huge kitchen. Her reprieve had arrived. Her mother had cut her off. It was finally over. She was free. And she was on the hook for a mortgage she couldn't afford.

She sat there a long time, brooding, sulking, and growing more worried.

She was in trouble.

Finally, she stood.

"You are not losing this house," she said to the empty kitchen.

Then she returned to the job of unpacking the last of the utensils from the final box, and thrusting pots and pans onto the rollout shelves with more force than necessary. She thought she was fine, that she could handle this blow, until she found herself seated, head down and sobbing on her own forearm.

Forward, my girl. It's the only choice.

She thought of Seth scrubbing the oven of their old place and remembered telling him not to bother.

Yesterday, she hadn't cared if the slumlord kept the money along with that hot little oven of an apartment.

Now she did.

SIX

What was she going to tell Seth?

Her mind tumbled like a child rolling downhill, misjudging the grade, and finding, too late, that she could not control her fall.

She was cut off from what Seth called, with some derision, 'adult child support'.

Who would catch her now?

The refrigerator was empty. Should she use her credit card to fill it? Charge what she could before her mother shut down her line of credit?

Her dad had done it again, choosing his wife's wants over his daughter's needs. The rivalry that her mother conjured in her troubled mind had haunted much of Taylor's childhood, and it appeared to be alive and well. As if her father had room for only one of them in his heart.

Suddenly, she remembered all their old furniture she'd left on the curb as garbage and the new furniture she'd purchased that had yet to be delivered. Her mind ran down the list—the outdoor patio set, the grill, the bedroom suite, the living room set, and the grand dining table.

Oh, no!

Taylor lifted her phone and canceled it all, losing her down-payment, which hurt, but it was unavoidable.

Next, she texted Seth and told him what she'd done. He already knew her parents' fight had been over her dad's decision to help put them in this house. She waited but there was no reply.

Her stomach rumbled. Taylor needed to eat. She found only the remains of the guac and chips in the fridge, which made an odd breakfast. Before noon, she headed out to the bank ATM and then to the grocery store, buying the essentials and scrutinizing the prices.

In the produce department, she paused, feeling someone's eyes upon her. Usually, this was grandmothers, asking the same general questions. But this time, when she glanced up, she saw the man from the hospital and froze.

What were the chances?

She scowled as he continued down the aisle and out of sight.

Taylor realized she'd squeezed the peach in her hand so tightly, the juice was dripping down her fingers.

What about him gave her the creeps? He hadn't been looking at her, or at least, she had not caught him staring. Was she becoming like her mother, all paranoid delusions and unfounded fears?

She shook off that terrible possibility. Her mother was so ill she needed a private nurse.

"Forget it," she said, heading to the checkout with her selections. Back in her vehicle, she locked the doors and then it struck her. "No cart. No basket. No groceries."

The man had selected nothing. But he might just have been there to pick up a few items. It was possible. The unease made her shiver, but it dispelled as she made her way home.

When she finally got back to the enormous empty house,

she found Seth waiting, and much of their old furniture, which she'd put out at the curb at the apartment, was now in their new home.

She stared at the green leather couch and coffee table all alone on the bare tile of the expansive hardwood floors, looking like an oasis in the desert. The television she'd planned to use in the family room sat on a board, supported by two cinderblocks. And the tiny kitchenette squatted like a toadstool under the enormous glittering chandelier. There on the acrylic surface were several takeout containers and a pink hibiscus flower in a red Solo cup.

Her bottom lip began to quiver at the sad furniture and the husband who was so willing to make things better.

"Someone took the carpet before we got there. But we got most of the rest of it. Lost a floor lamp, too, and our dresser. But Nathan spotted a bookshelf on the way home. We can use it in the bedroom, for now. You know, for our clothes."

"Nathan?"

"Yeah. He and Rubin helped me. Lucky timing. They just got back from a long haul."

"Where?"

"Don't know. They didn't say and I forgot to ask."

She could just imagine the bookshelf holding their T-shirts and underwear, there beside the full-sized bed in the suite that was designed for both a king-sized bed and a seating area.

Taylor lowered her head and wept.

Seth was there, holding her, hushing her, and rocking her in his strong arms.

"We're all right, Taylor. I'm sorry about, you know, everything."

She lifted her head. He didn't care about the money. He cared about her, and that knowledge filled up the empty places in her heart with hope.

He guided her to the kitchen where she found two stools.

"Where did these come from?"

"Rubin gave them to me. He said they have four and we can use these until we find something, you know, the right height."

His friend had given him half of his own kitchen set. Taylor was touched. She sat, rotating back and forth on the white pleather as Seth put away the groceries.

"This was very sweet of Rubin. We should have him and Gina over for dinner."

"Yeah, great idea."

His optimistic smile stole her joy and she frowned. They had a place to sit. But their money troubles still loomed.

And she had yet to tell him about her conversation with her dad.

With the last bag emptied, he led them to the dining room. If Seth had asked, she would have said she had no appetite. That she felt sick and sad and nauseous. But he dished her out some fried noodles and opened the container of wonton soup, offering a spoon. The smell was heavenly and by the time she had finished, she felt slightly better.

She didn't want to spoil his surprise, or the evening, and she had yet to come up with a plan, so she kept her bad news to herself until after they had finished their meal.

"I saw your dad was released," he said.

"Yep. He's home."

"Did you speak to him?"

She nodded.

"How's he feeling?"

"Better than before, so he said."

"See? I told you."

She cleared her throat, but the words stuck in her windpipe. She took another sip of water. "Listen, Seth, something happened."

"Oh, God, are you all right?" He shot to his feet.

"Yes." She motioned him to resume his place and he folded to the chair.

"The babies?" he asked, brows still tented with worry, but his voice no longer held that sharp note of alarm.

"Are fine." The pause stretched as he waited, and she tried to find the words. She squeezed her free hand into a fist and pressed it to her mouth.

"Taylor? What is it? Tell me."

Seth knew that an argument over this house had sent her father to the hospital, but she needed to tell him the rest. That her mother had given her dad an ultimatum. Taylor knew that her father loved her, but that everything her father had, originated with his wife's bankroll, and he would not risk his coveted lifestyle and outwardly successful practice with attempts to change Sabrina's mind.

Finally, she needed to tell Seth that she'd canceled the furniture to limit their debt and didn't know how to make the mortgage payment. Taylor drew a breath and plunged in.

When she finished pouring out the worst, she lifted her gaze to judge Seth's reaction to her mother's refusal and her father's desertion.

"Any chance she'll come around?" His flat, unnatural calm only added to her disquiet.

"I've never known her to do that. She's very stubborn."

"Like you."

He could not even imagine how much the comparison tore at her. She was nothing like her mother and if she was, she needed to make some changes.

"We could call our landlord and see if he'll let us move back."

"Then I'll be on the hook for the house *and* the apartment. We have one month grace before anything is due. That takes us through July and to the end of August."

"Rent it out for the year?"

She shook her head and let her chin fall to her chest.

"Taylor," his voice was coaxing. "We can't keep it."

"We can. How long does it take a bank to foreclose?" she asked.

"Honey. Listen to yourself."

She swiped at the tears now running down her cheeks. "I just want us to hold onto this place. Everything else can go."

"You sure?"

"Yes."

"All right then." He cast her a warm smile. "Everything you did was to help me reach my dream of being a doctor. You supported me, even when I knew you weren't too keen on having another doctor in the family."

She lifted her chin. She'd never told him that, but somehow, he knew. He leaned in and kissed her, slow and deep. The contact set off a firestorm of sensations. He cradled the back of her head and dragged her to his chest and their mouths parted.

When he drew back, they were both breathless.

"Every dream I had is coming true because of you, Taylor. So, if this house is your dream, I'll support you." He grinned down at her with that perfect look of adoration. "If anyone alive can pull this off, it's you."

Even with his support and confidence in her ability, she knew she'd have to be very careful and very lucky to keep them out of foreclosure on a house that was suddenly beyond their means.

She considered letting it go, resting a hand on her belly in time to receive a magnificent kick of protest.

Taylor chuckled. "Yes. All right. We're doing this."

"Thank you," he said.

"For what?"

"I can't even begin to tell you. Everything. My life now. It's all because of you," he said.

She tried for a smile, but the worry intruded.

"Seth, we're in trouble. You know that, right?"

"Yes. But the sun still rises, and the moon still shines."

"The bank doesn't accept moonlight as payment."

He seemed happy that her parents would no longer be acting as their financial backers. "So, we will live in a house we can't afford. We're hardly the first couple to face that problem."

That was true.

"Are you glad my parents aren't helping us?"

"In a way. Yes. I am. Give us a chance to make it on our own."

"Will we?"

"Of course."

If she hadn't been sure before, Seth's support, when her entire world was crumbling, was all the proof she needed that this man had her back and would protect her with everything he had.

But the clock was ticking.

What the hell were they going to do?

Seth took hold of her hand. "Let's unpack the rest of those boxes. Okay?"

They headed upstairs.

There was some confusion and then some rummaging in boxes to recover their pajamas. Seth slept in only running shorts and she now preferred voluminous nightshirts.

Taylor sat on the bed as Seth unpacked the luggage, piling their things in the cubbies of the white rattan bookshelf.

The job done, Seth climbed in beside her and managed to kiss her before dropping soundly asleep. Taylor lay awake, back aching and feet throbbing, as she listened to the unfamiliar sounds of the air conditioner rumbling on and off, and the frogs' croaking reminding her of the creak of many rocking chairs.

Unable to rest, she tugged at pillows and shifted, finally giving up and rising. She headed to the private balcony, opened the French doors, and stepped out to look at the stars.

The tree frogs' chorus was now deafening. Above her, the half-moon threw enough silvery light to shimmer off the leaves and branches of the palmetto palms that bordered the property and cast long shadows across the yard.

One of the shadows moved. Taylor frowned. Something or someone was creeping along the border of their yard, keeping close to the cover of the palm fronds.

The jolt of fear seemed to fix her in place as her breathing grew rapid and her hands squeezed the metal railing.

Who was out there?

SEVEN

The crackling sound of the dried undergrowth reached Taylor. Whatever was out there, it was moving deeper into the reserve.

She leaned over the rail and the shadow paused, retreating into the undergrowth. The tree frogs ceased their trill, and the only sound was the breeze rustling the dried palm fronds with a distinctive rattle.

Taylor opened her mouth, her breathing coming in panicked little gasps, and all she could hear now was her blood roaring past her eardrums like an express train.

The yard was still. Nothing moved. In a moment the frog chorus resumed.

What was that?

Too big for a bobcat. She was uncertain if the shadow had moved on four legs or two. A neighbor's dog? A teenager sneaking out past curfew?

She didn't know why, but her heart pounded painfully in her chest, telling her that something was wrong. Why did her mind go to the man in the waiting room and then in the hospital? Had he followed her home?

That was ridiculous and exactly the kind of wild presumption her mother would make. She refused to go there, down that dark corridor where no one could trust a word she said.

Taylor retreated into their room and locked the doors. Then she hurried downstairs and checked every door and window to be certain they were secure.

She knew she was overreacting. But the place was strange, and she wasn't yet comfortable here. That was all. When she peered out between the family room blinds, she saw something squatting between the two oaks that grew side-by-side beyond the pool cage. She leaned forward, her mouth going dry.

Taylor lifted her phone, preparing to call the police. When she glanced up, there was nothing between the trees but moonlight.

Whatever it was had disappeared. Taylor didn't know if that made her feel better or worse.

* * *

When she opened her eyes on Sunday morning, the room was bright with sunlight splashing across the floor. Seth was up and out of bed and had drawn back the curtains to the balcony.

Her worries descended as she stretched, wondering where Seth had gone. She called but received no answer.

Something was wrong.

She remembered the moving shadow creeping around their house last night. Taylor slipped out of bed and into the bathroom, calling again for Seth.

The house felt so empty.

Taylor scooped up her phone and headed downstairs.

Where was her husband?

This time she did not call, but crept across the empty living room, the hardwood floor cold on her bare feet, sweeping through the dining room and empty kitchen to the entrance to the garage.

Seth's Jeep sat beside her car.

Enough hide-and-seek. He could be on the lanai or in the pool, but the idea of going out back alone sent a frisson of fear dancing across her shoulders.

Instead, she lifted her phone to send a text when an unfamiliar chime sounded.

Glancing down, she saw a motion alert from the video doorbell.

Taylor tiptoed to the empty foyer, breathing fast and her scalp tingling as she peered out, hoping to see Seth sauntering up the drive. Instead, she discovered an unfamiliar red pickup truck pulling in.

Her fear morphed into uncertainty; maybe this *was* a sales call, someone canvasing the neighborhood trying to coax her into upgrading her windows or buying a water purifying system.

The scowl brought her brows low over her eyes. No salesperson would ever drive such a beat-up old truck. And the entire back was filled with bedframes haphazardly tied down with yellow nylon rope.

As the truck inched forward and reversed, she noticed the vehicle towed a flatbed trailer filled with a junk store full of old furniture.

"What in the world?"

Seth stepped from the passenger's side, swinging the door shut behind him as a man she did not recognize slipped from the driver's seat of the red truck.

Her relief was short-lived as she realized she was about to receive their first guest in a nightie and bare feet. Reversing course, she hurried upstairs to the main bathroom, tugged back her hair, scrubbed her face, and brushed her teeth. Then she tugged on her underthings, burrowed into a tent-like maternity dress and slipped into flats. Tinted gloss and a quick swipe of the hairbrush and she headed downstairs in time to hear an unfamiliar rumble.

The garage door, she realized.

Taylor stepped from the impressive front entrance and into the midday humidity.

Her husband waved like a little boy returning from the bus after his first day of school.

"Hey, honey! Do you remember my friend Jason?"

The man in question stepped up to Seth's side. Of course she remembered him. Jason McClellan was tall, wiry with dark brown skin and a receding hairline made less noticeable by an extremely short haircut. His glasses were overly large and bright blue. He had elegant long fingers that would have made him an excellent piano player had he not decided to become a thoracic surgeon. She even remembered that his motivation to pursue medicine had been the early death of the grandfather who'd raised him. And if she recalled correctly, she and Seth had attended his grandmother's funeral only six months earlier.

"Of course I remember Jason." She descended the steps to greet their first guest. "How lovely to see you again. How are your mom and your sisters?"

His mother had some personal troubles, which was why he and his sisters had ended up with their mom's parents. But she'd gotten through it and his teenage sisters now lived with her up in Gainesville.

"They're all good," he said, coming forward to accept a hug. "Goodness, look at you!" He stepped back to give her a once over.

"I know." She laughed. Her hand automatically cradled her descended stomach. "If I get any bigger, I'll need to wear a circus tent."

"You look great," Jason said.

"I'm big as a house."

He laughed. "Well, not this house, anyway."

A blue truck appeared on the street and the three turned to watch the pickup pull into their drive. This vehicle she did recognize.

"Right on time," said Seth, giving her a one-armed hug and a kiss on the head.

"Is that Rubin?"

"And Gina and Nathan."

EIGHT

Taylor frowned in confusion as the blue truck pulled to a stop in their drive.

"Are we having a party?" she asked.

"Not exactly," said Seth, in response to Taylor's question. "Well, yes. It's kind of a party. A moving party."

The blue Ford's engine flicked off. There was Rubin behind the wheel, Gina sat beside him, and Nathan had the window seat. They piled out and she hugged them each in turn.

Finally, she looked from one to the other. They all just stood there grinning at her with identical suspicious looks.

Taylor shifted her attention to Jason's truck and flatbed, her gaze landing on a couch that seemed to have time traveled out of the nineties. It sported a velveteen fabric and ghastly orange and brown flowers.

She wrapped an arm around her husband's waist and asked, "What are you all up to?"

"Well, I told Jason about our problem, big house with no furniture, and he told me about his mother's problem. A garage full of her parents' things. She can't even pull her car out of the heat."

Taylor's emotions ping-ponged between elation and worry.

"Oh, Jason. We can't. These are your grandparents' things. Your grandfather. You'll want to keep them for your place."

"My mom already took a few smaller things for my sisters to get set up at college. I've got a few items. But she was just going to donate the rest. Better for it to go to use here."

She wrapped Jason in another hug. "You're a lifesaver. Can't thank you enough, and please thank your mom."

"You can thank me by inviting me over for dinner. I'd love to sit at my grandmother's table again."

Seth interjected, his voice excited. "And it's not just furniture. There's kitchen stuff and bathroom stuff and even a sewing machine."

"My mom never learned to sew and neither of my sisters wanted it."

"This is just amazing." Taylor was beginning to think of all the things she could make on the sewing machine for two little babies.

Seth turned to Nathan and Rubin. The pair were of similar heights, and both had wavy dark brown hair. Rubin was bigger all around, and Nathan was blessed with blue eyes and the kind of long curling dark lashes that just were not fair for a man to have, in Taylor's opinion. In contrast, Rubin's eyes were so dark that they seemed nearly black.

Seth introduced Gina to Jason. The petite blond wore a short white tank top, cutoff jeans, and her hair in twin braids. She looked like she was off to milk a cow or serve beer at an Oktoberfest.

Seth turned to Taylor. "You just point where you want it." Then he raised his voice. "Okay, gang," said Seth. "Bring it in."

In a few moments, in came ten boxes of who knew what all. Gina helped with the directing, as Taylor could not keep up with the speed or quantity of new possessions.

Then the men unloaded two newish couches, a proper, if

dated, pine dining room table, six matching chairs with padded seats, upholstered with a faded tropical print harkening back to the eighties, twin bed frames with brass headboards, another couch, and a rocker. A rocker! She pictured holding her babies while rocking slowly back and forth. She stroked the wood armrest.

"This is lovely."

"I thought you'd like that. It was my grandmother's. Used to sit on the front porch."

"I adore it."

"Let's get it inside and you can try it out," said Seth.

She did, sitting in the living room as the men carried in another bedframe, this time for a full-sized mattress and with a pine headboard.

"This is amazing."

"My mom said to keep it or sell it. As long as it doesn't end up back in her garage."

The men placed the furniture as she directed from downstairs and Gina from the second floor. By the time they had finished, they had the orange monster of a couch in the family room with two barrel-chairs she hadn't even seen come in. A rust-colored area rug clashed with the couch, but clearly someone had tried to tie it to the orange floral velveteen overstuffed sofa that Taylor suddenly felt so lucky to have. Their television now sat on what had been the McClellans' coffee table beside the remote and an artificial fern in a basket.

She had no idea what Gina had done with the upstairs and didn't really care. Taylor had sent every bureau, bed, and dresser to her and hoped for the best.

With the truck and bed unloaded, Seth headed out to close the garage as a gangly teen with a shock of red hair the color of polished copper headed up the drive, with an older woman several steps behind him.

"Hi there."

Seth went out to handle their uninvited guests. Meanwhile, Jason carried boxes into the kitchen. Seth showed up in time to help bring in the rest of the furniture.

"Who was that boy?" asked Taylor.

"Neighbor. He was selling a discount card for local businesses. A fundraiser for his football team. I gave him twenty bucks."

Taylor absorbed the sharp stab of concern. Money was so tight.

Seth set the plastic card on the kitchen island. Taylor stared at the rows of punch-out coupons for the sort of restaurants she never frequented. But that was then, and this was now.

"I think that twenty dollars will help spread a little goodwill."

He was right. He was absolutely one hundred percent right. The money was not going to change their life, but it might help them join this community.

"He's a senior. Running back. And his mom wanted to know if we have any dogs because her two French bulldogs lost a buddy who lived in this house before we moved in."

"What did you tell her?"

"I told her we were planning to get a dog at some point."

"Are we?"

"I think it would be good for the boys."

She lifted her shoulders in delight at hearing him speak of their unborn twins as if they were already running around in the backyard. Yes, she could picture them with a new puppy.

"I've never had a dog," said Taylor.

"Until coming to Florida, I've never been without two or three."

"All right. As soon as I'm sure we can afford one," said Taylor. Even the lovely gifts didn't solve the main problem.

She had to cover that mortgage, and quickly.

He kissed her again, a quick peck on the mouth, and then carried two dining chairs into the house. The back of the pickup was also filled with goodies. There was a bench, a pine buffet, two bureaus, one stenciled with red hearts on a country blue background, a desk, another upholstered chair, and finally, a toy chest.

She was thankful again that home sales included window coverings because each window had either Venetian blinds, draperies, or both. She didn't know what such window treatments cost, but whatever it was, they couldn't afford it.

Out the dining room window, she watched the teen and his mom heading in the other direction.

Fundraising was something Taylor had never had to do.

Taylor might have begun life in a bubble of wealth and privilege, but being a rich kid had its downsides. So did having a mom with mental illness.

Her mother's moods came to mind. Sabrina Roth was like a seesaw, up and down and up and down. Did any other kid know what manic depression was by the time they hit first grade?

She often wondered.

Her energetic mom always emerged like the phoenix after long gray stretches. Her father said the downs were a depressive period and the ups were her manic period. A cycle. Taylor had her own names for them. She called the wired episodes the jumping jitters and the melancholy times the gloomies.

Those jumping jitters were happy and frightening and always followed by the gloomies of low energy, much sleeping, and the rise of grouchy, angry, paranoid, unpredictable Mom. That was the one that scared her. The one that made her hide.

She remembered sitting in the front of her mom's newest car. Another luxury sedan, cream colored this time. It seemed her mom got a new vehicle about every two years. The lease, her dad said.

During the jumping jitters, her mom wasn't really there. She was traveling or out with friends or home dancing with the music turned up so loud Taylor couldn't think to do her homework.

Her mother's public face was always haughty, well-mannered, so put together and on the go. Busy, busy with charity events and parties. Too busy to remember to pick up her daughter from dance class. Taylor hated that jittery mom nearly as much as the gloomies mom who spent all day in the house with the blinds drawn or laying naked poolside.

By the time Taylor was in sixth grade and at her new middle school, she began to excel and make new friends. Finally, she was creating a life and personality of her own. She loved changing classes and her new math teacher, Mrs. Miller, was a particular favorite. She wanted Taylor to join the STEM program. It was a club and they made actual robots and programed them.

One morning in October, on the ride to school, Taylor recalled her mom taking a turn too fast and getting tossed against the side door so hard she dropped her phone. The shock of her jolted landing caused her to forget for a moment exactly to whom she was speaking.

"Mom! Slow down. You're going to kill somebody."

Her mother had slammed on the brakes. Taylor's seatbelt engaged, jerking her to a stop before she faceplanted on the dashboard.

"What did you say?"

Behind her mother's car, a horn sounded.

"I said..." Taylor glanced at her mother to find her red-faced and panting. Her eyes were wide and her mouth grim. "Nothing."

"Get out," ordered her mother.

They were stopped in the right lane of a two-lane road still a mile from school.

"Mom, I'm sorry."

"Out!" Sabrina bellowed.

Behind them, horns blared.

Taylor released her belt and scrambled out onto the shoulder.

"I need my bag and my phone," she said, crying now.

Her mother stomped on the accelerator so hard the closing door hit Taylor. She watched her mother roar off.

She had no phone, no backpack, no lunch, and, oh man, no homework.

Someone shouted at her. "Get out of the road, you idiot!"

Taylor reached the sidewalk. If she had her phone, she would have called her father or their housekeeper, Regan, who had carefully packed her lunch this morning. But her phone was in the wheel-well of her mother's car.

The tears kept coming and she wiped them away. There was no way she would be crying when she got to school. The only thing worse would be fainting or puking. Everyone would be talking about it if they knew. So Taylor needed to be certain they didn't.

It turned out that her middle school had a program for kids who 'forgot' their lunch. But that was not the end of her worst day of middle school.

She'd told her favorite teacher that her mother had been acting erratically, only she had not used those words. Crazy, she'd said.

Mrs. Miller asked if Taylor had felt unsafe.

And Taylor had wept and told her about being left on the side of the road.

And had her 'narcing' on her mother helped?

It had not, because after Mrs. Miller called with her concerns, her mother was respectful, explained that Taylor's version of events wasn't exactly true. 'You know how imaginative teenagers can be.'

And before they reached the Christmas break, Mrs. Miller was removed from her classroom and had left the district.

All her students were devastated. They wanted Taylor to sign a petition to get her reinstated to her position. She didn't because she was the only one who knew why Mrs. Miller had been sacked and who had done it.

NINE

Flashes from Taylor's childhood sparked before her, memories she had ignored, avoided, and suppressed. But she tucked them away. She'd survived her youth. She could survive this.

"Put up or shut up," she whispered to herself, and shifted her attention from the mother and son to her driveway where Jason lifted out a final box. Seth followed him into the house.

"This one my mother packed for you. Gramma McClellan kept our baby clothes. And she could crochet like nobody's business. Mom sorted out what she wanted, mostly my sister's things, and that left mine."

He set the box on the living room floor and opened it, lifting out a beautiful blue baby blanket.

"This one was mine." He offered it to her.

Taylor felt the tell-tale burning in the back of her throat. The tears followed, streaming down her cheeks.

"Oh, Jason." She held the soft blanket to her cheek. "I can't take this. You need to keep it."

"I figure by the time I need it, you'll be done with it and can send it back. Besides, I want you two to have it."

She pressed her face into the blanket and cried. Seth

rubbed her back and Jason shifted uncomfortably from side-to-side.

When she got control of herself, she hugged Jason and then offered the makeshift movers a drink.

Gina wanted only water, thankfully, and Nathan, Rubin, and Jason accepted a beer, one of the few things in their refrigerator, and then they all headed upstairs so Taylor could see the bedrooms.

The men went to work putting together the frames for the twin beds that Gina had sent to the smaller of the three bedrooms and the queen-sized bed in the other. Their primary bedroom now included a six-drawer oak dresser, so each of the guest bedrooms had got a bureau, and the larger got the bookshelf.

"Maybe just one of the single beds in here," said Taylor.

"What about the other?"

"Garage for now?" she asked, feeling guilty someone had to carry it back downstairs again. As soon as they disappeared, she remembered the attic. Though she didn't want that to become a storage room for unwanted, unusable stuff. As they worked, Taylor realized something. With Jason's amazingly generous gift, and under Gina's direction, they'd transformed the upstairs from an empty shell to furnished rooms with framed artwork, desks, floor lamps, bureaus, side tables, and beds. And the age of the additions actually made them look inviting.

Gina plugged in the portable smart television on the bureau in the larger room and connected power. In the second bedroom, she'd set up both a boom box with a CD player, along with a wire rack of CDs, and a clock radio, set to the correct time. Both looked to have arrived from several decades past and worked perfectly.

Seeing the rooms set up this way gave Taylor the first inkling of an idea.

"I put the rocker in your room," said Gina. "Easier to feed the babies that way. It's near your bed."

"Thank you."

Jason grinned. "My grandmother used to rock my sisters in that chair. Oh, that reminds me. There are children's books in those boxes. *Where the Wild Things Are, Stellaluna, The Snow Day, The Very Hungry Caterpillar.* And my favorite, *Don't Let the Pigeon Drive the Bus.*"

Taylor clapped her hands in delight. "I love *all* of those." She thought of all her books, still on her bookshelf in her parents' home, with a trickle of melancholy. "My favorite was *Olivia.*"

Jason laughed. "Makes sense."

"Hey," she said, taking mock offense.

"My sisters loved those books, too," said Jason.

"Maybe Uncle Jason can come by and read a bedtime story," said Taylor.

Jason grinned. "It would make a nice change from biochemistry."

"And clinical anatomy," added Seth.

The mention of medical texts and studies lowered the mood in the room. Jason glanced at his phone, checking the time.

"Can I fix you all some lunch?" asked Taylor. She wasn't sure what she could whip up. There was a large container of wonton soup in the fridge.

"Gotta get back to the hospital," said Jason.

And their never-ending practicum hours, thought Taylor.

"Thanks for everything. I mean, this is amazing," said Seth.

Jason waved away the gratitude and gave a lopsided smile. "You're welcome."

They all headed downstairs.

Taylor turned to the remaining work crew.

"Gina, Nathan, Rubin, can I at least make you a sandwich?"

Rubin shook his head. "Nathan and I just got back and we're out again tomorrow on another long haul."

"Together?" asked Taylor. "I thought you each had a rig."

Gina broke in. "Usually. But it's better to have two on a cross-country run and they're on back-to-back turnarounds."

"Where to?" she asked.

The men exchanged a quick glance that activated her internal alert system. The pause stretched as the pair glanced out the window where Seth was waving Jason off.

Gina filled the odd silence. "Just back from Denver. Next one is Los Angeles."

Rubin flinched. Nathan continued to stare at Seth, who'd now returned to the house. Neither one looked at her.

This only added to Taylor's curiosity.

"Well, I'm sorry I can't at least feed you."

"We'll take a rain check," said Gina. "That pool is out of this world."

"We'll have a cookout. Soon," Taylor promised.

She walked them out, thanking them all again and giving the movers hugs.

As she watched them drive away, her notion solidified, and she knew exactly what she would do.

And it just might work.

TEN

Seth left her for the time it took to pick up a pizza from their favorite place. He sent a text upon return because he'd forgotten his remote for the garage door.

She opened the door with the remote in her purse and then waited until he'd pulled in and cut the engine before hitting the button to close the garage.

"Forgot the code, too?" she asked as he retrieved their lunch from the back seat.

"I did."

"Put it in your phone."

She accepted the pizza as he fiddled to add the information to his notes app.

They ate at Jason's grandmother's dining table. Taylor fingered the numbers indented in the soft pine, as if some child had pressed too hard while doing their math homework in some distant time and place.

Taylor smiled. Old things had character.

After supper, Seth ducked into their bedroom for a shower. He emerged in a T-shirt and shorts, slung low on his narrow hips.

"These towels are so soft," he said, holding up the end of the rose-colored towel that had been in one of the boxes along with bedding. She'd taken their old ones and moved them to the guest bathrooms. The place now looked as if it was occupied. And she loved that.

The sight of all that damp skin and tight muscle made her insides quicken. Meow, she thought, surprised at the visceral tug of attraction this late in her pregnancy. The sight of him made her want to do things her obstetrician discouraged.

But there were other ways. Taylor led him into the family room to christen that orange couch.

"Where are we going?"

"I wanted to thank you properly for feathering our nest."

"Really?" He looked so surprised it made her laugh. "What about..." His hand went to her belly.

"They won't mind." She pushed him back onto the sofa and dropped a couch pillow on the floor between his legs. Then she reached with eager fingers. Seth's head dropped to the cushioned seatback and his eyes fluttered closed as he gave a groan of pleasure.

By the time they finally returned to the kitchen, where their new-old dinette and his dinner waited, she had decided that she really liked that couch. It was more than comfortable, big enough to accommodate two, and there were things more important than a pulled-together interior design.

After their meal they returned to snuggle on the sofa. Taylor wondered if she should tell him her idea or wait and see what kind of a response her ad garnered. His soft snore answered the question.

Seth had promptly dozed off with his head back and mouth slightly open. They were working him so hard. And he'd driven up to Gainesville and back with Jason to surprise her. She was so lucky to have a man like him.

Had she not roused him from his doze, they might have spent the night there.

"Come on, baby. Time for bed," she said.

She offered her hand.

"I love that couch," he said.

"Comfy, right?"

"And big," he said.

They shared wicked grins. "Very."

Taylor guided him up the stairs to their room. Seth was half asleep and fell into bed and slumber the minute his head hit the pillow.

Taylor tried to sleep but her mind kept going back to the shadow she'd seen last night in the yard. She slipped from the bed to check to see that the balcony doors were locked. Then she wondered if Seth had locked the front door. Of course he had. She returned to bed and laced her fingers over her stomach. Why didn't the air conditioner shut off? It had been running steadily all evening.

She finally dozed and then jolted awake, the air conditioner still blowing and the room freezing.

What was it set at? She tossed back the covers. Seth rolled to his side as she headed to the hall to check the thermostat. It was set at seventy-two, which was right.

Taylor continued downstairs. She glanced out into the empty drive to the street, seeing no one. The streetlights were set well apart, leaving shadowy places between the houses across the way. She peered into the gap between houses. Then she looked back at their driveway.

The garage door was wide open.

Seth didn't have a remote yet. And she'd closed that door from inside.

So how did it get open?

Taylor took one step in the direction of the garage and then stopped. Her skin was crawling and the hair on her arms stood straight up.

She went back upstairs and shook Seth awake, her voice a rasping whisper and her mouth filled with the acrid tang of fear.

He roused slowly, dragged from the deepest sleep, his movements clumsy as he struggled to sit up.

"What?" he said.

"The garage door is open. But I closed it."

He had one hand on his head, swaying. "Okay. Just a minute."

Seth scrubbed his face with his hands and then stood. She held her phone.

"Do you want your bat?" she asked.

"My bat?"

"For protection."

He shook his head, awake now. "You think someone was in the garage?"

"I don't know," she squeaked. "But I closed it. Could they have snuck in there during all the moving? You know, the furniture? Then maybe let themselves out with the button in there?"

"Stay here." He sounded alert now.

"Like hell."

But she did let him go first. The door from the garage to the house was locked, thank God. But the garage door was still open. Seth stood in the open garage, hands on hips. Taylor hovered in the doorway to the house.

"Hmmm," he said.

"I closed it."

Seth flicked on the light. She blinked under the visual assault as Seth checked the overhead mechanism of the lift system.

"Looks okay. Hit the button."

She did and the door glided closed. Now she felt stupid.

"Animal?" she asked.

He shook his head, then made a slow circle around the cars, opening the doors to peer inside.

"Everything looks all right. Might have a wonky remote system."

"They don't open by themselves. Sometimes they don't open, but they never just go up on their own."

Her chest hurt from the wild hammering of her heart.

"Maybe you hit the remote accidentally when you were getting something from your purse."

She thought over that possibility.

"Maybe." She still felt uncomfortable.

"Come on. Work tomorrow. What time is it?"

She checked her phone. "Eleven-thirty." She stared at the door. "Did you hear it go up?"

"No. You?"

She shook her head. "Maybe we can't hear it from upstairs. But something woke me."

"Try it again."

Taylor hit the button. They watched the door rise. She hit it again and they watched it fall.

"Weird," he said. Then he shrugged. "New house. We'll get used to things."

"If you think I'll get used to a garage door opening itself, you're mistaken."

"I'll bet you hit it accidentally."

That was a reasonable guess. More likely than her theory. But not the only possibility. Taylor double checked the lock on the door from the garage and then rechecked the front door before heading back upstairs with her husband.

Once safely in their room, Seth headed into the bathroom and she settled back in bed, using her phone to check the garage details online. There was no way that door went up on its own. Unsettled, she checked the security system, viewing the house through each of the security cameras. First the doorbell-cam that showed the garage shut, then the one on the lanai that showed the pool's underwater lights turning the water a cerulean blue. Then the one in the entrance foyer that gave a view of the empty living room and hall to the kitchen. Then she stopped, puzzled. Where was the one for the master bedroom?

Taylor glanced at the camera mounted in the corner near the ceiling. Now that she really looked at it, she noted it wasn't even the same shape as the others.

Panic rose like a ball of ice in her throat, choking her words as she called out.

"Seth! Come in here please!"

ELEVEN

The camera wasn't connected to their system.

"How did some random webcam get in our bedroom?" she asked, still shivering from the aftermath of the flood of adrenaline.

Seth had gotten the camera down and removed the batteries. Whoever put it there no longer had a view of the interior of their bedroom. But it had been pointing straight at their bed. Her skin crawled at the thought of some voyeur watching them sleep. It was such a violation.

"The garage," she said. "Someone came in here and put that camera up."

Seth cocked his head, thinking about that. "Are you sure it wasn't up there before?"

She wasn't.

"Maybe it was just a random leftover from a previous system."

"And they just left it up there? It could have been broadcasting to who knows whom."

"It could have. And that's disturbing. But we've changed the router when we changed the house security system to our account. New password. Everything. So, that would stop it, wouldn't it?"

"I think so. I'm not sure. Probably."

"So it's a leftover. Someone before the previous owner had a different system."

She hoped that was true, but the disturbing image of someone watching her in her bedroom made her nauseous.

"It's okay, Taylor. Really. It's fine."

"Yeah. I'm sure it's okay," she said, but she planned to search every room for additional cameras.

* * *

"I'm going to rent the spare rooms." Taylor announced this at breakfast on Monday morning, as Seth was finishing up his egg sandwich. She'd searched every room, including the creepy, dusty unfinished attic and the interior of the garage, finding no more random cameras.

"What?" He swallowed the last bite.

"Boarders. We need two, at $1,600 a piece and I can almost cover the rest of the mortgage with my salary. If I can get three, I'll have more than half."

"How'd you think to fit three in two bedrooms? Are we sleeping in the garage?"

The mention of the garage made her shiver.

"No, silly. A couple, I'll ask for $2,700, and a single at $1,600. That's more than half the mortgage."

She grinned at him, so proud that she'd come up with a plan to allow them to keep this house.

He made a humming sound in his throat and shook his head.

Her smile dropped away, and her pride morphed into confusion. This was not the reaction she'd expected. Seth always supported her ideas, encouraged her, and had told her more than once that he admired her tenacity and ingenuity. He rarely said no and always hedged his refusal with explanation.

He pushed away his dirty plate, and folded his arms.

"Not sure I like that idea. Isn't it against the rules in this neighborhood?"

Off balance now, she proceeded with caution, using reason as she explained.

"Subletting is. I didn't see anything about boarders. But if it's the HOA, I'll handle it. Don't worry. I'll say they're my cousins, here to help with the babies. Besides, it takes community organizations months to get anything done and they have no teeth."

"Where are they going to park?"

"On the street."

"No overnight parking. They all have to fit in our drive."

Taylor thought about that problem. "It's a big drive. They'll all fit."

"We'll have to juggle vehicles to get out."

She nodded. This was true. "Anything else?"

"Well, since you asked, I've never lived with strangers. It makes me uncomfortable."

Seth had never been to prep school, sleepaway camp, or college, in the traditional sense, with dorm rooms and roommates.

"It's good. You can make some great friends and get exposure to different cultures. Keep an open mind." He looked unconvinced so she added, "If we don't bring in boarders, we won't have a house."

"We could move into a one-bedroom in Orlando."

"You just brought in all this furniture. And you told me you knew I'd work it out. Well, I have. This is the plan."

His jaw muscles bulged, and he frowned.

"We have two empty furnished bedrooms upstairs just going to waste. This will work. Trust me."

"I trust you. But I'm gone a lot and you'll be here alone."

"So?"

"I can't protect you."

"Protect me? Seth, what are you talking about? These are tenants, not cage fighters."

"Will you be able to even rest with three people creeping around upstairs?"

The mention of people creeping around reminded her of the moving shadow she'd seen on Saturday night, the garage door that opened by itself, and that damned webcam in their bedroom. Had someone snuck in here? She shivered and glanced out at the sunny yard. Now, in the warm, bright morning, the landscaping looked charming. She chided herself on letting her imagination run away with her. The shadow was a neighbor's dog. Or perhaps a deer. Nothing sinister. And the garage door and the webcam? Seth had reasonable theories.

Ones she just didn't buy.

Her confidence flagged yet again.

"They'll be responsible. Great. And you'll feel better having them there. Not worse. Because I won't be alone while you're gone."

Seth looked unconvinced. He opened his mouth, closed it then opened it again. "Taylor, please come up with something else."

"I can't. My income isn't nearly enough, and you won't have any income for several months. *This* is the plan. It's short term and we'll make it. We can keep the house and pay the minimum on our credit cards in the meantime."

"Where are you going to find them?"

"Here." She showed him the website specializing in connecting roommates and rentals. "They vet them for us. And they'll vet us as well."

Seth uncrossed his arms. "You sure about this?"

TWELVE

Taylor was sure. Seth talked her idea over with Rubin, his most trusted confidant and, after Rubin weighed in on her side, Seth climbed on board the boarder train with her. Seth's only provision was that he be there when she interviewed prospects.

That seemed an easy compromise. It couldn't hurt to have him there for a second opinion on the prospects.

She finally remembered to give him the remote to the garage, and they left for work together that morning. Seth again checked the mechanism of the door lift. Everything seemed to be working correctly.

"Can another person's remote open our door?" asked Seth.

"It's possible, I suppose. They work on radio frequencies or infrared signals that are unique and I'd be surprised if this place doesn't have rolling code technology."

He cocked his head. Seth knew medicine but not engineering.

"No garages back home?" she asked.

"We had a garage. Barns, too. Just no remotes."

"I'll check online and see what we have. Okay?"

He nodded and then kissed her goodbye. She headed for her car and waited for him to pull out before she did the same.

* * *

Her online ad got a lot of attention. She put in a lowball number for rent and when she received a call, she told them that the room at that property had been rented, but she had two rooms still available in her home that cost $1,600 a month for a single and $2,700 for a couple. More than half the callers dropped their offer then, but several were willing to move forward.

Of the five people still interested in immediate occupancy, only four were ready to lay down first and last month's rent and only one was a couple.

Wednesday afternoon they had two appointments, one physical and one virtual, to interview prospects. They'd meet the young couple virtually and a single woman they would interview at her jobsite. Taylor texted Seth and he said he could meet her at the office, so she'd juggled some appointments to clear her afternoon.

The online site she'd joined told her a lot of initial information and she forwarded that to Seth. The candidate for the single room was a woman, Zoe Furr, a museum curator at the once opulent hotel built by a wealthy northern entrepreneur who brought the railroad and tourism to Tampa Bay at the turn of the last century. She currently lived in St. Pete and said, via message, she hoped to find a place closer to work. She'd provided all the information Taylor requested and included several particulars she needed.

The virtual meeting was with Jules and Becca Currie, a newlywed couple. He'd been working up in Ruskin for several years as a mail carrier and finally got his transfer to Tampa. She had lived with her parents until her wedding, had done a lot of job-hopping in the service industry, and was a new hire as a barista at a place downtown.

Seth picked her up at her office and drove them to the museum lot. They walked up the sidewalk past mature oaks shading benches fringed by pristine flowerbeds, beside a long porch where potted ferns and rubber trees thrived beneath the continuous glide of fan blades. Brickwork and Victorian ginger-bread scroll work seamlessly blended beneath Moorish minarets and cupolas.

Seth clasped her elbow as they mounted the stairs, then opened the door.

Inside the cool dark interior, they paused to look around. Ornate didn't cover it. The Victorian aesthetic was everywhere, with dark wood, heavy carpets, statues, potted ferns, gilded accent pieces, period upholstered benches, Chinese porcelain, and the admissions desk. Mahogany, of course.

The woman working admissions listened as Taylor asked to see Ms. Furr. She was in her late sixties with short blond hair, sun-damaged skin, and pink lipstick bleeding into the deep wrinkles about her mouth.

Before the museum gatekeeper could answer, their meet-up arrived walking with the briskness of a New York City commuter.

"Thank you for meeting me here," she said, stopping well back from them. She did not extend her hand but turned to the woman at the admissions desk and said, "These are my two guests."

The receptionist smiled warmly. "Oh, I see. Well, enjoy."

"Such a busy time with the change in exhibits and the loan items arriving and needing my attention. Is this all right for our chat?" Zoe asked, motioning to a seating area adjacent to the admissions desk. "It's one of the only places guests can sit in the museum. So many period pieces with velvet ropes to keep folks from ruining them. And my office is very small and crowded."

"This is fine," said Taylor.

"Very interesting place," said Seth.

"Have you never been? You should. We have over six thousand pieces, just in this building, and I've cataloged each one. Decorative exhibits and local history. We even have some unusual taxidermy pieces."

They sat together and Zoe continued to fuss with her collar, repeatedly drawing the two scalloped edges closer together above the last button. Taylor noticed her nails were short and she had Band-Aids on the tips of two fingers.

"I haven't been since I was a kid," said Taylor. "My parents brought me. They're donors."

"Oh yes? What are their names?"

Taylor held her smile, but hesitated, wishing she'd filtered that detail. Finally, she said, "It's Dr. and Mrs. Roth."

"Sabrina Roth?"

"That's right."

"Oh my word. They're two of our most generous backers. The exhibit I'm working on now is due to their donations."

Nice they had money for museums, but none for their daughter, she thought, but then felt guilty at her pettiness.

Likely Ms. Furr had sent her mother a birthday card.

"Is that right?" said Seth.

"Yes! They're lovely people. Sabrina is just wonderful. So charming and well educated. And enthusiastic about everything to do with our museum."

Because she'd only seen her in her manic periods, Taylor knew. Her mother did not go out when depressed. But when she was up, Sabrina could channel those jumping jitters to appear effervescent and charming. Most people loved her mother.

"You're so lucky to have such a cultured mom, and your dad, well he just adores her. Who wouldn't? She's the picture of refinement and elegance."

Taylor wondered if she should ask the woman if she'd like an autograph from her mother. Or if she'd like to hear a few more personal stories of the donor who loomed so large in her mind.

She didn't, of course, because she'd been taught from an early age that she never discussed her mother's mental illness with anyone outside the family.

"Isn't it a small world?" asked Seth, giving Taylor a minute to remove the forced smile and get control of herself.

"Yes. It certainly is. Wait until I tell them here that I might be living with the daughter of Sabrina Roth."

Taylor rolled her lips together and bit down to keep from ordering Zoe to keep her trap shut. For reasons too personal to delve into, she did not want her parents to know the depths to which she was sinking to keep the house.

What would her mother say? Sabrina Roth might be either scandalized or delighted. Unpredictability was one of her mother's stronger suits.

She was certain that her mother expected her to either beg for help or lose the house out of stubbornness. Despite Taylor's excellence in school and high grades, her mother did not think her exceptional or even very capable.

In addition, she was certain that her mother would not approve of her daughter running a boarding house like some widow in a Dickens novel.

Why, after breaking free, had she ever allowed her father to lure her back and start up the Sabrina Roth Trust Fund machine again?

"But back to business," said Zoe. "I'm certain, knowing your parents, that your home is lovely. But I would need to see the room and your property before signing anything. And you got my requests. I'll bring an air purifier, but I must have my own bathroom."

"Yes. You'll have a private bathroom," said Seth.

"Shower or tub?" she asked.

"Large walk-in shower."

She nodded.

"Carpets?"

"No. Would you like one?"

"I prefer not. Allergies."

"Ah, well, it's a laminate floor."

Zoe nodded her approval at this.

Taylor took over and asked general questions about her work schedules, hobbies, habits. It seemed Zoe was an early riser, avidly practiced yoga, kept herself to a very strict vegan diet, and her hobbies included reading and playing chess online and with a local club. She was also active in her church.

All that made her sound like an ideal boarder.

"Oh, I need a place for my pot and skillet. I don't cook in anything contaminated by red meat, poultry, or swine."

"We can arrange a place in the pantry for that," said Taylor, trying to shake off her annoyance as she wondered if this woman would become a nuisance.

"What do you enjoy doing on the weekends or on days off?" asked Seth.

"I often work on Saturdays, but when I'm not, I enjoy visiting other museums and attending open houses. Sunday, I go to church, of course. As I mentioned. And there's Bible study on Tuesday evenings. And the chess tournaments. I've even competed nationally."

Taylor picked up on one activity that seemed out of place. "You mentioned open houses. Are you considering buying a home?" she asked.

"Oh, no. I just like to see how people decorate. This museum is largely ornamental arts. I enjoy seeing the artwork and furniture arrangement. I've been studying what modern families collect and am considering an exhibit comparing old versus new design aesthetics, collections, and games. And the open concepts of today are so different than the days when you hid the cooking and servants behind swinging doors."

Seth held his smile as he cast Taylor a side eye.

"Unfortunately, some lack taste. Money doesn't make up for that."

"Really?" asked Taylor, not understanding the thrill of exploring homes you did not intend to purchase.

"Yes. Oh, I wasn't referring to your parents, Mrs. Parker. I've never had the pleasure, but I hear from some of the executive board that their home is simply stunning."

"Yes. My mother has excellent taste." That she could say without hesitation.

Then a disturbing notion struck. "Do you ever attend open houses on new construction?"

"Never."

"What about unoccupied homes?"

"Rarely."

Her answer put Taylor on guard.

It seemed Zoe Furr was odd, a snoop, or both.

THIRTEEN

It appeared to Taylor that this pale, fussy, judgmental vegan was a bit of a voyeur. Not a deal breaker, but just a caution, like the yellow light warning of the red one to come.

"Any allergies?" asked Taylor.

"Dust irritates my sinuses, but that's all."

"What about pets?"

Zoe looked surprised. "I don't have any," she said. She was peeling and re-sticking one of the bandages on her fingertip now.

"We might be getting a dog or cat at some point. Would that bother you?" asked Seth.

Zoe sat back, having to think about this. Finally, she spoke. "It would have to stay out of my private areas. And be well-behaved, of course. No one likes a barking, slobbering dog, or a destructive clawing cat spraying the furniture with urine."

On that they could agree.

"Your bedroom and bathroom?" said Taylor, clarifying. "Those are the only private areas."

"Yes. That would be fine. To what rooms would I have access?"

"Parking is in the driveway. Not covered. You'd have access to the kitchen, living room, family room, lanai, yard, and pool. There is a private reserve behind the house if you like walking in the woods."

"I don't walk. Not outside. Would I have dedicated storage in the kitchen and refrigerator?"

"Dedicated?" asked Seth.

"I simply would not like my food blended with other tenants'. There will be others?"

"We're considering a couple for the other bedroom."

"I see."

"Yes, we can give you a shelf for food in the fridge and pantry."

"Lovely. Laundry privileges?"

"Yes," said Taylor. "But you'd need to wash and dry at one time. No leaving clothing in either washer or dryer. And dishes go in the dishwasher or washed, dried, and put away after each use."

"You needn't worry on that account. I'm very neat."

"Smoking?" asked Seth.

"Of course not."

"Would you like to come by to see the place?" asked Taylor.

"Yes. Would Friday afternoon suit?"

They gave her the address and left with her resume as if they were going to hire her to curate their belongings.

On the way to the car, Seth began tugging at his shirt collar.

"I know," said Taylor. "What's up with that? And her fingers?"

"The bandages?"

"Yes. And some were just cracked at the fingertips. What causes that? Eczema?"

"More like harsh chemicals. I'm guessing the woman's a clean freak."

"What do you mean?"

"Scrubs surfaces until her fingers crack. Might be a germaphobe. Did you see how far back she sat? And when we stood and I extended my hand, she backed up as if I were poison."

"Yeah. I can deal with neat," said Taylor. "What about her hobby with the open houses?"

"Odd. Voyeurism?"

"I'd say she's a first-class snoop."

He nodded.

"As long as she stays out of our room, she gets the okay from me. You?"

Seth nodded. "She's weird, but okay weird."

* * *

The couple appeared on Taylor's laptop right on time. She and Seth sat in a coffee shop across the street from the hotel museum, huddled close so the webcam could pick them both up. In the screen, Becca and Jules also huddled close.

Becca Currie gave them a big high, lively, and a double-handed wave. Unfortunately, the sound was off. The woman wore her long black hair in a loose braid that lay over one shoulder like a satiny scarf. Her huge pink sunglasses had the vibe of Janice Joplin from her *Pearl* cover and she wore bright pink lip stain and blue jean overalls over a tankini. Her shoulders were pale and narrow.

Jules reached forward to fiddle with the controls. Becca's husband was only slightly taller, broad, with a winning smile. He kept his black hair tugged up in a man-bun, or a manpunzel, as Seth called it, and wore a short beard. The plaid button-up shirt and absence of facial jewelry gave him a clean-cut, if hip, vibe. He frowned, squinting his gray eyes at the laptop, and then spoke.

"Is the sound on?" he said.

"Yes," Seth answered. "Nice to meet you both."

"Thanks," piped Becca. "You, too!" She clasped her hands beside her jaw and squeezed them as if giving them a virtual hug.

"I'm sorry we couldn't get there in person," said Jules. "I only finished at work a few minutes ago."

"Rushed home to be here. Just made it." Becca grinned at her husband and he beamed back.

"So you two are newlyweds," said Taylor.

"Yes!" Becca bounced. "A June bride."

"But we haven't found an apartment we can afford and still save for a house," said Jules.

Seth and Taylor asked their questions, set down house rules, and laid out what they could offer. Then they answered their questions. This pair were anxious to move in immediately to 'get out of my parents' house,' Becca admitted.

Taylor could hardly blame them. She informed them about the other boarder, likely Zoe, who would have her own room and bathroom across the hall from theirs. They were fine with that. They were young and energetic, and Taylor liked them both immediately.

"Did you get the photos from the listing and the virtual tour?" asked Taylor. Since they could not see the place before committing, she did what she could.

"Yes! Can't wait to see it in person," said Jules.

"You have the bedroom with the one navy-colored wall. The bathroom is private, and it has a tub and shower and double sinks."

"That will be perfect!" said Becca, clapping.

"I'm glad. The furniture you see is not ours. Ours is..." She glanced at Seth.

"Old," he finished. "Really, really old."

Becca laughed.

"Bed is full-sized?" asked Jules.

"It's a queen," said Taylor.

"Even better." Jules glanced at Becca in a meaningful way. She cleared her throat.

"Listen," said Becca, lowering her voice conspiratorially. "I have to tell you something. You know. To be totally honest. I have a cat. But, listen, it can stay at my parents'. I don't need to bring her, but she's very well behaved. No scratching furniture and she's clean, has all her shots, and uses her litter box."

Seth looked at Taylor. She thought about it and leveraged the pet.

"Two hundred in advance, a security on the cat, fifty more a month and I never want to see that litterbox."

"I'll keep it in my private bathroom. Don't worry."

"Also, we live on a reserve. There are coyotes and possibly bobcats. I wouldn't let your cat outside."

"Just inside the pool cage and the screened lanai. Would that be all right?"

Taylor nodded. "If you're there."

"Oh, thank you! You'll love Moon. She's amazing. Such a sweetie and, well, she's just a lovebug, is all."

Taylor added effervescent to Becca's list of character traits.

"Listen, Becca got the night off because the freezer broke, and the restaurant is closed. So we were wondering, could we drive down tonight, you know, just to see the place? Would that be possible? I know it's last minute. I understand if you have other plans," said Jules.

"That could work," said Seth. "When could you get here?"

The pair exchanged a look and then Becca answered. "Rush hour now, so it would be, like, after seven."

"That's fine."

Seth took down their contact information. "We'll email the agreement and you can autosign or print and sign and bring it along."

"Great!" said Jules. "We'll see you soon."

They disconnected.

Seth and Taylor glanced at each other.

"They seem nice," said Seth.

"Zoe is going to hate them."

* * *

Seth and Taylor drove home in separate vehicles and had time to change and have supper before their prospective tenants arrived.

As to the remaining prospects, one emailed that he'd found a place, and the credit check on the other, a single woman, showed a foreclosure and large gap in her credit history, so Taylor told her the single was already rented. If Zoe decided not to rent, she'd open the search again.

The motion sensor in the doorbell camera alerted them to the couple's arrival before the pair were even out of their car. They drove a late model Caddy, powder blue with a faded vinyl top and a bicycle rack on the back, carrying a Schwinn men's mountain bike.

Becca drove and fairly bounced out from behind the wheel. Jules met her as she rounded the car, a jute bag slung over one shoulder. They walked, stride for stride like a matched set of carriage horses.

"Look how cute they are," said Taylor.

Seth opened the door. The men shook hands and Seth welcomed them into their home.

"Oh my gosh!" said Becca. "You're having a baby!"

"Twins," said Seth, grinning with pride.

Becca stepped forward and ran a hand over Taylor's pregnant belly, as Taylor tried not to grimace. She simply hated it when people did this. When the woman's hand lingered a little too long, a shiver slithered down Taylor's spine and she stepped back.

"Congratulations," said Jules, striding up behind his wife

who had already cleared the entrance and paused in the foyer.

"Wow!" said Becca, looking at the high ceilings as she turned in a full circle. "Oh, wow!" She met Taylor's gaze and clapped. "It's beautiful!"

"Let me show you around." Taylor led the way.

Seth fell in beside Jules as they toured the family room, kitchen, and dining room. Neither commented on the odd collection of out-of-date furnishings. In fact, Becca appeared to love every single thing, while Jules seemed the more practical one, asking if they could use the grill and what time would be too early or late to use the pool. All his questions showed a man who wanted to make no waves and not overstay his welcome.

As they headed from the screened lanai back into the house, Seth paused to show them how to lock the sliders and then they proceeded upstairs.

"When are you due?"

By the time they reached the couple's potential bedroom, Taylor was puffing and out of breath from the stairs and all the questions. Becca's enthusiasm and high energy was slightly overwhelming. But she was so sweet and eager, Taylor was charmed.

Seth and Taylor remained in the hall to let the couple explore the bedroom. Becca looked out the window, excited to have a view of the wooded reserve. Jules opened and closed the drawers to the bureau and checked out the closet. They left the room to investigate the bathroom and Taylor heard them jabber excitedly about the large shower and bathtub.

"They seem so young."

"Just married," said Seth.

They shared a smile, each remembering their early days of marriage.

"I hope she's a better cook than I was."

"Actually, Jules does the cooking. Or that's what he told me."

"How progressive. You should take notes."

"I cook," he said, and she took his hand and leaned her head on his shoulder.

"What do you think of them?"

FOURTEEN

Taylor had taken only half a day off work on Friday to meet Zoe at the house. She'd given her the tour and they'd signed the paperwork. Her new renter had left before ten, satisfied with the accommodations and with plans to move in the following day. Having her and the Curries take immediate occupancy meant she was one step closer to making her first mortgage payment, which was a bonus. But traffic had delayed Taylor and she arrived at the office later than anticipated.

Her boss, Nicki Wakely, met her at her desk before Taylor had stowed her purse in the drawer.

She braced for a reprimand. Instead, the granddaughter of the founder of their business gave her a once-over.

"You look tired, Taylor. Why don't you take the rest of the day off?"

Taylor fought back the tears, but a few leaked down her cheeks making Nicki tut-tut.

Nicki was a mother of four kids, all adults with the last in college. She was thick in the middle, dressed in draped suits and low heels and had a kind face, expressive brown eyes and a wicked, cutting sense of humor.

"Thanks, Nicki, but I have a few things I need to handle. They can't wait."

She nodded and gave Taylor's upper arm a squeeze. "All right. Don't work too hard."

Taylor settled at her desk, pushed her problems aside, and attacked her inbox like the soldiers storming the beaches of Normandy.

Despite her zeal, she didn't leave the office until Nicki appeared at her desk and pointed toward the door just before six. At least the afternoon traffic rush had slowed.

Seth called as she was heading home.

"Did she get there?" he asked.

"Sure did." Taylor flipped on her directional and glided into the left lane.

"How was that?"

"Well, she looked everything over carefully, but did not touch a single thing. It was like she thought she was still at the museum or something. I mean, not even the doorknobs."

"Odd."

"And she kept hold of her shoulder bag as if she thought I would grab it and make a run for it. What's she got in there? The Hope Diamond?"

"I haven't heard it's gone missing."

Taylor smiled.

"And if I was in the doorway she waited until I was well past before stepping through. It was like Covid protocols all over."

"Germophobe," he said again. "Bet she's got hand sanitizer in her bag."

"So do I."

"No handshake?" He sounded incredulous.

Taylor made a huffing sound through her teeth. "No."

"She get the key?"

"Yes, and she's coming tomorrow morning, then heading to some church function."

"And the Curries?"

"Mid-afternoon." Taylor checked her speed and slowed to allow a Beamer, who was using other drivers as traffic cones, to zigzag across three lanes and zip past an eighteen-wheeler.

"Great."

"When are you coming home?"

"Soon. Listen, one of the nurses brought in a huge tray of stuffed shells for a goodbye party. You want me to bring them home?"

Taylor perked up. "Yes! But doesn't she want them?"

"She said no."

"Then yes, of course. Thank her for us."

"Will do. See you soon my little slumlord." His chuckle made her grin.

"It's hardly a slum." She tried for an haute tone of disdain but didn't pull it off.

"I'll say."

After the call, Taylor wound through the streets in their neighborhood, so happy to live in this area. Once inside the garage, she decided to waddle out to the mailbox to see if anything had been forwarded yet.

At the box she was greeted by the wet nose of an overly friendly golden retriever who flopped down on the street, waving its legs and thumping its tail in hopes of a belly rub.

Unfortunately, Taylor feared that if she bent that far over, she'd topple right beside the canine. The long lead line was tethered to an older woman, with a cap of white hair and huge sunglasses that nearly covered the large square bandage over her temple. She wore a baggy pink T-shirt, cutoff jeans and yellow crocs that made her feet look enormous.

"Oh, Candy, get up now, you're embarrassing yourself," she

said to the dog, who continued to wiggle and twist, ever hopeful.

Taylor collected her mail and closed the box.

"You're the new neighbor?" The woman grinned, showing deep twin lines bracketing her mouth and teeth that Taylor was certain came out at night.

"Yes, that's right." Before Taylor could even introduce herself, the woman chattered on.

"I'm Ella. Ella Brinkman. My husband is Larry. We live right at the end of the street. Gray house with the porch swing hanging from the live oak. He's retired, but I'm the school nurse at Jefferson Elementary. Larry is also the HOA president. One more year." She crossed her fingers as if anxious for Larry to step down. "You work in the area?"

Clearly this was the local busybody. It was funny, only a few days ago this conversation would have felt as natural as breathing. Now Taylor struggled not to reveal the awful truth, the one thing that was completely unacceptable among her friends and every person in this neighborhood. She didn't belong here because she was flat broke.

"Yes. Downtown Tampa." She'd managed to answer the question about where she worked without revealing what she did.

"What kind of work?"

"Construction projects." She smiled.

The vagueness seemed to give the woman pause, perhaps because she realized this conversation had become more inquest than introduction.

"Lovely. I expect you'll be off on maternity leave soon."

"Yes."

Taylor held her smile for the next long awkward pause. Her father had once told her this forced the other person to speak, because of the need to fill the uncomfortable silence.

"I saw you moving in. Small truck for such a big house."

Had she been watching them? Taylor's brow dipped. Perhaps Ella was more than a busybody.

"Yes, well we moved from a one-bedroom apartment, so we didn't have much."

"We? Are you married?"

It was the sort of question that, in a different time and place, you would not need to ask a new, pregnant homeowner.

"Yes. My husband starts his residency soon. And my cousins will be bringing the rest of our things." It surprised Taylor how naturally she delivered the lie. Too much like her mother, she thought, and her smile faltered.

"Cousins?" A line appeared between her brows as she took in this information.

"Yes. Two, raised up with me, so they're more like siblings, you know?"

"Oh, I see. So, four of you?"

"Five. Soon to be seven. We're having twins. And my cousins have agreed to stay, you know, until I get back on my feet. Well, my cousins and one of their husbands. I'm so lucky and I know I'll need the help."

That sounded like a reasonable reason to have long-term guests.

Ella lifted her hands and clapped. This caused Candy to roll to her stomach and stand, long tongue lolling and eyes half closed.

"Well, it's a big place. You can make that work. And congratulations! Twins! That's so exciting."

"Yes. We're very happy." That much was true. Though Seth seemed less happy since she'd ignored his suggestion to rent out this place and get something smaller in Orlando. The worry crept in. She'd been so set on this house, she just couldn't consider not going forward. But he was likely right. This might turn into a colossal mistake. Was she dragging them into bankruptcy?

No. She could do this. She knew she could. The boarders would make up the shortfall and she'd get back to work after her maternity leave so they wouldn't lose her salary. Maybe she could work from home part of the time.

"You know," said Ella, leaning in and dropping her voice conspiratorially, "the folks that had this house before you were flippers. But they thought they'd just use it as an Airbnb. Well, our association was after them the minute they saw that listing. We check them. Airbnb, Vrbo, even Zillow for rentals. Your place is still listed there, but that's likely from the old owners. Honestly, some people just can't follow the rules."

"Isn't that sad?" Taylor was happy she'd used a roommate-finding site that her new nosy neighbor had not mentioned and likely did not know of.

"I'd contact those sites. You don't want your address listed on those sort of places. Draws all kinds of trouble."

"Oh, I will. Soon as I get out of this heat." That hint was none too subtle but seemed to have no effect on Ella's need to gossip.

"I didn't catch your name."

"I'm Taylor Parker. Nice to meet you."

"Parker," she repeated. "Like Spiderman!"

Taylor held her smile, though she'd lost count of the number of times someone made that banal observation.

"Yes. I'm glad his first name isn't Peter. It's Seth."

Ella laughed at that, but then her mouth twisted into a snarl and her face flushed pink. She half turned toward the sound of the relentless pounding of a basketball bouncing on blacktop.

She growled and placed her hands on her hips. "Those boys have been playing in the driveway all summer. I can hear that dribbling from my pool deck. It's driving me crazy."

Taylor turned to see the redhead that Seth had spoken with, a running back, she recalled. He had three other boys with him. All were skinny as coyotes, looking gangly and underfed, perpetually hungry. There was a blond with hair to his shoulders and two boys of different heights but similar enough features that she thought they might be brothers.

"They all live there?"

"No, only the coppertop, Sean. The others just seem like they live here. Those two are brothers. Gus and Pete Fetterman. They live one street over. I dropped a hint to his mother that maybe they could play at one of the other boys' houses and do you know what she said?"

Taylor did not and shrugged her shoulders.

"She told me that the boys don't have a hoop in their driveway. Honestly. How hard is it to put up a basketball hoop? Just inconsiderate is all."

"Well..." She stopped herself from revealing that there would soon be two more boys in the neighborhood, though it would be many years before her twins could annoy Mrs. Brinkman with a dribbling basketball. But her words fell off. Ella's expression told her that her mind was made up on this matter. So she started again. "Well... boys need exercise. And they seem like good kids."

"Exercise isn't all they're up to. Mr. Todd caught them drinking out in the reserve, right behind your place, and April Baxter, she lives right over there, she said they were creeping around her property at night."

"Why?"

"Who knows."

Taylor did not like the sound of that.

"So don't tell me they're good boys. Good boys don't steal alcohol from their parents' liquor cabinets, trespass, or careen about the neighborhood on motorized scooters."

"I did."

This brought Ella's head around.

"Stole my parents' liquor. Their car, too." Why had Taylor

said that? It wasn't true. But some part of her was feeling contradictory and annoyed with this woman's grilling.

"Well, that's disturbing. Follies of youth?"

Taylor just gave her an enigmatic smile.

Ella's frown deepened.

The heat was starting to get to Taylor and she felt damp all over. She thought of that pool and wished she could plop in to cool off.

"What are your cousins' names?"

"Jules and Becca Currie and..." And, of course, she blanked on the museum curator's name. So instead of answering she lifted her phone and glanced down.

"I'm sorry. I have to take this call."

"Yes, all right. Nice to meet you, Taylor. It's Ella and Larry. We're at 106."

"So nice to meet you and Candy. I look forward to meeting Larry."

"If I could get him out in this heat. But it seems only a golf course can perform that magic."

But Taylor was already striding back up the drive, hurrying along the curved flagstone path and up the red brick steps to the extremely empty porch that ran the length of the front of the house. She'd pictured sitting out here and waving to the neighbors. But she'd be damned if she'd let them see her in a folding chair, so this space, and others, would stay empty for now.

With her phone pressed to her ear, as she pretended to take an important call, she darted back inside.

The gust of cool air made her sigh, and she closed her eyes to appreciate the relief from the blast furnace the July morning had become.

She pressed her back to the solid front door and leaned backwards, enjoying dry, chilled air from the vent in the foyer.

Then she opened her eyes to buttery colored walls and the crowned molding and the ugly wrought-iron carriage lantern chandelier that she had planned to swap out but would now be happy to live with if she could just keep this place.

Thank the Lord she and Seth had already purchased the crib, bassinets, stroller, rocker, and, well, everything for the babies' room. Unfortunately, the babies' room would now house renters. So she'd be setting the crib up in their bedroom, in the area designed for a seating space with views of the woods. She and Seth had decided on one crib for the first few weeks to provide some extra comfort. When the babies were a little older, it would be easy to add a second one.

But back to the problem with tenants and nosy neighbors. Taylor would need to figure out a way to not have them out themselves to the HOA but insisting her tenants claim to be relatives put her in such a bad light.

Well, she'd figure it out. She always did.

At dinner, she told Seth all about Ella Brinkman. He laughed when she admitted about claiming she'd stolen a car and again when she related her momentary panic after forgetting Zoe Furr's name.

"Not an easy one to forget. What time are they arriving?"

"She'll be here in the morning and the Curries in the afternoon. Jules has to work."

"Sure. Regular mail day."

"I guess. Do they work six days a week?"

"No idea."

After clearing away the remains of the dinner, Seth opened the refrigerator.

"Whoa," he said, looking at the neat labels for their roommates' use. "This will take some getting used to."

"Make sure you don't use their food or put anything on their shelves. Same in the pantry. Especially Zoe's. I get the feeling she's not a big sharer."

"I think you're right."

Taylor had taken extra care checking the renters' rooms,

setting out fresh towels, and Seth had cleaned all the surfaces in the kitchen.

Once they'd set the kitchen back in order, they nestled on the couch until Taylor found herself dozing. Seth helped her up and they headed to bed. Tonight, sleep came easily, but did not last long.

A sound woke her. Taylor pushed herself upright in bed, heart hammering. What was that? Not the garage door again.

She nudged Seth's shoulder.

"Hmm?" he said.

"I heard something."

There was another pop.

"There," she said.

Seth cocked his head. "Sounds like a rifle."

FIFTEEN

Except for movies and television, Taylor had never heard an actual rifle fire. But Seth had grown up hunting with his father. He knew guns and his initial assessment terrified her.

"Should we call the police?" she asked.

He was out of bed and drawing on his T-shirt. At the door, he lifted his baseball bat.

"Stay here," he said.

"Seth?" But he was gone.

Off went the covers and she tiptoed after him. Another pop sounded. It was coming from the reserve.

By the time she reached the living room, Seth was on the pool deck watching the woods.

She stood at his elbow as the popping came again, in rapid fire.

Seth snorted.

"What?" she whispered.

"Firecrackers. Someone is setting off fireworks."

As if to confirm his assessment, a whistle preceded a pink flash of light, followed by a green cascade of sparklers.

"Woods are too dry. They might just set the forest ablaze."

"Should I call the police?"

But the far-off wail of a siren told them that a neighbor had beat them to that. From the woods came the sound of boys laughing but there were no more explosions.

"They'll never catch them," said Seth.

"It's probably the three our neighbor told me about. Hellions."

"All boys are. Let's go back to bed."

* * *

Today was move-in day. She didn't mind letting her boarders move in two days before month's end because it made their lives easier and got them into their rental for the full month of August.

Rental agreements were signed, and deposits collected. Taylor felt more confident she could handle the first mortgage payment so soon after her parents had cut her off.

She'd never been so proud or so happy.

So here she was, with a boho interior design that was growing on her by the day. It was funny to realize that old furniture meant unexpected advantages. She did not need to worry about tenants spilling red wine on expensive upholstery or tracking dirt over expensive custom carpets. And if she and Seth really were going to get a puppy one of these days, that piddling, chewing, bundle of adorable fluff would have a chance to ruin only her shoes. And those she would keep well off the floor.

Her kitchen cabinets were largely empty as was the refrigerator. But each tenant had a neatly labeled shelf in the pantry and one in the refrigerator. That left her and Seth with the crisper drawers, side drawers, and the top one. Plenty, she thought.

Funny, she hadn't lived like this since college, in her first off-campus apartment. But before that she'd been away at prep school and that thought sent her right back to her father's study and that day in ninth grade.

Dad was at work and her mom was deep into her gloomies. Taylor had scored a solo in the holiday concert at school in early November. The night of the concert, she needed to report to the choral practice room at 5:45 in the afternoon. And had she known that her mother wouldn't take her, she would have just stayed at school. But stupidly, she had come home and now her mother refused to get off the sofa and drive her back.

So she tried her dad, but, of course, he was with a patient. He said he would be there, and she knew he would be, if he didn't forget or if there wasn't a mental health emergency. She didn't know if he would go right from the office and now worried that he'd be sitting in the school auditorium and she'd be here, at home.

Even if she left right now, she'd never make it in time for warm-up and she'd be kicked out of chorus, and Megan, who she harmonized with on the second half of the verse, would never speak to her again.

Her mother dozed on the sectional. Taylor hesitated, biting her lip. Finally, she spoke.

"Mom. You've to get up and take me to school right now!"

Sabrina did get up. Her eyes popped open and her face went scarlet. 'In trouble' did not begin to cover the look of unshielded fury Taylor saw glistening in her mother's icy gray eyes.

"Mom, I'm sorry." Taylor backed away feeling like those action heroes who open a case to discover it's filled with dynamite and a ticking alarm clock.

Her mother stalked forward like a hunting lioness, eyes fixed on her prey.

Taylor's heart hammered so hard it hurt her ribs and her

body felt jittery, as if she'd just drank that acid-green sports soda with all the caffeine.

"Mom, I need to get to practice. It's the concert tonight."

"Do you think that anything in your life is so important that it gives you the right to shout at me?"

She hadn't shouted.

Her mother's whisper held all the menace of a rattlesnake sensing prey.

Taylor wished she'd raise her voice instead of using that terrifying hissing whisper.

"Mom, I'm sorry. Please drive me to school. I can't be late."

"Late?" She scoffed. "You aren't going."

"Mom, I have a solo. I *have* to be there. Everyone's depending on me."

Her mother made a sound of derision in the back of her throat.

"Your father got you that solo. You didn't think it was your voice, did you?" She snorted. "He talked to your choral teacher, offered the use of our place in North Carolina over the summer recess. No one cares if you show up. I'm certain your understudy has a better voice."

The truth—and Taylor knew it was the truth—cut so deep she forgot her fear.

"I hate you! You're mean and crazy and sad!"

Sabrina's smile held a dangerous edge. She no longer looked lethargic or depressed. She looked enlivened and sparkling with energy.

Sabrina advanced and Taylor lifted her chin, determined to show no fear and finally, finally stand up to her mother.

Taylor was standing there, chin raised when her mother slapped her so hard her lower teeth gashed her inner cheek. Taylor cupped her hand over her mouth in shock, and to keep the blood from spilling onto the rug.

Her mother no longer smiled. Her lips were twisted in an ugly sneer.

"I'll never forgive you." Taylor ran off to her bedroom and slammed the door with all her might. In her private bathroom she rinsed out her mouth, but it kept bleeding and she got scared. She texted her dad again, begging him to come home.

Mom hit me

The three dancing dots appeared. Then disappeared. Finally, she got her reply.

Heading home

She'd waited and he'd arrived nearly an hour later, rapping gently on the bedroom door.

"Is it true?" she shouted at him.

Through tears and sobbing, she finally told him what her mother had said.

"Pumpkin, listen, I was just trying to help. I knew how heartbroken you were last year when you didn't get a solo."

"But I didn't earn it. You stole my chance to see if I could. If I'm good enough."

"You're not," said her mother from her doorway.

"Sabrina, give us a minute," said her dad.

Her mom remained where she was.

"She doesn't appreciate a thing we do for her. Just like my mother. My mother would have pulled a stunt like this. Making demands. Making me lose my temper. Keep jabbing at me until I finally exploded, then blame me for what she started. Now my daughter is doing the same thing. Trying to get me in trouble."

"I'm not doing anything," Taylor cried, then pointed at her mother. "She hit me." Then she opened her mouth. "I'm still bleeding."

Her father barely glanced at her as he spun on Taylor's bed to face his wife.

"She's nothing like my mother," said her father, his voice taking on an unfamiliar hard edge.

"She is. And she's going to tell them. Say I hit her and that I'm incompetent. Just like my mother said when she tried to send me away."

Taylor blanched at this. Her grandmother had tried to get her mother locked up?

"Taylor isn't going to tell anyone," said her dad.

She hadn't thought of doing that, but now she did.

Her mother pointed a manicured nail at her. "She even looks like her. Reminds me of her more each day."

Her dad stared at Taylor as if he'd never seen her before or like she had turned into some dangerous creature. What was happening?

"Sabrina, give us a minute. Please."

"She's going to tell."

"Please, Sabrina." His tone held obvious impatience.

Her mother rolled her eyes, uncrossed her arms, and spun away and out of sight.

"You still want to go to private school?" asked her father.

Taylor scrambled to sit up. "Yes!"

"Okay."

Ten days later, she was enrolled in a private school in Massachusetts and on a plane by herself for the first time. At fifteen and a half, she had begun her divorce from the pair of them.

* * *

Taylor stared out the dining room window at the wide driveway, watching the street for her tenant. Why hadn't she asked what kind of car the woman drove?

Zoe was expected any minute.

She didn't mind spending her Saturday welcoming the boarders. It was preferable to taking a personal day during the week. She knew she'd need every single one once she returned from maternity leave to handle doctor's appointments, ear infections, and other unexpected but predictable everyday catastrophes.

Soon she'd hand over the freshly cut keys to the house and then let them move on in. It did feel slightly uncomfortable to know they could come and go, enter her home whenever they liked. But it didn't make her as uncomfortable as seeing a foreclosure notice up on her front door.

Zoe's car was a four-door white Acura. The license was not the vanity sort, but just the plain oranges and green lettering with the state slogan, *Sunshine State*, at the bottom.

Taylor watched from the dining room as Zoe exited her vehicle, retrieved her purse, and locked the door. She made it halfway to the front entrance when she stopped, retraced her steps, and again checked the driver's door handle to be certain it was locked. Then she rounded the car, checking each door handle, finally returning to the driver's side only to repeat this process.

Taylor frowned.

Zoe, seemingly satisfied, marched toward the house and Taylor stepped back, so as not to be caught watching. But the pause stretched, and Taylor went back to the window to see Zoe now checking to be sure the trunk was closed. Finally, she left her vehicle and reached the steps. Taylor waited. Zoe looked back at her car and Taylor could almost feel her resisting the urge to check it again.

Seth appeared from the garage where he'd been putting away his tools after fixing one of the shelves in Jules and Becca's closet.

"Is she here?"

"Oh boy, is she."

The doorbell rang.

Seth let her in and then helped her carry in her suitcases, a plastic bin holding files, her computer bag, and a crate on wheels which housed an odd assortment of electronics and cleaning supplies.

Taylor was happy Seth expedited the move-in. The less time for neighbors to gawk, the better.

"Well," she heard Seth say. "We'll let you get settled."

"Thank you."

He appeared in the hall and rolled his eyes. Then he lowered his voice to a whisper. "She didn't want me to put anything on the bed."

Taylor shrugged.

They ducked into the bedroom, craning their necks to listen.

Zoe left her room, closing the door. Her bathroom was right beside her room and at the opposite end of the hall, past what would be the Curries' room and bathroom on the opposite side. Taylor risked a glance out the door and saw their single tenant carrying a full caddy of cleaning supplies into the bathroom.

"Look," she whispered.

Seth did.

"What's she doing?" He peered down the hall. When he spoke, his tone held a note of indignation. "I just cleaned that bathroom last night."

But Zoe went to work with the spray and sponges, scrubbing vigorously. She must have felt them watching because she paused and glanced at them before they could duck back out of sight.

A moment later, the bathroom door slammed shut.

What the heck was happening?

SIXTEEN

Less than forty-five minutes later, both their phones chimed with motion alerts. Seth checked the doorbell live view as he trotted down the stairs. Taylor focused instead on holding the railing and watching her step.

"Probably Jules and Becca," said Taylor.

Seth shook his head. "Looks like Rubin."

"Rubin? I thought he was on a long haul."

"Was he? Must be back early, I guess."

They reached the foyer and Seth was out and down the steps before she cleared the front door.

Seth waved as Rubin pulled in, grinning, his elbow resting on the door of the open window. There was a large piece of furniture in the back of his pickup.

"Hey buddy," called Seth.

Rubin rolled to a stop before the garage.

Out from behind the wheel of his truck, Rubin clasped Seth's hand and her husband tugged him in for a quick hug. These men always hugged. The embrace was more a bumping of shoulders and a rough thump on the back before release, but still, it was nice to see such genuine affection.

"What are you doing home?" asked Rubin, spinning his ball cap so the brim faced backwards.

"Roomies arriving today."

"Oh right. Move-in day. I forgot."

"Why aren't you driving?" asked Seth.

"I will be, as soon as I finish here." Rubin rubbed his neck and his gaze shifted to the ground. Seth did not notice Rubin's sudden quiet or the gesture that told Taylor something was off with him.

"What'd you bring us?" asked Seth, moving toward the truck bed and getting straight to the point of the drop-in visit.

"One of the other truckers got a wall-mount TV and wanted this out of his house." He motioned to the whitewashed television unit that had endured since the 1990s. "We take the middle shelf out and your television will fit, I think."

"Plenty of room for our DVDs," said Taylor, finally reaching the pair.

Rubin looked surprised. "You still have some?"

"No."

Rubin laughed. "Fill it with books then." He glanced at Seth. "You want it?"

"Sure. Beats a board and cinderblocks."

"That's what I thought." Rubin grinned.

"What else you got?" Seth peeked over the back gate, which was too high for Taylor to see over, thanks to Rubin's custom tires.

"Patio set. Only three chairs, but still..."

Taylor grinned. "That's wonderful. The lanai looks so empty."

"Not for long," said Rubin.

The men went to work. In came the television cabinet and out went the cinderblocks and board. They carried the patio set around the house and she told them where and how to place it. There really was little else she could do.

The men stood admiring their work, with hands on hips, looking similar in height and coloring, if not body type.

"You two look like twins," she said.

They traded a look and Rubin said, "I gotta go."

Taylor hugged him and Seth walked him out. A moment later her phone chimed a motion alert. She watched on her phone as the men stood talking for a few minutes, then exchanged the customary hug before Rubin pulled out.

Seth turned toward the house, paused, and then turned back. Rubin's blue pickup passed a late-model Cadillac. The car pulled into their drive. Seth lifted a hand in greeting.

Becca and Jules Currie had arrived.

Taylor could no longer run, but she shuffled at top speed from the lanai, through the house, and hurried down the three steps to the drive.

The Cadillac turned in, pulling a small rental trailer, and rolled to a halt. Becca leaned out the passenger's window and waved like a metronome gone crazy.

"Hi, Taylor? Are we early?" asked Becca.

"Not at all," she said, returning Becca's bright smile as she worried how much stuff these two thought they could cram into a guest bedroom. "Is this your only vehicle?"

"No, we have a scooter in the trailer," said Becca. "Jules uses it to get to work because he'll be leaving for the new job super early, and I work until sixish."

Jules was already out of the car and stretching.

"How was the trip from Ruskin?" asked Seth, giving Jules a firm handshake.

"Oh, fine. Usual traffic," said Jules.

Taylor was glad Seth was here to support her and welcome their new roommates. Becca gave her a hug and then did the same with Seth. She was one of the most energetic women Taylor had ever known. Perhaps it was just that lately Taylor felt slow and tired as a hippo with insomnia.

"He's home way before I am," said Becca. "As soon as he finishes his route."

Seth asked Jules which post office was his home base.

"It varies. Right now, I'm filling in for guys on vacation. Time varies, too," said Jules. "My shifts are longer in the winter because more traffic, more people, more holiday mail, and all the packages." He rolled his eyes.

"I might beat him home in December." Becca grinned at Jules then turned back to Taylor. "Okay to put the scooter in the garage, or do you want me to leave it with the car?"

"I think it will fit in the garage."

"Oh good. I worry, you know. Like, they're so easy to steal." Becca stared at their little trailer.

"No, they're not," said Jules, scowling.

"You just have to put them on a truck," said Becca.

"You ever try lifting one when it's locked?"

"No." She giggled.

Taylor waited for them to hug or touch, but they just turned to stare at her.

"Can we bring in our stuff?" asked Jules.

"Of course. I wish I could help," said Taylor.

"Don't be silly. You've got enough going on," said Jules.

Becca popped the trunk, revealing boxes and crates and several garbage bags.

"Big trunk," said Taylor.

"I call it my four-body trunk. You know, like I'm a mobster!" She giggled.

Taylor smiled at her humor while Seth and Jules turned to the trailer, lifted the lever, and placed the ramp. They had the scooter down first. It was gas powered, and looked more dirt bike than scooter, but she was sure it got the job done.

Becca wheeled a large suitcase toward the entrance and Taylor held open the door and followed her up the stairs.

At the upper landing, Zoe appeared from her room to stare at Becca and Taylor.

"Becca Currie, this is our other roommate, Zoe Furr."

Becca abandoned her suitcase and hurried forward, hand extended. Zoe backed up into her room and for a moment, Taylor thought she meant to slam the door in Becca's face. She did not offer her hand.

"Nice to meet you," Becca said, and nodded. Her hand remained offered but her smile dimmed.

Zoe said nothing but retreated another step before giving a short little bob of her head. Finally, Becca dropped her hand to her side.

Taylor said, "Zoe also works downtown. She's a curator at one of our most popular museums." She doubted very much the former resort hotel was more popular than the zoo, art museum, or children's museum, but there was no harm in the lie.

"Oh, cool! Um, I'll be working downtown, too. Maybe I could come see the museum before work sometime."

"That would be fine," said Zoe. "Well, this is my room and that is my bathroom." She pointed to be sure Becca comprehended. "I understand you and your spouse will have your own?"

"That's right. Your room is on this side, Becca." Taylor opened the door at the end of the hall on the left, as Zoe stood in her doorway like a hockey goalie guarding the net. The bedrooms shared a common wall, separated by their closets. The bathrooms sat on opposite sides of the hall and were similar except Zoe's had only a shower, toilet, and single sink, while Becca would have a tub-shower combo and twin sinks.

"The bathroom on the left is yours." She opened that door as well.

Becca swept inside. "Better than I remembered," she said.

"Well, it was nice to meet you," said Zoe, retreating and closing her door.

"She seems nice," said Becca.

Does she? wondered Taylor.

"The laundry is off the kitchen. Once you're moved in, I'll show you where you can store your groceries. Okay?"

"Super!" Becca retrieved her suitcase and hustled it into her room.

The room was welcoming enough, with a sunny yellow bedspread over a very simple queen-sized bed that had once belonged to Jason's grandmother. A metal desk with a tempered glass top that had been designed in the time of large tower-style desktops, a tall bureau, and a lopsided swivel desk chair completed the furnishings. The previous owner had painted three walls sky blue, and the accent wall a navy color. The carpet consisted of only a runner beside the bed.

Becca released the telescoping handle of her suitcase and moved to the window that faced west into their neighbor's yard. She peeked through the Venetian blind. "Sunset view. Cool."

"I'll leave you to unpack." Taylor set the keys on the dresser.

"What's that?" asked Becca.

"Two keys. They open both the front door and garage door into the laundry room. Check with Seth about where to park the scooter. Okay?"

"Yup. Sure will."

"The sticky note has the garage code."

"Oh, great. Thanks."

She had a nice kind of Central Florida accent, with a little drawl.

"Keypad is on the right side of the bay door. See you in a bit."

"Thanks, Taylor. This is going to be so epic!"

Becca's enthusiasm was exhausting. Taylor offered a wave and headed down the hall. At the stairs, she resisted the urge to continue to her room and lay down. Instead, she went downstairs to the kitchen and poured a large glass of water. She heard the garage door lift and close and the men appeared in the kitchen.

"Water?" she asked them.

"Later, maybe," said Jules, and headed out. Seth leaned against the counter as Jules and Becca shuttled their things in and up the stairs.

Taylor told him about Zoe and Becca's first meeting.

"And she said she seemed nice?" asked Seth, snorting in an effort not to laugh.

"An acquired taste, perhaps," said Taylor, and chuckled.

"It's all going well." Seth leaned in and kissed her. "You're a genius."

Becca headed toward them with a small animal carrier that bumped and shook in her hands as if it contained a Tasmanian devil.

Taylor braced for attack.

SEVENTEEN

Becca seemed unperturbed by the thrashing, furious furball trapped in the carrier.

"Guys, this is Moon." She held up the cage so they could see through the door's lattice.

But all that was visible was black fur, needle-sharp claws, and white fangs gnawing at the confining bars. Taylor inched back.

"Does she bite?"

"Oh, no. Never. She, like, hates the carrier is all. Can I put her food and water down here, or would you prefer it go in our bathroom?"

"Here is fine."

"Great. The litterbox is already in our bathroom. Let me just get her settled upstairs. Show her where she can do her business. Then I'll come get her food ready."

"Great."

Becca took the jolting, juddering carrier away.

"Wildcat," said Seth. Then his stomach gave a mighty gurgle. "Oh, boy. How about some lunch?"

It was so nice and such a rarity to share lunch with him. He made the sandwiches and got them drinks. They were about finished when something small and black shot through the kitchen.

Seth went to investigate, reporting a sighting from the laundry room. "It's between the washer and dryer," he said.

Becca headed to the driveway and returned with two food dishes, a bag of chow, and a mat. Taylor picked a place near the door to the garage and Becca set up the cat's food station.

"You might not see her for the rest of the afternoon. She does this. Like, hiding until she gets used to everything."

"Okay," said Seth as Taylor said, "That's fine."

Seth waited until Becca was out of sight.

"Mind if I go to the hospital?"

She blinked in surprise that he felt comfortable enough with their tenants to leave.

"Should I stay until you get back?" asked Taylor.

"No need to. I mean, you have to leave eventually. Right?"

"True." She pushed down the uncomfortable feeling squeezing her insides. This was her plan, and he was right. She needed to trust them at some point.

"Will you be back for dinner?" she asked.

"Not sure. Maybe."

She waved him off and then gathered her purse. If he felt comfortable enough to head out, she could get a few errands done as well.

Taylor left them. It was so weird to leave strangers in your house.

But it would be all right. It had to be.

* * *

Seth did make it back before dark. Taylor heard Jules greeting him in the kitchen.

It was just after seven and she heard Jules say, "Wow. Long day, man."

Taylor stepped up to kiss her husband and Jules turned back to his cooking.

Once in the living room, Seth said, "Something smells great."

"I think that's his dinner. Not ours. But I did put those stuffed shells in the oven to heat. Some of them. That was a huge tray," she said, referring to the bounty of leftovers he'd brought home.

Jules popped his head out from the kitchen. "Shells were browning so I covered them with foil and put the oven on warm."

Taylor gave him a smile. "Thank you, Jules."

"No problem." Then he lifted his gaze to the walkover and called out. "Becca! Supper."

A moment later Becca thundered down the stairs. She had a heavy tread for someone so small.

"Well, I'll let you get back to it," said Seth, guiding Taylor toward the stairs.

Once they were in their bedroom, he dropped his heavy bookbag on the ottoman beside the bed.

"Are you hungry?" Taylor asked.

"Starving. But let's have a drink on the pool deck. Now that we have a table and three chairs." He grinned. "Give him a chance to finish in the kitchen."

"See if he cleans up afterwards," said Taylor, glancing toward the closed door. "And that the shells don't dry out too much."

"They'll be fine. Boy, that was a lot of chili. Is he having a party?"

"They're not allowed visitors. It's in our agreement."

"Good." Seth headed to his nearly empty walk-in closet to

change. She waited for him to emerge in his sweatpants and a T-shirt, ratty and stretched out at the collar.

"Come on, I'll make you a mocktail. Tonic, mint, and some lime soda."

"Sounds perfect. Except we don't have mint and we're out of tonic."

That made Seth laugh. She joined him and her giggles made one of the babies kick.

They headed downstairs, Taylor to the lanai and Seth to the kitchen. The aroma of chili and onions was overpowering. The house now smelled like a taco stand and her mouth watered.

She sat on one of the three chairs Rubin had provided as she waited for Seth. He didn't turn up for nearly a half hour.

"Everything okay?" she asked when he finally returned.

"Just chatting. He's a Florida boy. Only been as far west as New Orleans."

Seth offered her the mocktail.

It was pink and there was a leaf in it.

"What's this?"

"Dragon fruit vitamin water over ice."

"The garnish?" she asked.

"Oak leaf."

She chuckled and removed the leaf.

Taylor wasn't a big drinker, but she did miss having a fancy mixed drink at a posh bar. But even after the twins arrived, she didn't expect she'd be frequenting her old haunts anytime soon, unless it was to pick up an extra paycheck. The trouble was that she couldn't afford childcare and Seth would not be around for, oh, say, three more years.

Lucky for her, the company where she worked had started a childcare facility right on site during Covid and it was so popular and had reduced absenteeism so much that they had opted to keep the perk. If they didn't have that, she would be job hunting right now.

Seth settled in a chair next to her. The used furniture creaked, and she worried it might collapse, but it held. She wondered if she should put this grouping of furniture on the porch out front instead of tucked back here inside the protection of the pool's screened cage.

Here, she decided. At least until the fall when the bug population flagged.

"I caught sight of the cat for an instant. Fast feline," said Seth.

"Really. I've only seen it once since it arrived."

Her husband stared past the pool to the wooded reserve.

"Listen," he said.

She did but heard only the basketball bouncing.

"That's a woodpecker."

"It sounds like a basketball player."

"No, up there. Listen."

She did and heard a bird call but would never have known it was a woodpecker. Early on he had shared with her his love of the outdoors. It was one of the reasons that she thought this place suited them so well. She had a nice safe neighborhood without all the restrictions of a gated community, and he had the reserve where he could enjoy the nature trails and birdwatch.

"It's nice back here," he said, then lifted his beer and took a swallow.

"I think so."

"Peaceful."

She ignored the basketball bouncing but noticed when it finally ceased. A palmetto leaf quivered. She sat forward pointing at the disturbance.

"What's that?"

He stood. From the undergrowth stepped a raccoon, followed by two babies.

"Brassy thing, coming out in full daylight," Seth said.

"It's nearly twilight. She's got little ones to feed."

"Better stay out of our garage," he said.

"When do you think you'll explore the trails?" she asked.

"Oh, I don't know. When I have time. Pretty busy right now. Also, it's kinda buggy in the summer."

The sliding door swept open, and Jules appeared.

"Nice evening," he said. In his hand was a large bowl with a soup spoon and he cradled a can of beer against his chest. Becca followed, carrying her drink and paper towels.

Taylor suddenly regretted giving the tenants access to the pool and lanai because they now had four people and only three chairs.

"Aren't you eating?" Seth asked Becca.

"This is hers," said Jules. "I ate hours ago." He held his easy smile as they settled at the table.

"You two don't eat together?" asked Seth.

"He's up with the roosters and home before I even have my first break," said Becca.

"I'd starve to death if I waited," Jules added.

Taylor frowned. She would have had a little something to tide her over so she could eat with her husband. But to each their own, she supposed.

"I took your shells out and I put what was left of the tomato sauce from the chili on the stove on low, you know, for a little extra with the shells," said Jules.

"That was thoughtful," said Taylor.

Seth offered his hand to help Taylor rise and Becca and Jules settled at the table.

"Enjoy your meal," he said, and guided her toward the door.

"Don't let us chase you off," Jules said, waving his dirty spoon.

Once inside, Seth turned and said, "Kitchen counter or dining room?"

"Let's eat at the counter. I'm starving." She offered a shoulder shrug and apologetic smile.

"Great."

Seth set out the plates and silverware as she retrieved their drinks. The shells were hot and crispy, and the extra sauce Jules left was just the right touch. The salad she'd bought from the store needed only dressing and soon they were digging in.

"This is so nice," she said. "Really great for that woman to offer these to you."

After their meal, Taylor stowed the leftovers and Seth cleaned up.

Taylor closed the refrigerator to find someone standing on the opposite side and gave a little shriek.

EIGHTEEN

She slapped her hand over her mouth to muffle the shriek and Seth whirled from the sink to find Zoe standing beside the refrigerator. Their female boarder backed away as if scalded.

"I'm sorry. I thought he left the door open."

Taylor pressed a hand to her chest, trying to contain the wild hammering of her heart. "It's fine. Let me get out of your way."

Zoe spun and headed out the front door without a word.

Seth twisted open his beer and dropped the cap in the trash. "She's so odd," he said.

They moved in unison to the dining room, flicking off the overhead light, and then watched her retrieve two bags of groceries from her car.

"Paper bags," said Seth.

"No plastic. And vegan. Got her pots on a separate shelf."

"Great."

Behind them, someone bounded down the stairs. Seth whirled and Taylor stiffened. Becca sailed past them and back outside to the lanai.

"I didn't hear her go back up," said Taylor.

This arrangement was going to take some getting used to.

Jules appeared, his step light and sure.

"Seth? Can you show me where to park the scooter?" he asked. "We've got to return that trailer before close or they'll charge us for another day."

The two men headed toward the kitchen and out of sight. Zoe returned with her groceries, carrying them to the kitchen and her assigned drawer.

Taylor followed.

"Can I give you a hand?" she asked.

Zoe shook her head. Then she proceeded to unpack a roll of paper towels and an organic kitchen cleaner. She sprayed and scrubbed her assigned shelf in the refrigerator. She did the same to her assigned drawer in the pantry, and the plate in the microwave. Taylor watched Zoe empty the bags of all the dried goods, lining them up in neat little rows like a platoon of soldiers, the labels all facing forward. Finally, she washed a bowl and dried it before opening a can of lentil soup.

Taylor's brow knit. Seth returned as Zoe was using a bleach wipe on a soup spoon. His smile dropped and he glanced at his wife. She shrugged.

Seth motioned with his head to the living room, scooping up his beer on his way through the kitchen. There, Taylor sipped her water as he set up the TV in the television unit that squatted against the wall.

He flipped to CNN to see what news they'd missed. It was still on when Jules and Becca appeared, Becca waving a yellow tube of raw cookie dough.

"I bought cookie dough!" she said, her words almost a song. "Chocolate chip. Would you guys eat some?"

Seth grinned. "I wouldn't say no."

About two minutes after they entered the kitchen, Zoe retreated toward the stairs.

"No cookies for you, Zoe?" asked Taylor.

She turned and looked down her nose at them. "I don't eat processed sugars or eggs."

"Ah, well. Goodnight then," said Seth, then to Taylor he made the aside comment, "Explains why she's thin as a rail and likely anemic."

"The absence of chocolate chips in a diet doesn't make you anemic."

"No, but the absence of iron does. It's in fortified flour in addition to red meat."

A short time later the air was filled with the aroma of baking cookies. Taylor's mouth watered. The oven timer lured them into the kitchen.

Becca scraped the spatula under the cookies and onto plates as Jules poured them each a glass of milk.

"Oh, none for me," said Taylor.

Jules paused. "It's good for the baby."

"Just water."

He complied.

"Jules tells me you are having twin boys!" said Becca.

They both looked thrilled.

Taylor flushed with pride. "That's right. Due in three weeks."

Becca extended a plate holding two ooey gooey browned cookies dotted with melted chocolate chips. Taylor accepted the treat with both hands and her thanks.

"Natural delivery?" asked Becca.

None of your business, thought Taylor, but answered. "C-section."

"Oh, that's a mistake. A natural birth is so much better for the babies. Washes them in natural immunities."

Taylor held her smile but something dark curled behind it. Why did everyone think it was acceptable to offer her advice on birthing, to touch her stomach, or share some delivery horror story?

"How many babies have you delivered, Becca?"

"Oh, dozens. I helped my mother. She's a midwife."

Taylor failed to hide her surprise at this revelation and Seth's smile fell away.

"Where?" he asked.

Becca paused, flicked her gaze to Jules, and then back to Seth.

"Up in Jacksonville. At a birthing center."

Seth's shoulders dropped and he took a bite of his cookie.

"These are great," said Taylor, trying to restore the congenial mood. "Thanks for making them." But now her intuition niggled. "They let you help out at a birthing center?"

"Well, I only got to watch. When the mother agreed, that is."

That sounded more reasonable.

"How nice," said Taylor, still frowning. "But I thought your parents were in Ruskin. Didn't you say you were anxious to get out of their house?"

"Sorry. I should have said my stepmom. My dad's place and his third wife," said Becca.

"I see."

Taylor lifted her water glass and thought of the nineteen more days until she was a mother. By then, they'd have the money for the mortgage.

Becca headed to the sink to wash the cookie trays. Jules collected empty plates and loaded the dishwasher.

Seth downed most of his milk in two large swallows and his gaze shifted as he lowered the glass.

Taylor startled as the black cat leapt on the kitchen island and sat, staring at Seth with yellow moon eyes.

They regarded the interloper.

He poured the last of the milk on his plate and put the plate on the floor. The cat leapt from the stone counter, emerging beside his chair to lap up the offering.

Becca noticed the feline.

"There she is!"

Their tenant retrieved Seth's glass and handed it to Jules who loaded it with the rest.

"The TV working?" asked Jules.

"Sure is."

The pair headed to the adjoining family room where Jules stretched on the couch and Becca folded into one of the bucket chairs with her legs crossed.

Seth asked Taylor if she wanted to watch some TV.

"I'm kinda bushed."

He nodded.

"You don't like cats?" asked Taylor.

"Not even a little."

"She's paying fifty bucks extra each month."

"I like it better already." He glanced toward the family room and the sound of canned laughter from something the couple was watching. "Let's go upstairs."

That space and their primary suite were private and nearly as big as their old apartment.

"That's odd," he said in a whisper.

"What?"

"Do you remember when we were newlyweds?"

She flushed and grinned. "Of course."

"We couldn't keep our hands off each other."

"So?"

"Look at those two."

She did, now noticing that, instead of cuddling up on that couch together, as she and Seth had done, they sat apart watching a rerun of a television show with the apt attention of a gamer trying for a high score.

"You'd think they'd never seen a television before," she joked.

"It's not normal."

"Zoe's the one who's not normal," she said, and took his hand, leading him away.

Seth called goodnight. Becca spun and waved, and Jules lifted a hand which appeared above the backrest.

Seth squeezed her hand as they headed upstairs. Taylor stopped at the walkover. From here she could see the living room only. The entrance was beneath them and the kitchen, dining, and family rooms lay beyond the arched doorway.

"You think it will be all right?" she asked, looking at Zoe's closed door.

"I think you're a miracle worker. Your parents pulled the rug out from under you, and you still landed on your feet."

"I should have done this sooner."

"Like before the wedding?"

Taylor rolled her eyes. "Don't bring that up! I didn't want all that nonsense. That was just another way for my father to show off."

"And to drag you back into indebtedness to him."

"You think so?"

"Positive."

She grimaced. Likely, Seth was right. "I didn't even know half those people."

"We should have eloped."

"Next time."

He chuckled and brought her palm to his mouth, planting a kiss there. The tingling sensation traveled from the point of contact all the way up her arm and to her heart, giving her that zing of desire.

"I'll take you up on that," he promised.

At the door, Seth flipped on the overhead light. There in the middle of their spotless comforter dozed a black cat.

Seth exhaled a growl, scooped up the cat, deposited the creature in the hall and then closed the door in its face.

"You'll have to explain the private versus public spaces to Moon in the morning."

Taylor locked the door. "Yes. I will."

"I'm going to take a quick shower," he said.

Seth stripped out of his clothes and Taylor washed up, changing into her cotton nightgown for bed. She propped up the pillows behind her and woke her Kindle. She hoped she'd sleep a few hours before her cramped bladder woke her.

She heard Becca's light tread on the stairs. She was talking to Moon. Then she closed her door, and the house went still.

It would be an adjustment hearing people moving about. But she was adaptable. She'd make this work.

* * *

At first, she thought the splashing was Seth, but the sound seemed to be coming from the other direction. The night was unseasonably cool, thanks to a tropical storm in the Gulf that had sucked away all the humidity and provided a nice northerly breeze.

Taylor rose from the bed and stepped out onto the balcony in time to see Zoe swimming laps in the small, kidney-shaped pool. How had she gotten down there without anyone seeing her?

In the silvery moonlight Taylor could see her boarder's clothing in a neatly folded stack on the pool deck and that Zoe had elected to swim naked.

Tomorrow, she'd need to go over a few house rules, including wearing swimsuits when swimming in her pool.

"Taylor? Everything all right?"

She turned to see Seth, his hair wet, his skin damp, wrapped in nothing but a towel.

Taylor closed the balcony doors. "Everything is perfect."

He came to stand beside her overlooking the pool. He

noticed Zoe, leaned forward to stare at her silvery body darting naked through the water and shook his head.

"Nope," he said.

Then she noticed a dark shadow moving along the pool cage, followed by another.

"What's that?" she whispered, pointing.

NINETEEN

Seth moved back inside and flipped on the floodlights that flanked the pool.

Below them, Zoe screamed and the three boys, including the tall redhead from earlier in the week, dashed from the hedges toward the reserve.

"We've got ourselves some Peeping Toms," said Seth.

Below them, Zoe had splashed out of the pool and was now wrapped tightly in her towel.

"Call the police," she shouted up to them.

"I'm calling their mothers," said Taylor.

Seth spoke to Zoe. "You all right?"

She scooped up her clothing and stormed toward the house.

Taylor found the HOA listing for the redhead's mother and made the call explaining what had happened. Thankfully, the woman took the incident seriously and gave her the name and number for the twins' parents. Taylor repeated the call and was again gratified that the father said he'd handle it and there would be no repeats.

On the upper landing, Seth was speaking to Zoe, who was

crying. She caught only the end of what their boarder was saying.

"...thought this would be a safer neighborhood," she sobbed.

Safer? That statement raised all kinds of questions in Taylor's mind.

She stepped out to explain that she'd contacted the boys' mothers.

"They should be arrested."

"You're free to call the police. But they are just high school kids," said Seth.

"And minors," added Taylor.

Zoe harumphed. "They're voyeurs."

Becca peeked out to ask what was going on and Seth told her while Zoe stood shivering in her towel.

Between the three of them, they got Zoe settled down and she withdrew to her room and Becca back to hers.

Taylor also headed to bed but she did not sleep well. Both her pregnancy and her worries tormented her. Seth slept like the dead and so he did not notice someone going downstairs at three in the morning and returning around four.

She had not heard the garage door but wasn't sure if the rumble of it lifting would reach all the way upstairs to her room. Maybe someone else couldn't sleep either and had just gone to the family room to watch television or perhaps to the pool deck?

It bothered her more than she'd anticipated, the doors opening and closing, worrying if they remembered to lock the front door or the rear slider and wondering what they were doing.

Despite her vetting them, they were still strangers and strangers were, by definition, outsiders.

Sometime in the night, Taylor woke to a sound that had her startling upright, hand pressed to her heart.

In the darkness, she could see little, but heard the sound again. It seemed someone was turning the knob to their bedroom door. Try as she might, she could not see the knob turning.

Everything went quiet and she strained to hear footsteps but heard nothing but the wind and a faraway roll of thunder.

Taylor flopped back to the pillows. Had she really heard something or was her imagination furnishing tangible concerns about this invasion of their privacy?

It was a long while before her heartbeat slowed and her eyes drifted closed.

Sometime later, Seth slipped from the covers and dropped a kiss on her cheek. She had meant to rise with him. It was Sunday, and she expected him to have to head into the library to study, or spend hours here, on his laptop or with his textbooks.

But her exhaustion got the better of her and the next time she opened her eyes it was nearly nine in the morning. She bolted upright and then swayed, feeling dizzy at rising too quickly.

"Seth?"

Her call met with silence. He'd managed to slip out without her hearing him. Funny how every strange sound last night had brought her to heart-pounding alertness, but she'd not been aware of his rising, using the bathroom, making his half of the bed, and creeping away.

Taylor hurried to the bathroom, only to reverse course to lock the bedroom door. Then she showered and dressed, reaching the kitchen to find Seth holding Moon in his lap while Jules told a story to him and Becca that had them all in stitches.

Taylor noted that the unfamiliar cat dish was now partially empty.

"Good morning," she called from the doorway.

Seth rose, setting Moon on his stool, and greeted her with a kiss.

"Good morning, sleepy head."

Jules and Becca both called their good mornings.

"I'd say I feel lazy as a cat," she said, "but I see even Moon has beaten me up."

Seth laughed at that, guiding her to his place at the counter.

Taylor glanced about.

"Has anyone seen Zoe yet?"

"She's up and gone. Filled a travel mug of tea and headed to church," said Seth.

"Chamomile," said Jules, and made a gagging gesture.

Becca punched his arm. It was an odd show of affection between them, and Taylor frowned.

"How is she doing this morning?" asked Taylor.

"Still rattled," said Becca.

"You want me to follow up with the boys' parents?" asked Seth.

"That'd be great." She offered the homeowners' list that had arrived with the community HOA's rules and regulations and pulled up the number for the twins for him. He stepped out of the kitchen, phone to his ear.

Taylor sat at the counter while her tenants ate their breakfast, Jules sitting beside her and Becca standing at the sink. Finally, Seth returned.

"Twins are grounded," he said.

"Gus and Pete Fetterman, right?" she asked. "What about Sean?"

"Left a message. Told them your cousin still wants to call the police."

Zoe returned from church while they were still gathered in the kitchen. She drew up short at seeing all of them assembled there. Taylor struggled to reconcile the naked water nymph she'd glimpsed last night with this buttoned-up woman in a knee-length gray skirt, blouse with cameo at her throat, practical flats and... were those tights?

"Taylor, could I speak to you?" asked Zoe.

Seth cast her a side-eye and quirked his brow. Taylor had the sinking feeling that Zoe was about to move out.

"Of course," said Taylor, slipping off the stool and following Zoe to the living room.

"Before you start," said Taylor, and she explained about the boys all being grounded and the parents' assurances that this would never happen again.

Zoe nodded stiffly, her expression sour.

"What did you want to speak to me about?" she asked.

"Someone was in my bathroom," said Zoe.

"Really?" asked Taylor. She wanted to ask how she knew but didn't.

"One of my supplement containers was moved. I had to throw out the entire bottle."

"Why?"

"How do I know who had their hands inside, or what they put in there?"

Taylor's eyes widened. Zoe sounded like her mother, all strange, irrational fears and paranoia. "I see."

"Am I correct that it was not you or your husband?"

"We weren't in there."

"Then will you please explain to our other roommates that they are not to be in my private spaces without seeking permission?"

"I can. Of course."

"And I expect them to replace the bottle. It's listed online for thirteen dollars and forty-two cents. That includes free shipping."

"Can't you use the rest?"

"No." Zoe extended the container. "They may have it."

Taylor accepted the bottle and Zoe stormed away. Interesting that she needed Taylor to confront the pair.

She returned to the kitchen to find all three hovering near the arched entrance, listening.

"It was me," said Becca.

"Why were you in Zoe's bathroom?" asked Seth.

"Oh, like, I had a headache, and we don't have any aspirin. I was looking for a painkiller, ibuprofen, or something. But she's only got weirdo herbal drops, lavender spray, and chlorella pills in there." Becca made a face.

"Well, now you own your very own superfood. She expects you to replace it." Taylor extended the bottle.

"Replace it? I didn't take anything."

"You moved it. Says it's yours now because she can't use it."

"Is she for real?" asked Jules.

Becca accepted the bottle and tossed it in the trash. "This is bonkers. Why didn't she come to me instead of tattling like a little coward?"

"I don't know. Uncomfortable with conflict, maybe?"

Jules retrieved his wallet and slapped a ten and a five on the table. "She can keep the change. You want to give it to her, or should I?"

"Probably need to disinfect the bills first," grumbled Becca.

"I will," said Taylor, collecting the money. "She's a bit territorial."

"I'll say. Did you see her bathroom door?"

Taylor frowned. "What about it?"

"She added a slide deadbolt. I saw her. Middle of the night. Like four in the morning."

Seth cast Taylor a side eye, his face grim. She didn't like it either and pressed her lips together.

"I'll have a look and speak to her." Taylor turned to Becca. "But you need to stay out of her bathroom and room and please don't touch her things, especially her food."

"Probably booby-trapped," said Jules into his coffee.

"Oh, don't worry. I won't," said Becca. "She might freeze me with those chilling death stares. Geesh. I've seen friendlier badgers."

Taylor watched Zoe head up the stairs wondering if she should follow or give her a few minutes to cool down.

"Taylor?"

Seth was speaking to her.

"Hmm?"

"I asked if you wanted some frittata. Jules made it with goat cheese and fresh asparagus."

"Oh, that's more than I can handle. Maybe toast with a little jam."

"Protein," said Seth.

"Almond butter?"

"Great." He rose and headed to the cupboard retrieving the jar then grabbed the bread from the refrigerator.

A few moments later Seth delivered her golden toast on a plate with a knife so she could help herself to the almond butter. While she ate, he had another cup of coffee and removed Moon from the table, twice.

"You going to the hospital today?" she asked Seth.

"Yes." He glanced at his phone. "Now actually. Walk me out?"

She finished her toast and rose.

In the garage, they passed her Lexus LS to reach Seth's Jeep.

"Does the cat bother you?" she asked.

"When it's on the table or our bed, it does."

"I'll work on that. And I'll speak to Zoe. She can't just take a screwdriver to my door."

"Let me know how that goes."

"I will."

"What about the Jeep? We need to turn it in?"

"According to what I read, the lease is my father's. Not ours. He pays it or he doesn't. But it's his credit and responsibility."

"He said he won't be paying it from now on," Seth reminded her.

"I know, but he's not very organized. Might take him a bit to spot that he's still paying. Or rather, it might take my mom a while. I'm going to leave it for now and cross my fingers." Taylor knew her father was lackadaisical about his finances. That came from always having enough and never having to worry about running out, overdrafts, and the like. "And even if he has stopped payment, it takes, on average, three months before they repossess these vehicles."

"Then what?"

"Then, we should have our feet back underneath us and be able to lease something, smaller economy vehicles."

"Will that ding our credit?"

"I didn't lease them. So, no."

"You don't want a flashy car?"

She lifted to her tiptoes and looped her arms about his neck.

"I want a nice safe house in a good school district. I don't care about cars or furniture. Just help me hold onto this place."

"There are good school districts in Washington, Chicago, and New York, too."

She pressed against him, as best she could with the inflated balloon of water that held their family between them.

"I know, but none of those places have the Gulf of Mexico."

"They have other things."

"You focus on finishing your hours for now and we'll worry about your practice after you get started on the residency. Okay?"

"You be all right with them?" He motioned his head toward the house.

"Sure. I've got this."

He grinned. "If anyone does, it's you."

They stood together a moment. Then Seth kissed her and climbed behind the wheel.

He extended his hand out the open window and grasped her fingertips. "I'll see you for supper?" he asked.

"Yes."

"What are you doing today?"

Canceling my nail appointment, hair appointment, and golf club membership, and figuring out how to get the lawn mowed, she thought, but said, "Just relaxing."

He released her. She stepped back and he hit the remote. The door trundled up and he started the engine. Taylor remained in the garage as the heat from the July morning rolled over her like a wave.

The door trundled up, revealing Becca's Caddy blocking Seth's Jeep.

"I'll go ask her to move it," said Taylor, giving him a kiss goodbye.

She returned to the house and sent Becca out to move her vehicle.

Then Taylor headed for the stairs to see what modifications Zoe had made to their home.

TWENTY

Upstairs, she checked Zoe's bathroom and found, indeed, she had added a slide bolt to the back of the door. There was already a normal lock in the knob.

In addition, she discovered that Zoe had covered every electrical outlet with a sheet of tinfoil, fixed to the wall with blue painter's tape. What in the world was that about?

On the counter beside the sink sat an orange and white paracord friendship bracelet, exactly the type and color Taylor and her best friend had once made at sleepaway camp. It didn't seem to fit Zoe's age or persona.

Taylor lifted it, still unsettled at the resemblance to the one she'd made for her friend. She was so focused on the bracelet that she nearly overlooked the hair clip still on the countertop.

It was hers. She was positive. The blue lapis heart and silver tone setting was unique. She'd purchased it at an antique fair years ago.

This was getting very weird.

Taylor left the bathroom, still holding her clip, and knocked on Zoe's closed door. She answered it, open book in her free hand, and then stepped backwards, widening the space separating them.

"Did you speak to her?" asked Zoe.

"I did." Taylor offered the money and Zoe stepped forward to take it, holding the bills between her thumb and index finger as if they were wet.

"And now I need to speak to you." She explained the problem with the locks.

"The existing lock was insufficient."

"Then you speak to me, but you do not drill holes in my door without checking first. No more modifications, and I'll be taking the cost of repairing the molding from your deposit."

"But the lock remains? While I'm here, I mean."

Taylor weighed her need to extract revenge against the worried little shifting of Zoe's eyes and her flaring nostrils.

You never knew what kinds of trauma people had suffered. She had her judgmental, unaffectionate mother. Perhaps Zoe had been attacked or suffered a stalker. Really, who was she to judge?

"It can stay for now. But nothing more."

"I put one here, too." She stepped forward, seemed to think better of closing the distance between them, and then pointed.

Taylor inspected the slide bolt and scowled. Then she scanned the guest bedroom noting that Zoe had unplugged the boombox, radio, and CD player, and these outlets, too, were covered with foil.

"What's that?" asked Taylor.

"The foil? Don't worry. The painter's tape won't damage the paint."

"But why?"

"It blocks the EMFs."

"The what now?"

"Electromagnetic fields. Outlets emit them. So do satellites, microwaves, televisions, smartphones. Even radios. Though that's a different kind of radiation. Most anything electrical. That's why I keep my tablet and phone in a mesh fabric case, when I'm not using them."

"Why are you blocking them?"

"Oh, they can do terrible harm. You should cover all the outlets, especially in the babies' room. Protect them from damaging radiation. You're not going to use a baby monitor, are you?"

"I'm not sure." But she was. The kind with the cameras, but that wasn't Zoe's business.

"They're terrible for infants. Babies are more receptive to radiation."

Taylor wondered if Zoe was serious. From her expression she guessed she was.

"Is this yours?" Taylor lifted the friendship bracelet.

Zoe reached, plucking it from Taylor's grasp. "Yes."

"Did you make that?" asked Taylor, finding the coincidence odd and wondering if Zoe had stolen that and the clip from her bedroom.

"This?" Zoe motioned to the bracelet. "No. My niece, Mia."

Taylor held her smile, but it now felt forced. "How nice. I have one like it, since I was a girl."

Zoe lifted her brows. "Do you?"

"And this?" Taylor lifted the clip.

Zoe flushed and dropped her gaze. The pause stretched. "I found it."

"Where?"

"In the garage."

That didn't make sense. Taylor kept her hair ornaments in the primary bathroom. Had it slipped from her hair? It was possible. But she didn't buy it.

And what possible reason did Zoe have to be in the garage? Looking for a screwdriver to install the lock?

"Were you in my room?"

"No." Zoe's eyes were wide and her expression sincere.

Taylor could not tell if she was lying. But she must be. Except... then she remembered the open garage and the random security camera in her bedroom. Suddenly the ground was turning under her feet, and she couldn't hold on. She swayed.

"Taylor? Are you okay?" asked Zoe.

"Nothing more. Understand?"

"Yes. I do."

"Great."

Taylor headed for her bedroom, determined to look for her friendship bracelet, but then something crashed downstairs, and she hurried to the kitchen to find Jules holding a broom and Becca crouching and gripping the dustpan.

"Oh, Taylor. I'm sorry. I broke one of your coffee mugs."

"Don't worry about it."

"I can get you another."

"That'd be great."

"We'll clean up. Don't worry," Jules assured her.

Taylor nodded and climbed the stairs again. In her bedroom she found their closet door open. Hadn't she closed it? She usually did. Inside her keepsake box, the friendship bracelet sat dead center.

Now she was sure that was not how she had left it.

Zoe had had time to return it. Should she go back and demand to see the bracelet?

"Let it go," she said to herself. But this time, when she closed the closet door, she placed a tiny scrap of paper between the jam and door. If anyone went in there again, she'd know.

She wondered if her mother had asked Zoe to do some snooping. But why take her things? It was reckless and stupid. Not at all the sort of behavior she'd expect from a careful, neat germaphobe. Something wasn't adding up. And if she caught Zoe in her room, she was throwing her out.

After that bumpy start, their routine began to take shape.

That Sunday Jules and Becca went out to visit friends and Zoe left to see some open houses in the area, which meant Seth and Taylor had much of the Sunday to themselves in their home.

Monday through Saturday, Jules was out first, before anyone was up. Seth left next. Becca left shortly after Seth, leaving Taylor to lock up. Neither she nor Seth ever saw Zoe leave, but her car was gone, meaning she was out after Jules and before Seth was downstairs. They'd worked out where to park, too, with Zoe close to the mailbox and Becca nearest the garage but not blocking Seth.

Jules returned first, followed by Zoe and then Becca, according to the doorbell alerts. Taylor was in next and generally found Zoe had eaten and was already upstairs in her room and Jules and Becca finishing their supper. She either fixed herself something or waited for Seth to return after seven.

Taylor had the house almost to herself between seven and eight in the morning except for the cat. Moon tended to follow her. The feline was an indoor cat but always managed to be on the wrong side of every door, meaning Taylor's routine now involved letting the cat in and out and in and out, et nauseum.

Seth usually got home last every night. He was developing bags under his eyes as the stress of logging so many hours at the hospital mounted.

All their boarders had been cautioned about the community's rules against having tenants, subletting, or leasing the properties and Becca and Jules agreed to pose as her cousins. Zoe said she wouldn't be talking to anyone.

Taylor got bigger by the week and became accustomed to hearing the doors open and close, the aroma of unfamiliar food cooking, water running, the laundry buzzer, and the toilet flushing.

On the first Saturday of August, the single member of the HOA's welcoming committee, April Baxter, arrived with a cherry Bundt cake, and Taylor answered all her questions about who was living here by again claiming her boarders were relatives.

April was well into her fifties, judging from the unnaturally dark hair, deepening lines around her mouth, and flowing top designed to disguise her apple shape.

She said she was married to an optometrist and had a labradoodle named Daisy, plus two daughters off at college.

"I heard from Ella Brinkman about your trouble with those Fetterman boys and that hellion, Sean Kingston." She shook her head as Taylor wondered at the speed of the neighborhood's gossip mill. "Not surprised." April reported they'd had trouble with them before, drinking in the reserve.

"Boys need constant supervision. I'm so glad I had girls."

Taylor promised to keep an eye out.

"What about you? Do you know the sex of your babies? I heard you're having twins."

"That's right. Boys."

"Oh! I'm sorry, I didn't mean anything by that comment. I hope I didn't offend you."

"Not at all."

"I mean, I'm sure your boys will be angels. I can't wait to be a grandparent, myself. Boys or girls, as long as they're healthy." April, red-faced and stammering after her awkward recovery, quickly changed the subject, offering to introduce her to her next-door neighbors, Jeff and Donna Owen.

"She likes to swim. Constantly in their pool. Even wears her bathing suit to pick up the mail," she confided. "Can you imagine? And she's not young. Her husband has one of those outdoor TVs on the back deck. You let him know if it's too loud. He can't tell because he's losing his hearing."

"I'll be sure to tell them, if it's a problem," said Taylor.

"Well, welcome again. We're real happy to have a young family in the neighborhood."

At last April handed over the cake, which surely wouldn't last until Seth returned home from the hospital.

Closing the door, Taylor sighed in relief but April's comment about grandparents made her realize she needed to call her father and tell him that Seth had turned down the residency he had arranged. She did not look forward to that conversation.

* * *

She put off the call until Monday and, as expected, her dad thought Seth ungrateful and short-sighted. She asked about her mother and was told she was a little worse. His health seemed to have improved since his incident, which was the only good news she received during the conversation.

Today marked the start of the second full week with tenants. Things were looking up because thanks to the boarders' rent payments and Taylor's bi-weekly paycheck, she believed she'd have enough to cover the mortgage.

Next month, she'd learn if her father's accounts still paid the mortgage or if he had shut down that payment already.

Taylor's worries and her pregnancy often kept her from sleeping well.

* * *

That first Monday in August, on a balmy summer night, under a crescent moon, Taylor sat on the balcony when she caught movement below.

Someone going for a swim?

No, the motion came from outside the pool cage, beside the bushes. The shape seemed like an animal, motionless now, as if perceiving her attention. It was big.

She sat frozen as her face flushed and her hands shook. Her eyes opened wide, trying to see into the deep shadowy places.

What was out there?

Were there panthers in this area? From what she'd read, most lived down in the everglades, but a panther had been reported in Ocala. Not too close and not in the Tampa area. Not for hundreds of years. But it looked bigger than a dog, almost like a person, squatting beside the privacy hedges.

Her heart jackhammered in her chest as she rose to her feet, peering into the deepening shadows.

"Daisy?" she called. "Candy?" She tried the names of the two neighborhood dogs that she knew.

The shadow did not move.

She opened the slider to the bedroom and called to her husband.

"Seth? Wake up!"

Something in her tone, the fear, leaking into her vocal cords, brought him up out of bed in one swift motion.

"What's wrong?"

"Something is out there." But she really thought it was a someone.

She turned, pointing. The shadow rose, standing. A person. Definitely.

Taylor gasped.

"Right there." She pointed, shivering all over, each tiny hair rising on her body as her skin went cold despite the warm evening air. Someone was watching the house.

The person—a man, she thought from the breadth of the shoulders—hurried across the lawn and ducked behind one of the trunks of the live oaks.

Seth was beside her, leaning over the balcony rail.

"Where?"

She pointed at the person, there in the deep shadows of the trees.

Seth flipped on his phone's flashlight and pointed it in the wrong direction. The light reflected back from the pool cage screening and off the metal frame.

The shadow disappeared, but Taylor saw the palmetto fronds moving.

"There." She pointed again.

Seth swung the light, but the foliage was still, and the shadow was gone.

TWENTY-ONE

There was no evidence of anyone lurking about on their property in the morning. Seth walked around the pool cage and all the way to the wooded edge of the reserve as the sunrise cast long sinister shadows across the yard.

She watched from inside the pool cage as he vanished into the living wall of vivid green. Here at the edge of the forest, all the smaller vines, palms, and scrub vied for the precious sunlight. A moment after he disappeared, the leaves stilled, and the only sound was the angry chittering of a squirrel.

Taylor waited, her back throbbing and her feet aching. She had not seen her feet in several weeks, but Seth told her that her ankles were swollen. Her obstetrician was concerned about her blood pressure and the rise in her blood sugar.

While she waited for his return, she called Mrs. Kingston.

"What time?" asked Sean's mother.

"Around ten."

"He was here in the living room watching a movie because I took away his gaming console. Grounded, as I said. It wasn't Sean."

She felt foolish now but still called the Fettermans,

receiving the same answer. The boys were at home with their family, grounded and miserable without their phones or access to their computers.

So, whatever she had seen was not the local hellions. Taylor stared at the wall of green, wishing Seth would come back, and resisted the urge to shout his name. Jules emerged from the house. She startled at his appearance.

"I thought you'd be gone by now."

"Mandatory training today. Late start."

She nodded, not sure what that all meant. He usually began his day at the post office quite early.

"Whatcha looking at?" he asked, coming to stand beside her, a can of his energy drink in his hand.

"Seth is checking out how far the walking trail is from the property line."

She certainly wasn't going to tell him that they might have either a stalker or a Peeping Tom skulking around.

"Oh, it's only about forty feet. I walk in from here all the time."

Had she seen Jules last night? But why would he squat in the hedge row and then vanish into the woods in the middle of the night?

"When?"

"I don't know. Mostly afternoons. But the bugs are vicious. Gotta use spray."

"Ever go out at night?"

"Mosquitoes are worse at night. So, no. I figure once the rainy season ends, they'll settle down."

"See anybody else?"

"All the time. Folks with their dogs, which isn't allowed. Trail bike riders, also not allowed, and I saw a bunch of teens drinking one afternoon. They took off when they saw me. Left all their cans. Quite a mess."

"Doesn't anyone patrol?"

"Not so much. Since the pandemic, less parks people to go around."

And less teachers, nurses, wait staff. The only thing they seemed to have plenty of were construction workers. The cranes were everywhere downtown and here in the suburbs they were knocking down bungalows daily to build ugly modernist cubes that loomed over their neighbors and ate every legally available square foot of property allowable into the footprint of the home.

It was why she felt so lucky to have this place. Though lately, it was feeling a little creepy. She was glad she was rarely alone in the house.

She thought having this wildlife reserve behind them would be an asset, giving them more privacy. But now it seemed to make it simple for anyone who walked the trails to creep into her yard.

Maybe they needed to put up a fence? She quickly abandoned the idea. Too expensive.

Soon Seth wouldn't be here to wake up when she got scared. He would begin his residency and she would see very little of him.

Seth returned, stepping out of the woods and swatting at bugs. He leaned over and ran his hands through his hair, shaking loose debris.

"Here he comes." Jules finished his drink and crushed the can as if it were a paper cup.

"Anything?" she called to Seth.

"Bloodsuckers by the million. Found a circle where someone had a drinking party and a campfire."

"I saw that. Teenagers. That redhead and the two brothers," said Jules.

Seth narrowed his eyes. "No work today?"

"Late start. Training day. New route. Finally getting my own."

This seemed to satisfy her husband, but Taylor still frowned.

"Nothing else but the empty trails. No one is out there this early."

"Too buggy," said Jules.

"You can say that again." Seth darted into the pool cage, bringing several mosquitoes along with him.

"Don't go out there," he said.

"Why?" she asked, heart still beating in her throat.

"Bugs will eat you alive."

"The rain is giving them plenty of breeding grounds. And we've got malaria cases down in Sarasota. Did you hear? Bet they don't put that on the travel websites," said Jules. He glanced at his phone. "I've gotta head out. Have a great day, you two."

He rounded the pool and returned into the house via the sliders from the family room.

Taylor turned to Seth. "Any footprints?"

"Not that I saw. Just thick underbrush. Thorns, too. Wild roses, I think. Tore me up." He showed the beads of blood across the back of one hand and another line across his bare shin.

"No wonder the bugs were after you."

Seth glanced toward the house. "I've finished my practicum hours and I'm cleared to start in Orlando."

Seth was so excited to finally get started handling actual patients. She was glad for his enthusiasm because everything she'd heard was that the residency programs were grueling and even more difficult than his final years of medical school. That was hard for her to even imagine. The fact that they'd recently imposed an eighty-hour limit on medical residents told her all she needed to know.

Soon she would see very little of her husband and when she did see him, he'd be exhausted. But he'd be making a few thousand dollars a month, which would help. At least they'd keep their heads above water.

"Let's get some disinfectant on those scratches," said Taylor.

"I can do it."

"You better be able to," she said, making them both smile.

Inside, he paused. "Are you really happy with this place?" he asked.

"Yes. I love this house. You?"

"It's a nice place. Just too far from Orlando."

"I know. I'm sorry."

"We'll work through it."

Seth's phone rang and he drew it from his pocket, scowling at the caller ID.

"Who is it?"

"It's Gina."

"Rubin's Gina?"

Seth nodded. Rubin and Nathan were often in touch with Seth. But she'd never known Gina to call him. And a call. Not a text. Now Taylor was also scowling.

"You better take it."

TWENTY-TWO

Seth tucked the phone away after speaking with Gina and met Taylor's gaze with a worried expression.

"Rubin was supposed to be back last night, but he didn't turn up."

The first flutter of apprehension danced over her skin with tiny bird feet.

"Should we be worried?"

"Maybe. He called Gina from the road last night. She said he was to pick them up some breakfast and be home before she left for work."

He looked worried.

"What are you going to do?"

"I'll text Nathan."

"Where is he?"

"He's supposed to be on a long-haul. With Rubin, I think, but I might have that wrong. Anyway, maybe I can get ahold of him and I'll try Rubin, too."

"Let me know if you hear anything."

"I will."

Seth left for the hospital within the hour but still hadn't heard back from Rubin or Nathan.

Becca appeared as Taylor was leaving the house early, heading to her doctor's appointment. She swore she saw her obstetrician more than she saw Seth. But everything was fine, and she made it to the office only thirty minutes behind schedule.

Seth called to check in and she said everything was good, except her blood pressure was up a bit.

"To be expected. Blood sugar?"

"Normal, Dr. Parker." She smiled. "Anything from Rubin?"

"Nada." Seth exhaled with enough force to be heard.

"He's been late before," she said, trying to reassure Seth.

"Not this late." Seth growled in frustration. "And he always checks in with Gina."

"Had he checked in with her dad?"

Gina's dad owned the trucking company and was Nathan and Rubin's boss.

"No."

"Maybe he just broke down." Her attempts to ease Seth's worry were failing.

"He would have called."

She tried again. "Phone was dead?"

"He has a charger in the truck," said Seth. "I'm texting him again. I don't like him taking trips back out west."

Taylor's brow knit in confusion. "Why not?"

The pause stretched. Finally, he said, "Longer trips mean more chances for things to go wrong."

Seth was there for them. She admired that.

It impressed Taylor how close the three of them were. Almost like brothers. And Rubin and Nathan now were driving together on long hauls. She wondered if Seth felt left out.

"Should you maybe call the police?" she asked.

He exhaled loudly again into the phone. "Twenty-four

hours. He has to be gone that long before they'll take the report. But I did check Florida Highway Patrol to see if there was any accidents or major delays."

"And?" Taylor asked. "What did they say?"

"None."

Now she was worried, too. "Then we should retrace his route. See if we can find his truck."

Seth's breathing was coming fast. This turn of events clearly had him rattled.

"He's on a long haul, Gina said."

"Maybe their phones are broken," Taylor said, grasping at straws. "Or off."

"Both of them?"

A wisp of uncertainty strengthened into concern as Taylor wondered if something had happened to the pair. "But you can't reach either one?"

Seth's voice rose with his obvious frustration. "No. I can't. Nothing from either one."

"Well, what can we do? Call the highway patrol in every state?"

"Yeah. Okay. Yes. Good idea."

Taylor was relieved she'd come up with something to help, though she was now genuinely alarmed. "Maybe we could swing by Gina's tonight."

"I'm sure she'd appreciate that."

* * *

After work, she planned to meet Seth at Rubin and Gina's place. They lived in Brandon, west of the University of Southern Florida off West Kennedy Blvd in a ground-floor apartment complex of four units.

When she pulled into the lot, Rubin's truck was not in their assigned spot, but Seth's Jeep occupied the space.

Taylor pulled to a stop and texted Gina that they were here.

The three dots appeared, danced, and then vanished. Whatever she had started to text, she didn't finish. Taylor frowned. Why had she stopped writing?

Seth met Taylor at her car door, and they headed toward the apartment. Someone drew back a curtain and then dropped it.

A moment later Gina stepped out to the landing dressed in an oversized T-shirt, brightly colored Spandex leggings, and no shoes.

Her tiny Pomeranian, Obi, danced out the entrance, waving his front feet as he twirled. Gina scooped him up under her arm like a wiggling football and closed the front door behind her.

"Hi you two. This is a surprise."

"We were worried about you," said Taylor. "Hi, Obi."

She gave the dog's soft head a pet and was rewarded with a lick.

Gina glanced back at the closed door as if to be sure it was shut.

"Any word?"

"Yes. He made it back. Everything is fine. Just fine."

It was that second assurance accompanying the fixed smile and glassy stare that set off alarm bells inside Taylor.

"What was the delay?" asked Seth.

"Oh, you know..." She waved her hand, flashing artificial nails painted a stunning shade of turquoise. "Just the usual. Stupid drivers. Construction delays. Spotty cell service in the mountains and a heavy load making slow going."

The color drained from Seth's face and his words were a hoarse whisper. "The mountains?"

Taylor knew there were no mountains in southern Florida. You had to drive north to see anything resembling a mountain.

"Yeah. Another long run. Denver, this time."

Seth's hand went to his forehead. "With Nathan?"

"Yes. They're both back."

"I'd like to speak to them," said Seth, stepping forward. Gina blocked his way.

"They're not here."

The curtain moved and Taylor saw the face of a teen with shaggy black hair. She wasn't sure if it was a boy or girl.

"When will they be back?"

"I don't know. I'll have Rubin call. Okay?" Gina absently stroked Obi's fluffy head as the dog panted and wheezed as if his tiny snout was too small to provide him with enough oxygen.

"Did they meet anyone out there?"

Gina blinked, her head cocked, as if thinking. "Like who?"

Seth didn't answer.

"You have a houseguest?" said Taylor, pointing at the teen in the window.

Gina turned and the curtain dropped back into place.

"Oh, yes. My nephew. Just watching him until his mom comes to get him."

"I see," said Taylor. "Well, we're glad the boys are home safe."

"Ask Rubin to call me," said Seth. He turned to go and Taylor hugged Gina and then followed.

At her car, Seth opened the door and Taylor hesitated.

"Did she say her nephew?" she asked.

He met her gaze, his expression still troubled. "Yes, why?"

"Gina is an only child."

TWENTY-THREE

"It's nothing you need to worry about," said Seth when he'd called her from the hospital later that night.

Now that was a sentence guaranteed to make a person worry.

He'd sent a text that he'd gotten a call back from Nathan. That was hours ago and Taylor finally sent Seth a text to ask if he was all right. His reply was a thumbs up emoji.

Wait up?

> *No. I've got nightshift. Go to bed. See you in the*
> *morning.*

* * *

Taylor woke to the sound of whispering in the night. Seth's side of the bed was still empty.

Still not back, she thought. Those three were hiding something. She was certain.

All those blank spots in the three men's history now seemed

a threat. At the time, she'd been so relieved not to explain about her mother's mental illness and the terrible rages her father tried to medicate away. But that had allowed Seth to skip all sorts of background information too.

Taylor tried to recall what he had told her when they'd first met. It had been September, after she had finished up the engineering job at the dam, and she had taken a trip out to Yosemite. She was on route to the Rocky Mountains and planning to head north from there to see Yellowstone when her father's call came in.

"Hi pumpkin. Where are you?"

"Somewhere in Colorado, I think, heading north. Why?"

"Are you driving?"

"Yes."

"Call me as soon as you find a safe place to stop."

"What? Why, Daddy? What's wrong? Is Mom okay?"

"She's fine. Just call me."

He disconnected. Taylor stepped on the accelerator. These stupid roads were so impossibly narrow. She barreled down a steep grade and up another. There was an emergency truck stop, but if she stopped there, she might get plowed into by an eighteen-wheeler.

The rockface to her right gave no place to pull over and several large stones in the road told of the danger of doing so. Finally, on a wide curve, she spotted a lookout on one of those impossibly steep, twisty roads in the mountains and steered into a spot. Before her was a small stone wall and then nothing but mountains and sky.

She made the call as all manner of horrible possibilities flashed like lightning strikes in her mind.

"Daddy? I'm stopped."

"Honey, don't be scared, but something happened."

Taylor's face went all sweaty and her skin tingled.

"What's wrong, Daddy?"

"I had a cardiac event."

Cardiac event... That meant a heart attack. Didn't it?

"Daddy! Are you okay?"

"Not really. I need surgery."

"Oh no."

"It's... it's, well, now. They're taking me right in. So, in case, you know, I wanted to speak to you before the surgery and tell you—"

"I'm coming, Daddy. I can be there, ah, soon?" How long did it take to drive from here to Winter Haven?

"Oh, I'd like that. I miss you."

"I'm programing it into the nav program now." But her fingers wouldn't cooperate.

He told her the name of the hospital.

"I'll see you soon, Daddy." Should she say good luck, or don't die?

"Okay, pumpkin, I love you. Drive safe. Bye-bye."

And then he was gone, and she got all turned around.

He never said *bye-bye* or *I love yo*u, for that matter. Did he think he wasn't going to survive surgery?

How long had she been driving? A glance at the nav program showed it frozen. There was no reception, and she didn't have a paper map. Really, who did?

But how long had she been driving without seeing the road or the road signs? Her compass in her rearview mirror said she was heading northeast. That was wrong. Wasn't it?

It got dark. It started snowing. She was sliding around on the road and wondering if she was going to pitch right off into space.

And then, there they were. The three of them. Like guardian angels, appearing out of the clouds of blowing snow.

What exactly had they told her that night?

Had they said they were heading for Florida, or had they said that after she'd said it was her destination?

She couldn't remember.

She did recall that she had picked up Nathan, Rubin, and Seth on a dark, lonely highway when she was totally lost. Icy roads in September. It was unbelievable.

Who knew there could be snow that early? In Florida it was still hurricane season with the warm moist air giving power to the tropical storms.

But in Colorado it had been below freezing before the sun even set. The desert had been cold in winter, but it rarely snowed.

And there they were, thumbs out, backpacks on. Something about the three men, freezing, miles from nowhere, had stirred pity. She'd pulled over, knowing her father would have killed her if he had even known. But he was in the hospital, and she needed to get home to him pronto.

She stopped, hoping they could get her back to the interstate.

Seth, though skinny and scruffy, had instantly caught her eye. She loved his voice and those eyes and how he had filled the long dark drive with calm, amusing, distracting stories that kept her from panicking over the icy pass.

When the weather grew worse, he'd taken over. He was an excellent driver, even on those icy, narrow roads. Once down in the plains, Rubin had driven them, and she'd fallen asleep in the back with her head on Seth's shoulder.

She supposed that was the first time they'd slept together.

The trio had said they'd been working on a sheep ranch but had decided not to spend another winter freezing. So off they went to Florida.

But now Taylor wondered... was the cold really all they'd been running from?

* * *

The whispering came again. What time was it?

She stepped out of her room to the walkover that gave views of the living room and backyard beyond. But in the dark, with no lights switched on, she could see only the nightlight she'd placed in the hall to guide her boarders along to their bathrooms.

The voices were coming from below her. The stairs or the living room, she suspected.

One male. One female.

Seth? No, the pitch was too low.

So Jules and, likely, Becca. Unless one of them had sneaked someone into the house. That was strictly against the rules, but possible.

She strained to hear but had to creep down a few steps.

The words were a jumble and the accent made them even harder to understand. But neither Jules nor Becca had an accent that she could recall.

Taylor's brow knit as unease seeped through her, making her skin pucker and prickle.

Had Zoe brought a guy home?

"What if... her time... a problem."

She sat and inched down another step.

"He won't be," said the male voice.

That was Jules. She was sure.

"Listen."

The two went silent. Taylor sat straining to hear in the darkness, one hand pressed to her thudding heart. A shadowy figure appeared at the bottom of the stairs.

Becca.

"Taylor?" she said.

Caught, she thought. "Yeah. I thought I heard voices."

"Sorry. Didn't mean to disturb you." The accent was gone. It had sounded like Texas, sort of, but not quite.

Jules stepped up beside her. "Did we wake you?" he asked.

From the living room, she thought she heard the slider to the pool open and close.

If they were both here before her, who was creeping out the back?

Zoe?

She dismissed the idea. Since the supplements incident, Zoe was barely civil to the pair.

Taylor stood, suddenly terrified. "It's fine. Lock up. Okay?"

She pushed to her feet and hurried to her room. Once inside she engaged the lock and rushed to the French doors.

With the lights still off, she drew back a curtain and peered out in time to see Jules step from the lanai and then duck out the screen door.

Someone rose from the hedge and walked forward to meet him. Together, the two crossed the yard and disappeared into the shadows.

TWENTY-FOUR

Seth had not come home last night and, when they'd spoken this morning by phone, he had been vague about his conversation with Nathan. He'd said that his friends had been held up on a stretch of I-10 that had no Wi-Fi.

What stretch was that?

"Did you ask about Gina's houseguest?" she had asked.

"Nathan said he didn't know anything about that."

"You believe him?"

Seth had paused a long while. Finally, he'd said, "He never lied to me before."

Had this been the first time, or did he mean he believed him?

She wasn't sure, but would get to the bottom of it tonight.

But when Seth dragged himself home after a night shift at his new job as a resident in Orlando, she didn't have the heart. He was just done in.

She was pleased that he'd taken the residency posting he wanted, but sorry it wasn't closer to home.

He was not too tired to eat, which was great, and he listened as she described the snippets of conversation she had overheard between Becca and Jules.

"She definitely asked if my time would be a problem."

"Time for what?" he asked.

"I don't know. My due date?" She looked away, suddenly embarrassed. Was she still the self-centered princess thinking every conversation centered around her? "It's stupid. Forget it."

Seth stopped eating. "How much background checking did you do?"

"I checked every reference they provided. And pulled a credit report, of course."

He took another forkful of the chicken and biscuits she'd warmed up for him in the microwave.

"What's his post office?"

She told him his base of operations.

"He has a route?"

"He said so. Why? What are you thinking?"

"Maybe I'll just drop in to see him at work. Make sure he is who he says he is."

"Who else would he be? He has a Florida license. I've seen it."

Seth chewed methodically, eyes no longer on his plate but fixed on the wall across from him.

"Not sure."

Taylor wondered if she should tell him about Jules' jaunt into the reserve. And she couldn't help herself.

"He met someone?"

"I think so. It was dark, but I thought there was someone else out there."

He was shaking his head. "I don't like that. Where are they now?"

It was eight o'clock on a Wednesday morning, so they were both at work. He was the only one eating supper. Then he planned to crash before reporting back to the hospital at five in the afternoon. She had him for nine hours, but that would be a rare phenomenon once the rotations really got underway. And that nine hours included the two-hour drive to the hospital and her eight-hour workday and her job. So she had him for about twenty more minutes.

"I'll speak to him when he gets home," he said.

She nodded and sipped her orange juice, fortified with calcium, downing one prenatal vitamin after another. Dressed for work and needing to leave in the next few minutes or be late, she still lingered. He'd only been gone a few hours, but she missed him. Especially at night.

"How are your ankles?"

She lifted one to his lap.

"Still swollen," she said.

"What did your doctor say?"

"Stay off my feet, of course."

"Good advice."

He massaged the arch of her foot, causing her to melt in a puddle in her chair. Gradually the motion slowed, and his hand dropped away.

She opened her eyes to see his head bowed as if in prayer, his arms at his sides and a soft snore coming from his side of the table.

After lowering her leg, she pushed to her feet and tugged at his arm.

"Come on. Off to bed with you."

He helped her clear the table and then she walked him to their room. He dropped his clothing before sliding between the covers. She kissed him and he rolled to his side.

"Do you want me to lie down with you for a little while?"

She'd actually just gotten up, showered, and dressed, but any time with him was precious now.

He didn't answer.

"Seth?"

The snore rattled through his nasal passages and his breath puffed from between his lips.

She crept from the room, closing the door. Only when she reached the overlook to the living room did she recall that she'd forgotten to ask if he'd spoken to Rubin, too, or just Nathan.

* * *

Taylor's afternoon chugged along as she played phone tag with job supervisors and fired off emails to various contacts. Her cell-phone chimed with a distinctive ring for Seth, and she realized it was already after three.

"Hi honey."

"Hi there."

The sound coming to her from the call told her immediately that he was driving.

"So I spoke to Jules by phone. He denies going into the woods. Said that was crazy, especially at night. Seems a bit of a city guy. Doesn't like bugs, snakes—"

She interrupted. "But he told us he's walked the reserve trails. That doesn't sound like a guy who's afraid of the woods. Plus, I saw him."

"Or someone. Jules says he's seen those teenage boys cutting through our lot to get to the reserve."

"Why?"

"Obvious answer is drinking."

"You believe him?"

"Not sure. Want me to call those boys' parents again?"

"No. But what about the conversation with Becca about my time and whether it will be a problem?"

"He explained that to me. Hey, you gave them a start, lurking on the stairs."

"I wasn't lurking. Pregnant women don't lurk. Besides, it's

my house." Or it might be in thirty years, she thought. "What did he say that explained them whispering about my time?"

"You misunderstood. They weren't even talking about you."

Embarrassment heated Taylor's face. That was exactly the sort of mistake her mother would have made, as she believed the world turned around her, orbiting around the sun, as was her right and her due.

Had she really made the same error?

"I'm not sure I believe him," she said.

There was a horn blast. Seth swore.

"You okay?"

"Yeah, yeah. I-4. Crazy, right?"

It was the deadliest highway in the nation and she was distracting him on this call. But he had called her.

"I'll tell you in person. Just trust me. It's okay."

"What about Rubin? Have you heard from him yet?"

The long silence was answer enough.

Finally, he said, "No. He hasn't returned my messages."

"Has he done this before?"

This also caused a longer than normal pause.

"Seth?"

TWENTY-FIVE

"He's never gone dark with me before," said Seth, obviously worried over his friend ghosting him.

Gone dark?

What was that, a military term?

"Can I do anything?"

"Yes. Don't work too hard. Eat. Rest. Keep your feet up."

"Yes, Dr. Parker."

He chuckled. "I like the sound of that. But seriously. Take it easy. I don't need to be worrying about you, as well."

As well as Rubin? Or as well as something else? Before she could ask, he told her he loved her and hung up.

Taylor went back to work, left her desk a little after five, and ran right into traffic.

By the time she left the car in the garage, her back throbbed and her feet were puffy as pink marshmallows. Tomorrow, she had an appointment with her doctor; she would ask if the due date was still the same. Earlier would have been better, but it was all up to the boy's development and her health.

She found the house to herself, so she heated up the final portion of chicken and biscuits and she added a healthy portion of steamed spinach. Not her favorite but for some reason, it tasted delicious.

She checked her blood pressure, a new part of her daily routine, and found it still about the same, slightly elevated, which was normal for a gal with more blood in her system and two little passengers aboard the 'soon to be mom' bus.

The smile came unbidden. Just thinking about those tiny little feet and hands and butts made her happy all over. She cradled her stomach, as a poor substitute for her babies.

"Soon, you two, I'll get to see if you have your daddy's eyes and your mama's nose. Or I suppose that's noses." She laughed.

Just over a week until her C-section.

It would not be long now.

After placing her dishes in the nearly full dishwasher and starting the load, she headed upstairs.

She stepped into her bedroom to put together the mobile she'd purchased during her lunch break with her credit card, which she really needed to stop doing.

She was sitting on the rocker, threading the cords through the frame, when she felt that uncomfortable prickle that told her she was being watched. Some primal remnant survival instinct had flicked on in her brain and she stilled. She was being hunted. Motionless, her hands stopped moving, freezing in place. Her nostrils flared as she sucked in a breath. Someone was behind her.

Why hadn't she locked the door?

Prey had only three choices. Freezing in hopes to go unnoticed—a variation of this was playing dead. The next was running, which was not an option, and the final, and her first choice in nearly every situation, was to fight.

Taylor made an ungainly push to her feet and pivoted, finding Becca standing in the doorway.

"Need a hand?" she asked as if she'd just arrived, instead of having been caught watching Taylor.

Had she?

"I didn't hear you." Taylor's pulse pounded at her neck and her face felt hot as her body struggled to abandon the preparations to defend herself.

Funny, it took only a moment for her system to roar into readiness but several minutes to restore equilibrium.

"You all right? You look flushed."

"You startled me."

"Did I? I'm sorry. I knocked."

Had she? Taylor didn't think so but she might have been so focused that she hadn't heard her. Was that why she felt she was being watched? Was it possible that Becca had done just as she claimed, and Taylor was the one at fault?

"Well, no trouble. Did you need something?"

"Toilet paper, really. But I'm happy to help you hang that mobile. I'm pretty agile and handy. Did you want to string that from an eyebolt?"

"I didn't get that far."

"Let me get my toolkit."

She had a toolkit?

"Great."

Why did having Becca in her private space feel like an invasion?

The woman was as narrow as Taylor was round. Long and lanky with her black hair coiled in an artful messy bun on top. Today she wore black lace-up boots like a new army recruit, super short khaki shorts, rolled at the waist to reveal her flat, tight stomach, and a jeweled naval ring. Her top was a lacy halter over a barely noticeable breast swell. The outfit might be created to drive tips at work. The combination of her gorgeous smile and the charm that Taylor had already witnessed would help her bottom line.

Side-by-side, Taylor looked like a fertility effigy compared to Becca who had stepped into adulthood still sporting the body of a gangly teen. Her license said she was twenty, but she didn't look it.

Zoe appeared in the doorway and paused to watch them. Taylor gave a little wave and Zoe nodded then continued to her room.

"She's in there all the time," muttered Becca. "Like the Unabomber or something."

That was a disturbing thought.

"Why would you say that?" asked Taylor.

Becca looked away and Taylor picked up on a vibe.

"Did something happen?"

Becca seemed about to say something, opened her mouth, closed it again, and then said, "No, it's nothing."

"If you are having any issues, I'd like to know about them."

"Okay. I understand."

But whatever was on her mind, Becca did not share it. Taylor gave up.

With the mobile hung, they both stared up at their handiwork.

"That looks great, Becca. Thank you."

Becca hugged her, spun with effortless grace, and vanished. Taylor pressed a hand to her heart. There was no reason to freak out. This was their home now, too, and it was at least possible that Becca had knocked.

"She didn't knock," she whispered.

* * *

That night, with the mobile spinning in slow circles, pushed by the current of air driven from the air conditioner and the vent in the ceiling, Taylor sent a text to Seth, who was working overnight on the pediatric floor.

On the job training to be a papa

He sent back a heart emoji and a kissy face emoji.

Goodnight, she typed and pressed send.

His message appeared a moment later.

Sleep well. Love U.

She put the phone beside her bed. He would not be home tonight or tomorrow. Would he make it home for the weekend? He'd told her that weekends were the busiest times for residents because the senior staff and attending physicians, surgeons, and other specialists were all on their boats or golf courses, leaving the new arrivals to hold down the fort.

Taylor shifted, then readjusted the pillow under her legs.

She fiddled with her phone, hoping Seth would write again. But he was gone, back to work. Her husband was such a health nut he rarely even drank coffee, let alone alcohol.

How he'd survive his residency was a mystery.

The phone dipped and she realized she had dozed. She set the phone on the charger beside her bed and glanced at the mobile, watching the ducklings continuing their restless spin and grinning.

She placed a hand on her stomach. "Goodnight, you two."

In reply, one of her babies pushed against her hand.

Her smile widened. This was going to be so great.

*   *   *

Taylor dozed but roused to something banging in her closet. Heart hammering, she grabbed her phone and the bear spray.

Whatever it was had gone quiet, but someone was in there. She just knew it.

Which of her new roomies would have the audacity to enter her room while she was sleeping and rummage around in her closet?

Zoe, if she felt it needed disinfecting or to steal something else. Her single tenant was a bit beyond odd and she made them all uncomfortable.

The next sound was something dropping from a shelf.

Taylor hesitated at the door to the walk-in closet.

"Hello?" she said, thinking how ridiculous it was to call a greeting to a closet. She listened to the quiet, then summoned her courage and threw open the door.

Moon darted past her as Taylor staggered back and just stopped herself from squirting the empty closet with the bear spray.

On the floor was her purse, upended, of course. Several pairs of shoes were also strewn about.

"Damned cat. Nearly gave me a heart attack." She collected her purse and tucked the contents back inside. Then she kicked the shoes toward the shoe cubbies and headed back to bed.

The cat had disappeared. After searching, she found it under her bed.

"How did you get in here to begin with?" she asked.

The cat stared with her yellow eyes but did not answer her query. Taylor tried opening her door to get Moon to vacate the premises, but she wouldn't go.

Taylor kept her closet door closed. So how did she get in there?

She wondered if one of her tenants had been in her room. Zoe came to mind first. Searching for another trinket, perhaps? But Zoe hated the cat and Becca had been lurking in Taylor's doorway. Plus, it was her cat.

Which one could have been in here and what might they have been doing? Stealing? Snooping. She had money. But no idea how much. If they'd taken a twenty, she doubted she'd even notice. Her jewelry was all sold, except for the wedding ring on her finger which she now spun in a circle.

"Come on, cat," she whispered. "Out."

Moon remained squarely under the bed and she gave up. It was at least possible that the cat had followed her into her room and into the closet when she retrieved her nightie.

But she didn't believe it.

Someone was creeping around in here. She felt it with that part of herself that sensed danger.

Why?

She left the door open a crack and eased onto the bed, watching for Moon to feel the coast was clear and make her exit. She set the spray and her phone on the table beside her bed, propped two pillows behind her and prepared to stand guard. But her eyelids dipped.

Taylor dropped into slumber.

Sometime later her eyes fluttered open. She had to pee. But that wasn't what woke her.

She was about to reach across the mattress for Seth, but remembered he wasn't there. But she did hear someone breathing.

Panic seized her, gripping her windpipe.

Taylor stared toward the partially open door to her room. There in the doorway was a large dark figure, backlit by the nightlight.

TWENTY-SIX

Taylor choked the bed covers as she peered toward the hallway, struggling to see in the near darkness. The figure in the open doorway stood stock-still.

That was not Seth. He was too broad.

Could it be Jules?

Why was he there, looming?

Suddenly she recalled leaving her bedroom door ajar for the cat. She'd left it unlocked.

Taylor reached for her phone, pulling it off the charger. The screen illuminated, so bright that it momentarily blinded her.

She pressed the phone to her chest, thinking whatever he was doing, he now knew that she had seen him. She had to keep him in view. That was as important as calling for help. More really because it would take help several minutes to arrive.

With the light quashed, her gaze shot to the doorway, and she found the space empty.

A cold sweat gave her a chill that slithered down her back and pooled at the base of her spine. She slipped out of bed on legs so stiff she could barely bend her knees. Toddling forward as if just rising from a coma, she staggered across the carpet.

Approaching the door, she tried to think. Lock the door or peek into the hallway?

In the end, she did neither, pausing just before the entrance, one hand on the frame. The solid wall did little to keep her head from spinning. Her stomach cramped. Braxton-Hicks contractions. Normal. Terrifying. She was not having these babies before her due date.

She reached out for the door latch and slammed the door and engaged the lock. Then she pressed her ear to the door and heard nothing.

"Jules?" she called. Her voice seemed breathy and thin, like some reed instrument warming up before the performance.

There was no answer. No sound.

Should she call the police?

Her fear was quickly morphing into outrage. How dare he come in here?

There was no reason for Jules to be in her room at night when she was sleeping.

It was so creepy. How long had he been doing this? Had he been lurking over her and Seth, or did he reserve his nocturnal spy missions only for her?

Tomorrow, first thing, she was showing him the door. He was not going to be creeping around when she was pregnant, vulnerable, and about to have two little souls to protect.

He'd messed with the wrong woman. He didn't know who her mother was. Being raised by a woman like Sabrina Roth gave her a unique set of survival skills that flowed in her blood along with the platelets.

"Oh, he will be lucky not to get arrested."

Of course, at this point she realized this was a 'he said-she said' situation. One he could easily, and wisely, deny.

Why hadn't she turned on her video instead of hiding her phone as if she was the one who did not want to be discovered?

Because she had been terrified and that thinking part of her brain had momentarily disengaged. The last thing she needed was to alert a possible attacker that she knew he was there.

Taylor returned the way she had come, sitting on the bed, still warm from her body. The cool air conditioning blew over her puckered skin, further lifting the hairs on her arms and neck. Each tiny hair stood at attention as she listened, but she heard nothing but the hum of the air system.

It would worry Seth terribly. He was two hours away and really there was nothing he could do.

She was on her own, just like the nights that her mother came into her room to stand over her bed and stare.

Taylor had become very good at feigning sleep.

She recalled the way her mother's breathing rasped as she loomed over her. Taylor would open her eyes just enough to see the shadowy outline of a figure silhouetted by the light in the hall. Taylor never knew why she did this, crept into her room late at night, stood smoking and watching. But she felt in that deep and primitive part of her that allowing her mother to know she was awake would be a mistake.

It was the door's squeak that alerted her to her nocturnal visitor. Once there, her mom never tucked her in or adjusted the covers. She never stroked her hand over Taylor's head or leaned to kiss her cheek. She just watched. Sometimes she'd whisper something.

"I know you're not sleeping." Or, "He's mine, you know?"

Had she meant Taylor's father? Did her mother see her as a rival for his attention? Yes. Of course she had, and she had been as anxious to be rid of her daughter as Taylor was to go.

But even back then, when Taylor was very young, she had recognized this for what it was—a test. And she never moved. After an eternity, her mother would turn and slip away, the hinges would creak, and the door would click shut.

Later, when she was ten or eleven, she never used her

pillows, but kept them under the covers between her and the door. When the hinge would creak, Taylor would drop to the ground and hide under the bed, or behind the big chair. Once she burrowed into the pile of stuffed animals in the corner. During the day, when her mother was in one of her angry moods, Taylor would run and hide. Like a game of hide-and-seek but with dangerous stakes. Her mother would storm and shout as she searched for her daughter. But Taylor had learned to be silent, still, and small. And if her mother got too close, she'd bolt like a rabbit for a hedgerow. Only when her father came home would she emerge to face her mother's silent glowering rage and her father's worried smile.

Hiding was one of Taylor's survival skills. Running. Hiding. Being very, very still. Now it all came flooding back. The fear. The sense of being trapped and the uncertainty of exactly what would happen if she wasn't quick enough.

Alone in her bedroom, the door securely locked, Taylor shivered with her phone gripped tight in her sweating hand. Taylor breathed slowly through her nose, trying to control her galloping heart and slow her frantic breathing.

"He's gone. You're safe."

But was she? What was he doing? Or planning to do?

Nothing good. That was certain.

It was such a violation. She'd let him into her home. Granted, for a fee, but not so he could creepy-crawl her room like some freaking Charlie Manson disciple.

"Uh-um. No way." She stood, dressed, considered what weapons she had in her room. None really, but nearly everything could be a weapon.

Wait until tomorrow during the daylight to confront Jules? Confront him by phone after he'd gone to work? Change the locks after the pair left the house?

First, he'd been creeping around in the woods. Then he was

lurking in her doorway. This guy was not staying in her house a minute longer.

What if he was bothering Zoe? Had he been in her room lurking and staring while she slept?

If her single roommate was aware of anything like that, she would surely have mentioned it. And Zoe had shrewdly increased her security by adding that slide bolt. That now seemed less annoying and more smart.

Taylor would be wise to follow her example.

And she would have to ask Zoe if Jules had bothered her.

Sometime after she had visited the bathroom and settled back in bed, the practical side of her brain reengaged.

They were a quarter of the way through the month. If she tossed him before month's end, she'd lose that cash and be on the hook for the money due to the mortgage company. If she told Zoe that Jules had been in her room, it would scare her and possibly make her move out.

Taylor wrestled with that moral dilemma.

"This is wrong. If he's a creeper, they have to go."

She flopped back on the bed but couldn't sleep. What if he came back? That stupid, cheap lock wouldn't stop him.

Taylor dragged her pillow from the bed. She took it and her bedding to the far side of the room, past the mobile Becca had helped her hang. Then she lay on the shag area rug with the triangle foam wedge she had used to stretch and exercise before she was as large as a beer keg.

Now, if Jules tried to get in, she had time to slip out to the balcony and call the police. There was no access to the deck from there, but she would not be where he expected. He might not find her right away. Hiding was a very viable strategy for a smaller, weaker animal, which she definitely was.

She had considered going downstairs, getting in her car, and driving away. But she'd be damned. He was not chasing her out of her home.

Her parents had done that to her once. She was determined not to let that ever happen again.

After her mother hit her and she'd finally been allowed to go to prep school, she'd decided to make her own home. It was better to be with people who cared about her and liked her than live under her mother's cold disapproval. And it wasn't hard.

Her father's contribution to her bank account was sizable. There was much that money could fix. But not everything.

She did not come home for Christmas or Easter or when the school year ended. By then she was seventeen and she could work. She took a position at a summer sleepaway camp in the Berkshires teaching riding to kids just like her—rich, entitled, smart, and driven. But she wasn't sure what she was driving toward.

At that point she was just driving away—from them.

Her dad called, left messages, and she texted back. It was the minimum, but it was enough.

After prep school, she'd attended Dartmouth University.

Her father came to visit her once during parent orientation in her freshman year. Her mother never did.

Taylor knew she was smart and decided to funnel that over-active mind into a challenging field of study. She finished her engineering degree with honors. Her parents flew up for graduation. She met them afterwards for an awkward family photo which she was certain would go on the wall in her childhood home or on her father's desk. Dinner had been strained and they'd left the following morning.

After college she debated graduate school, narrowing her focus to environmental engineering. Afterwards, instead of taking a predictable high-paying job, as her father recommended, she joined a government infrastructure project on the White Mountain Apache reservation in Arizona, helping plan and build a dam, treatment facility, pumping plant, and storage reservoir to distribute clean water.

It wasn't a resume builder. But it was a chance to do something valuable, necessary, and really, past due. After two years, she had more of an understanding of people whose lives and living circumstances could not have been more different than hers.

The budget was threadbare, and she'd had a chance to build something real, instead of theoretical. Her portion of the project was the water treatment facility. And she was proud of her contribution.

Then her father had called, and she was rushing home.

Seth had recently revealed that he believed this had been a ploy her father had used to drag her back. He was probably right. By the time her dad was out of the hospital, she was accepting help to get her into an apartment, driving a replacement for her old car and settling into a well-paying job in Tampa. And her dad had made a few calls to his contacts to help Seth get into college and offered his guidance on what to take. If not for her father's financial help and tugging on the correct strings, Seth might not have gotten into med school in Tampa because he had been homeschooled with only a GED to show for his efforts.

Then came the wedding plans. Taylor groaned in pain just at the memory. They paid for everything, but her 'special day' was not the simple, elegant affair she would have preferred.

By the time she finally reached her wedding day, she felt like a distance runner hitting the wall and unsure if she could even finish the race. She'd been tugged from the beauty parlor to the church, feeling ridiculous in a tiara, like a princess in some elaborately staged live theater production.

But she'd gotten through it and the reception, where the speeches and shenanigans with her garter meant she had not even eaten unless you counted the one bite of wedding cake fed to her by her new husband.

After dancing with her father and sharing a very public first dance with her new groom and then being passed from man to man like a dancehall girl, Seth finally rescued her.

"I need some air."

What would have happened if they had not gone out at that exact moment?

Seth held her hand and they made their way out to the lobby of her parents' country club, the yacht club being too small to accommodate this number of guests.

"This good?" he asked, steering them toward a bench.

"No, away from the music. My ears are ringing."

The band was some awful 1980s rock group that her mother had picked. Taylor swore she didn't know half the songs they played, but her parents' friends seemed happy reliving their youth.

"Outside it is," said her new husband.

Her husband. That thought warmed her heart and made her ribs constrict as if the corset of the gown were not enough.

"The cake was pretty," said Seth. "Lots of little pink flowers."

"Rosebuds," she said. "Made of fondant."

"Chewy," he said, and that made her laugh.

"You've been a very good sport about all this."

"I feel as if I have landed in a foreign country. I knew it would be a shock, but oh, boy. I had no idea. That cocktail hour was more food than I've ever seen in one place."

"You should have seen my sweet sixteen. I wondered how they'd top it. My dad got one of the Jonas Brothers to sing that Ringo Starr song. You know, that one about being sixteen and beautiful?"

"That's a little creepy. No?"

"Yes."

They were laughing as they reached the back exit. This led

to a formal garden with a central fountain. Beyond, the golf course stretched to a dark horizon. But here, the gravel paths were tastefully illuminated.

The first person they spotted was the father of their ring-bearer and a groomsman. Larry Wilson held a beer bottle and a nearly finished cigarette in one hand as he glanced nervously about.

He was a childhood friend from her neighborhood. He'd been called into service to make the fifth on the groom's side to balance her five friends from college and the project out in Arizona. He was married and had a very cute son, Artie, who had done as good a job at the wedding as any two-year-old possibly could.

"Artie!" called Larry.

"Did you lose him?" asked Seth.

"He was right here a minute ago." Larry's words were slurred, and Taylor wondered if he'd enjoyed the open bar a little too much.

"Where's Helen?" asked Taylor, mentioning his wife of three years.

"Inside. She will kill me if he gets that suit dirty. It's a rental."

"We'll help you look," said Seth.

They'd all taken different directions, with Taylor heading down the center path toward the fountain, all aglow with LED lights making the curtains of water change color by the minute. It was a big structure with three tiers of collecting bowls topped with a draped maiden pouring water from a jug. The bottom basin held three dolphins spewing water from their open mouths. The dolphins were the old-world sort, like you'd see in Italy or on the edge of a pirate map. But the LED lights did not quite fit, in her opinion.

She drew up short at seeing her mother, Sabrina Roth, statuesque in a blue-gray silk gown that fit her elegant form perfectly.

Taylor came alongside her. "Mom, what are you doing out here?"

Something dark and small caught her eye. It was like a ventriloquist dummy floating in the water.

TWENTY-SEVEN

Taylor's breath caught as she sprang forward. This was no doll.

It was Artie in his little tuxedo, waving his arms as he tried and failed to lift his head from the water.

Shrieking, Taylor lunged, snatching the boy up with one hand.

"Oh, be careful, darling," said her mother. "Your dress. It's satin. Water stains."

Taylor had the boy over her arm and was pounding him on the back.

Had her mother just cautioned her not to save a child because it would damage her dress?

"Seth! Larry!" Taylor cried.

She could hear someone pounding down the gravel path from the opposite direction.

Artie vomited up water all over her dress and then gasped and began to cry and choke. She squatted with him in her arms, rubbing his back and cooing reassurances.

Larry arrived first. "What happened?"

"He fell in the fountain," said Taylor, realizing as she spoke that she had not seen him fall. A more accurate answer would have been that she'd found him struggling face-down in the water.

Larry took his son, who was now red-faced and coughing.

"Oh buddy. Why'd you go in the fountain?"

His boy was crying vigorously, the sound rising to a howl.

Taylor glanced at her mother who watched with silent interest. She had not taken a single step in their direction.

"Thanks, Taylor. My God, my wife is going to kill me." Then to his son, "You're all right, buddy. You're okay."

Why hadn't her mother done something? Hadn't she seen the boy floundering? If Taylor was able to see him, her mom must have, because they shared the same vantage point.

The crunch of gravel announced Seth's arrival and Taylor explained that Artie had fallen in the fountain.

Now, her mother reanimated, stepping forward to criticize.

"Taylor, honestly, look at your dress. You're covered with gravel and mud and whatever was in that boy's stomach." She made a disgusted face.

Several guests were gathering. Artie's cries grew until they were ear splitting.

Her mother clapped her hands over her ears as Larry carried Artie away, the boy now demanding his mama. Seth followed along with the pair, leaving her with her mother.

"Why didn't you do something?" asked Taylor, exasperated.

Her mother shrugged; her brow knit in confusion. "Like what?"

"Mom," said Taylor in a hushed tone, "didn't you see him?"

"Of course not," her mother assured her.

Her words were choked with aggravation, and she waved her hands, while somehow keeping herself from shouting because no one shouted at Sabrina Roth. "How could you not see him?"

Her mother aimed an elegant finger skyward. "I was looking at the moon."

"But you must have heard him splashing."

"Over the cascading water?" Her mother waved a dismissive hand. "Don't be silly."

Taylor texted her father who arrived a few moments later.

"Dad, I just pulled Artie out of the fountain. He was face down and struggling."

Her dad glanced at Sabrina and the pair exchanged inscrutable looks.

"Oh, that's terrible," said her dad. "Is he all right?"

Taylor gave a quick, bobbing nod. "He will be, I think."

"Where were his parents?" he asked.

"Exactly," said her mother.

Taylor was not ready to deflect from her biggest difficulty.

"But Mom was right here before I even arrived."

"Sabrina, why didn't you rescue him?"

Her placid brow knit once more. "In my defense, I am wearing silk."

Taylor blinked at the non sequitur.

"And look at our bride. Covered in vomit and mud. She can't go back in like that." She clapped her hands. "Time to change into your traveling clothing."

That outfit was meant for Taylor's grand exit with her groom in a horse and carriage, then a private car to the honeymoon suite at the Ritz-Carlton, then, tomorrow, an early flight to Hawaii.

Her mother and father whisked her back indoors and to the private rooms they'd rented.

Her dad drew her aside. "Your mom is on some new mood stabilizers. She's not totally aware of her surroundings."

"Dad, she didn't lift a finger."

"They're powerful. She's more than a little spacy."

"I thought maybe she was drunk."

"She can't drink. Not with these medications."

It was an explanation that she really wanted to accept. But

even as she changed into the winter white linen suit, her mind was still back at the fountain.

Had Artie fallen?

Well, what else could have happened?

Even as she thought it, a terrible notion dropped, one that she could not voice.

What if...

No. Not possible.

Taylor shuddered thinking back on that moment. Whatever the reason, the boy could easily have drowned.

No. He *was* drowning.

* * *

Taylor pushed that memory down with the others. Lots of people had terrible stuff happen to them. That didn't make her special.

But Seth said they were the frogs in hot water. It was some experiment he knew of. If you toss a frog into very hot water, it will jump out. But if you put it in cold water and slowly increase the temperature, the frog will just sit there until it cooks to death.

She didn't like being the frog.

She didn't like knowing her parents once again had her so obligated that she'd sat right here, in the pot they'd given her, as the temperature went up and up.

Her parents' decision to cut her off financially had been the rapid temperature change she needed to leap clear.

Now she planned on finding her own pond and never letting herself get trapped by their money again.

Before dawn, Taylor roused to find herself lying on the floor. It was a struggle to get to her feet and to make it to the bathroom. But she did it. Survival instincts were not to be ignored.

She was awake, dressed, and downstairs before Jules. He left the house before five in the morning because of his postal job. But she waited, lights off in the kitchen, for him to appear.

Beside her, she had two things. A full can of Mace and her phone.

When he flicked on the light, she was pleased to see him notice her seated at the kitchen counter, yelp, and jump backwards.

Good start, she thought.

"You scared the shit out of me," said Jules, hand splayed on his broad chest.

"Good. What the hell were you doing in my room last night?"

TWENTY-EIGHT

"Your room?" Jules gave a very convincing impression of someone who was confused.

He stood by the light switch on the opposite side of the kitchen. She remained seated with a finger on the button to spray a chemical irritant in his puzzled face.

"That's right. Two in the morning. And you were standing inside my room. That means you did not knock, opened my door, and stood there for God only knows how long. How did you get past my locked door?"

He blinked stupidly at her.

"I know for certain you did not do that by accident. I want you out."

"But it *was* an accident. If I was where you said."

"If? You accidentally wandered through a locked door and into my room? That's your answer?"

"No. Yes. Listen. I have a problem."

"You sure do. You have no idea how big a problem. I could press charges. I could—"

"It wasn't locked. Couldn't be. And I sleepwalk."

She frowned. "You what?"

"I sleepwalk. Especially when I'm upset or in an unfamiliar place." He dragged a hand through the long tangle of his hair. "Usually, it's the kitchen. Once I woke up in my car in the parking lot of the post office at midnight."

"You sleepwalk."

"Yes. If the door is locked, I won't wander in. But you might hear me moving around."

She *had* heard someone moving around late at night. More than once. The frown deepened as her suspicions warred with his plausible explanation.

"I almost always end up back in bed. But once, my mom found me sleeping on the dog bed. The dog took mine." Jules rubbed the bristle of his chin, making a scratching sound like an emery board on a fingernail. "I'm really sorry, Taylor. I'm super apologetic if I frightened you or anything like that."

Now she didn't know what to believe. It was possible. It was also possibly a lie.

"Was your door locked?" he said. "It couldn't have been."

It wasn't. She remembered now that she'd left it open for the damned cat, which was probably now sleeping on her bed.

"What if I put a slide latch on the inside of your door?" Taylor asked.

He frowned, causing his forehead to furrow like a field ready for planting.

"That might work. But I need to get to the bathroom. And I'd probably just open it while asleep."

"I could put the slide lock up high or down low. Not the normal place. Is the lock a problem?"

"No. I mean, I never tried it before. But I think I'd just remember and open it anyway."

She regarded him, looking for anything that might indicate he was scamming her, but saw nothing. That only meant that he was either being honest or that he was a competent liar.

"We'll try the slide lock. Otherwise, you two might need to find other arrangements."

"I have a lease." This had turned into a stand-off. "We'll try the lock. But you need to lock your door as well."

"Oh, believe me, I will."

Becca sidled into the kitchen aiming right for the coffee maker.

"Good morning," she managed.

Becca was not a morning person. She was generally upbeat, but the early hours found her sullen and uncommunicative until after her first cup of Joe.

Taylor returned the greeting as she pushed up from the stool, using the counter to assist her. Once on her feet, she was fine, but rising with just her legs was becoming a chore.

"You're up early," said Taylor.

"So are you."

"Because I didn't sleep well. Your husband was in my room."

Becca's face relayed shock.

"Sleepwalking again," he said.

Was that an explanation or was he informing his wife of his cover story?

Becca blinked at him. "I didn't even hear you get up." She turned to Taylor. "I'm so sorry, Taylor, if he scared you. It's so weird when he's just walking around in his own world."

"Yeah, weird." And alarming.

Taylor left the pair but, as she crossed from the kitchen into the living room, she wondered again why Becca was already up.

Their normal schedule was Jules and then Zoe were up and out before she was awake. Becca hit the shower about when Taylor's alarm went off. She knew this because Becca had a lovely singing voice and sang in the shower. Oddly she sang mostly things Taylor didn't recognize. The only one she did know was 'Simple Gifts'. That one had to be at least a hundred years old. Becca was usually downstairs before Taylor.

But not today.

Still, why was Becca up so darned early?

Taylor had risen to speak to Jules. Had their conversation woken her? From downstairs?

Not likely.

She really didn't know when Becca got up. Only when she had her shower and when she left the house.

Taylor reversed course, returning to the doorway but keeping just out of sight so she could listen.

Jules was relaying his conversation with Taylor to Becca, accurately.

"This isn't good."

"I know, but I heard her crying. I thought maybe she needed us. You know? The babies?"

Needles pricked her skin, first hot and then icy cold. Why would she need them?

But then she remembered the nightmare. She *had* been crying. Had he heard her and come to check if she was all right? But then why not say that? Why tell her he was a sleepwalker?

None of this made sense.

"Next time, wake me up." There was a stretch of silence. "Her C-section is only a week away. Her twins might be on their own schedule. So why was she crying?"

"I don't know. But she's fine this morning."

They sounded like two nurses discussing a patient. Taylor found that thought disturbing. A shiver ricocheted through her.

"Are we still going through with it?"

Now Taylor's confusion crept toward panic. Through with what?

"It's all set."

There was that accent again. Both of them. Southwestern? She wasn't certain.

"The others?" Becca asked.

"They're ready. Just need to pick a date."

"Sooner is better," said Becca.

Taylor inched away. She needed to call Seth. He needed to be here. He'd been right to voice concern at the thought of strangers in their house. She'd been stupid and greedy and entitled. Why did she think she and her babies deserved a home they couldn't afford?

Because she'd always had everything she wanted. Everything but a mentally stable mother. Everything material that she wanted, at least.

Taylor reached the stairs and climbed to the second floor. There she paused, listening over the banister, but she could hear nothing but their murmured voices and the faucet flipping on and off.

The rattle of dishes confused her. Was one of them unloading the dishwasher?

She lifted her phone and texted her husband. The time on her mobile read 5:12 am. He might be sleeping, or he might have been awake for hours. Either way, she needed him. She tapped out her message.

Call me as soon as you can.

TWENTY-NINE

The ring of her phone startled Taylor awake. She was still in her pajamas and robe and had dozed on her bed with the door locked.

She glanced at the screen and accepted the call.

"Seth!"

"The twins?"

Naturally, he'd assumed that she'd gone into labor. Her body was unaware of her approaching C-section and might have ideas of its own about when she and her babies were ready to deliver.

"No. I'm fine. Nothing but the Braxton-Hicks contractions."

"Oh, phew. I'm on the floor. Understaffed. I wish I'd realized how many shifts they aren't able to cover. And the time off, it's barely enough to sleep. I get about four hours, if I'm lucky. Not enough to get home and back. And if I did that, I would have zero sleep time."

"Where do you sleep?"

"Here at the hospital. They have bunks."

That thought was even more depressing.

"When will you be able to come home?"

"I'll be there for the C-section."

"That's not until next Thursday!"

"I'm sorry, Taylor. You knew this was a possibility. It's why I wanted to get a place up here."

"My doctors are all here. The birthing center."

"I know. I'm not arguing. I'm just explaining, I have very little time off."

She was clamping her teeth shut to keep from screaming. This was mostly—all right, totally—her fault. She told him about Jules in her room and his explanation this morning. She didn't know how Seth even kept from saying 'I told you so!' But he did.

"So, what should I do?" she asked.

"Well, he may really have been sleepwalking."

She growled. "Then why say he heard me crying?"

"I don't know. Sleep with the door locked, your phone handy, and my bear spray on the nightstand. He comes in again, pull the trigger. It shoots several yards."

Seth had told her that the bears in the area where he grew up were dangerous. Grizzly bears were not to be messed with, but if he, or anyone else on the ranch, happened to get between a bear and cub, the spray might give them time to pull their rifles.

Her husband's youth and hers bore no resemblance to each other. Seth didn't tell her much about his boyhood except that he worked hard, was home schooled, and lived in a remote area. He said he didn't have many friends growing up, except his cousins.

They both had that in common, the need to escape that isolation.

"Meanwhile, I'll call Jules and we'll have a talk. Might help to remind him that you are alone, but not..." His words trailed off.

"Not?"

"Alone but not on your own."

"Oh, Seth. Really?"

"Can't hurt."

She breathed away a sigh. "If you think that will help."

"It might."

"All right. But listen." She explained about the conversation she'd overheard between Jules and Becca this morning.

"Go through with what?"

"I'm not sure but it sounds... I don't know, sinister."

"Taylor?" His tone seemed put out, as if she were making a big deal over nothing.

"I think..." This was hard to say aloud because it sounded crazy, like the wild, irrational accusations her mother often made. "What if, I mean, what if they're after our babies or something?"

"What?" He sounded incredulous. Like his wife had just jumped off the deep end. "What are you suggesting?"

"I don't know. It's stupid." She swiped at the tears on her cheeks. "I'm sorry. Forget it."

"Taylor, I'm very concerned. Why would you say that?"

"Because they also said it was all set and the others were ready. They just needed to pick a date."

"The others?" His voice no longer rang with incredulity. Now he sounded deadly serious.

"Yes."

He said nothing, but she could hear him breathing. Finally, he said, "I don't like the sound of that."

"Can you come home?" She hated the way her voice quavered.

"Only if I want to drop out of the program."

"Don't do that!" she said, anxious now for entirely different reasons.

"What do you want me to do?" Seth sounded vexed.

"Call Nathan or Rubin. Maybe both. Ask *them* to speak to Jules."

"Nathan and Rubin are dodging my calls," he said, clearly annoyed with his friends.

She gave a low grown of displeasure, then said, "That's not good."

"No. It's not. I'm really disturbed by it. This is so unlike them."

"Can I do anything?" asked Taylor.

"No. You have more than enough to worry about. I'll call Jules again now," he said, turning back to her problems.

"Great. That's good. Thank you." She had her fingers crossed that he reached Jules and gave him hell.

"Have you considered booting the pair of them?"

"I have, but it's... well..." She sighed. "We need the rent money."

"This is bad. I'm already worried about you and the babies. I told you I didn't want strangers in the house."

And there it was. The belated *I told you so* she had been expecting.

"I know. You were right. But can we sort it out after the twins arrive?"

Another sigh. Then the frustrated humming he made in his throat when exasperated. "Sure."

"Call me later?"

There was a pause. He spoke to someone else. She heard him say he was on his way. Then he returned to her. "I'll try."

"At least text and tell me how it went with Jules."

"Will do. Gotta run. Love you, Taylor."

"I got the mobile together." Why would he care? She was like a toddler showing off her toys to hold the interest of a busy, distracted adult.

"Great. Bye, babe."

The silence was consuming.

Her wake-up alarm sounded, startling her so greatly that she dropped her phone.

"Holy shit!" she said through a locked jaw. Then she scooped up the chiming phone, shut down the alarm, and headed for the shower. But she backtracked to her door, checking again to be certain it was locked.

When she left the steaming bathroom sometime later, she found a text from Seth.

Left Jules a message to call me. Will let you know what he says. Wish I could be there.

She sent back a text, hoping to catch him, but got no reply.

* * *

Somehow every single person in her office had some dire emergency that Thursday afternoon. Taylor was cranky, barely polite, answering all the calls now transferred to her phone and unable to have a moment free to even open the files she needed to work on.

Earlier, she'd been to her weekly checkup, and all seemed fine with the babies, her, and the delivery date. That much, at least, was going as planned.

"This is ridiculous," she said to her empty office.

At least there would be no further sleepwalking into her room, because she planned to take a tactic out of Zoe's playbook and swing by the hardware store on the way home for a slide lock. And she'd lock her bedroom door every night from now on. Was he sleepwalking or had Jules been checking on her because she'd been crying in her sleep?

Both scenarios were equally disturbing.

She didn't like it. Too many ready explanations and she wasn't buying them. Those two were up to something. Zoe was like a shadow, sneaking around when no one was up or hiding in her room. They all made Taylor uncomfortable.

But she reminded herself, as an only child of a woman with mental illness, her gauge of normal was way off.

Seth had called mid-afternoon, and he had been just as cryptic as his text this morning. All he'd said was that she'd find out soon. He seemed as comfortable as she was unsettled.

And wouldn't you know it, as she was leaving her workspace ten minutes early and heading for the door, her phone chimed.

Not Seth, unfortunately. It was a text from Becca.

Hey, I need a favor. My car died. Already towed to the shop. Could you swing by the coffee shop and pick me up please?

Great. Now she was a chauffeur. What a wonderful way to end her day. This was not what she had pictured when she selected three competent adults.

She tucked away her sarcasm and annoyance and texted back that she'd be happy to pick Becca up while secretly wondering why her tenant didn't just call an Uber or why she had no friends to help her.

Great! ETA?

On my way now. Five minutes?

Becca sent back a smiling face emoji, a thumbs up emoji, and a coffee cup emoji.

Taylor parked before the shop six minutes later and waited. Becca did not appear. She could see several people at tables, but the serving station and register were not visible from here.

"She's really going to make me heave myself out of this car and totter in there, isn't she?"

The annoyance flared and she tucked it away. Becca was likely behind the counter cleaning up. Or waiting for these customers to leave. According to the hours posted on the door, the shop closed fifteen minutes ago.

"People can be so clueless," she said as she slammed the car door. She carried only her fob and locked the vehicle, leaving her purse in the wheel-well on the driver's side.

Halfway to the door, she spotted Becca's car and paused. Hadn't she said it had been towed to the repair shop? She gave the Caddy a once-over and decided it was definitely Becca's car.

Taylor leaned, cupping her hands at each side of her eyes to better peek at the box in the back seat.

Diapers. Becca had a huge box of diapers in newborn size.

She stiffened as her fears mounted, choking her. Sputtering and blasting air from her nostrils, Taylor backed away.

What possible reason could her renter have for buying these?

She could think of no legitimate reason and several sinister ones.

Oh, she was getting to the bottom of this right now.

The door chirped as she entered the shop and marched, shuffled really, toward the counter, searching for Becca like a big game hunter gunning for bear. She was more than halfway to the register before she spotted a coworker, Lindi Vanderput, seated at a table, grinning, her red reading glasses still hanging on the colorful beaded cord on her cream-colored satin blouse.

Taylor frowned as confusion and an uncomfortable uncertainty dropped her stomach several inches. Her fury morphed into doubt. She hesitated as her skin crawled and she shuddered. Lindi had said she had an eye appointment. And there across the table was Charlotte Rahahan, another coworker, dressed in the same bright saffron blouse and hot-pink hijab she'd worn in the office earlier today, before she told Taylor she had to pick up her child who had been injured at soccer practice.

"Charlotte?"

Charlotte's smile widened and she gave a goofy little wave.

Taylor's mouth hung open as she turned to see that there at the counter was Milena Smigelski, the new hire. She was grinning and wiggling on her barstool. And standing beside her was Taylor's supervisor, Nicki Wakely, also wearing a bright smile.

Taylor shook her head with a slow sweep, trying to understand why everyone from her office was here in this shop.

"What's happening?"

THIRTY

"What is this?" asked Taylor, confusion mingling with a growing sense that a joke was being played on her.

"It's for you," said Nicki, waving her arms in her colorful kimono-style top that moved like the wings of a butterfly. "We weren't sure, because, you know, we thought your mom would be organizing..." Her words fell off and she broke eye contact but quickly rallied, continuing. But her smile now seemed forced. "Then Seth told us that you are having some trouble with your parents. And that they weren't giving you a shower."

Shower?

Taylor's gaze swept the room. There was Becca, behind the counter, face flushing pink. And Zoe, dressed in a tailored gray suit, standing nearly against the takeout window and holding in her hands a small package wrapped in brown paper and string.

Her attention fell on an empty table beside Nicki.

"It was your cousin's idea to have it here," said Charlotte, motioning to Becca as she took Taylor's elbow and led her forward.

The table was loaded with gifts wrapped in white and baby blue paper. Twin balloons said *It's a boy!*

Jules rose from his hiding place behind the counter, stepped forward, and offered his phone. There on the screen was Seth, smiling with circles under his eyes.

"Surprise!" he said. "Wish I could be there, babe!"

"Seth!"

"Enjoy your baby shower. Have some cake for me. But not too much. Blood sugar," he said, then grinned. "It's all okay. Just relax."

A baby shower!

And suddenly it clicked.

The conversation she'd overheard. *Sooner was better. They're ready. It's all set.*

Becca and Jules had been planning her baby shower.

Taylor's throat burned. She pressed her lips together as tears of relief drippled down her cheeks. Why did she always jump to the worst conclusions? Why was she so suspicious of everyone's motives?

Taylor wiped away the tears. Jules handed her a napkin. She blotted her cheeks again.

Milena swept forward and gathered her up in her arms, hushing her and rubbing her back.

"We know it's a difficult time. We understand. But this is important. You're going to be a mama. And we want to celebrate with you."

She moved to Taylor's side. Becca swept forward with a chair and Taylor settled into the seat of honor.

"This is such a surprise," she said.

Jules offered her several more paper napkins. Charlotte presented an ice cream cake and offered a wicked-looking knife. Taylor made the first cut and Charlotte took over, slicing and serving portions onto adorable plates covered with cartoon animals with a border of blue skies and puffy white clouds.

Taylor's cake melted on the plate as she was inundated with gifts. There were tiny little outfits, home knit booties, a changing blanket, twin soft, plush teddy bears, and a gift certificate for the largest baby outfitting store in the area.

Zoe stepped forward and placed her gift on the extreme outer edge of the table before stepping back.

"Thank you, Zoe. It's so sweet of you to come and to bring me something."

She unwrapped the gift and withdrew a soft little stuffed white bunny with floppy ears and stitched eyes that made the toy appear to be sleeping.

Taylor hugged the toy. "It's so cute. Thank you, Zoe."

"It's a cotton case, no dyes. The eyes are stitched, so no choking hazard, and it's stuffed with one hundred percent organic cotton."

"That's very thoughtful, Zoe." She considered hugging her, but thought better of it and nodded her thanks.

Jules offered her a tiny wash basin filled with baby bath products and squeaky toys. Becca's gift was a tower of rolled diapers resembling a three-tier cake, topped with a lovely stuffed zebra with pale blue stripes.

Diapers, Taylor thought. Newborn diapers, each tied with blue ribbon. She blushed, remembering that she'd been ready to confront Becca about the box in her car. This was embarrassing.

Was every expecting mother so twitchy?

No, she decided. She had her mother to thank for being so uber-suspicious. Why couldn't she accept things at face value?

Taylor tucked away her shame and admired each gift. Cried at the tiny booties and brightly colored socks. She ate some of her melting cake and hugged everyone. For the first time in a while, she felt supported and loved. It was an awesome feeling.

"So we guessed right?" asked Nicki. "You're good with this celebration."

"I think I needed it without even knowing."

"We're sure going to miss you around the office," said Charlotte.

"I'll be back as soon as the doctor clears me."

Not that she wouldn't enjoy more time at home with her babies. Or she believed she would. But she needed her income if she had any hopes of keeping that large roof over their heads.

She felt momentarily guilty at being so suspicious. Jumping to conclusions and just expecting her boarders to be up to some nefarious plotting.

It was her mother again. That woman never made a move without some ulterior motive. It had made Taylor distrustful and apprehensive. How many perfectly innocent approaches had she rebuffed because of her inclination to protect and guard?

She was going to be a mommy. Taylor needed to find a balance between mistrust and faith. She had just seen so little benevolence from her mother, so little approval. And her father, despite loving her, was equally self-serving.

"Speech! Speech!" Charlotte was tapping her coffee mug with her spoon.

Taylor wiped her mouth on a paper napkin and then mopped her eyes.

She didn't know exactly what she said, as she was still blubbering. But she did remember saying "I love you guys" in an unusual show of emotion. These hormones were wacky because she wanted to hug each one of these wonderful people.

So, she stood and grabbed Charlotte and then Nicki. When she finished, the party broke up. It was nearly dinner time and every one of these folks, except Nicki, had families to return to. Nicki had cats. Many, many, cats.

Jules, Becca, and Charlotte helped carry the gifts to Taylor's vehicle. Becca's Caddy had not been towed, she was not in need of a ride, and she had a perfectly rational reason for buying newborn size diapers.

Taylor stood outside the shop, hugging her guests again, except Zoe, who was already in her car. Taylor thanked them all for the wonderful surprise. Tomorrow, she needed to stop and get something for the office; perhaps she'd bring a coffee cake.

Jules hopped on his scooter and drove away first. Becca returned to the shop to lock up. Nicki, Charlotte, and Lindi waved her away, calling their goodbyes.

She smiled all the way home. Once in the garage, she called Seth, telling him all about the party. She didn't quite finish when he had to cut her off. But it didn't matter. She was thrilled. Floating on a cloud and so warm inside.

People weren't all plotting, scheming jerks. Well, they had been scheming, but in the best possible way.

Taylor left the gifts in the rear seat, but at the entrance to the house, Zoe, Jules, and Becca greeted her and effortlessly brought all the gifts upstairs to her room, putting them in the empty crib.

Back in the kitchen, Jules whipped up a dinner of spaghetti with a Bolognese sauce big enough for all of them, except Zoe, who had whole wheat pasta, organic sauce, and vegan cheese. The meal tasted like heaven and Taylor finally saw that she'd been holding these three at arm's length, when they were really lovely people. Thoughtful. Kind.

"I can't thank you all enough for today."

Becca reached across the space that separated them and gave her hand a squeeze.

"You deserve it," said Zoe, smiling.

Taylor finished the last of the spaghetti on her plate, feeling full and happier than she had been in weeks. Some of the stress rolled off her shoulders. She could do this. Everything would work out.

"You know, I heard you two talking and, well, honestly it scared the wits out of me."

Jules' fork paused midway to his mouth.

Becca smile faltered. "What scared you?"

"About you two 'going through with it' and 'picking a date.'"

Jules lowered his fork. "What did you think we were talking about?"

THIRTY-ONE

Becca and Jules stared at her with matching rapt expressions, waiting for her answer. Now she felt so ashamed of suspecting they were up to some foul play. The entire thing was so preposterous and an uncomfortable reminder to her of the sort of outlandish accusations her mother would make.

Delusions. Paranoia. No, she was not her mother.

Taylor straightened.

"Taylor?" Becca coaxed. "What did you think we were planning?"

"I don't know," Taylor lied. "It's embarrassing."

"Ooh! Embarrassing," said Becca. "Spill."

"Something, I don't know, to do with the babies."

Jules scooped another portion of pasta into his mouth and then wiped the sauce from his beard.

"Ooh," said Becca. "Did you think we meant to steal them?" She grinned, clearly joking.

Taylor flushed. She had, actually.

"Some people would find the idea of taking on twins rather a nuisance," said Zoe. "I've been worried about the crying and the smell. But your room is at the far end of the hall, so I'm hopeful they won't disturb me."

All three of them stared at Zoe, frowning.

At the long silence, Zoe glanced up from her plate and lifted a hand. "What? Babies are noisy and troublesome."

Becca shook her head and cast Taylor an 'is she for real?' look. Taylor smiled.

"I suppose that's true." Taylor set aside her napkin.

The pause stretched.

"I'm sure my sleepwalking only made that worse. And that maternal protective instinct is just acting as it should. You were right. We were up to something. Becca should be a party planner. I just delivered the invites to your office. We didn't invite anyone from this neighborhood. Didn't seem like you've had enough time here to really settle in, make friends. You know?"

She nodded. That made sense.

"You sleepwalk?" Zoe had her hand at her collar again, tugging at the edges of her blouse.

"Yeah," said Becca. "He does."

"Around the house?" asked Zoe.

"He can't get into your room. So relax," said Becca.

"I'm glad you could make it to the party, Zoe," said Jules, changing the subject.

"I'm not much for parties," said Zoe. "I like people, but they just... well, objects of art, my acquisitions, they are more predictable. Introverted, my dad used to say. Maybe you're like that, too, Taylor."

The reasons Taylor was closed off and constantly wary were too complicated to get into with them. She was more suspicious than introverted but she went with it.

"Introvert. Yeah. I think so," said Taylor. "Also, an only child. Makes it harder. I was alone a lot."

"I prefer that," mumbled Zoe.

Jules nodded. "And here we are encroaching on your space."

"Plenty of space here," Taylor said. And she was determined to keep every square foot. She could already see the playset in the yard that Seth and she would build once her ankles no longer looked like mush melons.

She yawned. "Oh, I'm sorry. My energy level has been just flatlining lately."

"Your body is busy. You need more rest. It's normal," said Jules.

How did he know so much about pregnancy?

Taylor tamped down her suspicions. They were not kind, especially after all these three had done for her, when they barely knew her.

So why do something so elaborate? How did they even pull that together so fast? And when had they started? Was it before or after she'd overheard that conversation?

That tiny suspicious voice popped up another conspiracy theory. Couldn't that baby shower have been an extremely effective way to divert her suspicions about the disturbing conversation she'd overheard?

Stop it.

But really. What if...

"You okay, Taylor?" asked Becca.

She shook off that line of thinking. "Yes. Let me help you clean up."

Becca sprang to her feet with the agility of a gazelle. She waved her hand and then collected Taylor's plate.

"Absolutely not." Halfway to the kitchen sink, she stopped and turned toward Jules. "We should have a family dinner every week. Next Friday. Okay?"

Taylor shrugged. Jules was more enthusiastic.

"Sounds great!"

"You all like tacos?" Becca asked.

"I can make my own," said Zoe. "But I'd be happy to eat with you all. I have no plans."

Taylor thought it was sad that Zoe was free on Friday night, but held her smile. It was different for Becca and Jules. They'd found someone. But her single boarder was so odd, Taylor feared she never would. Of course, that was assuming Zoe wanted a relationship.

"Friday, taco night," said Jules and laughed. "Perfect."

Satisfied, Becca continued clearing the table with Jules' help.

Zoe remained seated, her gaze on Jules and Becca, who were now loading the dishwasher. Then she leaned in conspiratorially, lowering her voice.

"I ran into your mother today. She came by to preview the exhibit before the private opening. When I mentioned that I was one of your new tenants, she seemed, well, frankly, shocked."

Taylor set her teeth but said nothing.

"She told me she was unaware that you were struggling financially, as you must be to open your home to... strangers. Yes, that's the word she used."

"Did she?"

"Yes. Well, I hope I wasn't speaking out of turn. I assumed she would know."

"Did you?" Taylor's face felt frozen in a mask of placid calm while inside her heart was thumping and her hands were damp.

"She confided about your struggles at school and the troubles you had as a teen."

Taylor broke eye contact, now wondering exactly what lies her mother had spun.

"I was miffed to hear that you have broken all ties with her. She was very upset, in tears, actually, she's just beside herself."

"I see."

"It really isn't my place. But Taylor, do you think perhaps

you need to mend fences? It's rather childish to hold her grandson hostage, especially when she's so anxious to be a grandmother."

"Her grandson... Is that what she said?"

"Yes. I believe so. Oh, but wait, you're having twins." Zoe now looked confused at how a grandmother could forget that little detail. "That can't be right."

Becca appeared at Zoe's side. "Can I take that?" she asked, motioning to Zoe's plate.

"Oh, that's not necessary."

Zoe rose, seemingly in a hurry to make her exit. She cleared her own dishes.

Taylor seethed at her mother for managing to still have her tentacles in her business and for turning the situation to put Taylor in the worst possible light.

She got up and paused in the door to the kitchen. "I'm going to head up to bed. Thank you all again, for today."

Her bladder seemed less and less reliable each day.

She hurried upstairs to her room, flipping the door lock on her way in. When she finished in the bathroom, her feet hurt and her back ached. So, she changed into her pajamas and switched on the television, but her brain kept replaying the conversation with Zoe about her mother and her hurt feelings.

How could she?

An unflattering thought struck again. Did her mother encourage Zoe to apply as a boarder specifically to have eyes and ears in Taylor's house?

No, that was too farfetched. And it went right back to the narcissistic thinking that everything that happened centered on Taylor.

"Just because you're paranoid, doesn't mean they're not out to get you," she said, repeating the quote she'd seen on a T-shirt.

Finally, Taylor's gaze flicked to the crib, now filled with gifts.

The tugging at her heart was so unfamiliar. She was not used to people being thoughtful and dear. Her chest hurt and she struggled not to cry. She was crying all the time now. Happy or sad, frustrated or for no apparent reason. It was exhausting.

From beyond the door, she heard a television coming on. Taylor crawled under the covers just after eight in the evening. She had no chance of sleeping through the night, but she could barely keep her eyes open.

She sent Seth a goodnight text, feeling slightly guilty that she had both a bed and several hours to rest. She pictured him sleeping sitting up in the doctors' lounge, with his forehead resting on his folded arms or on a bunkbed like a teenager at sleepaway camp.

Just as she was dozing, her father called. She considered letting it go to voicemail, but some intuition had her picking up.

"Hi Daddy," she said, as if she were still seven.

But she was not prepared for the bombshell he dropped on her.

"Your mother has left me. She's gone to a hotel and is not taking my calls."

"What? When did this happen?"

"Today. I need you to call her. Talk some sense into her or at least find out where she is."

"Okay, I'm calling now."

"Call me right back."

She hung up, heart now racing and feeling fluttery and discombobulated. But she placed the call to her mother who picked up.

Unfortunately, her mother was in her jumping jitters and no amount of talking could convince her to go home. She did figure out the hotel and texted that information to her father.

As she finally stretched out in bed, she hoped that she and Seth could do a better job parenting than her own parents had done.

The last thing she did before dozing was check her phone for a goodnight message from Seth, but there was nothing.

Taylor wanted to tell him about her parents' latest drama, but it would have to wait.

She sent him a few emojis and set the phone aside.

Sometime in the night, she woke to an unfamiliar thud, like something large falling from a shelf. She sat up listening for a long time. What was going on out there?

THIRTY-TWO

Taylor listened in the dark. There was a thump, like something above her in the attic.

She cocked her head, heart pounding and body rigid. That sounded too big for Moon. Had some animal gotten in up there? A fruit rat or raccoon, perhaps. They'd had a possum build a nest in the boathouse once.

Someone ran down the hall.

Taylor eased out of bed and crept to the door. When she opened it, she found Jules standing at the end of the hallway at Zoe's open door.

"Jules? Is everything all right?" she asked.

He didn't answer. Just stood there. He turned and walked silently past her, his eyes wide open.

Sleepwalking?

She followed him as he descended the stairs in the pre-dawn hours of Friday morning. He seemed not to notice her as he headed for the kitchen, opened the refrigerator, and then a drawer. He withdrew a dish towel and slung it over his shoulder. Then circled the kitchen island three times before returning to the stairs, now carrying a dish towel in one limp hand.

At the upstairs landing, he went back in his room and closed the door.

"That is so odd," she said to no one.

She stared at Zoe's open door and then headed that way. Taylor lifted her hand to knock but she paused, not wanting to wake her.

"Zoe?" she whispered.

Her reply was croaky, as if she had just woken up. "Yes?"

"You okay?"

"Yes. Why?" The reply came from just inside the door, as if the woman was standing in the dark, just out of sight.

"Your door is open."

"Because I heard something. Did you see Jules?" Zoe sounded as if she had a cold, her voice an odd rasp. Or was that fear?

"I did. He was sleepwalking again."

"Okay."

Taylor headed back to bed. She had just fallen into a deep slumber when she felt dragged from sleep again.

Beyond her window, the world was still dark.

What had woken her this time?

Now she recalled Jules' sleepwalking and then speaking to Zoe.

Taylor crept to her door and released the lock. Then, as quietly as possible, she inched open the door to peer out.

The hallway was empty.

What time was it?

Taylor returned to the bedside table for her phone and discovered it was four-twenty in the morning. Likely she'd just heard Jules getting ready for work.

She thought that after this much time the sound of people coming and going up and down the stairs at all hours would not be so troublesome. But last night had been worse than usual. Or perhaps her pregnancy made her so uncomfortable that she never really was deeply asleep.

Not much longer now, thank heaven.

Though she tried, she could not fall back to sleep. Finally, she gave up, slipped on a robe, and headed downstairs.

She found the kitchen lights on and Jules, bleary-eyed and his hair wet from the shower, as he made himself a cup of coffee.

He hesitated a moment when he saw the kitchen illuminated and Taylor sitting at the counter.

"Good morning," he said, his voice a little creaky from sleep. "You're up early. Everything all right?"

"I'm not sure. You were sleepwalking again last night."

"Was I?"

"Took one of my dishtowels."

"I wondered how that got in our room." He headed to the coffee maker and went to work.

"Did you hear anyone bumping around or moving stuff last night?"

"When?"

"I'm not sure."

He thought about that and shook his head. "I don't think so. Not Becca. Could have been me. But maybe it was Zoe. I got up to use the bathroom and saw the light on in her room. It was pretty late."

"Hmm." She thought about that. To her knowledge, Zoe did not bump around at night. She was extremely quiet to the point Taylor often forgot she was here.

"You want me to check on her?"

"Too early," said Taylor.

She pushed to her feet and headed to the entrance. From the foyer she flicked on the floodlights above the garage and found only Becca's car in the drive. Zoe's car was gone.

"Where's her car?" she asked.

"Whose?" Jules came to stand beside her and peered out. "Not there."

Taylor could see that. But where had she gone?

"Some kind of family emergency?" he asked. "Maybe working on that exhibition or another chess thingy, a tournament?" He pulled out his phone. "Let me text Becca. Have her check upstairs."

"Oh, don't bother her. I can do it."

Jules held his phone out. "You sure?"

"Yeah. I'll be right back." Taylor slowly climbed the stairs. She paused at the two identical doors at the end of the hall. Jules and Becca's room on the left and Zoe's on the right. She lifted her hand and tapped, hoping not to wake Becca.

There was no answer. She tried again and whispered, "Zoe? Are you awake?" Taylor figured Zoe would not be in there if her car was gone. But still she waited a reasonable amount of time before trying the latch. The door swung open.

The light from the hallway illuminated enough for Taylor to see that her bed was made and the room empty.

Taylor flicked on the light and stepped inside, checking the closet and dresser.

Not only was the room empty, Zoe had packed all her things. The tinfoil was gone from the outlets and the tape had all been removed as had the slide lock. It seemed her tenant had left without a word.

This was so odd.

Had Zoe skipped out on paying the rent? That was crazy. Taylor knew where she worked, for heaven's sakes.

She retrieved her phone and sent Zoe a text asking where she was and what was happening.

The answer came before she'd returned to her room.

I've found a place closer to the museum. Keep the deposit.

Taylor tapped out her reply.

Why didn't you tell me last night?

Didn't want to spoil the mood. Apologies

Taylor returned to the kitchen.

"Is she up there?" asked Jules.

"No. And her room is empty."

"What do you mean, empty?" he asked.

"She's moved out."

"Did she tell you?"

"No. But she answered my text. This is so odd."

He snorted. "Can't be any odder than she is. Listen, can you get someone, you know, kind of normal for her room? I was afraid to cough or fart, because she might come pounding on our door telling us to keep it down."

"Did she do that?"

"Oh, yeah."

"I'm sorry. You should have told me."

"You've got enough to deal with. Besides, I've lived with worse." He retrieved his mug and lifted another. "Coffee? I can make decaf."

"No thanks. I'm going to text Seth and then I need to get going."

"Okay. See you later." Jules gathered his things for work.

She stared at the microwave clock. Then she opened the refrigerator to see Zoe's shelf empty.

Taylor was back upstairs when she wondered if she should list Zoe's room again and if the HOA would see the post. How was she going to explain a new cousin and the disappearance of the old one to the two nosy neighbors?

She knew Zoe didn't like confrontation. Leaving without a

word fit her personality exactly. But confronting Jules with a noise complaint did not.

Something about that didn't sit right. Taylor finished showering and headed for her closet, wrapped in a towel. Should she grill Jules again about Zoe or call Zoe first? She dropped the towel and quickly dressed, remembering she needed to leave in time to stop at a bakery for a coffee cake for the office. Taylor groaned.

Then she heard something or someone in the hall.

For reasons she couldn't quite grasp, the sound made her stiffen and still as she listened.

Someone was outside her door.

The unfamiliar noise came again. Taylor crept from her bathroom into her bedroom, staring in the direction of the clatter.

Someone was rattling her doorknob. Taylor could now see the knob rotating. What the heck was going on? Should she call out? Ask who was there?

She lifted her phone, preparing to call for help, and then remembered the bear spray.

Baby shower or no baby shower, she was blasting whoever stepped through that door.

"Taylor?" The voice was hushed but familiar.

"Seth?"

She hurried to the door, still holding the bear spray.

"Seth, is that you?"

"Yes." His voice was normal now. No longer whispering.

"What are you doing home?"

"Let me in."

THIRTY-THREE

Taylor released the door lock, and he swept in, scooping her up in his arms and pressing his face into the nape of her neck, as he did when upset.

He squeezed her a little too tightly as the wave of nausea from her fear receded. Weak-kneed and dizzy, she clung. His panicky grip only increased her fear.

"What's wrong?" she asked.

Seth was shaking when she drew back. Seeing her husband so obviously upset set all her alarms ringing.

Seth was peering out at the reserve. He dropped the blind. Taylor took another step forward and accidentally bumped into the bureau, causing something on the top to roll into the ceramic dish where she kept her wedding ring, now that her fingers were so swollen she could not wear it.

"Seth, what are you doing here? You said you couldn't come home."

"Did you see Jules downstairs?" he asked.

"I spoke to him a little while ago. Zoe left last night."

"What do you mean, left?"

"Packed up and moved out."

Seth swayed. "She's one of them. Must be. Oh, God." His gaze lifted to the ceiling for a moment and then flashed back to her. "We have to go. Right now. Before they come. They already know where to find us. They could be here already."

He was pacing, nearly running, to the master closet then hurrying back to the window. She'd never seen him like this. It was terrifying.

"Seth! Stop it. Tell me exactly what you think is happening."

He paused and stared at her, tears welling in his eyes.

"Seth. Tell me right now," she demanded.

The muscles at Seth's jaw bunched but he said nothing. A strangling sound came from his throat as if he was unable to speak past the fear.

"What is happening that has you so freaked out?"

"Get your things together." He had her elbow now and was hustling her toward their closet.

"What things?"

Something was happening. Seth understood it and he wouldn't tell her. If living with her mother had taught her anything, it was how to perceive danger.

She resisted his insistent tugging. "Where are we going?"

"You're going. Visit a friend. Stay there awhile."

"What! I can't do that. I'm having a C-section in six days! And I need to be near the birthing center and my nurse practitioner in case I go into labor."

"*Please* Taylor, just until I know it's safe."

She flicked on the light between the closet and master bathroom. "Safe from what exactly?"

He ignored her question, rambling now. Jabbering in a hysterical clatter that set her teeth on edge.

"What about someone from work? You'd be close by." He snapped his fingers as if coming up with the answer. "That one with all the cats."

"Nicki? Why?"

"Because I have to go back to the hospital, and I don't want you here alone."

"I'm not alone."

Seth glanced toward the open door and the hallway.

"We don't really know them."

"Odd, I'm beginning to feel the same way about you."

"Taylor, that's not funny." His voice held aggravation and a hint of desperation. He was afraid. Of what?

His obvious concern amplified her unease, acting like a reverb pedal on an electric guitar.

"I don't want you here with them. I don't trust them."

Neither did she but she was now very curious as to why he didn't either.

"Why not?"

"I'd feel better if you came back with me. We'll tell them that they have to make other arrangements. And you can stay with me in Orlando."

"You have a place?"

"We'll get an Airbnb for now."

This entire conversation was so surreal. She felt like Alice, stepping through the looking glass.

"Or we could just get in the car and drive."

"You'll lose the residency."

"It's not important."

He'd killed himself to get through medical school. This was his dream. Now it wasn't important? Something was very, very wrong. Her pulse fluttered and she suddenly felt faint.

"What's going to happen if you don't go back?"

He dragged both hands through his hair. Then he reached, pulling her in, resting his forehead on hers. "I love you, Taylor."

"Seth... please! Tell me what's happening."

"I just want you safe."

"If you want me to feel safe, tell me what's going on."

Seth sucked in a breath, blew it away, and then nodded. "Yes. I'll tell you. You should know. Then you'll understand why we have to leave."

He took her hand and drew her to the bed, where they settled facing each other, him with one foot tucked under the opposite knee and her seated cross-legged, her body tight as a bowstring.

"You remember that night you picked us up on that road outside Telluride?"

"Of course."

"We weren't leaving a job. We were running." His voice was an anxious rasp. "But I think they found us."

"Seth, honey, who found us? What are you talking about?"

"They told him. He's coming."

She'd never seen him like this. Crazy-scared and trembling. His upset acted like a lightning strike to dead wood. She grasped his hand to ground her from the panic that jolted through her. Her teeth were chattering, and her entire body felt as if she'd been dipped in an ice bath.

It was suddenly freezing in here.

Seth shot to his feet and stood at the window beyond the crib, staring out at the backyard.

"Honey? You're scaring me. Who do you think is out there?"

He turned and, even in the gray light, she could see his face was ashen.

"You're acting as if the FBI is about to raid our house. As if we're some radical extremist group or something. Whatever it is, you can tell me."

She hurried to him, standing like a sentinel at the window.

When he spoke, his words bore an unfamiliar high-pitched frantic quality she had never heard before.

"My father," said Seth "He's coming for us."

THIRTY-FOUR

"Rubin and Nathan wouldn't answer my calls. So I went over there. I've been watching Gina's apartment since last night. And I just saw them. I saw them all!"

"Seth, slow down. You still aren't making any sense."

The sight of him coming to pieces caused her insides to quake. Her throat tightened as she took hold of his face in both hands and turned his gaze from the bedroom window to her.

"Look at me."

He did.

"Now explain what is happening."

"We aren't just friends. Do you understand? They're brothers."

"Nathan and Rubin?"

"Yes! And I'm their cousin."

"What?" Her hands slipped from the rough stubble on his jaw and her brow knit as she took in this new detail. It was a large oversight. No, an intentional deception because they didn't want her to know. But why?

His friends did look very similar. Similar enough to be brothers. Close in age, with Nathan a year or two younger than

Rubin. And Seth had a similar hair color but a very different body type, more athletic and less gangly. And neither had eyes like he did.

"Nathan and Rubin are brothers?"

He nodded. "We all lived up on the ranch. But it's not *just* a ranch. It's worse. It's so much worse. When we got the chance, we ran. They tried to get Matthew out, too, but they couldn't. We couldn't find him, and we had to go. So they left him behind."

What was he talking about?

She didn't interrupt, just gripped his quaking hand and bloodless fingers as they sat in the gray pre-dawn light.

"Who is Matthew?"

"Their younger brother. He was seven when we left him. But he'd be twelve now. About that, I think. We don't have birthdays. Just, you know, the big one, Christmas."

"So they left him. Is that right?" asked Taylor, trying to catch up.

"Yes! You saw him. The boy in the window. That's when I first suspected. You reminded me that Gina doesn't have a nephew so I wondered, who was he and why would she lie about it?"

"Could it be someone who looked like him? You haven't seen the boy in years. Gina might be babysitting?"

"Then why not say that? Why say he was her nephew? She lied to us." Seth raked both hands through his hair and gripped them there, elbows out as if trying to hold his head on his shoulders. "It's Matthew. He's missing a finger on his left hand. The index finger. I saw him. I'm positive. That means they got him out."

"That's good. Isn't it?"

"No. Because my uncle wouldn't let him go. No way, not with both his other sons gone. They'd have to give them something they wanted badly enough to give up the boy."

"Like what?" As she said it, Taylor knew she was not going to like the answer.

Seth dropped his gaze.

"Like me."

"You. Is your father planning on forcing you back?"

"Worse, I think."

"Tell me everything you can about them, so I can understand what you think is happening."

Seth folded back to the bed, shoulders rounded in defeat.

"We weren't just working on a sheep farm up in those mountains," said Seth. His brow was tented in worry, and he worked his hands as if trying to scrub some invisible stain from his palms.

"I suspected that," said Taylor.

His thick brows lifted. "Really?" He swiped a broad palm over his mouth. Finally, he continued. "I was raised on that mountain. But it's more of a compound than a ranch."

"A compound?" She didn't like the sound of that. She folded her hands together and pressed them to her lap. Listening.

"Yeah. I guess you'd call us preppers or a survivalist group. My father was born there. My great-grandfather bought the land during the Cuban Missile Crisis, you know? In the 1960s? After the September 11 attacks, my grandfather and father began recruiting people. They started a newsletter, then a radio show, which is still going. But my dad added a podcast. He was my grandfather's second son and I'm his, which is really important to my family."

"And they got recruits?"

"Some people, a few, showed up. Like-minded folks."

Taylor's frown deepened. "All right. How many are we talking about?"

"Maybe two dozen including my uncles and their families

and maybe ten or so are new arrivals. I don't know because I've been gone so long."

"What are they prepping for?"

"Armageddon. Christ's second coming. The end of the world. Civil unrest. Invasion by armies of immigrants. Lately they've been focusing on the threat of nuclear attack by China launched from Cuba, again."

"So basically, everything."

"Yes." This he delivered on an exhalation of breath.

"All right. So how many people listen to this podcast?"

"It has over nine thousand followers."

She tugged on her bottom lip, unsure where this was going.

"I was born there, on the mountain. My dad and Pops, that's my grandfather, filled my head with all the dangers out here in the world. When my older brother ran off, I began to doubt them. Question what they were telling us. You know?"

"That was wise."

"Yeah, well, I wanted to see for myself. I trained as a medic, up there with what emergency guides they had, but I knew they were dated."

She tried to picture that—him up on the mountain with some old, tattered army field guide on triage.

"The night you picked us up, we were running from them."

"Running? From your family?" Ironic, as she had done the same. "Couldn't you just leave?"

"No. You can't ever leave. Our family is very religious, very clannish, and, looking back on them from out here, pretty crazy. Rubin and Nathan are my first cousins. Both are my father's sister's boys. Anyway, we all left, together. We thought that if we went all at once, we'd have a better chance. Rubin was a tracker. He knew their routine."

"You mean like a hunter?"

"No, not like hunters. Once you come of age, once you take

the oath, you can't leave. If you do, they send the trackers after you."

She straightened. "What? What do you mean? You were a prisoner?"

"Yes, sort of."

"I can't believe you hid this from me."

"I'm so sorry. We thought, if we went far enough, if we eliminated all contact between us and them... But Rubin and Nathan went back. Must have. They'd never know where to look otherwise. And the night we left, they planned to grab Matthew from the children's compound, but we must have tipped them off somehow, because he wasn't there. Rubin looked everywhere and that triggered some alarm. We ran. They nearly caught us."

"To that road where I found you?" Her tone had taken on a hysterical note.

She moved her hands to her aching lower back; the throbbing muscles seemed to be in a constant state of spasm. She shifted and heard something in her lower back pop, easing the discomfort.

Taylor shook her head. She'd known something was off, even suspected they were running. She'd been running too, and it takes one to know one. But she thought it was from the cops or something more... normal.

"So what do they do, keep you locked up?"

He broke eye contact and looked away.

"It's worse than that."

She reached out and touched his hand, now bunched in a fist. He startled.

"We're recruits. You understand? It's an army. A survivalist army destined to live through the apocalypse. My father's people believe they're chosen. Special."

Special, all right, she thought, but said nothing.

"They believe it with everything they've got. And they also

believe that keeping off the grid is vital to their existence. If outsiders know about us, it puts us all at risk. The ones who we fear, we believe they'll find us. Hunt us down. Or stragglers who survive the attack will attack us for our supplies."

"You said 'us'."

"Yes. I mean we were a part of them. They're our kin."

"And they all hid up in that mountain pass? They never leave?"

"Just for necessary supplies. And that is always with an elder, like Pops or my father."

"Where do they get the money to live up there?"

"Ad revenue from the podcast. And... other things."

She snorted at this. "So they have Wi-Fi?"

"Not at the compound. Location of the internet connection is secret. I don't know where they broadcast from."

"And only the elders leave?"

"Mostly. There's one exception. Young men are allowed to leave for up to six months, only to find a wife. But they have to come back. And they know that if Armageddon happens while they are gone, they won't be allowed back in. So, most of my uncles took less time than that."

"How do you get a woman in less than six months?"

THIRTY-FIVE

Taylor's question hung in the air. The longer she waited to learn how men from his family managed to 'find a wife' in only a few months, the longer he delayed, the more anxious she got.

"Seth? How do they find a wife? You're not suggesting... They come of their own free will, don't they?"

His face was grim.

"Sometimes they come willingly," Seth said.

"Are you talking about kidnapping?"

He could no longer meet her gaze.

"Yes," he admitted, head hanging.

She felt physically sick.

Human trafficking, she realized, her throat now tight with the bitter combination of fear and disgust. Who was this man she had married?

Taylor's ears buzzed as she grappled to comprehend what Seth was telling her. She knew his family was strict, rural, isolated. But it was much worse – he grew up in a fundamentalist, prepper community.

He shifted in place, clearly uncomfortable. "They think they're saving their brides from certain death."

She pressed her hands together, clasping them tight. "Being a deluded, religious fanatic doesn't make it legal."

"I know. But I was raised that way. I didn't question it." He looked miserable.

"Don't they try to escape?"

He gave a slow nod and dropped his gaze again. "Some did. Most are indoctrinated. Think they've been liberated."

"Brainwashed," she said. Stockholm syndrome, she thought. "What about your female cousins? Are they kidnapping husbands?"

He snorted. "Of course not."

Taylor frowned, confused once again. "Then what do they do? Never marry?"

He grimaced. "One made that choice. But it's discouraged. The others, they just leave for up to six months and come back..." He couldn't seem to meet her gaze.

"Back what?"

"Pregnant. They leave to get with child and then come back alone to raise them."

"Oh my God." She couldn't believe this. All of it was so warped.

"But since my brother ran off, the elders refused to let me go."

"Why?"

"I'm... It's hard to explain."

"Seth, if you're in danger, if we both are. I need to know everything."

He nodded. "I wanted out. I wanted to go to medical school. But it just wasn't possible. So I made a plan to run. Nathan and Rubin found out. They wanted to run, too, and bring Matthew."

Taylor's body went cold.

"But when they tried to get their brother, things went sideways. They lost the truck, and we ran on foot."

"To the road where I found you."

He dropped his gaze and nodded again.

"But once we got out, once they saw how things were..." Seth threw up his hands. "Our elders lied to us. Everything they said about our mission and the threat. It's just bullshit. That's why they set a time limit. Up until we turn twenty, we can leave for six months. Longer than that and you might have time to start thinking for yourself."

She hadn't realized Rubin and Nathan were so young.

"You were over twenty."

"Because I wasn't allowed to leave to take a wife."

"What do you mean?"

"I had to choose from within the compound, because of my position as the son of our reverend father."

"But you've taken a wife."

"You're not from the compound."

The chill shook her again. "So?"

"They won't recognize our marriage."

"What do you think they will do? Chase you?"

He didn't chuckle or deny. He just stared at her with those stunning bi-colored eyes, now filling with tears.

"We're recruits. It's an army. My dad and his brothers, they've become more paranoid. And I'm the second son of the second son," he said. "That makes it even worse that I left. A complete betrayal."

"What will they do?"

"You know what the punishment for desertion in the army is?"

"Imprisonment and dishonorable discharge?"

He shook his head. "Deserters are executed."

"What do you mean? They kill them?" Taylor's mouth was so dry, and she was freezing, so she rubbed her upper arms in a vain attempt to warm up. Impossible. The cold was coming from inside herself. Cold horror at what he was telling her.

He nodded. "Every time."

"Seth, if Rubin got his brother, that means…" She couldn't even finish the sentence. Her mind was reeling. Her face felt numb. "What did they do?"

He was shaking his head again. "Rubin was out there. He and Nathan both. Once you saw that boy at Gina's, I called her father. He confirmed that Rubin and Nathan had made two runs to Denver. I think they might have contacted my father and cut a deal."

"What kind of deal?"

"A pardon and their little brother in exchange for my location."

The pieces were falling into place. Rubin and Nathan had traded their lives and that of their brother's for Seth's.

She grabbed hold of his shirt and pulled.

"Are they sending someone to kill you?"

"I can't be sure. But I think so."

She scooted off the bed, heaving herself to her feet before him. "Then you have to go. You have to leave right now."

Taylor grabbed his hand and pulled. He didn't move.

"Seth, you are scaring the wits out of me."

He squeezed her hand. Tugged her forward. "I know. I'm sorry, Taylor."

"This is crazy!"

His expression was earnest and his face pale.

"So, your father is hunting you and he might have sent others to kill you."

He nodded.

"But if they're here, they could have done that already," she said, pointing out the obvious.

"Yes. It gives me hope," he said, not looking hopeful at all. "They might be here to bring me back to be judged and chastened."

It occurred to her that his parents were more screwed up than hers.

"Why didn't you tell me any of this?" Taylor struggled to keep her voice down as panic and exasperation merged.

Seth's head dropped forward, seeming ashamed. "I should have. But I didn't want to worry you, freak you out, and when you got pregnant, it wasn't planned. We were using protection to avoid having kids just yet."

That was true. This pregnancy had surprised them both.

Her husband scrubbed his face with his hands. "When I told you I wanted to finish my residency before we started a family, it was a lie."

Taylor's breath caught.

"The truth is, I wanted to be certain that I'd escaped them and we were safe."

"And you trusted your cousins." The rage at Nathan and Rubin's betrayal burned bright inside her chest and she locked her teeth tight.

"I did. Yes."

"Has anyone ever escaped your family?"

"I don't know." He thought about this a moment, his gaze cast up to the tray ceiling. "My brother maybe. It's possible they just lied to us. They always report the kills."

Taylor's scalp tightened as the ramifications of this detail shuttered through her.

He noticed her panic and hurried to add, "But they might make that up. I mean, some of them must have gotten away. But few try."

"Why not?" Taylor braced for his answer.

"My father, he's very charismatic."

Most cult leaders were.

"They feel safe there. Believe the end is coming and they are chosen."

"What does he look like?" she asked.

"My father?"

She nodded and Seth drew out his phone and began tapping. Then he reversed the screen showing her a mug shot of a man with bi-colored eyes and a stony expression. Taylor's scalp tingled as she recognized the man from the hospital waiting room. The one who had asked about her babies and then showed up while she was shopping.

"This is about ten years ago. He's sixty now."

"He's here. I saw him." Taylor struggled with her breathing as her heart pounded painfully in her chest.

Seth straightened, bracing. "You saw him?"

"He was wearing glasses. So I couldn't see his eyes. But yes. That's him."

She told him everything as her husband's face went pale.

"We have to leave," he whispered in a voice that lifted the hairs on her neck.

"Yes."

She was shivering now, as if the bedroom had turned into a refrigerator car.

"He was following me. So he must know my name. Where we live," she said, pushing the panic down and thinking of the shadowy figure she'd seen watching their home.

"Let's go," he said, standing.

How could he just leave everything behind? How could she?

"But you're schooling. The residency."

"Can't finish if I'm dead."

The calm with which he delivered this observation made her breath catch. One look told her how deadly serious he was and how grave their situation.

"But we're both going?" she clarified.

Seth dragged her into his arms. "Of course. I'm going to protect you and our babies with everything I have."

"What about the house? Our boarders?"

Seth drew back and his eyes rounded.

"It's Zoe," he said.

"She's one of them?" Taylor had had suspicions about her odd behavior. Growing up on the mountain could explain her social ineptitude. And she'd been sneaking around in their bedroom, had stolen that hairclip. Creeping around at night. Had she let Seth's father into their house?

"Oh, God," whispered Taylor. Then the doubts rose in her mind. "But she's been here, working here in Tampa for a long time."

"According to her?" asked Seth.

She paused and thought about that. "Yeah, right. I only have her word."

Taylor recalled their first meeting in the museum, how Zoe had greeted them in the reception area, telling the admissions worker that she and Seth were her guests. She could have been just a visitor who paid their admission. And they'd never even seen her office. Did she even work at that museum? Or know Taylor's mother? All the references Taylor had checked might have been fabricated.

Now she was angry, and her voice rose. "God! I'm so stupid."

"Plus, you said she packed up and left last night," he added. "That could mean she's one of them and the others are close."

"What about Jules and Becca?"

"Becca seems too comfortable out here in the world. Tech savvy and she knows how to drive. And I've never seen either Becca or Jules at the compound."

"Do all the members of your community live in the same place?"

"It's not a community. It's my family. My father, his sister and two brothers, his brother's wives, and their children. My cousins. You understand? Nearly every one of them is a relative."

"You said you take recruits," she reminded him.

"A few men and only after a long vetting process. They don't even see the compound unless they marry into the family."

"What about the wives?"

"Their vetting is... shorter."

Taylor paused, scowling at that information. "Have you been to wherever the recruits stay?"

He shook his head. "No. Never."

Then he hadn't seen them. Wouldn't recognize them.

Taylor thought of what she'd overheard, and all Seth had just revealed.

"Taylor, we have to leave. Leave everything. Even the cars. Especially the cars. It's our only chance."

She believed him, but some part of her was desperate to hang on. To fight this. "Can't we stop them? Turn them into the FBI or homeland security or something?"

"I can't."

"Why not?"

"They're my family. My sisters. My mom." The forlorn expression on her husband's face broke her heart.

"You said they'll kill you!" Her words were too loud, and she clamped her hand over her mouth.

"Try to understand. They think the end of the world is coming and they're saving their people. And now they know about you."

The furrows in his brow deepened.

"What will they do? About me, I mean?"

He shook his head. She longed for reassurances, but he offered none.

"I don't know." Finally, he added, "I think it will make them more dangerous. Taylor, we have to go right now."

THIRTY-SIX

All those warning signs that she'd tried to ignore. The sense of being watched. The shadows moving around their house. Zoe creeping around in her bedroom. Taylor checked their references, but now wondered who she had spoken to when calling the list of former employers. Did Zoe even work at the museum? Was Jules a postman? Shock rippled through her as she realized she knew for certain only where Becca worked and only because her shower was at the coffee shop.

Seth left her to duck into his closet, returning with a pistol.

"What's that?" Taylor screeched.

"It's for our protection. They might try to stop us."

"How are we going to leave without a car?"

"We'll get to the airport, fly somewhere, and buy a vehicle there. Maybe an RV. We could live in that. Bring whatever you can sell or pawn."

"I already sold most of what I could to keep this place."

"Okay. I can hot wire something if I have to."

"What? This is crazy. I'm due to deliver next week. I need to be near my doctors."

"Trust me, Taylor, if we don't go right now, we won't be able to leave."

Seth grabbed her carry-on bag from the closet and tossed it on the bed.

Then he rushed around, hurriedly snatching up random clothing from the closet and throwing them on the bed. Meanwhile Taylor watched in shock, her fingers tingling and her ears buzzing.

"I've got to get our paperwork out of the safe downstairs," he said. "Get your things packed."

Taylor did as she was told. Was this even happening? There had to be some other way than to run. Wasn't there?

It felt as if she were moving underwater. Sound was muffled, movements were clumsy and slow. She couldn't get enough air.

She wasn't supposed to fly. She wasn't supposed to be more than a few miles from the birthing center. What if she went into labor at 30,000 feet?

Taylor glanced toward the carry-on bag, open on the bed amid the few items Seth had tossed on the coverlet. She felt suddenly frightened to have him out of her sight, so she hurried toward the door, already dreading descending and climbing the stairs. But she hustled out and then drew up short, her breath catching in her throat.

Jules stood in the hallway, just past the stairs, watching her with an intent gaze and downturned mouth.

"What's going on?" he asked. Why was he still here? It was past time he left for work. Unease rippled down her back. Did he see her trembling?

Was he working with Zoe?

"Nothing," she said, hoping he'd ignore the squeak in her voice. She was now desperate to get to her husband.

Jules silently watched her as Taylor hurried downstairs, gripping the railing to ensure she didn't fall.

She reached ground level as the prickling at her neck darted down her spine and jabbed at her stomach, making her breath catch. Her ears rang, drowning out all other sounds as tiny spots sparked in her vision.

Were Jules and Becca a part of this? She'd suspected it. Now, knowing what Seth had kept from her, she was beyond confused and way more frightened.

The fury splashed against the fear. No time for that now. If they were quick and lucky, she'd have a chance to be irate later. Right now, she had to get to Seth.

She glanced out into the drive and saw Becca's car, but she had not seen Becca. She must be here if her car was. Unless she'd taken Zoe's car.

Where was Becca and where was Zoe?

Not knowing was unnerving.

Taylor went searching for Seth.

She located him in the laundry room, crouching before the floor safe the previous owners had installed in the utility closet floor. Her husband hastily shoved files of taxes, identification, and insurances into a cardboard box.

Seth used his free hand to hood his eyes and his shoulders rounded, sagging.

Taylor stood, her skin flashing hot and cold as she fought off the dizziness. Somehow, she made it to the kitchen and a dinette chair before her knees gave way.

The front door opened and closed. A moment later Becca appeared holding a set of keys.

"What's going on?" she asked.

"Nothing. We're just trying to find some paperwork," said Taylor.

"Are you going somewhere?"

"No. Of course not." Taylor thought she sounded insincere and that her reply was a little too hasty. "Have you seen Zoe this morning?"

Becca shook her head, then chewed on her upper lip a moment, watching them.

"Where's Jules?" she asked.

"Upstairs," said Taylor, anxious to be rid of her.

Finally, she left, heading out of the kitchen in the direction of the living room. Taylor turned to follow her but Seth was there grabbing her by the elbow.

"Don't go upstairs," he said. His color was terrible. His face was gray, his eyes red, and there were pink blotches on his neck. The sight only added to her panic.

"Why?"

"What if my father sent them? After he saw you. He might have..."

Taylor's breathing came in desperate little pants as she wondered the same thing.

"Becca was outside," said Taylor. "I heard the door."

"Taylor, go get in your SUV. Lock the doors. I'll get our bags and meet you there."

She glanced toward the garage. "You said to leave the cars."

"No time. We have to go."

"Now?" she asked, her whisper rising with her panic.

"Yes. Right now."

Seth turned to go, and Taylor grabbed his arm.

"Don't," she begged. If it wasn't safe for her, it wasn't safe for him.

"I have to get our things."

"You'll be outnumbered."

"I have a gun. I'll be fine. Get in your vehicle. Now."

"No. Come with me!"

He hesitated, his expression grim. Then he nodded. "Okay."

Something flashed across the ceiling. Taylor glanced up. Another flash of red light darted from right to left. Then a blue light flared.

"Seth?" she said, her heart pounding in her throat so painfully, she could barely get the word out. "What's happening?"

He was closing the box, eyes down, but now he stared at the kitchen ceiling, mouth dropping open.

"Oh, no," he whispered.

The pounding on the door made them both jump.

From outside came a shout. "Police. Open the door."

"Seth?"

He released her and left the kitchen. Together they reached the living room. From there, Taylor saw both Becca and Jules peering over the railing from the overlook. Their expressions showed shock.

Jules called, "Taylor, what's going on?"

Seth was halfway to the door when Becca said, "Seth, there's something in Zoe's bathroom. I think... I think it's drugs or something."

Had Zoe set them up? Taylor wondered. Planted something incriminating and called the police?

Seth gaped up at the pair as the pounding came again.

"Police. Open the door."

Seth pressed a hand to his heart. "Oh, God."

"Taylor, what should we do?" asked Becca.

Seth had gone ghastly pale again. He grasped Taylor's shoulders. "Wait here. Don't open the door yet. I need time to..." He released Taylor, then charged up the stairs. The boarders stepped aside as he rushed along the walkover and out of sight.

The banging changed. It seemed the police were now trying to batter the door down.

Taylor did not stay put, but followed her husband at her top speed, which was a shuffling hustle favored by old people with brittle bones and very pregnant women.

She hurried toward her gaping tenants.

"Taylor?" asked Becca, her eyes wide and her voice trembling.

She didn't stop. Just rushed up to where the pair waited on the landing.

What had Zoe done?

At the top step, she paused long enough to see Becca pointing in the direction of Zoe's bathroom.

"He's in there," she said.

Taylor hurried to Zoe's side of the hallway.

"Seth?" she called, pushing open the bathroom door.

The noise from downstairs told her that the police were now inside. That was good, wasn't it? They could help them. Except she had not called them, and she didn't know why they were here.

"What are you doing?" she said as she crossed the threshold to find Seth hunched over the toilet, tearing at a firm packet of something white wrapped in plastic wrap and secured with gray duct tape.

"Taylor, get out of here," Seth shouted.

He was dumping the contents into the toilet and quickly flushed. But there was now powder on the toilet seat and the floor and on his hands.

"What is that?"

"I don't know. It was on the counter. Drugs. I think it's drugs."

"But that's not ours," she said, her voice all but deserting her.

Taylor glanced about the empty bathroom. The only thing in the pristine space was the packets of powder.

"It's in our house. Zoe must have done this," he said.

For just a fleeting moment, she considered that her husband might have been lying. That whatever was in that package, he knew about it. But she dismissed that. She believed Seth.

Despite his lie of omission, she believed him. Someone had set them up and they were in real danger.

"Stop it," she said. "That only makes you look guilty. Tell them the truth, that you don't know where this came from."

"They won't believe us. She called them. That's why they're here!"

"Seth! Stop!"

He didn't. Just kept trying to dispose of the drugs as he babbled. "Zoe's room. She did this."

Had she?

The pounding now sounded like someone running up the stairs.

Two police officers charged down the hall and rushed into the room, darting past her, as they seized Seth, yanked him from the floor, and ran him backwards across the room until all three were stopped by the wall beneath the textured glass window.

Her scream did not stop them from spinning her husband around. He struggled, which only made the two officers more forceful. Seth was not a small man or a weak one, but the pair eventually overpowered him, bringing him face down and folded at the waist over the counter and basin.

"Let go," he yelled as they kicked his legs out from under him, forcing him to the floor where he sprawled with two officers falling on top of him.

She rushed forward, pounding on one of the men's backs. He stopped her with one extended arm, driving her backwards and off balance. They handcuffed her husband as she collided loudly with the wall and towel rack, leaving an indentation in the Sheetrock.

"What are you doing?" she howled as they cinched the handcuffs on Seth's wrists.

"You stay right there," said the officer who'd shoved her.

This one had light brown skin and was short and broad with a thick neck supporting a head like a bowling ball. He had one hand on his Taser and so Taylor stilled and raised her hands in surrender.

"Do you have any weapons on you?" the bigger of the two officers restraining him asked Seth. The guy's bulging muscles flexed, showing the bluish ink of a tattoo mostly covered by the stretched sleeve of his polyester uniform. His hair was black, thick, and frozen in place by some hair product, resisting any movement as he manhandled her husband.

The gun, Taylor thought. Seth had a gun. Had he left it in the bedroom, or was it on him right now?

"Front pocket," Seth wheezed from between clenched teeth. Obviously, it was difficult to breathe with the man's partner kneeling on his back.

"Anything sharp in your pockets?" he asked as the two cops hauled Seth upright.

"You can't just barge in here," shouted Taylor.

"Ma'am, you need to step back," said the stocky cop with the shaved head that looked shiny as waxed fruit.

"You're in my house!" she bellowed. "You tell me why you broke in here," she shouted. "You tell me right now or I'll... I..."

Or what? said the voice in her head. Was she going to call the cops? Call her daddy?

The other cop retrieved the gun and held it for his partner to see, as if this was some proof of wrongdoing.

"Seth Parker?" asked the one now patting him down.

"Yes," he said.

"You are under arrest for possession."

"That's not mine!"

They weren't listening to his denials.

Taylor's support network had crumbled. She had only her husband, now handcuffed.

Once finished with his search, the cop grabbed Seth's arm and hustled him past Taylor and his partner. She followed as far as the landing. Down the stairs the two went and vanished out the door. The other officer had remained behind. With the evidence, she guessed.

"Why are you here?" she asked the cop, whose name badge reported he was Anderson.

"We got a call from a tenant here."

Why did Taylor's mind go to the fact that she wasn't allowed to have tenants in this neighborhood? This was not the reason they had forced their way into their home.

"I don't understand."

"The call was from Zoe Furr. She said your husband is armed and dangerous. And she witnessed narcotics sales at this address. She alleged she'd been threatened at gunpoint."

"That's ridiculous. My husband is a doctor."

As if that excluded him from all suspicion.

Anderson did not look impressed.

Oh, boy, was she going to get Zoe for this. And then it struck her. The woman had succeeded in getting Seth handcuffed and dragged from their home. The police were here to search their premises and Taylor was no longer sure what they might find. The anger dissolved in a sea of dread, cresting over her like a rogue wave, tugging her down. Floundering, she struggled to catch her breath as the police began their search.

What else would they find?

THIRTY-SEVEN

"Do you reside here?" Officer Anderson asked Taylor. They'd arrested Seth, ordered Becca and Jules downstairs, and moved her to the primary bedroom.

Anderson stood between her and the door.

"I'm his wife."

"Name?"

Taylor told him. He wrote it down.

"Going somewhere?" asked Anderson, nodding toward the open suitcase on the bed and the clothing dumped beside it like dirty laundry.

Taylor knew when to keep her mouth closed. This was one of those moments.

"We're going to have a look around," said Officer Anderson.

"You absolutely are not!" said Taylor. "I need to see a search warrant or something."

"A report of narcotics sales gives us the right to search these premises. Probable cause."

"That's just not true." She said this, knowing there was something powdery and white all over the bathroom down the hall.

Officer Anderson motioned to the door. "Downstairs," he said.

"I need my phone," she said, glancing toward the charger and phone beside her bed.

"No, you are going to wait downstairs as instructed or we'll arrest you, too."

"On what charge?"

"Obstruction. You're delaying my investigation, interfering with my ability to perform my job. You need me to go on?"

Taylor left her phone and slowly descended the stairs, sitting, as directed, on the shabby couch in the living room, stiff and frozen as an opossum facing a bobcat.

Meanwhile the detective directed his men to search, beginning with the upstairs.

This could not be happening.

A glance outside showed that the morning was rapidly turning to afternoon.

"Where are Jules and Becca?"

"The other couple is being interviewed in the family room."

Over the next two hours, law enforcement officers swarmed her house. Seth was gone and she was not permitted to retrieve her phone or leave the green leather couch in the living room except to use the powder room.

Taylor heard one of the officers report that the other bedrooms were 'clear'. Did that mean empty, empty of narcotics, or just empty of people?

"May I go upstairs?" she asked the female officer assigned to babysit her.

"I asked. You just sit tight."

Sit tight while they raided her home and arrested her husband, Taylor thought.

Four men descended the stairs carrying evidence bags with gloved hands.

The bags were clear, making it easy to see the cakes of something wrapped in tinfoil and gray duct tape.

"What is that?" she asked.

They didn't answer. Taylor watched them leave the house. The entire street was wall-to-wall police cars, lights flashing. Taylor imagined the number of neighbors standing in little groups, speculating what was happening at the home of the newest residents.

"I want to speak to my husband."

The woman got up again, engaged in a brief discussion with the officer stationed in the foyer, and then returned to her, sitting opposite in the worn green and white checked accent chair.

They waited, Taylor craning her neck and listening for all she was worth to the conversation going on in the kitchen. Finally, both Becca and Jules were escorted through the living room.

Taylor rocked to her feet.

"Where are they taking them?"

Her keeper gave no reply.

Becca glanced back, her expression worried, and then the pair were swept from her sight.

The blond officer used her head to convey something to a comrade in the entry. He called out into the yard. A few minutes later a man in plain clothing stepped in. He was small, mid-thirties, with light brown hair and thick brows that seemed to have once joined in the middle judging from the very exact line between them. His cheeks showed a dark stubble totally absent from his neck. A gold badge flashed from the waist of his gray slacks. His neatly tucked white button up shirt was bunched near the holster and gun at his hip, as if he had hastily dressed. He scanned the room with intent dark eyes, spotted her and stepped forward with sure authority.

"Mrs. Parker, I'm Detective Antonio Vasi with the narcotics division."

"This is a mistake."

"I'm afraid we found narcotics in a guest bathroom and in the hallway linen closet."

"That's ridiculous. It must have been planted."

"By whom?"

She told him. Told him that her husband was fleeing a cult and that she suspected her boarder, Zoe Furr, had done this.

He listened, but his expressive eyebrows told her that he didn't believe her. As she rambled on, his gaze flashed from one officer to another as if silently asking 'are you hearing this nonsense?'

"Do you have any evidence?"

She didn't. Of course she didn't. But she knew in her heart that while she was sleeping, Zoe was planting those drugs. Was this on orders from Seth's father? The retribution and judgment her husband had anticipated? Sending his own son to prison for narcotics was not a death sentence, it was worse. Seth would never be a doctor. And depending on the amount of drugs, he might be in prison for a lifetime.

"Mrs. Parker, I asked if you have any evidence to support your allegations?"

"No."

"I see. Well, we have arrested your husband. He'll be arraigned on drug charges on Monday. You can come to the arraignment."

"You tested what you found?"

"The loose powder only, yes. Cocaine."

She recalled Seth saying his family had done 'other things' to raise money. Were they mules for some Mexican cartel? Did his family traffic drugs as well as women?

"Can I post bail?" she asked, miserable now and her voice all but deserting her.

"The unregistered gun, quantity of drugs on premises, and the fact that they are narcotics will make the court less likely to set bail. They'll see your husband as a flight risk."

Ironically, they were in flight when the police had arrived. But Zoe had stopped that.

"Am I allowed to leave?"

He stared at her in silence for a long time. Finally, he said, "We are not charging you at this time. But don't leave the state."

"Leave the state?" This could not be happening.

She sat for another forty-five minutes according to the clock on the home audio system.

Detective Vasi returned to stand at a respectful distance from the sofa. "We're finished searching these premises."

"My home," she corrected.

"My people will be leaving. Your husband was transported to the jail for processing and then will be incarcerated."

"Where?"

He provided the address.

She was going there. She had to get to Seth, get him out of jail.

Vasi stood. "When are you due?"

"Next week. Thursday."

He nodded, his expression showing the first hint of regret.

Outside, car doors slammed, engines roared, and the lights that had been dancing on her ceiling for hours finally disappeared.

She glanced about. Had they taken Becca and Jules to the station or were they still here?

Where are they? Where is Zoe? And where is Seth's terrible father?

She didn't trust any of them.

Vasi cleared his throat.

"Detective?"

Vasi turned.

"Will you walk me to my car?"

He scowled but nodded, escorting her.

"Mrs. Parker, I want to repeat, you are not to leave the state. If you do, I'll issue a warrant for your arrest. You understand?"

"I do. But I'm going to the jail."

He nodded and fell into step behind her.

Once inside the garage, she opened the automatic door. Becca's Caddy was gone.

"Do you know where Becca and Jules are?"

Vasi nodded. "The station. They have to read and sign their statements."

"I see."

Vasi waited until she was in her vehicle with the engine running before he said goodbye and walked down the drive and out of sight. She put her SUV in reverse.

Taylor drove away from the house.

Could it be possible that just yesterday her tenants had thrown her a baby shower and now at least one of them had framed her husband for a drug arrest?

Any one of them might be part of Seth's family, or they were recruits, as he'd called them.

She briefly considered going to Gina's but thought better of it. Seth suspected Rubin had brought this trouble to them. If he was correct, his two cousins had traded him and his family for the release of their brother.

What about her parents? She winced at just imagining the blame they'd heap upon her, and honestly, with their separation, she wasn't sure she had a home there anymore. Taylor imagined showing up at her mother's doorstep and shuddered.

Seth had asked her to leave. Go visit a college friend up north or stay with one of her coworkers. Either prospect was so embarrassing. But perhaps her best option.

Except she couldn't leave the state.

Taylor made it to the jail but was unable to see Seth or get any more information from them about his arraignment.

It was then that she realized her purse, phone, and wallet were still in the house.

"Oh, no." Taylor considered her options. She could book a hotel, then go to the jail. Seth's arraignment was Monday. And her C-section was Thursday.

But to book a room she needed, at least, her phone.

Taylor turned back toward the house. The prospect of going inside filled her with panic. Could she get in and out before Jules and Becca returned? Was Zoe really gone or was she waiting with Seth's father to trap her?

Taylor parked in the drive and called the police, reporting that she feared someone might be in her home. They arrived in less than four minutes. She let the two officers inside and waited on the landing as they checked the house. Only when they reported that the premises were empty did she venture within.

Her first stop was the garage, for a screwdriver. Back outside, Taylor busted the outdoor keypad from the exterior. Now none of her tenants could use the code to gain entrance to the garage and house. Once back in the entry, she threw the deadbolt on the front door. Only then did she breathe a sigh of relief.

Her skin still prickled as she hurried upstairs for her purse, retrieving it from the master closet. Then she rolled out her largest suitcase. But it seemed uncharacteristically heavy. She couldn't even lift it to the bed.

So, she flopped it onto its side and unzipped the luggage and only then recognized this wasn't hers. She hesitated another moment, wondering who had switched this suitcase with hers and what she might find inside.

Then she flipped open the top. Taylor sucked in air through her nose as her eyes bugged. She shook her head wildly back and forth as the fear bolted up and down her spine like an electric current.

Desperate to escape, she staggered back, stumbled to her seat, and then scrambled like a crab away from the horror before her.

"Oh, God. Oh, no. Oh, please no!"

THIRTY-EIGHT

Twelve hours earlier...

Zoe was reading in her room when she became aware of something going on in the hallway. A glance at her phone showed it was nearly midnight.

Today had been pleasant enough, with the loan items arriving. She loved opening the boxes and cataloging the contents, noting the condition and any imperfections. This was her favorite part of her job. Like Christmas morning all day long.

And the party for Taylor had been nice. Uncomfortable, but still worth attending. She certainly had a lot of coworkers. And Taylor seemed to appreciate her gift. If it were her babies, she would never dress them in those terrible outfits, just loaded with synthetic dyes, or use diapers that would impact landfills well after her little ones were dead and buried. Cloth diapers. Definitely the right choice.

She'd speak to Taylor about her babies' environmental impact later.

Another thud. Those two were up to something again.

She'd caught them before, creeping around at night. Going up and down the attic stairs.

Zoe rose from the floral accent chair dressed for sleep in her oversized green satiny pajamas that made her feel like Claudette Colbert in *It Happened One Night*. She placed her book on the dresser beside her charging phone. This sort of nocturnal thrashing was simply not to be borne. She would complain to Taylor in the morning.

Another bump came from above her head. What in the world were they up to?

Her curiosity brought her across her bedroom where she slid the bolt back, cracked open the door, and peered out.

Those two were carrying a narrow bedframe up into the attic. It was the bed she'd seen stowed in the garage, when she'd helped Taylor bring in some household supplies. That did not belong to them.

Were they planning on sleeping in separate beds? They were newlyweds, weren't they?

They never kissed. She knew that much.

And the attic wasn't even air-conditioned. Was it?

Zoe had not meant to leave the safety of her room, but she did. She followed them, silently. The entrance to the attic stairs was on the opposite side of the hall, just past Taylor's room and the linen closet. If it were her house, she would have put the washer drier there. Much better function than having to drag things up and down the stairs.

She hesitated at the open door. They were talking in hushed voices. Zoe felt like Nancy Drew as she crept up the stairs.

When her head emerged above floor level, she glanced about.

The ceiling was just joists and fiberglass insulation on a slanted roof. It was musty and hot, far hotter than downstairs. A single bulb revealed Jules sliding the mattress onto a twin bed frame as Becca lowered a diaper pail to the ground beside a padded changing table.

Zoe's eyes bulged and a gasp escaped her lips.

Becca turned, glaring. Her face flushed and her eyes narrowed, pinning Zoe with a look that felt threatening.

"Company," she said.

Jules turned, spotted Zoe, and took a menacing step in her direction. Becca lifted a hand to stop him.

"What are you doing here?" asked Becca.

Zoe meant to say that she could ask them the same thing. Instead, she just shook her head as if she'd suddenly gone mute and retreated, descending a step.

"Here's what's going to happen now," said Becca, aiming a finger at her. "You're going directly to your room. Pack up all your shit and be out of here in an hour. Understand?"

Zoe nodded. Why did Becca sound so different? She'd never heard that Texas twang before.

"If you aren't gone, something bad will happen. And if you say a word to anyone about this, I'll make you sorry. Clear?"

Zoe gaped, hand at her throat.

"Are we clear?" Becca repeated.

Zoe nodded again and backed down the stairs. At the landing, she turned and ran to her room.

Inside she went to the closet to retrieve her large suitcase. The shock made it hard to think and her hands shook as she lifted each neat stack of folded garments from the dresser drawer and loaded them into the case.

When she reached her underwear drawer and began rolling her panties, her brain re-engaged.

They couldn't order her out of her home. And she needed to tell Taylor. What were they even going to do with that room?

Nothing good.

No, something terrible.

Zoe glanced around. Why hadn't she even locked her door? And where was her phone?

THIRTY-NINE

Taylor's scalp tingled and her ears buzzed. This could not be happening. She craned her neck to take another look.

There, folded into the bottom of the suitcase like a contortionist, was Zoe Furr.

Zoe's skin was gray, and her body unnaturally still. Taylor held her breath in terror at the horrible lifelessness. The immobility momentarily stopped Taylor's own breath. Her heartbeat marked the seconds as the air returned to her burning lungs, coming in ragged gasps. She collapsed to the floor, battling the dizziness and dangerous gray spots swirling in her vision.

"Don't black out," she cautioned herself.

Zoe wore lime-green pajamas. Her head was bowed and shoved tight to the top portion of the luggage. Her arms were bent, and her fists curled above her forehead. Her knees were jammed against her chest and her bare feet were pointed as if she was trying to stand on her tiptoes on the bottom of the case.

Taylor reached and her fingertips touched Zoe's arm. It was cold and stiff as a chunk of dried clay. She snatched away her hand as if it had been burned and drew back. When she finally came to a stop, she found herself crouching against the wall, panting and shuddering, with the hand that had not touched the body balled in a fist and pressed against her mouth to keep her from screaming.

Her purse was on the bed. She needed to call the police back here. How had they missed this body? They'd searched the entire house.

Keep breathing, she told herself. *Think.*

"It wasn't here."

Becca had brought it back to the house.

Taylor looked more closely at her luggage. Her set was hardshell black, and this was a hardshell black. But the manufacturer was different. This wasn't her bag.

"Zoe's."

She was panting now.

"She never left. She's been here. Where..." Why hadn't the police found Zoe's body when they raided Taylor's home?

They must have hidden it. But where?

Becca's car. That trunk. What had Becca called it? A four-body trunk. And it was private property. They couldn't search it without permission or a warrant because they didn't have probable cause.

"Oh my God."

Taylor crawled on her hands and knees to her purse. She had to get out of here right now.

She didn't even remember flying down the stairs or through the house. But she made it to her vehicle. She was so nervous she started the car with the garage door still closed. A tap on the remote and the door lifted. She tugged the SUV into reverse and the obstacle alarm chimed.

A glance showed nothing, but then the garage door was descending again.

The alert sounded, indicating some obstacle behind her again. A glance at the rearview camera showed Jules standing inside the garage at the rear fender of her vehicle. In her periphery, she caught movement. Becca stood at the top step, with one hand hovering at the button as the garage door rolled down, trapping her inside with them.

Taylor stomped on the accelerator. Jules jumped aside as the SUV collided with the heavy metal door, denting it outward. She prayed the sound would bring help as Jules threw open the driver's side door and hauled her out.

Becca darted down the steps and looked out the window in the garage door.

"I don't see anyone."

"Turn off the engine," he ordered.

Taylor shook Jules off, inching backwards toward the side door leading to the front yard.

"She's trying to run," said Becca, pointing.

Jules rushed past her, blocking her retreat. Taylor spun, finding herself trapped between the two of them. He blocked the side door. Becca blocked the entrance to the house.

Of the two, Becca seemed the better gamble. The woman was wiry, strong, and young, but Taylor had the benefit of mass. Taylor charged her. The collision caused Becca to spin, hit the running SUV, and stagger out of her way.

Taylor did not stop. She only needed to reach the front door. There she could start screaming.

She cradled her belly as she swept along. But she never cleared the kitchen. She had just one tantalizing glimpse of the living room and the foyer beyond before she was pulled up short.

Jules grabbed hold of her arm. She tried and failed to shake him off.

"You let me go, Jules. Let go!"

"It isn't Jules. It's Joshua. Good Old Testament name."

From behind him came Becca's voice.

"Careful. Don't hurt her."

"I'm not." Jules started for the stairs, dragging Taylor along as if she were the family dog reluctant to go to the vet.

"Turn off the SUV," he ordered over his shoulder.

At the stairs she tried to sit, but he just scooped her up in his sweaty arms and continued up to her bedroom, pushing her inside.

The moment she found herself alone, she twisted the lock. The knob turned and then stilled. She knew that the gorilla she'd selected as a tenant could kick the door down and that realization caused her to inch back until she folded on her bed. Beyond the door was only stillness.

Then she turned and saw the open suitcase and Zoe, motionless in death. Tears burst from Taylor's eyes and she sobbed.

What were they going to do to her?

They had Seth, had extracted their revenge. Her husband was in jail because of their lies. What did they want with her?

Confusion etched her brow. Was this another way to punish Seth?

Taylor straightened. She couldn't sit, quaking like a captured rabbit. She needed to get out of here. Her first move was toward the French doors. There was no easy access to the pool cage, and she was well past the time when she could have hung from the balcony and dropped to the concrete pool deck. But she could scream. The houses were close enough. Her neighbors—what were their names again?

It didn't matter. What mattered was that she liked to swim. And her husband had an outdoor TV on the lanai. She could scream for help, and he might hear her.

Taylor reached the hurricane-grade French doors and tugged, but they did not open. She tried the deadbolt, twisting it one way and then the other. It wasn't locked. But the doors were stuck.

What had they done? Bolted them from the outside?

She recalled her parents getting hurricane-grade windows for their home. No more shutters for approaching hurricanes, her father had said. Two pieces of glass with a shatterproof membrane sandwiched in the middle. The salesman had boasted that not only would these windows stand up to wind-borne debris hurled by a category-five hurricane, they would also withstand repeated impact from would-be intruders.

"Seals them out. Seals me in," she said quietly, her shoulders drooping as the defeat settled heavily there.

Taylor hustled to the window, determined to open it, and screamed for help. But the window would not open. She saw why immediately. A small, flat sheet-metal screw had been installed on each side.

Taylor next tried the bedroom window facing her easterly neighbor's yard and found the same tampering.

Why had neither she nor Seth noticed?

Perhaps because it was summer and hot and humid as blue blazes outside. The summer here was like the winter up north. Windows stayed closed, people stayed largely indoors and the air conditioning blasted twenty-four-seven. Why would either of them have tried to open a window?

Her captors had made her a secure little cage.

She went back to the bedroom, in a stupid, vain attempt to recover the phone before discovering it missing. Had Becca stolen it off her charger when they planted the drugs?

This was so bad. Taylor began to shake. A check for her tablet and MP3 player found them missing, too.

She stumbled into the bathroom and leaned against the sink, peering at the terrified, wide-eyed woman staring back at her from the mirror.

"I'm trapped."

Her stomach heaved. Taylor made it to the toilet as the acid in her empty stomach scalded up her esophagus. When she'd finished, she glanced at the mess, not of her making, but by the police search.

They had not cleaned the bathroom of powder but seemed to have smeared it everywhere. Taylor grabbed the bathroom cleaner and then recalled she was not supposed to do physical labor or use harsh chemicals.

So, she stumbled into the shower area, huddled in a ball, rested her forehead on her arms, and wept.

The high-pitched whirling sound of a power tool brought her head off her forearms.

What was that?

FORTY

Taylor rushed to her bedroom door where the sound was louder.

She placed her hand on the lock, hesitated and listened, one hand pressed to the door. Just above her index finger, a tiny hole appeared, and the tip of a drill emerged.

Her heart slammed against her ribs like a squash ball. What were they doing?

But she knew. The sinking sensation, the dropping of her stomach, told her. They were locking her in.

A quick twist released the lock and she tugged at the knob. She caught just a glimpse of Jules, power drill in hand, before he slammed the door shut in her face.

"Hold the door," he said, likely to his little evil assistant, Becca. Were they even married?

"Becca? Please let me out."

"It's Rebekah," came the muffled reply.

Jules' voice was a murmur and then came Becca again.

"Are you hungry?"

She was, but she wasn't eating anything they might give her.

"No. Let me out."

"You should get some rest," said Jules, and then the power drill started up again.

"With Zoe's body in here?"

"She found it," Becca said, seemingly reporting to Jules.

Taylor tugged and strained but could not even crack the door. Either Becca or Jules' handiwork had her trapped inside this room, surrounded by hurricane-grade glass and doors and windows that were screwed shut.

Without her phone, she had no way to judge the time but thought the afternoon had crept into evening.

"What are you going to do with me?"

"With you?" called Becca. "Nothing."

And then both of them laughed. Laughed as if keeping her prisoner was a lark, just some hilarious practical joke.

"How did you know I was back here?"

Silence.

Finally, Becca answered. "Your phone gave us a doorbell alert."

"But I locked the doors. Disabled the garage remote."

"But you didn't check the sliders from the pool," said Jules. "We left them unlocked."

Taylor stepped back, released the doorknob, and skulked to her bed.

Seth should have told her about this threat. Why hadn't he? Now look what he'd brought down upon them.

No, she realized as she slunk away from the door. It was her fault. Hers for not listening to Seth's objections and taking on the financial risk of a place now well out of their reach. Her fault for not adapting when the rug was pulled from under her feet, adjusting her plan to accommodate the change in their finances. And Seth's fault for not trusting her enough to tell her the truth. Had she known, she could have made plans, contingencies. If he'd said, 'Honey, I'm running from my family,' or said, 'I don't want strangers in the house because they might be recruits of my family's dangerous extremist group,' yeah, that likely would have made a difference.

But would it? She was so desperate and determined to have this house, she had ignored all warning signs, her husband's pleas, and her own good sense.

He begged me to wait. But I did what I pleased, without his approval, and couched it as a surprise.

And that was no way to be married. She'd make it up to him later. After she escaped this room, overpowered two maniacs, had her babies, brought them to safety, and got Seth out of jail.

Her chin sank to her chest, which gave her a great, close-up view of her stomach.

Her hands went automatically to cradle her distended belly. Her poor babies. The panic nearly overwhelmed her but some fierce rage ignited deep in her heart.

She rocked them, cooing assurances—to them and to her.

"They are not keeping me here. I'll see them both in hell first." Then she whispered to her twin boys. "All this excitement. You two must be upset. Me sending you all those stress hormones. I'll settle down. Just breathe. We're safe."

For the moment. But for how much longer?

The tears dripped down her cheeks. Seth must be going crazy. Out of his mind with worry. And with good reason.

How long did they plan to keep her here?

She was so thirsty. Taylor lifted the bottle she kept beside her bed and guzzled it down. Only after she had lowered it and replaced the cap did she detect a strange aftertaste. Was that flavored water?

No. It shouldn't be. And it had been sealed.

But it hadn't been. She had twisted off the cap without noticing that she had not broken the seal.

Her scalp tingled as suspicion bloomed into certainty.

The seal had already been broken. She popped to her feet and scurried into the bathroom, flicking on the powerful lights over the sink. She held the clear bottle up and examined the last remaining drops in the bottom.

They were not clear, but slightly cloudy and there was some particulate at the bottom.

"Oh, God, what did I just drink?"

Taylor hurled the plastic bottle.

She leaned over the sink and stuck her fingers down her throat, bringing up the vile drugged water. Had she been quick enough? How much of whatever was in there had reached her bloodstream and what would it do to her and to her babies?

Her fingers, slick with spit and the contents of her stomach, went back in her mouth and she shoved them hard against the rear of her throat, vomiting again but bringing up very little.

The weariness crept silently forward, dulling her concentration, and making her eyelids heavy. Had they drugged her with something to render her unconscious? But that was so incredibly dangerous. What did they want?

She needed to think. She needed to lie down.

Taylor stumbled from the bathroom and stretched out on the bed to do both, flicking the coverlet from Seth's side of the bed and over herself.

There, her body and the drug took over, dragging her unwilling mind into sleep.

She woke sometime later with her first labor pains to find Becca and Jules standing over her bed, watching her.

The sharp pain brought the collision of possibility with horror. If they wanted to punish her husband, what better way than by harming her or...

Were they after her twins?

FORTY-ONE

What time was it?

Taylor blinked open her eyes to a dark room where bars of moonlight stole between the panels of the Venetian blinds.

Someone stood beside the window.

Her breath caught as she realized she was not alone but had been unconscious and vulnerable. Her pulse pounded in her neck and lightning bolts of panic streaked along her nervous system, making every muscle twitch.

Becca stood at the window just beyond the light while Jules hung in the shadows closer to the door.

Somehow, she kept from startling upright, and her eyes remained half closed. But the fear made her mouth dry. She repressed the urge to swallow as her heart slammed into her breastbone.

"She's awake," said Becca.

There was a long pause, before Jules spoke. "I know."

He flicked the light switch and eight LED puck lights flared on with the intensity of a flashbulb, momentarily blinding her. The stabbing pain behind her eyes caused her to throw one arm over her face, to shield her from the visual assault.

Jules wore an unfamiliar pair of green coveralls, as if planning to put in a vegetable garden. Her throat constricted like a snake squeezing the life from a small rodent. She couldn't draw a breath until little bursts of light exploded before her open eyes.

The suitcase that had rested beside her bed and housed Zoe Furr's dead body was gone and Becca stood in the same spot.

She was garbed in the sort of green surgical scrubs worn by medical professionals in an operating room.

Or a delivery room.

Terror bit into her with tiny sharp teeth.

She was certain now.

They were never after Seth. They were after her babies.

Her pulse pounded in her ears as sparks of light exploded in her vision.

"Any contractions?" asked Jules.

It took a moment for Taylor to realize he was speaking to her. Alarm bubbled up in her throat like poison, making her voice sharp as a needle point.

"Get out of my room," she shouted, hoisting herself up on her elbows.

The two said nothing to this but just exchanged a look.

"You can't keep me locked up. Someone will notice I'm missing."

"Yeah. Likely your work," said Becca "But you've already sent a text saying your doctor wanted you on bed rest until Thursday. We don't expect it'll take you that long to deliver."

That accent was back. The one that she'd thought was Texan. Now it seemed less a drawl, more Wyoming or Colorado.

"How did you unlock my phone?" asked Taylor.

Becca lifted her index finger. "Used yours while you were out."

"We should just take her now," Jules said to Becca. "Easier to travel with them in her belly."

She lifted a hand, clearly in command here. "No, I want complete privacy for delivery. Can't have that in the back of a van."

Complete privacy? A van? This information sent a finger of cold dread skittering down Taylor's spine. There were few things that required complete privacy. Delivering her babies was not one of them.

"Why are you doing this? What do you want from me?"

Becca's smile chilled Taylor's blood. "They're twins, so we need to be here when they're born. Understand? Know which is which."

Becca's answer confirmed all of Taylor's worst fears. These two demons wanted her children. Seth had said a second son was important to his family. Her husband was a second son, and she was carrying two boys. But why did they want her second son? It didn't matter. Taylor's protective instinct roared to life. She would not let this happen.

"Let me go or you'll both end up in prison," she said, waving a finger at the pair and wishing she had something more threatening than a manicured index finger.

The bear spray.

A glance showed it was missing from her bedside table. Of course it was.

"You'll be going with us after you deliver," said Becca.

"I certainly will not."

"We can leave you behind, but I'd prefer you be the one to feed your babies until they're weaned."

That timeline gave her the first glimmer of hope. They didn't plan to kill her after the delivery then.

"Eventually they'll be assigned to a righteous woman to raise."

Taylor glowered. She'd be damned first.

Becca narrowed her eyes. "But if you cause us trouble, I'll just get them a wet nurse and leave you behind."

The hope died under the weight of this detail.

"Who are you? Why do you want my babies?"

"I'm Rebekah and this is Joshua. We're members of the Second Son Second Coming Disciples out of Coyote Creek, Colorado. The original community. We are devout Christians."

Christians don't steal babies, Taylor thought.

"Dedicated to worship, fellowship, preparing for Christ's second coming, and the survival of the chosen."

The chosen, meaning their wacked-out community of kidnappers and human traffickers.

"So why are you here?"

"Your husband abandoned his vows. He left us and that sin means his return to the community to face judgment before his fellows."

"But he's in jail."

"Charges won't stick. We used a tiny amount of cocaine on the toilet seat. Not enough to get popped for trafficking. The rest of those packets were baby powder. He'll come home and we'll be gone."

"He'll follow," said Taylor.

"We're counting on that," said Becca.

"Bring him home to face the tribunal," said Jules. "He'll come because you'll be there."

"Only you aren't the army, or a court. And US citizens have the right to come and go as they please."

"No. He forsook his pledge to God to be here to welcome his only son's second coming and to prepare our people for the apocalypse."

"This is crazy," said Taylor. "You're crazy."

Even as she said it, and watched the accusation hit Jules, darkening his expression, she knew this was a bad response. She should have said, *Oh, tell me more.* Or *I believe in*

Christ's second coming. Anything to give her time to escape them.

"What about Nathan and Rubin?"

"They're free."

"Because they betrayed my husband."

"They did their duty, reporting to the reverend father."

"In exchange for the release of their brother."

Jules shrugged as if this made little difference.

She'd never forgive either of them for what they'd done.

"Why did you kill Zoe?"

FORTY-TWO

The pair exchanged a look and then Becca smiled. It was a dangerous, evil kind of smile and it chilled Taylor's blood. Her question hung heavy in the air. Why had they killed Zoe?

"She saw us setting up your nursery and tried to do something stupid," said Jules.

"So you killed her?" asked Taylor, her blood pulsing in her neck so violently, it was making her feel faint.

"No. Becca did. Fast. Stopped her heart with a knife. Very little blood."

Taylor covered her eyes with one hand at the image this made. She saw Zoe, shocked and staggering as the blade sliced through the cartilage between her ribs, the spongy lung, and into the heart.

"Becca's quite a hunter. Skinned her own elk every year since she was seven. Knows her anatomy." Jules continued his explanation. "What was there was cleaned up before Seth got home. So good, the cops didn't even spot where we killed her. After, we tucked her in her suitcase and dropped her in her own trunk. Becca drove Zoe's car up the road before I called the cops."

Taylor imagined Zoe's body, folded to fit in that tiny box and thrown in the dark trunk. The police had been searching in the wrong place.

Had they seen nothing in her room? No evidence of her violent end?

"But she parked in the sun. That's no good for a dead body. So, after the cops finished with us, Becca and I drove back and picked her up, moved her to Becca's trunk. When you left, we stowed her up here in your bedroom. Cooler. Gives us more time."

Where had they left Zoe's car? Wherever they'd parked it, Taylor had never seen it again.

"How'd you know I'd come back?" she asked.

Becca held up Taylor's phone. "Also got your wallet, ID, credit cards. Knew you'd come here or the jail."

Taylor hated being so predictable. "Zoe will be reported missing at work."

"It's Saturday."

"Monday, then. They'll come looking for her."

Becca shook her head. "I got her phone, too. Opened it with her fingerprint and changed the password. Already texted her work. She's got the flu. At least that's what I told them. Out of work for seven to ten days."

That was very bad news. How long would the police hold Seth? How long until they discovered there was nothing but baby powder in those packets?

Becca held up Taylor's phone and pointed it at Taylor's stunned face.

Her phone unlocked and Becca began tapping. When she looked up, she was smiling.

"Changed the passcode. Now I've got access to yours, too."

Taylor glowered at how easily Becca had taken control of her phone. Then she asked, "Are you two married?"

They glanced at each other and laughed. The sound was so inappropriate it made Taylor shudder.

"Rebekah's my sister and she's only sixteen."

"I'm turning seventeen," she said.

"Old enough. 'Bout time she set out and brought home her own baby."

Taylor recalled that the women left to conceive and then returned with child. She grimaced. Then her stomach muscles clenched. Her eyes rounded.

"I've been with a few already. Might just be with child right now."

"That's fine," said Jules.

Taylor felt sick, gradually realizing that the disgust might not be the only thing tightening the muscles at her abdomen. This felt deeper and more unfamiliar.

"Did you put something in my water?"

Becca, or rather Rebekah, nodded. "Mild sedative and a natural tincture to start your labor."

Oh, no. Just as she'd feared. She laced her fingers around her belly, as if that might keep the drug circulating in her bloodstream from completing its task.

"Should have worked by now. I might have to give you a second dose. Injection this time."

Taylor tried to control herself, but the animal instinct engaged, and her breathing raced, coming in frantic little pants as she inched farther from the side of the bed where Becca stood. She loomed like a vulture, her beady eyes ever alert.

"I saw your ID. I ran credit checks," she said.

"Identity theft. It's one of our best fundraisers," said Jules. "Mostly credit card numbers, but they can make pretty fair copies of licenses and such."

"Very good," agreed Becca.

"Tell her about the testimony," said Jules, leaning his solid bulk against the only way out of the room.

Becca glanced back at him. "She doesn't believe."

"But she's the mother of the rebirth."

Becca sighed and then sat, uninvited, on the foot of Taylor's bed, like a parent might do after a child's nightmare. Meanwhile, these two *were* the nightmare. And she'd invited them into her home.

"Our founder, Ezekiel Parker, had a vision. He recorded his revelation on reel-to-reel tape in the mid-1960s. These recordings were later transcribed by the wife of his second son, Abraham."

Taylor wondered why the wife didn't even get her name mentioned in this unholy origin story, but said nothing as she pushed the pillows behind her and sat up. She felt sweat beading on her body as she tried to hide the fact that her labor was beginning.

"Abraham's second son was Seth, your husband, who is required to select from amongst our righteous women. Your marriage is not sanctified. You're no more than his concubine. A mere vessel. But you carry his second son. We learned this from Rubin when he revealed Seth's whereabouts."

If Seth was at fault, she was equally. She'd done this to them as surely as he had. Brought these two inside her home. Had they been back in their apartment, with the security guard at the gate, would this pair of zealots have even gotten past the entrance?

She supposed she'd never know.

Focus on what she's saying. Focus on escape.

Becca had been speaking and Taylor reengaged her attention in midsentence.

"...prophesized to lead our people through the dark times of famine and plague to emerge as God's chosen. Your son, David, will welcome God's second coming. He'll choose a wife and his descendants will lead us forth to repopulate new earth. We'll build a paradise of devout, righteous people. We'll..."

Taylor's cry of surprise and pain stopped Becca.

"It's started," Becca said.

"Get her upstairs?" asked Jules.

That question confused Taylor and then the pain tore all her thoughts away.

"She can deliver here. Easier to clean up," said Becca, reaching for Taylor's stomach. Taylor batted her hand away and Becca straightened, her mouth tight as she stared down her nose at Taylor.

"You want my help, Taylor."

"I want you both out of my house."

"No more than we do. This prideful house should be burned to the ground," said Jules. "The deadly sins of greed, sloth, envy, and pride. The downfall of man. And here you are committing these sins. How God chose you to be the mother of our prodigal son, I do not know. All of you deserve to burn."

"Out of sin comes salvation," said Becca.

Taylor watched as Jules moved to the end of the bed, her gaze flicking to the door and calculating her chances of escape. Her estimates showed zero chance. Even if she got through the door, she'd need to escape the house and run for help while in the early stages of labor.

The next contraction took the wind from her lungs. The muscles of her midsection jerked as if she'd been kicked.

"The drug intensifies the labor. More painful, but quicker. And quicker is safer for the babies."

"Adam and David," said Jules.

As the contraction eased, Taylor's indignation flared. How dare they name her babies?

But they'd already dared to move into her home. To watch her day by day, force her into labor, and plan to steal her children. Naming her babies seemed minor by comparison, but it infuriated her.

"Those aren't their names," she growled.

Becca chuckled. "Oh, no. What are you planning to call them? Herod? Cain?"

"None of your business."

Now Jules smiled. "It's our business all right. We're bringing your babies back to their granddaddy."

"What about Seth?"

"He'll be judged by our reverend father. It will depend on whether his second son survives. If your child survives, they'll have no more use for Seth."

"What does that mean?"

"It means they'll kill him for abandoning his vow."

So Seth's son's life would cost his father's death.

"Isn't murder a sin? You killed Zoe. Becca is hell-bound."

Becca scoffed. "I was protecting the chosen. My hands are clean."

Taylor wondered if Seth knew what was happening here. He'd at least suspect. Could he get help to her?

As the morning crept through afternoon, she no longer cared about their doomsday cult's beliefs or what they planned. Her focus had shifted to her body and what it was doing.

The squeezing pain of the contractions broke her water. Becca had predicted correctly. Once the contractions came faster and more powerfully, Taylor had little choice when they placed several pads beneath her backside. She kicked at Becca as the woman stripped away her sodden panties, landing a blow to her ribs.

Becca raised a hand to slap Taylor and Jules grabbed her wrist.

"No," he said, and Becca's shoulders sagged and some of the fury in her eyes hardened into hate.

Taylor bit her lip and groaned as another contraction tore through her. When she stilled, Becca drew on a headlamp before checking between Taylor's legs.

"You have to take me to a hospital. This is a high-risk pregnancy."

"I've delivered dozens of babies. They all come out the same way," said Becca. "Now save your strength. You'll need it."

The next contraction proved she was right.

Taylor screamed and Becca and Jules watched her with matching cool dispassionate expressions.

In the shorter and shorter periods of rest, Becca mopped her forehead and offered her sips of water. Jules stood at the door like a bouncer at some elite club. Beyond the blinds, the sky turned dark as evening overtook the day.

Where was Seth?

Jail, she remembered. Her mind was playing tricks now, her vision tunneling and then closing to a pinprick.

As her body heaved and stretched and resisted, Becca continued to share the crazy collection of conspiracy theories, religious double-speak, and paranoia necessary to justify their sins. This was God's will. Taylor's life or death already preordained.

Her first boy was born in those deadly hours before dawn, when a soul is least attached to the body. Taylor, blacking out, rousing, still managed a howl of delight when her firstborn gave a weak little cry. Becca suctioned out the infant's mouth and dragged away the caul before resting the baby on Taylor's chest. His eyes squeezed tight, he cried and whimpered as his color went from blue to a healthy pink.

"Should she be bleeding that much?" asked Jules.

FORTY-THREE

Taylor did not hear the answer because her body heaved with yet another ripping contraction. Time slipped with her consciousness. She woke with Becca slapping her face. Her abdomen jerked and the metal bands of muscles gripped again.

She sobbed in agony and screamed as her second son was born.

"To have lived to see this moment," said Becca.

"Praise the Lord," said Jules.

"Give him to me," ordered Taylor, reaching for her second son.

Becca cleaned the fluid from the infant's mouth and nose and rubbed him vigorously with a linen towel. Taylor strained to see some movement or hear a cry.

The baby was purple, and still.

"Give him to me," Taylor cried.

But Becca, now looking panicky, glanced at Jules and then gave a whimper. Jules lifted the boy over one forearm, cradling the baby's head in his open hand as he lowered the infant's head. The baby gasped and then cried, sucking in air with each wail.

Taylor's body pulsed with fatigue, demanding rest. Still, she reached for her baby.

Becca sagged with relief as she took possession of Taylor's second son. Jules took something from his pocket. It was a wide black zip tie. He cinched it on the boy's ankle as Becca cradled her son.

"Welcome, David, son of Seth, son of Abraham, son of Ezekiel," he said.

Taylor's vision blurred as her body jerked again; it was the afterbirth, she remembered, still needing to be expelled. She prayed to a more merciful God that it would dislodge without tearing. But the blacking at the periphery of her vision crept forward, leaving her staring down a tunnel at the pair, now rubbing something yellow and oily over her son's body.

She ordered them to stop. Or she tried, fighting the dragging blackness that beckoned. If she passed out or if she died, she'd be leaving her sons in the hands of these two zealots.

No, she told herself. *No. Stay awake.* But the blood still flowed from between her legs, and she feared she was dying. Taylor fought to stay alive as the darkness dragged her down to the depths once more.

"Well done, Taylor," said Becca with a tender tone.

Taylor could not see her, but for some reason, she could still hear, and the quiet, gentle tone terrified her, making her shiver.

"You delivered both boys alive and can seek your reward."

She shook her head, wanting to beg her captors to stop the bleeding, to help her live for her babies. But whether they treated her or not, she did not know.

* * *

Taylor dragged her heavy eyelids open to see dazzling daylight streaming through the slits in the blinds. She recognized her bedroom. Shifting, she was uncertain why everything hurt.

Then, as sleep receded, memories rose with her consciousness. Both her hands went to her stomach, and she cried out. Her babies!

Becca was there beside her, emerging from the mist that seemed to cloud her vision.

"Easy, Taylor. You had a difficult time bringing those two."

"Give them to me."

"They're sleeping. You rest. When they want you, I'll bring them."

"Where?" She meant to ask where they were, but the exhaustion tugged. "Thirsty."

She could not keep her eyes open or her body from the jerking fall into sleep.

When she roused again, her stomach muscles ached, her back throbbed, and her mouth was dry as cotton. She blinked, hearing something, an unfamiliar stuttering cry, thin and reedy.

There was Becca cradling her babies as Jules held open the door.

"Wake up, Taylor. They're hungry."

She pushed herself up on one elbow and spots spun like flies before her vision.

"She's going to faint again," Becca said to Jules. "Help her up."

He did, tugging her upright and thrusting several pillows behind her with all the gentleness of a man loosening a lug nut.

Taylor groaned.

"Water," she begged.

"First you feed them," said Becca.

Now she understood the sound she had heard. One of the babies was purple as he howled his fury at the world for not meeting his needs.

Her heavy-laden breasts responded, soaking the front of her nightie. When had she changed into this?

She hadn't, she realized. Nor had she changed the bedding,

but here she was in a clean bed on clean sheets in one of her nightgowns. Taylor reached and Becca handed her the twin that was not howling.

"Him first."

Taylor blinked in confusion. "I can feed them both."

"David first," said Jules.

Were they just going to stand there with her baby crying and watch her feed the twin that was sound asleep?

Yes, she realized, they were. Gritting her teeth, she yanked down her gown, exposing herself, and brought her second-born to her breast. He roused, rooted, and latched on with a very good grip. Her milk flowed with sweet relief. But the moment of bonding was sullied by Jules lurking at the foot of her bed and Becca bouncing her gasping, weeping firstborn.

Taylor reached with her free arm and Becca relented, helping her draw down her gown and get the one they called Adam into position.

That wasn't his name. She and Seth had already settled on the names Aaron and Brodie for the pair, A&B, based on birth order.

"You want to name this one?" said Becca, as if offering to have her name her own son was some kind of treat.

Taylor glared at her with all the malevolence she could muster.

"The placentas?"

"Whole."

She exhaled a breath of relief. Perhaps she'd survive this ordeal.

"This is wrong, you know?"

"It's God's work."

It was kidnapping and imprisonment, but Taylor needed to think how to play this. Should she ask to hear about their religion to stay with her babies until she could run? Protect them until Seth could bring help?

But her husband was in jail. And if they dropped the charges and released him, would his father be waiting to capture him? Bring him back to face their warped form of justice?

Tears rolled down Taylor's cheeks and she hated this sign of weakness.

"She's crying," observed Jules with the compassion of a small boy holding a magnifying glass over an unsuspecting ant.

"Baby blues. It's a common form of depression."

"I need water."

"Later," said Jules.

"If I don't hydrate, my body will stop producing milk."

The pair exchanged a look. Becca motioned to the door with her head and Jules trundled out. Once in the hall, he closed the door, and she heard an unfamiliar click.

Taylor frowned.

"We added a deadbolt to the outside. You can't get out. But now that you're awake, we can move you."

"Move me where?"

"Your new digs."

She didn't like the sound of that.

Aaron lost the nipple, fussed, and then latched on again. The moment Brodie finished, Becca collected him, rubbing his back as she marched beside the bed like a guard at Buckingham Palace.

Aaron finished a moment after his brother and Becca ignored him.

Taylor turned him onto her lap, face down, and rubbed his back with gentle strokes. His skin was wrinkly and pink and soft. The baby's faint burp made her smile. She righted him and cuddled him close, glancing up in time to see Brodie bring up some curdled milk all over Becca's shoulder.

"Oh, yuck," she said.

"I'll take him."

Becca hesitated and then turned him over. Taylor cuddled both her babies, joyful and full of love, despite her circumstances. *Look at them.* They were pink and perfect, and they both stared up at her with dark blue eyes. She wondered if they'd keep them. Her eyes were blue, and Seth had the bicolored, mainly blue with a splash of amber near the pupil in each, central heterochromia, they called it. So, chances were good her boys would be blessed with blue eyes. She could already see some differences.

Aaron had a tuft of blond fuzz on his head. Brodie's hair was also blond but longer, straight, and downy. She leaned down to inhale the wonderful smell of each of their soft heads. So, they were fraternal and not identical twins as she'd been told by her obstetrician.

The click of the deadbolt sliding back brought her out of her reverie.

Had she forgotten that Becca was here? That they held her captive and that they were planning on stealing her babies?

Yes. She had.

Jules appeared and paused to find Becca in her bra, gripping her shirt in one hand.

He frowned.

"David puked on me. Watch the door." She headed for Taylor's closet, returning with a T-shirt, which she slipped into. It was a maternity shirt, tie-dyed teal and white, and miles too big for her. But it was clean.

Seeing her so casually take that shirt made Taylor lock her teeth to keep from screaming. These two had no right to come into her home, misrepresent themselves, and steal her children.

She had to stop them.

"You look ridiculous," said Jules.

"It doesn't matter. Give her the water."

He did. She held the bottle up for him to twist off the cap. It took him a moment to realize she couldn't do that with one arm wrapped about her babies.

Once the cap was removed, she chugged the contents like a frat boy at his first kegger.

Nothing ever seemed so refreshing. Her body seized the liquid, and she closed her eyes, feeling stronger already. She'd need that strength and a clear head to fight them.

Her stomach gave a mighty gurgle, the water in her belly sloshing around like a tiny, troubled sea.

"I'm hungry."

"We'll get you something." Becca turned to her brother. "Take the other one."

Jules reached. Taylor turned, using her shoulder to block him.

"If you make Joshua take your baby from you, he will."

Taylor stilled as hot repulsion splashed through her. But she lifted her firstborn baby and offered him to her captor.

"Support his head," she instructed.

Jules took the baby, his massive hand supporting Aaron's head and much of his back.

"Take him out," said Becca. "Come back for David."

Jules strode away. Taylor heard him thumping down the hall. And then she heard him above her, his footfalls heavy on the ceiling.

Why was he taking her baby to the unfinished attic?

FORTY-FOUR

Taylor had her answer soon enough. Becca handed off her second-born to Jules, who again thumped up the stairs to the attic.

"What will happen now?" she asked Becca.

"That's up to you." Her kidnapper was very confident in her tone and in the arrogant lifting of her chin. "If you cooperate, you can stay with them, at least until we get home. If not..." She shrugged. "We'll leave you behind."

Would that be better? Taylor could get help. Go after them. Get her babies back. But could she? What were the chances she could find them and that the authorities could safely recover her twins? Then another thought struck. They'd never leave her behind because she *would* call the police. A perfect image of Zoe's body folded to fit into the suitcase sprang to her mind.

They meant they'd leave her body behind.

Icy panic gripped her heart, washing her body cold.

She needed to convince Becca she was no threat.

"I just want to be with them," she said, forcing down the anger and trying to channel weak submission.

"Good. That's real good, Taylor. We want that, too."

Jules returned.

"Ready," he said.

Becca's smile sent a shot of terror right through Taylor's middle like the thrust of a sword. Ready for what?

"Go ahead," said Becca. "I'll follow."

Jules approached. Taylor scuttled away, her body protesting at the movement. The throb and ache in her middle frightened her nearly as much as this man looming over her.

He reached. She kicked. Jules captured her leg and tugged her toward him.

"Careful," said Becca. "Don't get her bleeding again."

He grunted and then scooped Taylor up in his arms.

"I can walk," she said, twisting away.

His arms were iron bands.

"Stop it, Taylor. You're weak. You lost a lot of blood. You need to do as you're told."

"Let me go!" she shouted.

Jules squeezed tighter. It hurt. Taylor gave up. This was pointless.

"You lack discipline," said Becca. "You've been pampered and indulged until you think you're the center of it all. Well, you're not. Best learn that now. God is the center. You serve Him." Becca turned to Jules. "Take her."

Becca held the door and Jules carried her out to the hall and then up the attic stairs to the unfinished bonus room that she once pictured filled with a playhouse, climbing wall, a swing, and all her boys' toys. When they were older, she pictured sleepovers, a video console, beanbag chairs, and a mini fridge.

Instead, she saw rough ceiling joists. Pink fiberglass insulation with brown paper backing. Two-by-fours holding up the slanted roof. Two naked lightbulbs in cheap, white ceramic fixtures, secured to the framing. A plywood floor and a bed.

A bed. That had not been here before.

Taylor shivered in the stuffy, hot attic.

Beside the bed was a small table and lamp. The only seat was the kind of toilet chair used in hospitals.

Oh, no. This was a prison cell.

She struggled again. Jules' hold slipped and she got her bare feet on the rough wood floor.

His other hand supported her around her back and beneath one arm. It was only then that she realized he was all that kept her standing.

She sagged with weariness but glanced back to the door leading from the attic and to freedom.

Then she heard a little sound, like a hum. Her gaze swept the room and she saw something, a crate. She tried to move forward, toward that crate. Jules helped her along. What was wrong with her legs? Her knees were like jelly, refusing to lock and support her.

Another step and she could see past the single bed, the sheets with the tiny blue anchors and the cotton blanket. One pillow. Brass headboard.

But she could see into the crate. There they were. Her two precious boys, swaddled in individual linen blankets, both staring up at her with wide blue eyes. One blanket was blue. The other white.

"David will be in blue," said Becca.

Taylor tried to continue forward, but Jules did not comply.

"Put her on the bed," said Becca.

Jules scooped her up and carried her, depositing her on the mattress.

"Feel free to feed your boys." Becca pointed at the side table. It had one drawer and one cupboard.

"The changing table?"

"Over there." Becca pointed.

Taylor glanced in the direction she indicated, seeing a diaper pail, the white changing table she'd purchased for the nursery, and the vinyl pad.

"Diapers and wipes are still inside."

"It's too hot up here," said Taylor, already damp from the heat.

"It's insulated. It's private."

Taylor had planned to have this space air-conditioned and add a big window right over there. But that was before her father's phone call. Back when her only worries were what color to paint the nursery and which stroller was safest.

"You can't keep me up here."

But they were already leaving.

"Hey. I could die up here."

Becca called back. "Jules will bring you some food. Be a good girl, or..." She paused at that and cast a smile back at Taylor. The glitter in her eyes and the look of anticipation and malevolence curdled Taylor's blood.

She drew up her knees and hugged them, the simple protective move touching off a stabbing pain deep inside. Had she torn something? Was this normal to feel so depleted, sore, and weak? Or was something seriously wrong?

There's nothing wrong, she told herself. *You're healing. You need to get strong but act weak. Becca thinks you're a spoiled, incapable, weak little princess. So be that. Be that until they give you a chance.*

The door shut, the bolt slid home, and Taylor was alone, locked in the attic of the house she once thought they so desperately needed.

It was hard not to let the darkness overwhelm. Hard not to give in to tears. They fell, of course, but she wiped them angrily away. She brought these two into her home.

But Seth had never warned her.

"Stick with now," she said. *Plenty of time for blame when you and the babies are safe.*

Taylor slipped off the bed, holding on as the dizziness made her head spin. But her knees held her. She shuffled forward, bent like an old woman making it all the way to the bedpan. This was humiliating.

The plastic lid thumped up and she sat, emptying her bladder into the stainless-steel bowl, her urine ringing on the metal.

It already smelled like dust, mold, and wood up here. Soon it would smell like urine and feces, too. As if summoned by her words, one of her babies started crying.

White blanket. It was Aaron.

She hurried to him but found that simply leaning over the crate and lifting him brought another stabbing pain to her middle. Still, she cradled him close, asking him what was wrong and cupping the back of his tiny, perfect head. Her nose told her the problem.

Over at the changing table she found the supplies Becca promised and placed Aaron down on the pad for her first diaper change, but likely not his because she found a tiny little diaper snugly fixed about his lovely little belly. Swiftly, she removed it, cleaned him, and then inspected him all over, checking his drying red umbilical cord, his fingers, toes, ears, and genitals. Everything was perfect. Aaron kicked his spindly legs and waved his arms, wide awake now.

"My wild child. Is that it?"

Taylor diapered him and wrapped him up once more. She returned him to the crate, fury igniting again. Would it have killed them to bring up the crib?

Brodie was next. He gurgled happily at being clean and unfettered.

"Who's my happy boy?" she cooed.

Brodie waved his arms. She laughed and then diapered and swaddled him. Smiling, she brought him back to his brother.

"You two are my angels," she said. "And we are getting out of here."

Taylor rummaged in the drawers of the changing table but

found nothing but tiny soft clothing, diapers, and supplies necessary to clean them.

In the small drawer beside her bed, she found one book. The Bible.

The sight of it did not bring comfort, but rage. How dare they do this and blame God? Not one thing about this was God's will.

There was nothing else here. No tools. No weapons. Nothing more dangerous than a foam pillow and a bedpan.

Taylor slumped, admitting defeat—for now.

The sound of heavy footfalls alerted her to Jules' arrival before he even slid back the lock. He entered with a tray in one hand and a folding table, the sort used at parties or to eat before the television.

He erected it beside her bed and then placed the tray. The aroma of chicken soup caused her to inhale deeply. Her stomach growled, anxious for food.

The tray included chicken noodle soup, crackers with peanut butter, apple slices, and, oh no, a vanilla yogurt and a large glass of milk. The glass was already sweating in the heat of the attic, and all dairy products upset her stomach.

"Eat," he said, pointing. Then he stepped away, looming over the makeshift crib.

She did, quickly putting away the meal that looked to be prepared for a child's lunch, leaving only the milk and yogurt.

"Do you think you could bring me some clothing and the crib?"

"No."

"Why?"

"You don't need clothing up here. It's too hot. And Becca says cribs are vain and dangerous. They can get their heads stuck between the bars."

That wasn't true because she'd done research on that. But she didn't bother arguing over product safety.

"Slippers? A book?"

"You have the only book you need."

"What about a book on caring for babies?"

"You don't need it. One of the women at the compound will raise them."

That thought chilled her.

"And what happens to me?"

The corner of his mouth twitched. The cold now seeped into her bones. They needed her milk, for now. But the minute they got to the compound, her purpose would end.

"You going to kill me, like you killed Zoe?"

"Maybe." He smiled. "But I didn't kill that busybody. I would have, but Becca was there first. Caught that little freak with her phone in her hand and after we told her what would happen if she called for help. Becca told her she could go. But she made her choice."

"Would you have let her go?"

"Probably not. Once she got away, she'd feel safe enough to call the police. Best not to take that chance."

"But I received a text from her." Even as she said it, she recalled what they'd told her about using Zoe's phone to report to her work that she was sick with the flu.

And then Taylor remembered Zoe's text and that she'd misspelled 'apologies'. At the time she'd thought it was just a typo.

And so it was. But Zoe, so exacting and well educated, would likely not make such a mistake. But Becca, with her limited education, most certainly would.

"What about her car?"

"After the police and after we got her body out of the trunk, Becca drove her car to some hotel parking lot. Left it there with all her crap inside. Then thumbed back."

"Where's her... her body now?"

"Still in that big old suitcase at the bottom of Tampa Bay."

There was no remorse there. He looked pleased with himself. This monstrous pair had killed a woman and he was gloating. Taylor's stomach knotted and she failed to keep her mouth from twisting in revulsion.

He saw it and his smile vanished as he narrowed his eyes on her.

"What day is it?" she asked.

"Still Sunday."

So, she'd delivered Saturday night or Sunday morning. That made their birthdays either August 12th or 13th.

"Abraham? That's Seth's dad. Right?"

"Yes. And the second-born son."

Taylor held back her opinion on that bit of rhetoric.

Now she was sweating, all over. Droplets rolled down her back and between her heavy breasts.

So, Jules was not in control. Becca made the decisions, as she'd suspected.

"How long will I be up here?"

"Are you finished?"

She scooped the last bit out of her dairy-free yogurt and nodded.

"Drink your milk."

The milk was Seth's. She never touched the stuff.

"I can't."

He lowered his chin and glared.

"I'm lactose intolerant." An unwelcome gift from her Italian ancestors, she thought.

"Drink it," he insisted, snapping his jaw shut and aiming a finger gun at her.

She drank the milk. The sour taste was unpleasant as always and the moment it landed, it came right back up again.

Taylor just made it to the potty chair. The smell of urine finished the job. The milk came up and out her nose. After heaving, she lost the rest of her lunch.

The need to vomit again began with the reflexive contractions of her sore stomach muscles. This time she brought up only bile. She sagged on the floor before the stupid metal potty chair, the taste of acid and milk coating her mouth and tongue.

"What's wrong with you?"

With her head hanging, she answered from her place in a crumpled heap on the warm plywood floor.

"I can't digest milk," she whispered. Not only did milk products upset her stomach, they were disgusting, in her opinion. Though Seth loved them. Ironic.

"You need calcium."

"Vitamins or fortified almond milk or fortified orange juice. And Pedialyte to keep me hydrated." She'd need that most of all up here in this airless, stifling attic.

Sweating and gagging, she tried to rise. Jules hauled her to her feet and helped her to bed.

"Stay there. I have to talk to Becca."

Her stomach gurgled. Thankfully, it was just hunger and not the upset.

"I need Pedialyte. And I need another meal. If I get dehydrated my milk will stop."

There it was, the uncertainty that caused his eyes to widen and that flicker of panic. He didn't want her milk to stop. Not yet anyway. Likely he knew how important a mother's milk was to give her babies immunity, in addition to nutrition.

"And I need water to bathe. A face cloth. My toothbrush. Plus, it's too hot up here. It's not good for the babies."

"Maybe we'll take them. Just bring them for feeding."

She glared.

Jules went to the bedpan chair, lifted the lid, and stared down.

Taylor flushed with shame. Why, she didn't understand. She'd peed and been sick. Big deal.

Jules lifted the pan and poured the contents into the empty soup bowl.

Oh, yuck.

Then he returned the pan, retrieved the tray and table, then headed out.

"What about my lunch?"

He didn't answer. Just kept going until the door clicked shut and the bolt slid home. Taylor followed, waiting by the door until the sound of his footsteps faded. Then she counted to twenty and tried the knob.

Locked as she'd suspected. She shook the hardware. Then she banged her shoulder into the barrier.

"And the doors are solid wood. Not made like those cheap hollow core ones," Taylor said, repeating the selling detail related by the realtor.

She rested her head against the quality construction and wept.

FORTY-FIVE

Taylor had no window. No clock. No phone.

But her babies helped her mark time. The books she'd read while waiting for her twins to arrive said that newborns need about twelve feedings a day. One every two to three hours. Based on that, Taylor thought she had been locked up in her attic for four days, but couldn't be certain.

She didn't know. Four days to think and plan and mourn. Where was Seth? Was he still locked in a jail cell, falsely accused of selling narcotics? That charge alone might be enough to ruin his career.

Did her parents even notice she had not called to tell them of the birth of their first grandchildren?

Had they settled their differences? Was her mother back home?

What about all her friends at the office? Becca said she had texted them, using Taylor's phone, reporting she was on bedrest. But today might be her scheduled C-section.

Her doctor!

She'd miss Taylor for sure. What would she do, exactly?

Since her fiasco following her first meal, her captors served no more milk products and did supply her with Pedialyte, as much as she could drink. Also, vitamin supplements and a fan, thank heaven. She was getting stronger.

Her attempts at pounding on the roof and shouting had not brought help. It had brought Jules who slapped her so hard across the face her teeth sliced her cheek.

Taylor spent much of each day pacing in her prison, searching for a stray nail, a roofing screw, or something that might be fashioned into a weapon. Her meals were intentionally weapon proofed. She was certain of it. Why else would all her utensils be disposable, and her glass be the Styrofoam sort used to keep drinks cold? And Jules checked the cutlery as if she had any means of melting the cheap plastic into a shiv.

How long until they took her babies? Would they separate her from her twins and just leave her up here to die?

The only bright spot was her twins. Since their birth, their heads had returned to their normal shape. Their reddish skin had changed to healthy pink. Beyond that, her two bright boys were experts at eating, pooping, and sleeping. When they were awake, they stared up at her as if she was the most fascinating creature alive. And, in their world, she certainly was. And they could already grip. Her heart melted at seeing their tiny, perfect fingers coiled around hers.

Aaron managed to get his fingers in his mouth to suck. And Brodie would smack his lips when he was hungry. They were her only joy and when not napping herself, or caring for her babies, she was moving. Trying to strengthen her depleted body. Getting stronger. Preparing to escape. She did not know how or when, but there'd be an opportunity. And she'd take it.

Her food came only once a day now. That also helped her mark the time. She assumed they came around mid-afternoon with her hot meal. She wondered if Becca still worked at the coffee shop and if Jules had ever really worked for the post office.

When they arrived, Jules carried her meals. Two, both delivered together, one in a paper bag as if she were going somewhere and a hot meal served on a paper plate. Becca checked the babies. She weighed them daily as Taylor hovered, her heart pounding and her skin flushed and damp as she wondered if this was the day they took her twins.

Meanwhile, Jules waited until Becca was ready to depart, then carried out the bedpan and diaper pail, returning them shortly thereafter.

Becca always weighed Brodie first and then Aaron. Brodie got everything first. The treatment was so clearly lopsided, Taylor began to wonder if they would take Aaron at all.

Would they just leave him with her in this attic to die?

"What will Aaron's purpose be?" she asked.

They didn't answer.

That was the day Taylor chewed the plastic zip tie off Brodie's ankle. The hated thing reminded her of the sort of house arrest devices used on convicted criminals. Then she removed their swaddling.

On her return, Becca noticed immediately, screeching like a furious parrot. This brought Jules running.

"Look what she's done!"

Jules glanced at the babies, back to Taylor and then to Becca, confusion etched on his face.

"The anklet! She's removed it." She pointed at the twins, there upon the bed, naked, kicking and crying and neither with the black zip tie fixed to an ankle.

"How?" he said, only just noticing the absence of the marker revealing which was Taylor's second-born.

Taylor didn't need that external marker because Aaron's baby hair was shorter than Brodie's. The two were fraternal twins and she was certain the changes would grow greater with each passing day.

"I don't know!" Becca rounded on Taylor. "What did you do?"

Taylor stiffened as the pair abandoned the twins and stalked toward her. She took one step toward the doorway, which she knew was locked. They always locked it when they were up here with her. She then glanced at her babies and moved forward, toward the threat and her children.

Becca grabbed her shoulders and shook. Taylor punched her in the stomach and her attacker doubled over. But before she could scoop up her babies, Jules shoved her. She staggered, dancing backwards on bare feet and then tripping and falling hard to her seat.

They stood over her.

"How much longer do we need her?" Jules asked Becca.

Becca didn't answer. Just stared down her nose at Taylor, her eyes cold as any executioner.

"Get the scale," she said. "David weighed more than the other one."

They didn't even bother to use the name that they'd given her firstborn.

"It's Aaron," said Taylor, her outrage momentarily overcoming her injuries. Her cheek still stung from the slap Jules had given her yesterday, and the gash inside her cheek was swollen and raw. Now her tailbone throbbed.

"The scale," said Becca.

Jules lumbered off as Becca lifted Aaron and gently cradled him, carrying him to the changing table.

Despite the throbbing in her back, Taylor could not sit by while Becca handled her baby. She dragged herself up, wincing at the jolt of pain that zipped down her leg like an electric shock. Had she pinched a nerve?

No time to worry about that. She could hear Jules on the stairs.

He arrived with the scale and Taylor stood by as Becca weighed Aaron and then Brodie.

"This one," she said, correctly identifying Brodie.

Then she lifted him to her shoulder and started for the door. Something snapped inside Taylor. She raced forward and grabbed Becca, spinning her around with a mighty yank. Becca's eyes widened. Taylor reached for Brodie, and something clamped around her waist.

Jules hoisted her off the ground.

"She's strong enough to travel," he said, staring down at her.

Becca cast her a nasty smirk and sailed out the door, carrying her baby.

Taylor screamed and struggled. With one foot on the floor, she twisted and managed to rake her nails down Jules' face. He released her and shoved. She tottered and fell on her hip, sprawling across the floor, sobbing. Jules followed Becca, stomping over the plywood and then down the stairs.

When the tears abated, she heard a familiar stuttering cry and pushed herself upright. Aaron lay on the bed, naked upon a bath towel, his face purple as he howled his outrage. She crawled to him, gathering up her firstborn and cooing. But he would not be comforted. She tried feeding, but he would not take her nipple and continued to cry, his hands balled in tiny fists. She swaddled him and still he protested.

"It's your brother. Isn't it?"

This was the first time they had been separated, she realized. And somehow Aaron knew.

Taylor carried him to the door, and they waited in the stifling heat of midday for some sound that told of her captors' return.

During her first few days she had not noticed the change in temperature. The attic was always overly warm. But it did cool slightly at night. Now, she suspected the summer sun blazed down upon the shingles above her.

How long before anyone at the office called to check on her? How long before a neighbor noticed her absence? How long until the doctor raised the alarm?

Becca had taken her phone. She could be listening to all voicemails and replying by text. That would work. If she figured correctly, her due date for the C-section had come. Her friends would be in contact but respectful of her requests to restrict visits with her newborns to direct family. Most recommendations she'd read indicated that a newborn's interaction with outsiders should be limited. She'd imagined her father holding her babies, but not before washing his hands.

"Will your grandma and grandpa even want to meet you?" she asked Aaron, and then wondered if she wanted her babies to meet them.

Grandbabies were a powerful lure and a chance to get back into her mother's good graces. But just imagining her mother with her twins made her shudder and drove a nail in that coffin.

Her mom's mental illness warped the idea of all the normal grandparent visits into something dangerous. It was awful to have to protect your children from their grandmother, but that was her reality.

No. They were done with her, and Taylor with them. It was a door she was glad had slammed shut in her face and one that she would not be opening again. Her mother wasn't a bad person because of her illness. She was a bad person in spite of it.

Aaron's cries were weaker now. She tried feeding him again. He rooted and finally sucked. She sighed in contentment as her milk flowed, bringing comfort to her and nourishment to her baby.

One of her babies.

Taylor kicked at the door.

By the time she'd finished feeding Aaron, changing him, and tucking him back in the swaddling to sleep, she heard Becca's quick, light tread on the stairs.

When the door opened, she was there, waiting for the chance to attack Becca, but Jules was right behind her.

In her arms, she held Brodie, naked and howling his upset as he waved his spindly arms. There was something wrong with his hand.

What had they done to her baby?

FORTY-SIX

Brodie's cries twisted Taylor's heart. Milk flowed from her breasts, soaking her soiled nightie. Becca offered the baby and Taylor snatched him from her jailor, rushing across the room with him and dropping to her seat on the single bed.

"What have you done to him?"

Taylor extended his tiny fingers. They were black with something. It looked like ink. His feet were similarly black.

"I took prints of his palms and feet. For now, I'm using the ink stains for quick identification. Don't wash it off or I'll just take him again."

Jules dropped something on the bed beside Taylor. Clothing. Her heart stuttered with excitement followed immediately by her stomach dropping. This meant they were taking her. She'd be out of the stifling attic, but then what?

Taylor lifted the familiar garment. It was a satin robe. She stared at Becca.

"That nightgown is soiled and..." She waved her hand and looked away, as if the sight of Taylor was offensive. "It's sheer when it's wet and that's most of the time."

Because she was breastfeeding. Of course it was wet. That was why she had several new nursing bras in her bureau. Perhaps she'd misjudged. Maybe she wasn't getting out of this attic.

"Your husband called." Becca drew Taylor's phone from her pocket, opened the voicemail app, and tapped play.

It was Seth. Taylor covered her mouth with her hand as she heard her husband's voice.

"Taylor. I'm out. Why didn't you call or visit? I'm worried. Are you okay? Are you safe? Are the babies all right? God, I don't even know if you had the C-section. Are you in the hospital? Are the twins in the NICU?" She could hear the stress in his voice. Her throat burned as she choked back the tears. *"Your doctor had said it was a possibility. Should I come to the hospital? Are you safe?"* There was a pause here and he spoke to someone else. *"Yes. I am. Just a second."* Then back into the phone, his voice strangled. *"Call me, Taylor. Please. I need to know you are safe."*

Becca drew back the phone.

Taylor absorbed the gut punch of her husband's message. Did he know what Jules and Becca were up to? Would he get to her before these two stole her and their babies away?

"He'll be coming. Here or the hospital. We have to go."

Taylor gaped, then lifted a hand to wipe her eyes, swiping her fingertips over her wet cheeks.

Seth was coming. Finally, someone would know she was gone. He'd know she hadn't left him. Wouldn't he?

But would he know that it was Becca and Jules who had taken her? Would he know where they were going?

She wasn't sure. But Becca had said they were counting on Seth following them. He would. She knew it. And once back at his family's compound, what would they do to him?

"Come on," said Becca. "Shower time. You stink."

Becca tugged her to her feet. Taylor collected her babies and followed Jules down the stairs into the blissful cool of the air-conditioned second floor.

In the bedroom, Taylor finally glimpsed daylight and from the angle she saw it was afternoon. Friday? She wasn't sure.

Once they'd marched her into her room, Becca turned to Jules.

"Lock us in and go clear out the attic. He can't see any of that."

"We could just, you know..." Jules shrugged.

Taylor understood and her chest tightened as she realized Jules was suggesting they kill Seth. They'd killed Zoe after all. Why not murder her husband? He couldn't come after them if he were dead.

"Because," said Becca, her voice full of frustration as she dragged out the word, "if you hurt Seth, and then something happens to David, there will be no more second sons."

Jules pressed his lips tight as he ground his teeth. At last, he said, "Fine."

Taylor's breathing was coming so fast, she was seeing spots. She forced herself to slow her intake of breath.

"Inside," said Becca, pointing toward Taylor's bedroom door.

Becca told her to put the babies in the bassinet that had been sitting here, unused, for nearly a week, while her precious babies had been sleeping in a crate like a litter of pups.

"You could have brought me this," said Taylor, her annoyance leaking into her voice.

"You're too proud. You need taking down."

Taylor gritted her teeth. Her babies were safe and swaddled and sleeping.

Becca leaned over the bassinet and snapped a photo of the twins using Taylor's phone.

"Why?" asked Taylor.

Becca pointed. "Shower."

Taylor complied, her gaze sweeping her surroundings for something to use as a weapon. She had scissors in her bathroom drawer. Maybe she could get ahold of them. Should she attack Becca if she had the chance? That would mean she'd be locked in here when Jules returned.

It was a weak plan. Jules could easily overpower her, even if she killed Becca, and she wasn't at all sure she could kill her. Physically, she could. But emotionally? Taylor doubted very much she had that... that something, that feral spark.

For that she should be very glad. But just now, it seemed a vulnerability.

Then she glanced at her sleeping children and thought she might have that necessary brutality after all.

In the bathroom, Becca ordered her to strip and shower. She didn't leave Taylor and watched as she turned on the taps and used one hand to test the temperature. Taylor stepped into the warm spray. Nothing ever felt so good as the needles of water bouncing off her dirty skin and soaking her hair. She tipped her head back, unconcerned about her guard. She grabbed the shampoo, lathered, and rinsed. Then she did it again, before using the body wash. She had not showered since before giving birth. Either Becca or Jules had washed away the blood after her delivery, but she didn't remember and woke feeling dirty.

She lathered her hands, arms, and feet. Then she rinsed away the soap. The water went cold, and she yelped. Her eyes flashed open to find Becca with her hand on the faucet. The water flicked off.

"Out," she ordered. She thrust a towel at Taylor.

Taylor dried her skin and then her hair, wrapping the towel around her head. She knew the sight of her body made Becca uncomfortable. Maybe she'd score another towel.

She strode to the bathroom mirror, fogged now from the steam. With one swift motion she drew open the drawer which held the scissors. It was empty.

"Cover yourself," said Becca.

"I only have this towel."

Becca turned to the linen closet to retrieve another as Taylor quickly opened and closed each drawer, but she was unable to find anything more dangerous than nail clippers.

"Just what's on the counter," Becca said.

Beside the sink sat her toothbrush; oh, how she'd missed it. A comb. Deodorant and toothpaste.

Taylor used one hand to wipe away the condensation and then gasped. She hardly recognized her own reflection. Purple bruises covered her cheek and had crept beneath one eye from the slap Jules had given her. Her face was gaunt and her cheek swollen, as if she'd had a tooth extraction.

Another swipe widened her view, and she shook her head in astonishment at the dark circles under her eyes.

"No time for that. Finish up. We're leaving."

Taylor's hand dripped from the condensation, but she lifted her toothbrush and went to work on her teeth. Then she dragged the comb through her hair, releasing the tangles and wishing for some of the product she used to style her hair.

From the bedroom came a call from Jules.

"Becca?"

"In here." Then she repeated herself to Taylor, thrusting the bath towel at her. "Cover yourself."

Was Becca worried about her brother seeing Taylor naked?

It wasn't much, but it was something.

Becca walked to the doorway of the bathroom. "Wait there."

Taylor spit in the sink and Jules said something.

"What?" said Becca, stepping out.

With Becca out of the room, Taylor realized she had an

opportunity and she seized it. She dapped white toothpaste on one finger, then she wrote on the mirror below eye-level and as small as possible to still be legible.

Delivered twins
Taken
Abraham

She listened to Becca and Jules arguing as she flipped on the vent fan. As the condensation on the mirror evaporated, the words became less obvious. Taylor hustled to the window, flipped the latch, and tried and failed to push up the bottom pane. Screwed shut, she belatedly recalled. Still, she stared out the window as the steam cleared. Her view of the world seemed so normal, as if everything had just continued without her.

Sunshine filtered through the palmetto palm and the blue sky held a few cotton-ball clouds. She had a partial view of her neighbor's pool cage, empty in the middle of the day.

"What're you doing?" screeched Becca.

Taylor spun.

Becca called over her shoulder. "Jules, get in here."

Taylor's gaze flashed to the mirror. Her message was there, still legible in streaks on the bottom of the glass.

Jules stormed in.

"Take her out," ordered Becca.

He clasped her wrist and tugged, pushing her after Becca. Taylor's message was still there on the mirror, faint but legible. Neither captor had seen it.

She followed Becca and, behind her, Jules flipped off the fan and lights, then closed the door to the bathroom. They hadn't wiped off her message. But would Seth see it?

Becca rummaged through Taylor's closet, selecting a maternity dress and a simple denim jumper with shell buttons up the front. Then she added a plain white T-shirt, underwear, and a maternity bra.

"Put that on," she ordered, pointing to the offering. "Jules, wait outside."

"But she might try something again." His eyes were on Taylor now, slipping down her damp, naked legs and lingering on the skin exposed between her shoulders and the top of the towel.

His sister was having none of that.

"I'll handle it. Is the car packed?"

He nodded.

"Good. Go on. Git."

He hesitated a moment longer and then withdrew.

Becca rounded on Taylor. "What're you looking at? Get dressed."

Taylor complied, wondering again, as she slipped into her clothing, if Seth would see her message.

Taylor grabbed a pair of Dockside boat shoes from her closet, thinking them a good choice if she had to run, and slipped into them.

"You ready?" Jules asked from the hallway.

Becca called out, "Okay. Come in."

The bolt slid back with an audible click.

"Get the twins," Becca said to Taylor, and then stomped out the door.

They marched Taylor down the stairs and to the kitchen. There, her matching set of luggage waited.

"What's in there?" she asked.

"Enough of your clothing, jewelry, and makeup to make him think you've left him."

Her breath caught.

"No."

"Now you're going to write him a goodbye note."

Becca offered a pen and a sheet of paper from the notepad in the kitchen drawer.

"Write exactly what I say."

"No," said Taylor.

Becca turned to Jules. "Take her firstborn."

Jules stepped forward, hands outstretched. Taylor hunched around her babies and backed away.

FORTY-SEVEN

In the garage, Taylor paused at seeing that both Jules' scooter and Becca's vehicle were gone, and parked in Seth's spot was an unfamiliar, dingy white van. It looked like a million other work vans, as indistinctive as a leaf on a tree.

Of course, they wouldn't take her SUV because using her vehicle was a risk. If Seth thought she'd been taken, if he saw the message, then highway patrol would be searching for her. And all those windows, she might easily signal a driver for help.

Signaling would be impossible from the windowless back of that van.

Taylor descended the three steps leading to the garage.

Becca opened the rear door to her SUV. Inside, the two infant car seats waited.

"Put them in," she ordered.

They were taking her vehicle after all. It was a very lucky break. Carefully, Taylor secured her babies into their car-seat bassinets. She remembered wondering where she would take them on their first outing. She recalled thinking of Seth, proud and tired, bringing home his wife and their children from the birthing center. They'd be parents then, she realized, someone's mama and papa.

Instead, her twins' first trip was a kidnapping. Seething, she stood beside the SUV.

Becca extended a familiar key fob, the one that belonged to Taylor. Confusion took her as she grasped her keys.

"You're driving," said Becca.

"What? Why?"

"So Jules can keep an eye on you, and I ride back here with your boys as insurance that you don't do anything stupid, like signal for help. If you want your babies to stay safe, you'll do what I tell you. Understand?"

Becca was threatening to hurt her boys. Taylor bit down on the pulsing fury beating through her blood vessels.

"Understand?" This time, Becca's question held a harsh edge.

"Yes."

"Great. So, you drive. I watch the twins. Jules watches you and you watch the road. Then everyone stays safe."

Meanwhile, Taylor's phone, still in Becca's possession, chimed with text after text.

Would she have a chance to signal to a cop that she was in trouble? Could she motion the help sign to another vehicle?

Her female captor pulled out the cellphone and glanced down.

"We have to go. He's left the jail."

Taylor gripped her useless keyring, wishing it held some weapon instead of a fuzzy pink cat, a tiny phone charging cable, her AirTag, and a bottle opener.

A glance showed Becca scowling at Taylor's phone as Jules carried luggage from the kitchen and loaded it into his van.

"We're taking hers," said Becca.

He paused. "That's not a good idea."

"You can drive the van somewhere and ditch it. Hers is nicer. And the baby car seats are in there."

"It's nicer all right. And it has built in tracking."

Becca paled and her expression went blank. Then she narrowed her eyes on Taylor, the blame clear as her hatred.

"Gotta take the van," he said.

Becca nodded. Jules lifted the largest suitcase into the back of his van.

Taylor's phone continued to ping and chirp as Jules hefted the remaining cases into the back.

"Your parents again. Damned pain in my ass." She tapped away and pressed send. The phone made a distinctive swooshing sound of a text sailing off into cyberspace.

Taylor fingered the AirTag, then released the snap that held the leather case to the ring and slipped the tag inside her bra.

Before she glanced at Jules, she felt his stare.

"What are you doing?" he asked.

Her face went hot. "Nothing," she lied.

"Get the car seats," he ordered.

She did, releasing them from the rear seat and transferring one and then the other to the smaller of two bench seats of his shabby van. The interior smelled of motor oil and fried food. Taylor wrinkled her nose.

"Won't he know she didn't leave him, if her car is here?" asked Becca.

"Uber to the airport," said Jules.

"Maybe." Then she tucked away the phone.

Taylor resisted the urge to ask who had texted and what they had said.

"Turn off her phone," said Jules.

"It is off."

"No. It's not. Do a hard shutdown or he'll track it."

Becca tugged out the phone and did as he asked. Then she turned to Taylor, extending her hand.

"Keys?"

Taylor hesitated just a moment and then pressed the keyring into Becca's palm. She swallowed, waiting to see if her captor noted the missing item. Instead, she opened the passenger door of Taylor's SUV and tossed the keys on the dashboard.

"Get in," Becca ordered, pointing at the van.

"What about Moon?" she asked.

Becca grimaced. Jules answered. "Don't need her. And it's a stray, anyway." He pointed at the van. "In," he ordered.

"Why even bring her, then?"

"Because a pet made us look more like a responsible couple. Worked, too."

Taylor slipped into the driver's seat.

Jules climbed in beside her and glared. "So, you know, if we get pulled over for speeding or any other reason, Becca will smother your firstborn."

Taylor's eyes bugged and she could not draw a breath. She felt as if he'd punched her in the stomach. Finally, she gasped and stammered.

"You wouldn't," she whispered.

"Don't test us," said Becca. "Now drive."

Jules hit the remote to open the garage. Taylor depressed the brake and, with numb fingers, turned the key in the ignition. The van chugged and then started, and she slipped it into reverse, backing onto the drive as Jules pushed the garage remote button and tossed it beneath the closing door. On the street, Taylor pulled the lever into drive and crept down the road, feeling she might be seeing this neighborhood for the last time and surprised that she felt relief.

When she got away from this pair, she would come back here only to collect their things because nothing on earth could convince her to stay in this house now.

They passed only one car, an SUV. The driver, female,

lifted her hand from the wheel to offer a greeting. Taylor did the same.

Taylor followed Jules' directions, taking the main route to I-75 and heading north to Ocala.

This was not the way she had planned to leave Florida.

For the moment, she'd focus on their survival. Then she'd figure out how to free Seth. After that, she'd see that Becca, Jules, and Seth's father were held accountable.

But to do all that, she needed to stay alive.

FORTY-EIGHT

Taylor set the cruise exactly at the speed limit, surprised this old rattletrap even had that feature. Then she flipped her attention from the road to the rearview which gave her a glimpse of the top of the car seats and Becca glaring back at her.

Sometime between the Ocala and Gainesville exit, her stomach began growling. Jules shook his head.

"Give her some crackers or something," said Jules.

Becca passed up a granola bar.

"A drink," Taylor asked.

Becca sighed but offered a Pedialyte. Taylor drank sparingly, not wanting to have to pee.

Well before the babies woke and began to cry, her breasts grew heavy and aching, as her body prepared for the scheduled feeding.

"Becca? What will happen to me when we reach the compound?"

This question was met with silence.

But then Jules answered. "Once your second son is returned home, we'll await the end times. You'll perish knowing you birthed the son of God's chosen and he will grow, take a wife, and repopulate the earth."

"What about you and Becca?"

"We'll be raised to God's glory as all true believers."

"When will this happen?"

"Reverend Father Abraham has assured us that his grandson will be old enough to care for himself before we are called."

Terrifying, thought Taylor, but said, "Thank you for telling me."

Taylor glanced around at the dash for something to use to disable Jules. The cardboard air freshener shaped like a pine tree dangled from the rearview. And she had nothing but her Pedialyte, now clamped between her thighs, the AirTag tucked in her bra, and the keys to Jules' van dangling from the ignition.

She turned to find him staring at her.

"Are they sore?" asked Jules, his voice so low she barely made out his question.

"What?" she asked, her heart pounding in her ears like a galloping herd of mustangs.

"Your breasts. They're so heavy. Full. Does it hurt?"

"The milk?" There was something so creepy about his interest.

"Yeah." He flushed. "I was just curious."

"They feel uncomfortable sometimes. Like your bladder when you can't relieve yourself." And of course, the mention of her bladder made her immediately have to pee.

"What are you talking about?" said Becca.

Taylor realized that Jules had spoken in a low voice, nearly a whisper. Of course, Becca couldn't hear from the back seat of this rattly old van.

The first indication that one of the twins was awake was the familiar cry. It had been two hours since their last meal, but someone wanted another. Her breasts responded, contracting and soaking her bra. The pads inside absorbed the worst of it, thankfully.

"Can I pull off?" asked Taylor.

"How much gas left?"

She glanced at the gage. "Half a tank."

"Keep going until David wakes up."

And so, Taylor drove on, her breasts aching, her baby crying, and her rage burning brighter.

Finally, twenty-four minutes later, when Taylor had set her teeth to keep from screaming, Brodie roused and began to cry in unison with his brother. Thank goodness.

Taylor moved to the right lane and looked for the next exit, signaling her turn and gliding down the ramp to a stoplight.

"Right," ordered Becca. "Chevron station."

Was this her chance? Could Taylor get hold of both her twins and run?

She pressed her hand over her breast, assuring herself that the AirTag was still in her bra.

Please Seth, check my location.

She pictured him arriving home to that empty house. Seeing her SUV there. Would he see the remote? In her mind she pictured him reading the terrible note Becca had made her write. She'd dotted each *i* with a heart. Would he realize she never did that? How long until he spotted her missing luggage? Would he see her message on the mirror?

They parked in the back of the station. Becca hopped out.

"You be all right alone with her?" she asked.

Jules nodded, his expression inscrutable.

Becca motioned to Taylor. "Okay, come on back here and feed them. Change them too, before I get back, because we aren't stopping again." Then to her brother she said, "You throw out the diapers in that dumpster. If I'm not back, take the keys and one of the babies with you."

Taylor's heart sank as she climbed between the seats to

reach her babies. When she was settled, she found Jules kneeling so he could watch her over the headrest.

She hesitated with one hand on the top button of her jumper.

"Well? Go on."

Taylor finished the awkward process of feeding her babies with Jules watching like some pervert in a peep show. Becca's return was nearly a relief.

Together, they changed the diapers and Becca took them to the trash. Taylor was so hungry and thirsty her throat was dry. But most pressing was her need to pee.

"May I use the restroom?" she asked.

Becca laughed. Then she pointed. "Go behind the dumpster."

"I could get arrested."

Becca snorted. "You won't. Hurry up."

And so, Taylor withdrew to the dumpster. From behind the green metal bin, she had a clear view of the Denny's and its parking lot. This was good. Maybe someone would see her urinating and call the cops.

She drew down her panties and lifted her skirt, then squatted in the late afternoon sunlight, wondering if she stood and waved her arms if someone in the restaurant would notice her. She lifted her gaze to find Becca watching her.

Taylor gritted her teeth and finished her business.

They have to sleep sometime, and Colorado is a long way from here, she thought.

Back in the van she slipped into the driver's seat, which was cracked and the yellow foam padding flaking. Once underway she wondered if she should try to get the AirTag into the babies' swaddling. But how? The simple linen blanket had no nice satin trim and she had only her teeth as tools. No thread. No needle.

Where was Seth? Had he gotten home?

Please let him see my message on the mirror, she thought.

"What are you doing?" barked Jules. "North!"

Had she almost taken the ramp heading south? She had, and it was not a bad idea to try again when Jules was sleeping. A U-turn at one of the rest stops situated in the center between the two sides of the interstate would work.

Other ideas came and went as she took the correct ramp, rolling up and into the three lanes of light traffic.

Ram another car? Too dangerous.

Signal highway patrol? Had to get the window down for that and it, too, was too dangerous.

Grab the babies when feeding and make a run for it? Becca always kept hold of one of her boys when she fed the other. She was no fool.

Wait for Seth to figure out what happened and come for them? She hated the damsel in distress option. The unpredictability and the time it might take for him to find her made her discard this option.

She was so thirsty. Taylor chugged the Pedialyte and was still parched.

"Joshua, could I have another drink please?"

Jules heaved an audible sigh and turned to his sister.

"Another drink?" he asked.

Becca lowered her phone and passed forward a new clear plastic liter bottle of the grape-flavored fluid.

Taylor stared at the bottle as an idea struck.

"What's the matter? You don't like grape?" asked Jules.

FORTY-NINE

Seth collected his personal items from the jail during the discharge processing. He'd been in jail a week by the time they worked out that the drugs they'd discovered did not rise to felony charges and his public defender managed to get him before a judge so he could set bail.

His phone was dead, and his charger was at home. There was no way to contact an Uber or Lyft, so he used a credit card and the payphone, first calling Taylor and getting her voicemail.

Chief among his worries was what was happening with his wife. She had not contacted him since his arrest. He prayed the reason was her delivery, that she'd gone early, but he feared it was the other reason.

His family had her. That thought made his body shake and his breathing come in shallow little pants. He'd kill them if they hurt her or his babies.

His second call was to the birthing center. He was connected to a receptionist who asked for his wife's date of birth and then he waited as banal music played in his ear, as if everything in the world was as it should be instead of lilting dangerously to one side. All his internal warning bells were jangling, and he knew in his heart that something was very wrong.

"Mr. Parker?"

"Yes!"

"This is very odd. Your wife missed her appointment for her C-section. She did not respond to her reminder text, and we have been unable to reach her."

"What do you mean, unable?" His heart was slamming around inside his chest as if trying to beat its way out of his ribcage.

"Multiple attempts. Text, calls, and numerous messages. As I said, we have not been able to contact her or you. I reached out to her father, but if he called us back, I wasn't notified. Her physician even requested the sheriff do a safety check. They reported no answer at your home address."

"Did they check inside?"

"I'm sorry. I don't know."

Seth pressed his sweating palm to his forehead. It was what he feared. Oh, God, they had her.

"Mr. Parker, do you know where your wife might be?"

"No. No, I don't. I've got to go." He hung up.

The desperation made it so hard not to run from the station and head for home.

"Think," he said to himself.

His next call was for a taxi. Nineteen minutes later, according to his watch, which was the only electronic device in his possession that did work, the taxi arrived.

He drummed his fingers on his knee all the way home and jumped out of the car before it had come to a complete stop. The house had a cold kind of emptiness to it. Nothing moved. The garage door was shut. The lights were all off.

"Hey, buddy, you gotta pay."

Seth held out two twenties. "Keep the change."

Then he ran up the drive to the front door, finding it locked, so he used his key and banged open the door.

"Taylor?" He spoke, then shouted.

His call was greeted with only ominous silence.

Then he ran from room to room, downstairs, lanai, upstairs.

A cry came from Zoe's room. He opened the door. Moon appeared, winding about his legs as he stared at the vacant space. Moon kept meowing loudly and Seth ignored the cat.

Every sign that Zoe had stayed here was gone. The bed was made, the dresser empty. He checked the drawers and found them cleaned out.

Seth checked Jules and Becca's room and also found it empty.

He headed back to the primary bedroom with Moon.

It was in their walk-in closet that he noticed Taylor's purse and most of her luggage was missing. The racks held many empty hangers. He charged into the bathroom and saw her cosmetics bag, the one she used only for traveling, was still there. But her toothbrush and deodorant were gone.

He ran back to the bedroom, glancing at the side that Taylor planned to use for a nursery. The crib was there and empty. But the bassinets, stroller, and car seats were missing.

"Oh, God. They took her."

Was it Zoe, or Jules and Becca? He didn't know. But he did know where they were headed—the ranch.

Home.

The cellphone could bring answers. He dropped his on the charging pad and watched the bottom portion of the charger turn from red to green.

"Too long." He rummaged and found one of his mobile chargers and the cord, plugging it into his dead mobile.

The phone finally showed signs of life.

He had thirty-eight voicemails, dozens of texts, and messages on social media. But not one was from Taylor.

Where was his wife?

FIFTY

Seth dropped to the bed and began sorting through messages and listening to voicemails. His hospital supervisor had called a number of times and told him that if he didn't call back, his appointment would be rescinded.

And then the final blow. His supervisor had heard the news of his arrest. He was suspended pending a disciplinary hearing for his unexcused absences.

Moving on, several of his fellow physicians had tried and failed to contact him. His wife's obstetrician had left him an urgent voicemail yesterday and today inquiring after Taylor.

He called Rubin, the traitor, hoping he'd pick up, needing answers more than vengeance. But he got no answer. He'd have to find him if he wanted to give him a chance to explain.

"Find My Phone," he said, remembering the app. It took a few minutes to figure out how to find Taylor's cellphone, but the tracking software went to work and could not locate her signal. If she had her phone, it was dead or switched off.

Hopes flagging, Seth headed downstairs to check to see if Taylor had left him a note. He found Moon already at her food dish gulping down all that was there as he checked the counter.

They always used sticky-notes and left them on the coffee maker. This was the one sure place that neither of them would miss seeing.

But he found no note.

Turning, he spotted the white page, torn from the notepad there on the center of the counter, trapped beneath a saltshaker. He lifted the scrap, read the note. Read it again. And then the letters blurred, swimming through the tears. Seth collapsed onto one of the two kitchen stools and rested his elbows on the stone counter.

Taylor didn't write this. He knew it in every fiber. It was her handwriting, but not her words. They'd made her write it. And they'd taken her, surely to the ranch.

All the time in that terrible jail, denying the charges, refusing to admit responsibility for the drugs found in his home, insisting they were planted there and waiting as the detective's case finally unraveled. What had been happening here at home?

He didn't know.

Because he'd been locked up. The DA elected to drop most of the charges, according to his public defender, because the bags did not contain narcotics but simple baby powder, wrapped to look like heroin. That left only a charge of possession which gave him the ability to post bail.

And through it all, he had not wept. But now, the tears he had forced down burst forth with the pain in raw, rasping sobs. Outside, the sun dipped toward the horizon, sending gold light pouring through the kitchen window of their house, no longer a home.

They'd taken her. Or worse, they'd killed her and stolen his babies.

Seth cradled his head in his hands and let the tears fall. If they'd killed her, it was all for nothing.

Where were his babies? Where was his wife?

Seth straightened. He hadn't checked the garage.

He darted to his feet and hurried to the entry from the kitchen, throwing open the door.

There was her SUV. He leapt down the two steps and hurried to her vehicle, spotting the garage remote on the floor. On the dashboard sat her key fob. He peered in the back. No car seats. He rounded the SUV touching the hood. Cold.

"They took the car seats. They took the babies."

Had she delivered or was that simply in preparation?

Again, he had only supposition, and the torture of the unknown pricked at him with sharp barbs.

Exhausted, he paused, head hanging and shoulders slumped. He was calling the cops and reporting her kidnapping.

But wait. How much time would that take, filing a report? He needed to go after them now.

Maybe Taylor's captors had used her credit cards. He could check the recent charges. It was something. A chance to find her.

Seth headed upstairs to retrieve his wallet and phone.

They'd take her to the ranch. He knew where they were heading but not when they left or even which state to start looking.

So he would call highway patrol from the road. Report her missing as he followed.

Good. He had a plan.

Upstairs, he used the bathroom. After finishing, he glanced at his reflection, horrified at the purple bags under his red-rimmed eyes, and shocked at the amount of weight he had lost in only a few days.

Seth glanced toward Taylor's side of the large mirror. A streak on the glass caught his attention and he paused.

FIFTY-ONE

Taylor drove them through the night, taking I-10 west toward Tallahassee. Interstate 10 went all the way to the California coast. If she didn't do something, they'd have her out of the state and on to Alabama.

At this time of night, the highway traffic was mainly tractor trailers delivering goods. They roared past her as she hung in the right lane, going as slowly as she dared.

Her back ached from sitting on the worn, uncomfortable seat. Any time now her babies would need feeding. Her captors provided her with a burger and fries. The greasy meal upset her stomach. But she'd kept it down. She had to.

"Listen to this," said Becca. She held Taylor's phone and tapped the message to speaker and increased the volume.

Taylor recognized the sound of her father's voice.

"Taylor. Something has happened. You need to call me right now. Do you hear me? No more ghosting my messages. I need to speak to you immediately. Immediately, young lady! I mean right now!"

Becca giggled and then replayed the message.

"Young lady!" she said. "That's a laugh. He thinks you're

ghosting him. Can't blame him, what with your parents in the news. Oh, but you haven't seen the stories, have you?"

"What happened with my parents?"

"Wouldn't you like to know?"

Was Becca just torturing her or had something really happened? It was a distraction. Something meant to make her even more crazed. And it was working, too. Taylor breathed through her nose and tried to channel calm. She needed to think.

"Is that her phone?" asked Jules. "Shut it down."

"All right!" Becca snapped and complied, then tucked it away.

Wise, thought Taylor, because it meant that Seth could not use the Find My Phone app to locate them. Would he remember to check the AirTag or not even try because her vehicle and keys were both still in the garage?

"Oh, I sent your coworker a photo of the babies. She said they're adorable and everyone at the office wishes you well on your maternity leave. Won't expect to hear from you for weeks."

Taylor did not think it possible to feel any lower. But she did. The headlights and taillights blurred as the tears filled her eyes and rolled down her cheeks.

"I need to pee," said Becca.

Taylor flicked her gaze to Jules who she believed was close to dozing, his arms folded and his gaze unfocused. Becca's whine roused him, and he scrubbed his face with both hands.

"How much gas?" he asked Taylor.

"Light came on a little while ago."

"You need to tell me that," he growled.

She needed to tell him nothing, she thought, and pressed her lips together to keep from saying something she'd regret. Her cheek still throbbed when she spoke, thanks to the last time she'd upset him.

Jules turned. "Next exit," he promised Becca.

"How far is that?"

"Not far."

Taylor knew it wasn't close, and by the time the green and white exit sign for Tallahassee and Lake City finally appeared, Becca was hunched over and jiggling her leg with her anxiousness to relieve herself.

The amenities sign indicated that gas and food could be found only to the left, toward the west. The twin blue and yellow signs at the bottom of the ramp read *Madison County* 255. One sign pointed east and the other west.

"Left. Pull into that truck stop," ordered Jules.

Taylor did as instructed, using her blinker, gliding to the gas pumps and putting the vehicle in park. The stop advertised a restaurant and a convenience store.

Becca did not wait but hurled open the slider and dashed toward the store that offered scratchers and beer and advertised the pot for the Powerball jackpot.

With her exit, the dome light flicked on and Taylor got the first look at her babies since their last feeding. Aaron stared with unfocused eyes at the light above him and Brodie scrunched his eyes at the visual assault.

"Pop the gas door," Jules said. Just like he had the last time they'd stopped to fuel up.

"I have to pee, too," she said.

"Not here. Up the road a bit."

Apparently, the station was too busy for him to allow her to relieve herself behind the dumpster.

They'd been through a rainstorm and the resulting spray from trucks had covered the windshield with grime. Only one of the wiper blades functioned, and it had been hard to see, especially with the glare of those halogen headlights.

"You fill it this time," Jules ordered. He stepped out of the vehicle and into the place Becca usually sat. She turned in the bucket seat to stare back at him, looming over her babies.

"Well? Hurry up. And clean off the window."

"How am I paying?"

"Becca will pay inside. Just wait for the tank to switch on. Do the windows first. You talk to anyone, and I break one of their arms."

It would be Aaron's arm, she knew. The thought made her stomach twist as if in a wringer.

She slipped out into bright light that illuminated the gas pumps and attracted moths. They flapped futilely against the covered bulbs and died on the pavement all around her. Taylor left her door open, resisting the urge to speak to the young man filling up his motorcycle tank on the opposite side of the pumps. He was already screwing on the cap. Taylor retrieved the squeegee out of the reservoir of filthy water and cleaned the front windshield. She batted at a moth with one hand as she worked the squeegee with the other.

The stained and cracked concrete stank of gasoline and motor oil.

She peeked into the rear seat where Jules was yawning and paying her no mind. He had her babies, after all.

She grabbed her drink and lifted the release for the fuel door that flapped open. The tank made a ringing sound. In the brightly lit store, she could see Becca at the counter, paying for her purchases, now with an empty bladder.

Taylor scowled. Then she released the cap and dumped the contents of her drink into the gas tank.

FIFTY-TWO

Becca returned from the gas station convenience store carrying a plastic bag. Jules moved to the front seat as Becca climbed in the back.

"What'd you buy?" asked Jules.

"Baby stuff."

He heaved a sigh. "Nothing for the grownups?"

She offered a foiled packet. He peeled it open, filling the car's interior with the odor of hot dog and mustard.

Jules tucked in, seemingly satisfied with the offering.

Becca closed the sliding door and settled beside the babies in the backseat as Jules crumpled the empty foil and dropped it out the window. Then he pointed in the opposite direction of the interstate.

"That way," he said.

Taylor pulled out, away from the tractor trailers lined up for a break from the road. They passed the last station on the opposite side, and a defunct convenience store that was just a bit too far from the highway to compete with the offerings earlier on.

Next, they came to a turnaround where several RVs parked.

Taylor put on her blinker.

"Keep going," said Jules.

They drove on. The lights from the stations disappeared in her rearview.

"Where the heck you taking us?" said Becca, leaning between the seats.

"Somewhere private."

"There's nothing here," said Becca, lifting her arms in frustration.

She was correct. They drove on a narrow two-lane road, County Road 255, according to the signs. Huge oaks formed a dark wall on either side of the cracked, sun-bleached blacktop. Taylor caught the glint of barbed wire fencing beyond the narrow patch of trimmed grass that constituted a shoulder.

"You go any farther and you'll hit pastures and houses," said Becca.

Jules gave up. "Pull over."

She did, gliding off the two-lane highway and bumping onto uneven ground. She flicked on the hazards.

"Turn those off," ordered Becca. Then to Jules, she said, "Don't want some do-gooder stopping to help us."

"Get out and do your business," he said to Taylor.

She did, rounding the van and squatting near the rear tire. As her hot urine splashed onto the hard ground, sending droplets onto her ankles, she wondered how long it took for water and sugar to stall an engine.

The answer came when she was back behind the wheel.

Taylor pulled onto the empty road. Not a single car had come this way. If there were pastures and farmers, she couldn't see them. Taylor continued the way they were headed, away from the highway, praying to see one of those farms, a barn, a trailer. Anything that might mean help.

"What are you doing?" Jules asked. "Turn around."

She took her foot off the gas, her chest heavy with a blanket of despair that nearly snuffed the tiny flame of hope. The road was too narrow for a U-turn, but she slowed, preparing to make a three-point turn. The motor stuttered. She pressed the gas. The acceleration was rough.

Taylor smiled.

A glance in the rearview showed white smoke billowing from the tailpipe. Her grin widened. She pressed the accelerator and the engine responded, slowly.

"What's going on?" asked Becca.

The check engine light flicked on.

"Something's wrong with the engine," said Jules.

"Oil."

"I checked the oil."

"Air intake stuck again?" asked Becca.

Taylor enjoyed this exchange as much as anyone could while being kidnapped. As Becca continued to shout possibilities and instructions, the vehicle stalled.

"Start it again," said Jules.

Taylor tried. The engine gasped and wheezed like an asthmatic. She tried again. The third time, the engine turned over. Damn it.

"Get going," ordered Jules.

She did, but the acceleration was still slow to respond and now the engine misfiring caused the van to stutter and jerk.

"Pull over!" shouted Jules.

The engine stalled, but Taylor managed to glide to the same side of the grassy shoulder that led away from the highway. The headlights revealed gray, weathered posts, and barbed wire, leaning haphazardly before a wall of thick brush and tall trees. The perfect place to disappear and to be eaten alive by mosquitoes. In the summer months the bugs were terrible, especially in damp swampy places. And speaking of swampy, there were still alligators this far north, all the way up into southern Georgia, so she'd read.

Her plan had holes. Huge holes.

"Turn off the headlights," said Becca.

She did. *Now*, she thought, *let's see what they do next.*

What they did was argue and find fault. But the finger of blame never pointed in her direction. So, she remained still and quiet. Jules ordered Becca to get his flashlight. She scooted to the rear of the van and Taylor heard the clank of a metal toolbox flipping open.

Tools, she thought. Weapons. A hammer would be just the thing, or a crowbar. She hoped they'd ask her to bring them something from that box.

Becca passed forward the flashlight. Jules checked it and then got out.

"Stay here," he said, but it was unclear if he meant Taylor, Becca, or both women.

The hood creaked open, and the pair waited as Jules muttered and the light bounced.

"Becca, I need you to hold the light," he called.

Taylor stilled, holding her breath as she waited for Becca to comply. Then she'd scoop up her babies and run. It was possible she would get through that fence before they caught her. And once into that thick vegetation she might tuck under a bush or behind a tree and hide.

Until her babies woke and started crying.

A better plan was to overpower or otherwise disable her captors. She needed to get to that toolbox.

Taylor peeked back at Becca. Instead of seeing the woman reaching for the door, her captor aimed a pistol at her.

"Becca!" he shouted.

"No. I'm guarding her."

Jules cursed and banged, and the light fell on the ground.

"You did this," said Becca to Taylor.

"What?"

"You did something to the engine. Didn't you?"

Growing up with a narcissist for a mother had taught her

many things. One of these was lying effectively. No additional words, good eye contact, clear denial, repeated with as few words as possible.

"I didn't."

"Liar."

The air conditioning ceased with the engine and the interior rapidly warmed. In the dome light, Taylor could see beads of sweat on Becca's upper lip. The dark eye of the pistol's barrel continued to point at Taylor.

Jules stomped back to them and slid open the side door, pausing at the scene before him.

"What are you doing?" he asked Becca.

"She did this. She's gonna run."

His gaze flicked to Taylor and his eyes narrowed.

"Did you?" he growled.

"No. I didn't."

"She's lying," said Becca.

"Don't shoot her in the chest," said Jules.

"What's wrong with the engine?" Becca asked.

"No idea. The air intake is good. I can't get to the spark plugs. There's plenty of oil and transmission fluid."

"You let her fill the tank," said Becca.

"Yeah."

"Did you watch her?"

It took him a minute, but he caught up. His brow descended as he growled at Taylor. "What did you put in the tank?"

"Unleaded. That's all." She held his fixed stare until he shifted his attention to Becca.

"Could just be bad gas. Or a spark plug is misfiring."

"Whatever. What are we going to do?"

He pressed his lips together. Becca waved the pistol at a mosquito circling her head.

"Close the door, Joshua. You're letting in the bugs."

Aaron chose this moment to wake, fuss, and then cry.

Jules climbed in, closed the door, and sat on the rear seat behind Becca.

"Gimme the gun," he said.

Becca did and then tried again to kill the mosquito. Brodie, roused by his brother, decided to join in.

"Switch places with her," Jules said.

Becca moved to the front passenger seat and Taylor slipped in beside her babies. She placed Aaron on his belly on her lap and offered Brodie her breast. He latched on and sucked. Becca watched with a look of cold fury.

If hatred had an expression, this was it.

With Brodie fed and burped, she scooped up Aaron and fed him as well. Brodie waved the one arm that he'd managed to free from his swaddling as he reclined in his car seat.

Taylor cradled Aaron's soft, fuzzy head and closed her eyes, breathing in calmly. Once they were fed and changed, they'd sleep. And if the past was any judge, they wouldn't rouse even if their mother was running for her life.

She replaced the baby's soiled diapers. Cleaning and cooing at them made her momentarily forget her captors and situation. Once they were swaddled tight, she returned them to their car seats that more resembled bassinets. Should she put them together in one and take that when she ran? Or would she have a better chance if she just scooped them up? Either way, she did not clip either of her sons into their seats.

"Get rid of them diapers."

"Where?" asked Taylor.

"Toss them," he said, holding his nose. "Hurry up. They stink."

It was a chance. Once the door was open, she could run. But Jules had a gun, and he was right behind her.

She opened the door and placed the diapers to her right. With luck, Jules or Becca would step right on one.

"What now?" asked Becca.

"Walk back to the station, maybe," said Jules.

"Use her phone. Call Reverend Father Abraham. He might be in Tallahassee by now."

Jules retrieved Taylor's phone and she eyed the sliding door that she had not shut completely.

They were calling Seth's father and the cult's leader. He was also, unfortunately, the grandfather of her babies and he might be close by. She thought of the mugshot Seth had shown her and the man in the hospital waiting room and shuddered.

One thing was certain, she did not want him near her sons.

Behind her, Jules swore. "No service," he said.

Taylor repressed a smile as she petted the soft fuzz on Brodie's tiny head.

"One of us has to go to that station to call him," said Jules.

"Well, I'm not going. I'll get eaten alive out there," Becca said.

"You think you can guard her alone?"

"With a gun? Ah, yeah," Becca assured him.

Jules hesitated, pressing his lips tight. He exhaled like an angry bull but then nodded.

"All right. If she tries anything, shoot her here." He leaned over the seat and pointed to Taylor's thigh.

She flinched and Becca smiled.

"Love to."

"Only if she tries to escape."

"Yeah, yeah."

"Becca. I mean it. You can talk to the reverend father when he gets here. Make your case."

Becca's voice was sharp. "I said all right!"

Uncertainty stirred. Make what case? Were they planning to kill Taylor here and take her sons? She'd been told they would bring her to 'the compound' where she could join or die and that her babies would be raised by... a righteous woman. Her gaze flicked to Becca. Of course, she wanted to be the mother of 'the chosen one'. The position of being the mother of the child destined to lead them through the apocalypse would likely be the highest status position for a woman in their doomsday cult.

Becca was more than her captor. She was her rival.

FIFTY-THREE

Jules heaved himself from the rear seat and crawled to the slider, stepping out onto the grassy shoulder. Taylor glanced back hoping to see headlights. A good Samaritan might distract Becca long enough for her to run.

Jules checked his pockets.

"Don't use her phone," said Becca.

"I'll use a payphone."

"If they have one."

"It's a truck stop," he said. "They'll have one."

"Wallet?"

He exhaled loud enough to convey his annoyance.

"You just watch her and don't worry about me."

"You calling a tow truck?"

"No. We'll wait here for the reverend father."

"It's hot."

"It's Florida," he said, and slammed the slider closed.

Taylor watched as he appeared behind the van and then walked west along the road until he was out of sight. Becca watched as well, her attention fixed on the rear windshield. Taylor took the opportunity to glance over the seat, too, but the second bench-seat behind her blocked any view of the toolbox.

Her foot hit the plastic bag, causing it to rustle. Becca swung around, aiming the pistol again.

"What are you doing?"

"Nothing," said Taylor.

"Gimme that." She motioned with the barrel of the gun to the white plastic bag on the floor.

Taylor lifted the bag, taking the opportunity to see what was inside. Becca had purchased more than a hot dog. She'd also bought plastic baby bottles, a gallon jug of water and... baby formula. Taylor drew out the container of powdered milk, her heart flipflopping in her chest. Her breath caught. The label read: *Infant Formula, Newborn.*

Her skin tingled and her fingertips went numb as she dropped the container.

"Careful with that! It cost over fifty bucks."

Taylor gasped now, her mouth wide open as she tried to think.

"Figure it out yet?" Becca paused, her smile widening. "Once I know they'll take the bottle, I don't need you."

Taylor's voice was breathy as the panic closed her windpipe.

"May I have some water?"

"Ha! Drink your electrolytes. This water is for David."

"What about Aaron?"

"I'll keep him alive if that's what you're asking. He's fore-told to be his brother's right-hand."

Taylor slumped. At least Becca did not intend to stop feeding her firstborn.

"He was supposed to choose an honorable wife. Instead, he picked you—a godless woman."

Had Becca hoped to be Seth's chosen? That possibility made Taylor grind her teeth.

"Why would your leader let a woman who couldn't keep his grandson's mother alive raise her babies?" asked Taylor.

Becca's mouth tipped down at the corners.

"You don't know anything," Becca growled. "You're tainted."

And you're a crazy, thought Taylor.

Taylor kept her mouth shut, waiting for a chance. Wondering if Becca was psyching herself up to shoot her. Wondering if she should ask what her brother would do if he came back with Abraham and found Taylor shot to death.

"Get out," said Becca, motioning with the pistol.

Taylor hesitated.

"If I shoot you here, I might maybe hit one of them."

She got out. Becca followed and closed the sliding door.

Taylor's heart beat painfully in her chest and her legs seemed cast of lead. She could barely bend her knees. Her skin was damp, and her vision tunneled. A hand pressed to her chest did not stop the painful throbbing of her heart.

"What are you going to do?"

"See if your boys will take the formula."

The possibilities made Taylor's stomach flip. "Then what?"

"Kill you."

"You don't even know if they'll take the bottle."

"Let's find out."

Taylor needed to stall. Delay until Jules returned because if her babies did accept the formula, she was certain Becca would shoot her.

"What will you tell Jules?" Taylor's brain didn't seem to be working right. The fear was rising over her head, like quicksand. She could barely breathe.

"I'll say you ran off."

"They'll know it's a lie. I'd never leave my babies."

"You're right. I'll say you went for the gun, and I had to shoot you," said Becca, revising her plans on the fly. "If you do run, I'll shoot you in the back and tell the truth." She raised the pistol, gesturing with the barrel. "Why don't you run?"

"I'll mix the formula. See if they'll take it."

"Fine."

The dome light flicked off and the world went dark.

Taylor sprang at Becca, reaching.

She grasped Becca's wrist and the gunshot exploded with a flash that lit up the night. Taylor's ears rang from the auditory assault, but she did not let go. The pistol now pointed upward as they grappled. Another shot and the side mirror of the van shattered, raining glass upon the ground.

Her twins howled in protest. Taylor wondered if the sounds had damaged their still forming inner ear. The fury at this thought was all the fuel she needed. She yanked and the gun flew from Becca's grip. An instant later there came a thud of the metal striking the ground to their left.

Becca stared after it and then threw herself down on the ground, her hands out as she patted the grass. Taylor kicked her in the head and watched Becca sprawl.

Then Taylor tugged at the handle in a vain effort to reach her babies but found the door locked.

"Where is it?" Becca cried. "Got it."

The next shot was so close Taylor felt the bullet brush her hair.

She turned and ran, charging for the fence, pausing to slip between the upper and middle wire, and slithered into the brush. Run and hide. Just like when she was a girl. She could do this.

Her shirt caught on one of the barbs. The rusty metal tore the fabric of her denim jumper and the skin beneath. She didn't stop, just turned to push backwards through the dense cover of brush and briar, heedless of the thorns and branches tearing at her skin. She hunched, shielding her face from the worst of the assault.

"Taylor!" Becca's high-pitched shriek reached her. She could see nothing at first, but then she noticed the light. Bright white light coming closer. Not a flashlight.

It was headlights.

Deliverance or capture, Taylor wondered, crouching low to the ground.

A battered, late-model pickup truck pulled in behind the van on the north shoulder of the highway. Doors opened and two men stepped from the vehicle.

FIFTY-FOUR

"Rebekah?" The voice was low and unfamiliar.

"I'm here," said Becca.

Taylor huddled on the ground, afraid to move for fear the rustling would give away her position. She was close to the fence, perhaps ten feet back and blind to her surroundings. Was she far enough in that they would not see her if they shone a flashlight in her direction?

"Where is she?"

That was Jules. She'd recognize that voice anywhere.

She could see them now, silhouettes in the headlights of the truck as they approached the van. But if she could see them...

Her T-shirt was white. They'd spot it. She was certain.

Carefully, she unbuttoned her dress and dragged off the white T-shirt. Then she wadded the shirt in a ball and shoved it further behind her and under the groundcover.

"What happened?" asked the unfamiliar male voice. "Where is she?"

"She grabbed for the gun."

"You shot out the mirror?" asked Jules.

"I didn't mean to," Becca whined.

"My grandsons?" This voice was low and menacing. So, this was Abraham, Seth's father. The man he never spoke about. Now she understood why.

"They're here," said Becca.

There was rustling as the three turned their attention to the van. Taylor knew she should take the opportunity and crawl farther into the undergrowth, but her babies were in that van.

The murmur of voices reached her. They had her sons.

Taylor snaked forward like one of those grunts in the army training exercise, crawling under the barbed wire fence and onto the mown shoulder. She could see them now. The dome light was on again.

Becca and Jules were in the van. Abraham stood beside the open slider, his head and shoulders in the vehicle.

Taylor crouched, then ran, reaching the back of the pickup. She crept forward along the driver's side of the truck, glancing inside. Keys dangled from the ignition. She reached through the open window and took them. Then she rolled under the truck.

"We need to find her," said Abraham.

"Yes, sir," said Jules.

"She went that way," said Becca.

Taylor lay on her back beneath the vehicle, the heat from the muffler and exhaust system blazing down on her.

"Stay with the babies," said Jules.

A flashlight flicked on. She watched the two men move forward to the fence line and the place where she'd been hidden only a few minutes before.

The older man held the flashlight and swept it back and forth.

"There! There she is." Jules pointed. "Come out, Taylor."

She didn't. But she did army crawl forward until she was under the van.

Now she could see Becca's feet. She'd moved away from the vehicle to get a better look at the search efforts.

"She there?" she called, taking another step toward the men.

"Yes. I think so," said Jules.

The flashlight moved. "Go haul her out of there," ordered Abraham. He held the light in one hand and lifted the top wire of the fence with the other. "Go on."

"Yes, sir."

Becca took another step. She was ten feet from the van now. Closer to the men than the open slider.

Taylor slithered forward and rolled to her back, her head now out from beneath the van. Becca turned and Taylor froze, still as a rabbit beside a hedgerow. But Becca looked back to the wooded area.

"You see her?" she asked.

Jules would find that shirt any minute.

Taylor scrambled out from the van and reached inside, scooping one baby in each arm. And bless them, they did not make a sound.

Taylor dropped to her knees and then her back, wiggling her way beneath the van. The cuts on her back and arms stung, but she did not slow, moving as fast as she could while still remaining quiet.

"It's just her T-shirt," said Jules.

"Well, look around. She didn't go far," said the older man.

The light swung back in her direction. Taylor closed her eyes and looked away, afraid they'd see her eyes glowing from her hiding place.

"Rebekah. Did I tell you to stay by the van?"

"Yes, sir."

"Then get on back there."

Becca stomped toward Taylor and the light swung away. How many seconds until Becca checked on the twins?

She had to move. She had to hurry.

Taylor inched back and away from Becca's feet silhouetted against the glow from the flashlight.

"Anything?" called Abraham.

"No. I can't see nothing in this brush. Ouch! Thorns on the vines."

"Keep looking."

Becca's feet moved. Taylor reached the back of the van, but with her precious bundles, it was a challenge to scramble upright.

Taylor stood now, hunching over the babies, illuminated by the headlights from the truck parked behind the van. She ran to the driver's side, juggling one of the babies to hold them both in one arm. Her hand was on the latch and the door squeaked open.

Becca turned. Their eyes met.

"Hey!" Becca ran at her. "She's got David! She's taking them."

FIFTY-FIVE

The flashlight swung in Taylor's direction, blinding her as she scrambled into the truck. In an instant she had both her babies lying on the wide bench seat.

The men were only forty feet away. The light bounced as they ran in her direction. Taylor reached inside her bra and yanked out the key to the truck. She took her gaze off her pursuers long enough to shove the key into the ignition and twist.

A standard, she realized, thankful for her time in Arizona when she'd become an expert at driving this type of vehicle. The engine roared as Jules reached the passenger door.

Taylor leaned across the seat and slapped down the lock just as Jules reached the latch. He drew back his fist, preparing to smash the window.

She seized the gearshift and yanked it into reverse, then eased on the gas as she backed off the clutch. The pickup rolled backwards.

The dash lights showed the emergency brake was still engaged. And she knew exactly where to find that.

All three of her pursuers were shouting now as she ricocheted backwards. The three charged after her, but she kept going until she had enough time to throw it into drive without them reaching the doors. Then she stepped on the gas. Jules dove clear of the grill and Abraham slammed his palms on the hood as she jerked the wheel, bringing her onto the pavement.

She held her breath as she passed the van. Then the rear windshield exploded.

One or more of them were shooting at her.

Taylor scanned her sleeping babies and hit the gas, flying over the road. A glance in the rearview showed all three standing in the center of the highway illuminated red in her taillights.

But she was heading away from the interstate. She was heading in the wrong direction.

Taylor debated turning around but couldn't risk it. At least one of the three had shown themselves willing to shoot at her. She had no choice but to continue forward away from help and into the darkness. The road didn't have a streetlight in sight. What time was it?

She didn't know. Well past midnight, she thought. Closer to dawn. The first sign of civilization was so dark and so far back from the road that she noticed it only after she was parallel with the building. It was a small cracker-style house, dark and possibly abandoned. That didn't bode well. Next the woods on the left fell away and she could clearly see a pasture beyond the string of fencing. A barn came into sight, and she resisted the urge to pull in. There was a single trailer up on cement blocks on the right and then, finally, a house and garage. The garage had a security light blazing down like a homing beacon.

She slowed, glanced in the rearview, and pulled in. She'd gone a few miles. It would take them time to get here, especially without a vehicle.

For a doomsday prepper and demigod, Seth's father certainly didn't have the power of foresight.

But she wasn't safe yet. They were still out there, hunting.

Taylor swung the old truck close to the house and laid on the horn. She wasn't leaving her babies, even for the time it took to knock on a door.

She leaned until lights flicked on inside the house. Then she waited, panting, sweating, and feeling sick to her stomach. Her back was wet. Was that perspiration or blood? It didn't matter. Nothing mattered but getting these babies to safety.

Her headlights shone on the front door. The screen opened and a man peered out. In his grip was a shotgun.

Taylor opened the door and lifted her hands, illuminated in the security light.

"Help! I need help!"

The barrel of the weapon now pointed to the ground.

"What's wrong with you?" he called, not leaving the safety of the doorframe.

"I was kidnapped. Please. I have two babies with me."

He stepped out and a woman appeared beside him, older with a tight cap of gray curls. She cinched the tie to her robe and called.

"Babies?"

"Yes. Twins. I just... I need help!"

The woman spoke to the man, who wore only sagging shorts beneath his round belly. White chest hair sparkled in the light like a bed of cotton.

"Put the gun down, Jerry."

He didn't, so the woman slipped past him.

"Carrol, get back here," he said.

She didn't, but hustled forward, speaking to the man Taylor assumed was her husband. "Look at her. She's bleeding."

Carrol reached the truck and Taylor turned to retrieve her sons.

"Oh, Jerry, she's got two babies. Come quick."

He did, still gripping the shotgun which was now cracked open at the center.

"Oh, my word," said Carrol. "What on earth? Come on, honey." She wrapped an arm around Taylor's shoulders. "You're safe. We got you."

Taylor retrieved her sons, and they walked back toward the house, passing Jerry who trailed behind them. Once inside, Carrol hustled Taylor through a narrow, tiled foyer and into a large farmhouse kitchen complete with knotty pine cabinets and blue gingham curtains.

"Jerry, call the highway patrol."

Her husband set the shotgun aside and moved to a wall phone. Taylor blinked at the ancient device complete with a push-button dial.

"Here, let me just get something," said Carrol.

She drew out a drawer from above a cabinet and dumped the contents into the sink. Potato mashers, peelers, a ladle, and various other kitchen utensils clattered against stainless-steel. Then Carrol opened another drawer and tugged out several dishtowels, lining the bottom.

"You put them in here for now," she said.

Taylor did as she was told. Meanwhile Jerry spoke to someone on the phone.

"Just look at you." Carrol tugged a stick from her hair. "Are you cold?"

Taylor's teeth were knocking together and she shivered violently, but not from cold. The fear was catching her. She swayed.

Carrol guided her to a chair at the pine table and then placed her babies right before her. Taylor looked down at the twins. Aaron had his eyes open and stared with interest, though likely he could see only blurry images at best. Taylor leaned forward and stroked his cheek.

Were they safe? Were they finally safe?

"Mama's here. You're fine. We're all fine now."

Carrol wrapped a brightly colored crocheted lap blanket around Taylor's shoulders.

Something large and heavy hit the front door. All three stiffened and turned toward the intruder filling the foyer.

Jerry dropped the phone receiver and made a lunge for the shotgun.

FIFTY-SIX

The intruder reached the shotgun first, snapped the barrel closed, raised it to his shoulder, and pointed the weapon at the center of Jerry's chest.

"Step back," he ordered, motioning with the barrel.

Jerry cast a glance at his wife and lifted his hands.

Taylor shot to her feet. "Seth!"

Somehow, he'd found them.

She pointed. "That's my husband!"

The shock was receding now, and she understood. Seth thought these sweet, helpful, good Samaritans were her captors.

"No!" She raised her hands. "Seth, they saved me. It's not them."

He kept the shotgun raised.

"Step away from them," said Seth.

She didn't. Instead, she stepped before Jerry.

"They're back there on the road. The van. Did you see them?" Taylor was walking forward. "I got away. I made it here. They're helping me. They've called the police."

He glanced back at them, the hard set of his jaw easing as his gaze flicked from the couple, now huddled together, he in his sagging gym shorts and she in a nightie and robe. There had never been a couple who looked less like kidnappers.

"They did?" He was shaking now as he lowered the weapon, then rested it beside the shattered doorframe. He opened his arms and Taylor rushed into them.

"I was so worried," he said at the same time as she said, "I was so scared."

Seth squeezed her so hard, one of her ribs popped. She hugged him right back. Then he pulled away to hold her face in both hands, studying the bruises and split lip.

"They hurt you." It wasn't a question. Tears welled in his eyes as he dragged her forward again. Then he lifted his face from the crook of her neck and spoke to the couple behind them. "Thank you. Thank you so much."

Taylor stepped beneath his arm, and he pulled her close, pressing her to his side. Suddenly everything seemed different.

"Seth, this is Jerry and Carrol. My saviors."

Seth extended his hand. Jerry stepped forward to clasp it.

"I'm very sorry about your door, sir. I'll see it's repaired."

"It's all right, son. Man's job is to protect his family." When Seth released Jerry's hand, the homeowner retrieved his shotgun, cracked it open, and removed the two shells, which he tucked into the pocket of his shorts.

Carrol was there before them, smiling.

"Seth, would you like some water or a cup of coffee?"

Taylor laughed. The hospitality seemed so out of place for the situation. The laugh was somewhat hysterical, as if all the fear and pain had doubled back on itself and turned into madness.

"Taylor," said Seth, "you all right?"

"No. I'm not. But I will be. How did you find us?"

"Your AirTag. You have it. Don't you?"

"I stuck it in my bra."

"Well, thank God. That was fast thinking."

"Could you track my phone?"

"I tried. Couldn't get a signal."

She recalled that, except for a few occasions, the pair kept her phone shut down which was a blessing because Seth might have first confronted her kidnappers all alone.

"Thank goodness. Becca has it."

He took hold of each of her shoulders, his gaze sliding rapidly from her face down her body and pausing on her middle.

"The babies?"

"Here," she said. "Safe."

He exhaled his relief and his eyes closed for a moment. He swayed.

"Come see your babies, Seth," Carrol said, motioning to the kitchen.

Behind them, Jerry stood near the entrance, holding the shotgun, and casting a glance out toward the road. He remained there, a silent sentinel as Seth and Taylor followed Carrol along the tiled portion of the living room to the kitchen.

Seth leaned over the drawer to peer at his two sons, lying on a mattress of brightly colored terrycloth dishtowels, head-to-head and feet pointing in opposite directions as they slept with hands joined.

"Oh, Taylor." Seth's words were just a breath. A whisper filled with wonder and the quiet required around sleeping babies. The pair had not roused during the explosion of the front door kicking in or the shouting that followed. Taylor knew that when they needed sleep, little would wake them. But they should be hungry soon.

The thought made her breasts ache, and she anticipated being relieved of the milk that now filled them.

"Look how perfect," Seth said, crooking a finger to touch Aaron's cheek.

The boy turned toward the touch, staring up at his father

with wide blue eyes. He kicked his spindly legs and Brodie roused, scrunched up his face and smacked his lips.

"Someone is hungry." Taylor lifted Brodie from his place and sat at the dining table, unbuttoning the denim jumper, and dragging away the bra.

Aaron began to fuss.

"Pick him up," said Taylor. "Give him your finger to suck."

Seth headed to the kitchen and scrubbed his hands. By the time he returned, Carrol was holding Aaron on her shoulder, patting his tiny bottom.

"Here's your papa," she cooed, and passed Aaron carefully to Seth.

Taylor wished she could put her husband's expression of wonder into a bottle and keep it forever. She smiled, finally feeling safe and happy.

Seth cradled his son's tiny head and sat in the chair beside Taylor.

"That's Aaron," she said. "He was born first." Taylor glanced down at the baby sucking at her breast. "And this is Brodie."

"I should have been there," he said.

"Yes. And you should have told me, Seth. Warned me about them."

His head hung. "I should have. I thought they'd never find us. I never would have believed that Rubin and Nathan would betray me."

"I met your father," she said. "He's here and he wants our children."

Seth turned back toward the open door, staring out into the night.

"He's here?"

"Yes."

"When they released me, I checked for you at home. Saw your message on the mirror. Good thinking."

Taylor glowed under his praise. "So that's why you checked the AirTag?"

"First, I tried tracking your phone. Then I went to find Rubin. But he and Nathan took off. Been gone since that night you saw his brother. Gina was there. After being dumped, she was happy to tell me everything she knew. She said that Rubin and Nathan went back to Colorado, twice. The first time to make the deal. Gina thought they sent someone east to confirm your location."

"Your father in the hospital and then the one I saw in the woods," said Taylor, sure now this was who she had seen that first night in their new home.

"Yeah, and remember how I bounced the idea for renters off Rubin? He told my father about the house, your plan to take in renters and, most importantly, that you were pregnant with twin boys. He also gave them our address."

Taylor locked her teeth, thinking what she'd like to do to Rubin.

Seth bounced Aaron.

"And your father sent Becca and Jules to apply as tenants?" she asked.

Seth broke eye contact and nodded. "Yes."

Taylor tamped down the rage. Then she said, "I'll never forgive him."

"On the second run, they picked up their little brother."

"Your father kidnapped your wife?" asked Carrol, rubbing her forehead in confusion.

"Yes," said Seth. "He and his brothers, they have ideas, dangerous ones, about God and the end of the world."

"It's a cult," said Taylor.

"It's my family." Seth's voice was hoarse with emotion.

"Becca and Jules weren't family."

Seth grimaced, inclining his head to one side. "They might

be one of my younger second cousins. I don't know, but I'm sure they wouldn't have sent someone outside the family."

"They said their names were Joshua and Rebekah," said Taylor, watching her husband for his reaction to this information.

His brows lifted as surprise spread over his face. "Rebekah? But she'd only be..." He paused, calculating. "About fifteen, maybe."

"Sixteen, so she said."

"Joshua." Seth nodded. "Yeah, second cousins. He's her older brother. Is that who he sent?"

"Yes. Didn't you recognize them?"

"No. Kids are kept in a separate area. More secure. It's why we couldn't get to Matthew." He scrubbed his knuckles over his jaw, thinking in silence a moment. "But Rebekah and Joshua... yeah, I only saw them at their baptisms. The entire family gathers for that."

That explained how he could have failed to identify his own kin. As they were still considered children when he'd left the compound, he never saw them.

Taylor recalled her confusion that the pair never touched. "Looking back, it seems so obvious now that they weren't married."

"Surprised they let them out." Seth slowly shook his head, as if struggling to wrap his mind around what she had told him.

"Surprised, because it's a big chance they'd never come back?" Taylor asked.

"That's right. Plus, we all thought it was too dangerous. And they're so young."

"Not too young to be killers."

Seth's eyes rounded in an expression of shock. "Killers?"

"I found Zoe's body." Taylor shivered at the recollection. "Becca said she stabbed her, and Jules carried her out of the house in one of Zoe's suitcases. Becca put her in the trunk of Zoe's car and drove it off before they called the police on you. After the police left, I went upstairs to get my wallet and phone and I found... I..." Taylor couldn't finish. The image was too terrible.

Seth gathered her up. "Hush now. It's over."

"Let me get you a drink," said Carrol. Then she turned to her husband. "Jerry, maybe put on a shirt."

"You be all right?" asked her husband.

She nodded and shooed him away. Jerry headed out of the kitchen carrying his shotgun.

"Highway patrol is on the way," said Carrol. "In the meantime, I'll make coffee. You both look about spent."

Seth stared down at Aaron and offered the knuckle of his index finger. His son latched on.

"Wow!" he said.

"Tell me about it," said Taylor, and chuckled.

After a few minutes, Aaron grew wise to the fact that his father's finger was not providing the customary nourishment and began to fuss and then cry.

Taylor's heart squeezed with joy at seeing her husband comforting their hungry baby. And when Brodie finished his meal, she switched the younger for the older brother, in an exchange that she knew would become as routine as breathing.

Aaron wasted no time tucking into his meal. Brodie, meanwhile, was quite content to stare up at this new face in wonder.

Seth stared down with a look of astonishment that exactly matched his son's. Taylor giggled and Seth's attention shifted to her.

"They're so beautiful, Taylor. So perfect and I'm so proud of you."

She smiled as the glow of his praise warmed her inside and out.

"They are beautiful. Aren't they?"

She reached with her free hand, and he clasped it with his,

then leaned in to kiss her. As the kiss deepened, Seth crowded Aaron's space, causing him to squawk in protest. This made both parents laugh.

From somewhere out there in the dangerous night came the sound of sirens.

Jerry, now dressed in the same shorts and a red T-shirt, stared out his shattered front door. "Here they come."

FIFTY-SEVEN

Seth suggested taking Taylor and the twins to a hospital in Tallahassee, but she just wanted to go home. It wasn't until they saw the Tampa exit that she realized she had no home to go to.

Florida Highway Patrol had picked up both Joshua and Rebekah, along with Abraham, Seth's father, before they even arrived at the residence of Jerry and Carrol Persinger.

After giving their initial statements and contact information, Seth had driven his family south, taking Taylor and the twins to the hospital near the place Taylor should have delivered their sons. Her obstetrician was there to meet them. All three were remarkably healthy, despite their ordeal, but they kept them overnight for observation and because the twins had slight fevers after their first round of vaccinations.

That evening two homicide detectives had visited Taylor, after a phone call from Seth.

The next day, Taylor called the realtor who had sold them the property.

"We can't afford it," she said.

Seth did not argue. After they signed the necessary papers

to get their former residence listed and left the realtor, Seth asked, "Where to?"

"A hotel."

"Not home?"

"It's not home. It was a mistake and a bad dream."

And now again a crime scene as the police searched for human remains. Last night, Taylor had told the homicide detectives all she could from Becca and Jules boasting over murdering poor Zoe and dumping her in Tampa Bay.

"Tomorrow I'll call a moving and storage place to get our things cleared out because I am not sleeping there again," said Taylor. "Ever."

"No big house?"

"We don't need it." She shivered.

"I understand."

"What about the cat?" Taylor asked, suddenly recalling Becca's stray, chosen to make the pair seem more settled.

"Jason's mom will take Moon or find her a good home."

"Great." Taylor never wanted to see that feline again.

"Oh, Jason's baby blanket!" cried Taylor.

"Movers will pack everything up for us. Don't worry."

"Oh no, all of Jason's grandmother's things are going right back into storage."

"That's true. For now."

Once in their SUV, she and Seth locked the babies' carriers into place.

She stared down at her sons, both sleeping with feathery lashes brushing soft pink cheeks.

"You know, those bumper stickers are right. All the best things aren't things at all, are they?"

"Nope. And home is with you and my boys," said Seth.

Over the next week, the story of Taylor's abduction made national news. And after hearing of his family's ordeal, his hospital supervisor called to reinstate Seth in his residency.

The news reported that the FBI had stormed Seth's family's compound. The charges were extensive. Seth's childhood home had been raided and the children removed to the hands of social services thanks, in part, to Seth's statements regarding the lack of education and healthcare, and the tenet that forbid any member of the family to leave on threat of death.

Rubin and Nathan had also been arrested on a host of charges and Taylor found it very hard to muster even an ounce of sympathy. They knew what would happen to her and they let it happen. In her mind, they traded their cousin's family for their little brother, who was now in the foster care system.

The worst news was all the events that she had missed with her parents because of her abduction. Becca had not just been torturing her with hints of her parents' troubles. Their ordeals mingled with hers to create a supernova news event combining everything tasty in a lead headline.

Seth comforted her and promised to help her pick up the pieces. Her parents' misfortunes just made her more eager than ever to leave the area because the ghosts haunting her here were multiplying.

Taylor's father had tried to contact her again this week, but she needed time to process everything that had happened with her and with them. Seth said it was her right to expect some privacy, even from her father and his problems and demands.

Seth pointed out that her dad had not come to her aid when she asked but told her to figure it out. His view was that her father could now do the same.

Since coming back to Florida, she'd forgotten about making a difference and choosing important projects. She'd taken the job her father had suggested; it came with good pay, nice people, but she had zero job satisfaction planning concrete overpasses and overseeing bridge repairs.

Changes needed to be made. Drastic ones.

She was through with things. She wanted community,

connection, and family. She wanted meaningful work. She wanted her husband. And all that was impossible living in a home with high hedges and neighbors she did not know. This place where she had been raised was too toxic and it had been too easy for her to fall back on old bad habits. She needed the desert again, or something similar.

Now she wanted to ask Seth to find a position somewhere far from the Gulf of Mexico and all the darkness that clung to her past and clouded her future.

Orlando was a start. And after Seth's residency, perhaps Chicago or Boston or New York?

Yes, a big city. One that was as far from the Gulf Coast as she could imagine.

Over the next two months, as the details became public, Taylor decided to make her separation from her parents complete.

Seth and Taylor worked out a very conservative budget and moved into a one-bedroom rental a quarter-mile from the Orlando hospital in a building with great security. Then they turned in both vehicles and bought a late model Volvo wagon. They planned to stay in this apartment until after Seth's residency.

Because of their downsizing, Taylor no longer had to return to her job once her maternity leave concluded and she was happy to extend her time with Aaron and Brodie who were growing and changing by the day.

She could find a new job in a new place here in Orlando, or perhaps apply to work with another infrastructure project, instead of managing yet another overpass replacement or bridge repair.

Her boss, Nicki Wakely, had accepted her resignation and offered a glowing recommendation, which was much appreciated.

"How long can we afford for you to stay home?" asked Seth

one night when he somehow managed to return in time for supper.

"At least the first year," she said. "The budget is working out."

"That's great." Seth paused to stare at his boys, sleeping in the eat-in kitchen. "Oh, one of the nurses is having a yard sale this weekend. She said she has tons of baby clothes and some furniture."

Taylor glanced at the large dresser drawer where Aaron and Brodie slept side-by-side.

"Maybe I'll stop by. But they seem happy for now."

"How long have they been asleep?"

At ten weeks, the twins no longer spent most of the day sleeping, but could be expected to nap for a solid stretch after feeding.

"I just put them down before you came in."

Seth gave her a warm smile and her heart rate increased.

Her husband slipped from his place at the small kitchen table and leaned in for a kiss.

She hummed her pleasure at the pressing of his mouth to hers and then stroked his cheek.

"How long do you have until you need to head back to the hospital?" she asked.

"Why? You have something planned?"

"Not planned. More impromptu."

The speculative quirk of his brow and that devilish smile told her immediately that he understood her completely. It had been a long time since they'd been together, and her body felt ready. No, her body felt demanding and needy. She wanted him, so she grabbed hold of his collar and tugged him back for the kind of kiss that left no room for speculation.

She drew away, breathless and hungry for more.

"So, how long do we have?" she asked.

He grinned. "Six whole lovely hours."

"What are we waiting for?"

A LETTER FROM JENNA

Dear Reader,

I want to say a huge thank you for adding *The Patient's Daughter* to your reading list. If you enjoyed Taylor's story and want to keep up to date with all my latest releases, just sign up at the following link. Your email address will never be shared, and you can easily unsubscribe.

www.bookouture.com/jenna-kernan

I hope you loved *The Patient's Daughter* and if you did, I would be very grateful if you could write a review because your honest opinion helps new readers discover a book you enjoyed.

Writing *The Patient's Daughter* was great fun and I enjoyed asking my friends what experiences in their homes had really creeped them out. Some of those stories found their way into this book. One that did not make the cut was the entire uncooked roast beef that one of them found, covered with bird-seed, sitting in their backyard. Some real-life experiences are too unbelievable and not all that creepy. Am I right?

I love hearing from my readers – you can get in touch with me through social media or my website.

Be well and happy reading!

Jenna

KEEP IN TOUCH WITH JENNA

www.jennakernan.com

facebook.com/authorjennakernan
x.com/jennakernan
instagram.com/jenna_kernan
bookbub.com/authors/jenna-kernan

ACKNOWLEDGMENTS

This novel would not have reached you without the help of my support network. Here are just a few of the people I depend upon.

My husband, Jim, offers encouragement and snacks, while the work of building a compelling story occasionally overwhelms me. Even if I'm in a muddle, he makes me believe I can work my way out and is there to help me celebrate each release!

Thank you to my siblings for making the occasional fuss over me and for buying paperback versions of my stories for their keeper shelves!

Special thanks to my agent, Ann Leslie Tuttle, of Dystel, Goderich & Bourret, for looking out for my best interests in publishing and for being such a good friend.

My editor, Nina Winters, for her indispensable feedback. She always seems to spot what is missing from the story and what isn't missing that should be! I'm so blessed to have this talented editor working on this book.

Thank you to the Bookouture team for another stunning cover, promotion campaigns, packaging, and marketing efforts and for your dedication to books, authors, and readers.

The Patient's Daughter was available for early reviews, and I need to thank all those reviewers who took the time to offer their honest opinions via their reviews. These first readers are critically important to help make books better and to help new readers find this story.

Thank you to these organizations for educating, encouraging, and advocating for writers: Sisters in Crime, Gulf Coast Sisters in Crime, Mystery Writers of America, Mystery Writers of Florida, Thrill Writers International, Authors Guild, and Novelist, Inc.

Finally, I am grateful to my readers. This book only comes alive in your hands.

Thank you!

PUBLISHING TEAM

Turning a manuscript into a book requires the efforts of many people. The publishing team at Bookouture would like to acknowledge everyone who contributed to this publication.

Audio
Alba Proko
Melissa Tran

Commercial
Lauren Morrissette
Jil Thielen
Imogen Allport

Cover design
The Brewster Project

Data and analysis
Mark Alder
Mohamed Bussuri

Editorial
Nina Winters
Sinead O'Connor

Proofreader
Jennifer Davies

Marketing
Alex Crow
Melanie Price
Occy Carr
Ciara Rosney

Operations and distribution
Marina Valles
Stephanie Straub

Production
Hannah Snetsinger
Mandy Kullar
Jen Shannon

Publicity
Kim Nash
Noelle Holten
Myrto Kalavrezou
Jess Readett
Sarah Hardy

Rights and contracts
Peta Nightingale
Richard King
Saidah Graham

Printed in Great Britain
by Amazon

36227763R00216